W9-BCN-540

"My God, John!"
Amelia screamed
"What are you doing?"

He did not look at her but gripped the knife even more firmly in his hand as he advanced toward the paintings—his paintings—paintings he had created in passion.

"If I can't paint any new paintings, I can look at these old ones cold-bloodedly, see their faults—and cut them off!"

She gripped his wrist which held the knife, gripped it with almost maniacal force as she cried out, "Cold blood! You painted these pictures in hot blood! They're part of you! They're alive! You can't kill them!"

He forced the knife slowly toward her bosom overpowering her strength as he whispered, "Would you rather I killed you?"

Her eyes glowed with defiance. "Go ahead!" she challenged him.

Other Books by Irving Stone
in SIGNET Editions

☐ **THE AGONY AND THE ECSTASY**
(#E5189—$1.75)

☐ **THOSE WHO LOVE**   (#W5339—$1.50)

☐ **THE PRESIDENT'S LADY**   (#Q5191—95¢)

☐ **THEY ALSO RAN**   (#Y5192—$1.25)

☐ **LOVE IS ETERNAL**   (#Y5185—$1.25)

☐ **IMMORTAL WIFE**   (#Y5186—$1.25)

☐ **JACK LONDON, SAILOR ON HORSEBACK**
(#Q5190—95¢)

☐ **ADVERSARY IN THE HOUSE**   (#Y5188—$1.25)
with Jean Stone

☐ **I, MICHELANGELO, SCULPTOR** (#Q5028—95¢)

☐ **DEAR THEO: THE AUTOBIOGRAPHY OF**
VINCENT VAN GOGH   (#W3836—$1.50)

☐ **CLARENCE DARROW FOR THE DEFENSE**
(#J4851—$1.95)

THE NEW AMERICAN LIBRARY, INC.,
P.O. Box 999, Bergenfield, New Jersey 07621

Please send me the SIGNET BOOKS I have checked above.
I am enclosing $_____(check or money order—no
currency or C.O.D.'s). Please include the list price plus 15¢ a
copy to cover handling and mailing costs. (Prices and numbers are subject to change without notice.)

Name_____

Address_____

City_____State_____Zip Code_____
Allow at least 3 weeks for delivery

Irving Stone

THE
PASSIONATE JOURNEY

A SIGNET BOOK from
NEW AMERICAN LIBRARY
TIMES MIRROR

Copyright, MCMXLIX, by Irving Stone

All rights reserved. For information address Doubleday &
Company, Inc., 277 Park Avenue, New York, New York 10017.

This is an authorized reprint of a hardcover edition
published by Doubleday & Company, Inc.

Fifth Printing

 SIGNET TRADEMARK REG. U.S. PAT. OFF. AND FOREIGN COUNTRIES
REGISTERED TRADEMARK—MARCA REGISTRADA
HECHO EN CHICAGO, U.S.A.

Signet, Signet Classics, Signette, Mentor and Plume Books
are published by The New American Library, Inc.,
1301 Avenue of the Americas, New York, New York 10019

First Printing, March, 1969

PRINTED IN THE UNITED STATES OF AMERICA

FOR JEAN
(Artist in her own right)

CONTENTS

BOOK ONE

Wichita — The Hunger 9

BOOK TWO

Paris — The Search 98

BOOK THREE

Brittany — The Treasure 179

BOOK FOUR

New York — The Reward 236

Book One

WICHITA

The Hunger

HE LAY rolled in his blanket, watching the North Star brighten. Down by the creek Wichita Bill was munching rhythmically on the grassy bank. John Noble leaned up on one elbow, gazing at the fire over which he had boiled his coffee, ruminating that in its fullest sense the trip had been a failure. He had traced down every clue, followed trails through wild Comanche-Kiowa country that no white man had ever ridden, but nowhere had he caught a glimpse of his objective.

He told himself that he should not be too disappointed; no one he knew had ever seen a white buffalo. Perhaps they were simply a part of the legend of the old West. The closest he had come was a tale told by a chief of the Comanches over a fire in the Antelope Hills:

"Many suns ago, when my father's father was a boy, we were at war with the Piutes. The warriors of both tribes were riding either crest of a narrow valley, shooting their arrows at each other. Through the gorge suddenly poured the buffaloes, thick as black smoke. Then, as though from the skies, appeared a white buffalo at their head. The braves could not stay their bows; arrows entered the white buffalo from both sides.

"The black buffaloes swept over him and vanished down

the end of the canyon. The Comanches and Piutes put aside their weapons and walked toward the center of the valley. All that night the braves sat in a silent circle about the white buffalo. At dawn the two chiefs stripped off the fur. The warriors, the women and children then gathered about the luminous robe, dancing, chanting, supplicating the sun. When night came again the tribes intermingled, feasted, slept. By morning the white buffalo was gone, drawn up into the sun. Since that hour our tribes have lived in peace."

Nineteen-year-old John Noble tossed aside his blanket, walked in his stockinged feet to the fire and took some drawing paper from a saddlebag. He pushed the sticks up from the ground so that they met again over the stones, then sat with his legs tucked under him, sketching rapidly the narrow valley with the Indians riding either plateau, and the first of the black buffaloes sweeping into the mouth of the canyon. He covered a second sheet solid with the bison, at their head one beautifully formed white buffalo, caught at the instant when the arrows pierced him from either side. Then he roughed in the tribes joined in the ceremonial circle about the white robe, offering the sacred symbol back to its Maker.

The sticks had burnt down to the periphery of the fire and gone out. John shivered. He laid the three drawings before him, facing them in the near-darkness with unsentimental eyes. He sensed why they were bad: he simply could not believe the old chief's story. There was no more truth in it than there was in all the other leads he had pursued a thousand miles during the past three hot summer months. Yet hadn't Dave Leahy of the Wichita *Eagle* assured him that there was hardier truth to be found in a legend than in a whole barrelful of facts?

He rolled himself in the blanket, pointed his Winchester toward the North Star and fell asleep with the cold night fragrance of the creek, the buffalo grass and the prairie sod in his nostrils.

2

At the first grayish-purple light of dawn he lifted himself stiffly into the saddle. Wichita Bill headed north with an easy single-foot.

He was eager to be in Coffeyville before the village settled down to its day's routine. He had sketched many settlements looking upward at the people and the buildings against the inverted blue-bowl sky; this had given his studies the feel of the transitory, as though the town, the horses and the people were not rooted in anything. Perhaps he had been looking up too much, the way the farmers of the Kansas plains squinted into the sun, achieving little from their search except permanently half-closed lids. He thought, There's mighty little connection between the towns that men build and the mysterious sky against which they are silhouetted. But if I sketch the town looking downward toward its anchorage?

It was a little before eight o'clock when he came to the first outlying farms of Coffeyville. He recognized a gray frame house sitting back from the road as the one the now notorious Dalton brothers had occupied a couple of years before. He thought of the Daltons as romantic outlaws trying to keep alive the tradition of the old West. Frank, Bob, Grat and Emmet hadn't always been bandits, they had started out as United States marshals, fearless young men trying to preserve the law in the badlands of the Oklahoma Territory. Frank had been killed while making an arrest; Bob and Emmet had failed to receive their marshal's wages; Grat had been arrested in California for the alleged holdup of a railway express car and had broken out of jail when he learned that the defending attorney was in the pay of the express company. Only that spring Bob Dalton, the leader of the gang, had bought John a drink in a Wichita saloon while the peace officers of some twelve states were hunting for him.

John gave Wichita Bill a clucking signal as Coffeyville spread before him, the white houses gleaming in the sharp October sunlight. A few children were already making their way toward school. On Union Street he passed a number of young Negroes who were converting what had formerly been a cow trail into a main road, singing as they swung their picks. He entered the plaza, glanced up at the roof of the First National Bank to see if it would afford a good perspective, then walked the big bay horse to the alley which ran west off the square, leaving him at a feed stable to get a meal of hay and oats.

He crossed the length of the plaza to the First National building. Richard Schweiter, president of the bank, had been a house guest of the Nobles in Wichita that winter when he was trying to buy a strategic corner lot from John's father. As John entered the building he saw Schweiter sitting at his desk at the very rear, where he had a full view of every transaction. What a wonderful drawing Mr. Schweiter is, he

11

thought as he made his way toward him: that square-cut white beard, the thick head of white hair brushed flat on top and cut square on his neck; he's all planes and rectangles.

"Good morning, John," said Schweiter in a patriarchal voice. "I trust you brought your father with you, and the deed to that Wichita lot."

"I haven't seen Father for several months, Mr. Schweiter. I been down in Texas and New Mexico."

"Then how about coming to the house with me, my boy, and scraping off that stubble? Mother could give you some salve for those cracked cheeks. And what about breakfast?"

"Breakfast!" John's face lit up. "Now there's an interesting idea. Don't believe I've eaten anything solid for three or four days."

Schweiter looked at John's hollow cheeks and his eyes sunk deep in his face. "Run out of cash? Want to float a little loan?"

"As a matter of fact I did get taken about a week ago, up in the Osages." His smile had a touch of shyness. "Say, Mr. Schweiter, have you ever played cards with the Indians? A squaw held four deuces against my full house, and I would have sworn she was bluffing."

Mr. Schweiter set his hat gingerly on his head so as not to spoil his haircomb.

"Let's go down to the Acme Café. If your father hears that you passed through my hands and came out with that flat stomach, he'll add another five thousand to the price of the corner lot."

They sat at a front table with the autumnal sun flooding bright over their faces. John's head was massive, with a shock of cornsilk hair worn long and cut straight on the neck. His features too were on the ponderous side: a broad, rounded brow, wide, high-boned cheeks, a large nose, almost sensual mouth, and heavy, bony chin; but all of the massiveness ended in well-molded curves, and the gray-blue eyes were intensely alive.

Now that he was once again within the sight and smell of food he became ravenous. He ordered a steak, fried potatoes, a half-dozen eggs, wheat cakes with sausages, hot muffins, jam, apple pie and milk.

"You're like an Indian, my boy," commented Mr. Schweiter in an awed voice; "when you kill an animal you gorge yourself. Then you go lean and hungry between feasts."

He settled himself on the parapet of the First National

12

roof, listened for a moment to the school bells toll nine o'clock, then began drawing the brick-paved square with its imposing banks at either end, the Wells Fargo office, the Opera House, the hardware, drug and clothing stores. Quickly he hollowed out the scenes surrounding the town: the forges, stables, factories to the west, the residential districts north and south with their schools and church spires, the outlying farms, and stubble fields merging into endless prairie.

He had a strong draftsman's fist and the rough sketch took him only a half hour. Against the earth, as against heaven, these structures and these men seemed temporarily placed. Into his mind flashed the picture of the buffalo wallows he had seen that summer, depressions in the earth where millions of buffalo had rolled, over countless centuries, to wear off their unwanted wool in spring; buffaloes now extinct, the whole species destroyed.

Five men came quickly into the plaza from the end of the alley where Wichita Bill was stabled. They were carrying rifles and moving with purposeful steps. Pleased at this sudden appearance of the old West, John picked up his pencil from where it had fallen onto the roof and began drawing them into his sketch. He watched three of the men enter the Condon Bank on their left, the other two more swiftly toward the building on which he was perched. A drayman who had been drowsing on the seat of his wagon yelled:

"The Daltons!"

Then he half jumped, half fell to the brick pavement and scurried to safety.

Through the tall glass window of the Condon Bank John could see the employees standing in strained positions, their arms in the air. Gazing down over the parapet, he caught a glimpse of Bob Dalton, his drinking companion from the bar in Wichita, just as Bob and his brother Emmet entered the First National Bank. Because of his vantage point high over the square, he was the first to realize that the brothers were attempting a feat that had never been risked even by the daredevil James brothers: they were holding up two banks at once.

The plaza below him burst into furious activity. Someone in a doorway shouted, "The Dalton gang's holding up both banks!" and emptied his revolver into the air. The drayman's hitched teams broke loose and darted wildly. Men ran at converging angles over the brick pavement, some with guns, some

13

without. A saddle horse careened about the square, its eyes wide with terror.

John's fingers flew over the paper. A dozen shots rang out from the far end of the plaza, thudding around the door and the plaster just a few nicks below where he squatted, as Bob and Emmet Dalton emerged from the bank, Emmet carrying two heavy sacks of money. John recognized Bob's cool voice saying:

"Bum shot! Come on, Emmet, let's get out the back way."

John ran quickly to the rear of the roof, reaching there just as the Daltons stepped into the alley. A young clerk from Boswell's hardware store suddenly appeared with a revolver in his hand, a glaze of fear on his face.

"Hold up, there!" Bob Dalton commanded.

The young clerk kept running toward the Daltons. Bob raised his gun. An involuntary, half-muted cry came out of John, "No, no, don't kill . . ."

Bob Dalton fired. The clerk fell. John felt cold inside.

He watched the Daltons cross a corner of the plaza and make for the back of the Condon Bank. Flashes of gunfire could be seen from every store lining the square. Two men stepped from a doorway at the west end of the plaza; the one carrying a Winchester drew a bead on Bob Dalton. Bob fired with a lightning shot. The man's companion picked up the Winchester and aimed. Bob felled him too. The shooting was almost continuous now, an acrid smoke rising from the pavement and burning John's nostrils.

The two Daltons made the far alley where their horses were tied. Instead of mounting and riding to safety with their loot, they again stepped into the sheet of fire, heading for the Condon Bank just as Grat Dalton and his two companions, Bill Powers and Dick Broadwell, appeared. The five men regained the alley and unhitched their horses. Within a matter of seconds they would be out of danger.

Someone barked a command inside Isham's hardware store. There was a split-second pause, then a heavy volley of fire. Grat Dalton fell dead, his face in the dirt. Bob sank slowly to his knees. Emmet dropped his rifle, clutching at his shattered arm, then managed to get away. Powers toppled from his horse, dead before he hit the ground. Broadwell managed to reach the outskirts of town before he died of his wounds.

Silence fell. The greatest of all Western street battles was over. Seated on the parapet of the First National Bank building, surrounded by his sheets of drawings, John knew that he

14

had witnessed the end not only of the Dalton gang, but of the wild West itself.

By the time he got down from the roof and made his way across the plaza, the Daltons had been laid out on rough wooden planking, their wrists shackled. He gazed down into their faces, feeling a great poignancy. For years he had followed their every move as they lived off the land, admired and protected by cowboys, ranchers and pioneer settlers. If they had had a private quarrel with the railway express company, held up their cars, took nothing but money that was insured anyway, if the daring and resourcefulness of a handful of brothers could hold the whole law-enforcement body of the federal government at bay, paralyze railroad travel, furnish vicarious adventure to an excitement-starved country, all that had been in a great tradition.

Once again his fingers fumbled for pencil and paper. Into his drawing of the Daltons went his nostalgia for the romance he had loved, which to him now seemed gone irretrievably. In his portrait he tried to catch the brothers halfway between two worlds: the last eager, excited expression of life still on their faces, combined with the first sure knowledge of death.

3

The last hundred-mile stretch from Coffeyville to Wichita had done in both man and horse. Wichita Bill was favoring his right hind leg, in which he had pulled a tendon, and an old saddle sore had come alive again.

John rode a few blocks down Market Street, then turned the horse off toward Doc Saug's stable. It was Doc Saug, the town veterinary, who had summoned young John to see Wichita Bill an hour after the colt had been foaled. Saug was bandy-legged, with a weather-lashed face and short gray hair. He lived only for his animals, sleeping on a cot in the tack room and fixing his food on an old chuck-wagon cookstove which he kept in a rear shack. He smelled like a compound of all the liniments and medicines he used on his patients.

Doc Saug paid no attention to John's lean face or the ribs poking roundly through his thin shirt, but quickly ran his fingers over Wichita Bill's pulled tendon, examined the hoofs and the worn shoes.

"Not bad, John, considering how many miles you've covered."

"Wichita Bill was doing fine up to two days ago in Coffeyville. I had him stabled not twenty yards from where the Daltons tied their horses. That fracas started us both home, hell for leather."

Doc Saug was already brushing the horse down with expert strokes.

"Leave him with me for about three weeks. I'll fill him full of oats and clover and turn him out fat as a cat."

John lifted the roped saddlebags, threw one over his right shoulder, holding the other on his chest. He reached into the front bag, groped around for a moment and pulled out a very dry apricot. He fed it to Wichita Bill, stroked the horse's soft nose affectionately. Wichita Bill whinnied forlornly.

"Summer's over, old boy. You know how it is with a cowboy's horse. You're out for months driving three thousand head of Texas longhorns up the Chisholm Trail. You push the herd twelve miles every day, over mountains and plains, across icy-cold rivers at flood tide; and at night you ride circle around it. When it rains, you stand up to your knees in mud, cold, tired and hungry, and when those crazy critters get frightened and start running in the dark, chasing down strange canyons until the dawn, you've got to ride after them, hold them together, maybe break your leg in a prairie-dog hole. But that's what you're born for, eh, Wichita Bill? That's the best part of life. There's nothing for a cowboy or his horse to do in winter except sleep and eat, and dream about the next spring drive."

His horse was the only living creature with whom he would permit himself any display of sentimentality. As he rubbed the horse's nose his thoughts went back to the almost unendurable excitement of eight years before when his father had agreed to buy Wichita Bill. The boy would let no one feed or water or brush the colt except himself. It was not long before he was able to drop a light rope around the pony's neck and lead him through the fields beyond the town, and along the riverbank. At no time over the succeeding years had he permitted anyone to ride Wichita Bill. It was not jealousy or pride in personal possession; except for his books and pictures he had no desire to own things. When his father had become piqued at his refusal to let his sisters or young brother ride the horse, Mrs. Noble had quieted her husband by saying:

"It's that terrible loyalty he has to everything he loves.

He's monogamous by nature, and I think that promises well for his marriage."

"What marriage?" snorted the father. "I never saw a boy with less interest in girls. He bolts whenever a strange female heaves into sight."

"Give him time. All young men can't be as recklessly romantic as you were."

Vaguely flattered, the father abandoned the argument.

John walked from Doc Saug's stable to Douglas Avenue. Across the street was the Wichita *Eagle*. He made his way up to Dave Leahy's second-floor cubbyhole. From the doorway only Dave's shoulders and back were visible as he crouched over his wooden desk, holding the rickety table steady while he poured out a torrent of words on the rough copy paper before him.

Dave Leahy was that rare species in Kansas, the black Irishman, a big rambling-bodied fellow with coal-black hair, deep blue eyes, a jutting Roman nose and a jutting chin with a dimple slightly off center. He had a witty tongue and the Irishman's indigenous gift of storytelling. He had found his way to Wichita by helping to push the railroads westward; now he was the best-known journalist in the region, loved for his tall tales out of the Oklahoma Indian territory which were passed by word of mouth through thousands of miles of prairie. He had first made the important Eastern papers with a yarn about a party of tourists going through the Wichita mountains; they had run out of water and were dying of thirst when they passed over a field of stones, uniform in size and shaped like loaves of bread. The wagon wheels broke open one of these stones, and there was found to be water in it: ice-cold water. The first drink was given to a beautiful young girl. She had drunk deep and instantly turned to stone! John Noble had illustrated the story with a group of poignant albeit highly imaginative drawings.

The conspirators not only received telegrams from all over the United States asking for further technical information about the terrain, the chemical composition of the water and apparent age of the stones, but cablegrams from London, Paris and Berlin as well. They had managed to keep their story going for several weeks at five dollars a column and five dollars a sketch.

Dave had said, "It's a strange thing, m'boy, but most of these letters are from college professors and scientists. Why are they the easiest to fool?"

"Because they got the openest minds, I guess, Dave. They're always looking for something new and exciting."

The hoax for which Dave was most famous was *The Baby in the Well*. The wells in Kansas sometimes went down one hundred and fifty feet, with an opening of only eight to nine inches. Dave conceived the idea of having a baby crawl around the edge of the well and fall in. As he and John finished graphic accounts of the furious digging by night and day, of the food lowered into the well and the faint cries rising from the bottom, frantic suggestions for its rescue poured in from every state. All America prayed for the baby.

"Look, Dave," urged John, "that baby's been down the well for three weeks now. We can't get away with this any longer. Let's pull it up."

"How?" asked Dave. "We built such an airtight case that there is no possible way of rescue."

"What are you going to do, let the poor kid die?"

"Now, Johnny m'boy, there's no baby down that well. We invented it, remember? We're not going to fall for our own fiction, are we?"

That had been the year before. Now John stood in the doorway, the heavy saddlebags across his shoulder, watching Dave as he pounded out his latest story. After a moment Dave felt the eyes boring into his back and whirled about.

"By God, Dave, I've been gone all summer, and this office reeks worse than when I went away."

"I haven't been out in the clean open air," replied Dave with a warm grin. "I've been sitting here in my little cell, trying to earn a dishonest dollar, while you've been carousing around the country."

John shook his head. "No carousing, Dave. Haven't had a drink. Not even after the Dalton killings."

Dave pushed aside piles of clippings, magazines, pamphlets, almanacs, ash trays, bags of tobacco and blocks of matches, clearing a dusty plateau for John to sit down.

"My fingers have been itching to get at that Dalton story, Johnny. See this wire from the New York *Star*? They'll run as many sticks as we can give 'em. I didn't want to write just the stuff that every fresh-water cub had access to. I knew from your telegram that you'd bring me back something good."

"From where I was, Dave, up on the roof of the First National, it was like a quick succession of lantern slides. I've got a hundred wonderful scenes, flashes of movement against light and shadow etched on my mind, every detail as clear as

18

the Daumier prints in that book you gave me last Christmas."

"You confounded artists," broke in Dave disgustedly, "you're not human, you don't see people as people, but only as objects on a landscape. Eight men die before your very eyes, and all you can think of are problems of perspective. How do you expect me to write a story about the lantern-slide pictures you've got in your mind and that no one else can see?"

"I have one picture you can see, Dave."

Dave took his legs off the desk, scattering papers all over the floor. He held out short, squat, nicotine-stained fingers.

"Give!"

John reached into his saddlebag and took out the death drawing he had made of the Daltons. Dave's heavy figure relaxed; he pushed his squeaking swivel chair away from the desk and over to the window, where the light shone on the single sheet. It seemed a long time before he looked up again.

"You confounded artists," he murmured softly, "you can say more with one picture than we writers can say with a trunkful of words."

His eyes went back to the drawing, and he continued to speak musingly, as though to himself.

"It's all there, Johnny boy: the lean tense months of hiding out in the mountains; the ecstasy of those few frantic moments when they struck and faced death; their love and loyalty to each other and to the code of the West. Yes, and something more; something I would never have suspected about the Daltons: they were confused, troubled, unhappy . . . searching for something. But somehow it always eluded them; and there they lie, manacled, silenced forever."

John walked to the window and stood gazing down onto Market Street. Dave jammed his big yellow meerschaum pipe full of tobacco, filling the room with enormous blasts of smoke.

"What were the Dalton boys looking for, Johnny? It couldn't have been merely revenge on the railway express, or quick and easy money. These brothers had some deeper kind of hunger in them. What causes that terrifying look of loneliness you've caught on their faces as they lie on that crude plank platform, neither crushed nor unbeautiful even in their violent death?"

John turned back from the window, a baffled expression on his face.

"I wish I knew, Dave. I've thought of little else since I left Coffeyville."

Dave rose, put an arm about John's shoulder for a fleeting instant.

"I think I've got the story now, boy. Can I send this drawing East with my copy?"

4

He had not intended seeing Frances before he went home, but when he came to Oak Street he found that instead of crossing it his feet turned left and were carrying him rapidly to the neat red brick house of the Birchfields. He knocked loudly.

Frances opened the door. She had not been expecting company. Her hair was pulled back tightly from the brow and braided almost to her waist. Her full warm lips opened in delight at seeing him. They found themselves clasped in each other's arms, her firm young breasts against his chest, her mouth moist and sweet on his. When they parted they stood awkwardly: for this was their first ardent embrace.

He looked up, saw their reflection in the wall mirror and thought what an interesting contrast they made pictorially: her deep black hair against the corn-silk whiteness of his own, her pink-tinted olive complexion against the pale sunburn of his light cheek, her deep black eyes against his, drifting, smoky blue, her long slender face and finely modeled features against his solid bulk.

She slipped her hand into his, then led him to the dining room.

"There's one nice thing about October and the first rains," she murmured, "they always bring you back to us. After some three months and . . . eight days."

It did not occur to him to be astonished at her having kept such close track.

"Is that how long it was? They don't have any clocks or calendars down in the Territory."

"You wouldn't know how to read them, even if they did."

He chuckled. "Well, the concept of time is a form of slavery, anyhow. Men thought up the system to keep each other chained to counters and desks. I'm content to know what season it is and whether it's night or day. But I sent you frequent messages."

"Did you really, John? I never receiv . . ."

"At night, as I sat alone by my fire I tapped out smoke letters."

She replied laughingly, "I shall press your smoke messages into my memory book, along with my other love letters. By the way, when did you eat last?"

"Couple of days ago, in Coffeyville."

"Do you think your mother would mind if I fed you?"

"Ma never gets mad at you, Frances. She likes you."

Her eyes moved to his, quickly, to see if he were teasing: for she and Mrs. Noble had decided several years before that she and John would make an admirable couple. But John's face was innocent. He followed her into the kitchen, unable to take his eyes off her slim body moving so easily and rhythmically beneath her woolen dress.

Frances was an even six feet tall. She carried her well-proportioned figure proudly, disdaining heelless shoes or the stratagem of walking all scrounged down at the ankles and hips so as to seem an inch shorter, sometimes even accentuating her tallness by braiding her hair on top of her head. There were few men in Wichita who felt comfortable with her, or with whom she was completely at ease. Had she been willing to belittle her height, talk it down, poke fun at it as a kind of affliction for which she would strive to compensate, some of the young men might have been able to stomach the disparity. But to wear it as a badge of glory!

Frances was a bit taller than John, yet neither of them had any sense of this when they were together. Since their grammar school days he had admired her independence, her long-legged grace, the easy way she sat a horse.

She spread a crisply ironed tablecloth, placing him near the window where the sun from the rear garden warmed his back, and after a few minutes set before him an enormous plateful of fried chicken. She drew her chair up close to him, fascinated by his unabashed carnal appetite. The two top buttons of his shirt were off, so that she could see the powerful disks of his chest; she was almost repelled by his brutal and stark maleness, as though there were something indecent about so much carelessly worn strength. His vitality swept over her and made her momentarily faint, so that she had to turn away.

"I bet this chicken was for your brother Charlie's supper. Now wasn't it?"

"Yes."

"Better not tell him who got it. He'll hate me worse than ever."

21

"Now, John, my brother doesn't hate you. It's just that he doesn't understand . . . after all, he hasn't missed a day in our stationery store for eight years, since he graduated from high school. He just can't figure what you're working toward. Once he knows that . . ."

"You have my assurance, Frances, that if I ever find out your brother will be the first to know."

She grimaced, then said, "Did you have a good summer, John? Did you find what you were after?"

"Not a trace."

"When I was visiting in Dodge City last month I saw a white buffalo."

She had spoken in a quiet voice, but his body stiffened.

"A white buffalo . . . in Dodge City?"

"It's in the museum there."

He slumped back into his chair.

"Why are you angry, John? I thought you would want to know."

He rose, stood behind her and put his hands affectionately on her shoulders.

"Frances, the white buffalo I'm looking for has not been felled by a buffalo gun, skinned and nailed to the wall of a musty museum. My white buffalo is running free over rugged mountains and through green valleys; it is strong and beautiful, so beautiful that a man's eyes are hardly capable of seeing it!"

5

Elizabeth Noble heard her son's footsteps coming up Wichita Street. She hurried to the front door and leaned against the railing of the south porch, watching as he strode toward her. He had her hair, so blond it was almost white in the afternoon sun, and he wore it thick and long on his neck, mountaineer fashion, so that it seemed to gather there, the way she caught her own hair under the long flat clasp.

He's good-looking, she thought, as pleased as though it were the first time she had made this astonishing discovery.

Yet even the mother, waiting with a warm smile of welcome, had to perceive that her son's face carried a dozen contradictions within its modest compass. The strong bony structure of his brows, cheeks and chin gave the semblance of dominant massiveness, yet actually its contours were lean; his mouth appeared hearty but the lips were taut; and the lid of his right eye fell too sharply toward the bridge of the nose. To the mother it appeared a searching rather than an assertive face, amused by life and yet perplexed and harassed by it.

She thought, It all depends on which side of his face you happen to be gazing at; just as it all depends on who is looking out of his eyes: himself or his demon.

For Elizabeth Noble understood that behind her son's opaque blue gaze lurked some kind of submerged force. Always, if she looked deep enough, she found a brooding, haunting quality. What was it, unrest? Unhappiness? His eyes seemed crowded, as though inhabited by more than one person. There were times in the past few years when she had thought her son possessed. But by what?

She could foretell the seizures; the ridge of his nose sharpened bonily, his cheeks sank in, his skin became drawn. He seemed consumed by the fires of an unnamed conflict; his eyes retreated into his skull, he became enigmatic, seeing little, saying less. These were the hours she dreaded most, for she had found no way to help him in his torment.

But now as she took her older son in her arms and gazed at him across the long summer's absence, she saw that his expression was clear, his body lean from the days in the saddle, but with a healthy leanness that spoke of much purposeful movement. When she kissed him, murmuring her joy in having him back home again, she realized that she loved this big lumbering boy with a fierceness mothers reserve for children whose happiness, and very lives, are endangered. Her two daughters and younger son were such bright, cheerful, normal creatures. Why couldn't John have been born that way too?

"Son, you smell like a cowboy who has just driven a herd of Texas longhorns all the way up from Waco. I'll bet you haven't bathed in weeks."

"You lose, Ma. I fell off Wichita Bill while he was taking himself a long drink at Deep Fork."

"Sure, with all your clothes on."

"Now, Ma, you wouldn't have wanted me to be riding in the raw."

"Take your bag upstairs and come back to the kitchen in about ten minutes. I'll have a tub of hot water."

His room was not large, but it was hung with a buff wallpaper which his mother had let him pick out for himself. Tacked to the wall were dozens of pictures cut out of books,

23

magazines, brochures, catalogues: crude colored reproductions of oils by Rubens, Delacroix, El Greco, Frans Hals; line drawings by Michelangelo, Leonardo da Vinci, Rembrandt, etchings by Daumier. Covering the door wall were bookshelves with the works of Edgar Allan Poe, William Blake, Shakespeare, Balzac, Dante's *Inferno* illustrated by Doré, Milton's *Paradise Lost*, Homer's *Iliad, Pilgrim's Progress*, and several of Scott's historical novels.

The bed was placed at an odd angle in the room, against no wall, but in juxtaposition to the window so that when he put his head on the pillow at night the last thing he saw before he closed his eyes was the North Star. Elizabeth Noble had moved the bed into this position in the most desperate hour of his childhood, when he had been betrayed by his classmates. They were his friends, they were trustworthy; that was why, when they had suggested a great hoax for the Fourth of July, he had agreed to play the principal role. There was a bridge across the Arkansas River with high trestlework above it; the boys were to inform the whole town that on the Fourth of July John Noble would make a death-defying leap from the very top of the structure into the shallow water below. But just as he was about to dive his cronies would cry out:

"No, no! It's too dangerous! Come down!"

Then they would all climb the structure and drag him back to safety.

On the Fourth of July, after the barbecue and firecrackers had been exhausted at Island Park, a crowd gathered on the banks of the Arkansas to watch John make his heroic dive. He climbed to the top of the superstructure while below his co-conspirators were giving portentous rolls on a drum. Then it was time for him to leap. He gave the signal for the rescue. To his amazement the children laughed and shouted:

"Jump! Jump! Make the dive!"

He clung to the top of the supports, sick at heart and stomach. He knew that he would be killed if he jumped into the shallow river below; yet surely that was preferable to a humiliating retreat, accompanied by the jeers and catcalls of his betraying classmates and the Wichita folk as well. Then he remembered his mother, knew what grief she would suffer if he threw himself into senseless death to save his pride.

He crawled slowly downward; there was a roaring in his head which closed out the laughter of his friends. He ran home as fast as he could and locked himself into his room. It was not until midnight, when the rest of the family had gone to sleep, that he let his mother in. She sat on the edge of the bed, stroking his finespun hair, wiping the tears from his cheeks.

"It's not the humiliation I mind, Ma. Not even their calling me quitter and yellow-bellied. It's just that I . . . I'll never be able to . . . trust anybody again."

His mother sat in silence for a moment, then rose and walked to the window from which she could see the North Star shining brightly. She went back to the bed and pulled it on its casters to the center of the room.

"You see that star, son? That's the North Star. It's always there. No matter what happens to us, or to the world, that star is steadfast. It will never change, never fail you. As long as you can find the North Star, you'll know that you're secure."

Elizabeth Turner had been brought from Grasmere, England, when she was four years old. The family settled at Todds Point, Illinois, an English settlement where the Nobles owned considerable farmland. Elizabeth had an exquisite pink and white complexion and soft blond hair; as the oldest child in a family of six she was trained to help raise the other children and to consider the care of one's home and family a fine art. At the age of nineteen she had married John Noble, ten years older than herself, and moved with him to the raw, crude cow town of Wichita, terminus of the Newton and Southwestern Railroad. Here John Noble had invested every last dollar of the money he had secured for the farm left to him by his father, sunk it in business lots and town acreage in what had seemed to Elizabeth to be the end of the earth. Her husband then built a three-room house and surrounded it by a white picket fence; Elizabeth drew water from an outside pump, planted maples and cottonwoods, tended her garden and bore four children in seven years.

The Nobles were a happy family; Elizabeth's only misgivings had come from the wild and lawless life of the frontier, for the signs outside town read:

EVERYTHING GOES IN WICHITA

and the cowboys, like sailors home from a long voyage, wanted to spend their pent-up pay and pent-up craving for pleasure in the few hours vouchsafed them. Fights, shootings, killings, these were everyday occurrences in the rival dance halls of Rowdy Joe Low and John Red Beard, and in the sporting shanties in Delano down on the riverbank. She

25

would never forget the night of June 3, 1877, when a fight broke out in Red Beard's saloon between the Seventh Cavalry and the Texas cowboys. To nineteen-year-old Elizabeth the continuous gunfire made it seem as though John Brown and the Civil War had returned to Kansas.

During the years she had made no concessions to the fact that she lived on the edge of civilization. The wilder the town grew, the more her children were exposed to drunken street brawls, wide-open gambling halls and sporting sections, the more she insisted upon preserving in her home and family life all that she had learned from her mother at Todds Point. She never gave in to the rough frontier or was influenced by it.

Eventually the railroad had been extended beyond Wichita. The town was no longer the end of a longhorn trail. Wichita grew rapidly, peacefully, acquiring schools, churches, paved streets, a library and even a permanent theater. Now the Nobles lived in a two-story house in the best part of town, its interiors beautifully wood-paneled, with a big barn at the back for horses and handsome carriages. On Thanksgiving the house was decorated with mistletoe, holly and California pepper vines, with red carnations on the dining-room table. At Christmas and New Year's there were big parties. Bluff John Noble was proud of the way he could swing his smallish wife off the floor in the Virginia reel and schottishe. The youngest daughter, Elizabeth, played the piano for these dances and the neighbors came in to play violins, clarinets and French horns. The Noble children were always allowed to hold open house, and they and their young friends had soon danced all the nap off the heavy carpet.

Twenty years had cost Elizabeth Noble neither her lovely complexion nor the perfection of her piecrust; nor had they in any way depleted her fund of vitality and humor. She was up early, generally at six, and she was the last to bed, immersed in an endless series of chores which flowed effortlessly into each other, each task as good and important as the next. She was quick to help when her neighbors were ill or in difficulty, but she went out little socially; she had all the company and social life she required right in her own home. Nor was she one for fads; the year before she had been criticized for her refusal to join in the mad Sunday after-church carriage race through town to see who could leave the most calling cards in their friends' elaborate silver dishes.

Over the years John's bed had remained at its strange angle in the room; and over the years he had rarely gone to sleep without first sighting the North Star. In some mystical sense it had become synonymous with his mother: for she too was steadfast, unchanging.

So far as John knew she was a woman without dark corners of unhappiness, without fear, envy, bitterness or unrequited desires. How often he wished he could be like her.

6

It was suppertime before his father came home; for John Noble, Sr., had forced himself to remain at the Eaton Bar in order that his son might not know how eager he was to see him again. John threw his arms roughly about his father and embraced him. They were good friends, only occasionally antagonists. Every summer during his childhood his father had taken him on camping trips over the flat plains of Kansas or deep into the Rocky Mountains of Colorado. His father had taught him how to shoot and fish and live off the land, how to make camp, kindle a fire and sleep with his head pillowed on the saddle.

John Noble, Sr., was a big man, big in the shoulders, chest and back. His face too was big, and on the homely side, for his skin was coarse, and the enormous nose, mouth and chin looked as roughhewn as a sculptor's first model in damp clay. He walked as though he were carrying a heavy physical weight, yet there was no matching heaviness in his manner; he was gregarious, fun-loving and had more friends than any man in town. His instincts had guided him rightly about Wichita; when the village had begun to grow he put up buildings on his land. With the rental money he had bought residential plots, and then outlying farms and ranches, always buying, never selling. No one knew exactly how much he was worth, but the town had computed his income at more than a thousand dollars a month.

Independent as a wild horse, the elder John Noble had set up his own standards. As a boy he had refused to remain in school, insisting upon finding his education in the writings of the world's great minds. After his marriage he had been unwilling to remain in the midst of his prosperous and influential family, and had set out for a new, exciting frontier, as his English grandparents had before him. During all these twenty years he had never had an office, conducting his business on the streets, in the bars, and on the long buggy rides to and from his outlying properties. When friends remarked that it was hardly respectable for so important a citizen not to have an office, he laughed a thunderous laugh and replied:

"If I had an office, I'd have to go to it regularly. Once I was there I'd be obliged to answer the mail on the desk and talk business to people who came in. I'd have to close deals even when I didn't want to. But when you're just walkin' around town, you got no obligations to yourself or anybody else. Besides, offices are for men who get tired easy and need to sit down."

He was the most difficult man in the world to locate when somebody wanted to make a deal. He seemed disinterested in business, but actually he was a shrewd operator. Business was a game to him, an endlessly amusing sport; he liked to prolong the contest as long as possible and drive a hard bargain. Once he had won he would ease up on the terms and cry out from his permanent table at the Eaton Bar, his barrellike voice loaded with good humor:

"Jerry, set 'em up for the house! I just made me a horse trade."

Over the bookcase in the Noble living room hung a gentle landscape painted on ivory, a present from one of the Noble uncles back in Illinois. The shelves were filled with the novels of Dickens, Zola, Bulwer-Lytton, Mark Twain, Sir Walter Scott, with Darwin's *Origin of Species,* Haeckel's *Riddle of the Universe*. John, Sr., waged monumental arguments with young John over Darwin, Huxley and the meaning of disputed passages in *Love's Labour's Lost* or *Twelfth Night*. His son rarely won, but he put up increasingly stiff forensic battles as he grew older, to his father's delight.

Father and son had had their only serious row when the boy was fifteen. John had grown tired of school; his wide reading and philosophic turn of mind made the elemental lessons seem childish. He spent most of his time sketching on the margins of his notebook. One Monday morning he simply refused to go back. His father waited patiently for several months to see what the boy would do.

"Why are you wasting your time on this woman's work?" he finally had growled. "First thing we know you'll be painting china dishes."

This was the insult supreme; only spinsters painted on china.

"Would you rather I took a job somewhere?"

"Yes, if it's a good one."

"Like managing your office, for instance?"

The father let the impertinence pass; it was fair repayment for the dig about china dishes.

"There are lots of good opportunities around."

"Do we need the money?"

"No, son, we have enough money. It's just that I don't like to see you . . . floundering. You got to start thinking about growing up. Now if there's any school you'd like to go to, even if it was out of Wichita . . ."

"I don't like schools, Pa. I want to learn for myself."

"But just what are you learning from these scribblings?"

"My drawings are bad, amateurish, because drawing is the hardest thing in the world to get right. But if you do your best, then every drawing is important."

John Noble, Sr., had rarely disciplined his children; he left that regrettable task to his wife. Nor did he permit himself to grow perturbed in his home, for when he became excited froth bubbles formed in the corner of his mouth. But he was growing angry now, more from young John's resolute attitude than anything the boy was saying.

"I'll give you till fall. Then you'll either go back to school or go to work!"

"No, Father."

"No, what?"

"I won't go back to school or take a senseless job that I can't do well and nobody needs me for."

"Then you're defying me?"

"Only if you're determined to make an issue out of this."

The father showered his unyielding son with cold saliva and hot words. At the end of the five-minute outburst he stopped abruptly in the middle of a sentence.

"John, you're not listening to a word I'm saying."

"I'm listening. I'm just not agreeing."

"I don't care a fig for your agreement. You're only a fifteen-year-old boy and you'll do what I tell you!"

"You're wrong, Pa. I'll only do what I feel I must do."

Blind with rage, the father struck his son. Slowly the temper drained out of their tightly drawn mouths, and they had stood gazing into each other's blue eyes, equally aghast at what had happened. Then, without a word, they had turned and gone their separate ways and both had gotten thoroughly drunk.

Since that day they had enjoyed a healthy deference for each other. Whenever differences arose the father and son fought them out under cover of the supper table, the disputed

29

point artfully concealed beneath barbed humor, the family hearing only the surface contest.

7

Marty Buckler had learned from Frances that his friend John had returned. He came in just as the Nobles were about to sit down to supper. He was promptly invited to join them. Mrs. Noble liked Marty for the unswerving quality of his devotion to her son. Mr. Noble liked him for the inexhaustible flow of business schemes that poured through his head.

Marty was as thin as the Atchison, Topeka and Santa Fe rails which ran through Wichita. In grammar school the boys had called him "Stringbeans." He had a flat chest, arms and legs like piston rods: plenty of bone and grit, but little flesh. He had been brought out to Kansas when he was a year old and settled in a sod house, dug into the earth by his impoverished parents with their bare hands. He had seen his mother work herself into a shallow prairie grave, watched his father grind himself ever deeper into poverty and hopelessness, lose his homestead and have their paltry, pathetic personal articles, broken furniture and tools acutioned in public disgrace.

Marty was the same age as John. He had short-cropped, fiery red hair and red eyebrows that grew without a break across the bridge of his nose. His face was bony, but he had big and expressive purple eyes, flecked with spots of mustard brown. His day and night dreams were infested with thousands of schemes to make money, big money. Every time he came into the Noble house, or John rode his laundry wagon around town for an hour of companionship, Marty had new plans, bigger and brighter than the ones of the day before.

"From money," said Marty, "you get respect, security, long life. From poverty you get insults, bitterness, a miserable and lonely death. Ask me, I watched my parents."

Marty had as yet found no way to implement even the most modest of his ideas; but he was saving his money, nickel by nickel, occupying the smallest bedroom in Wichita, apparently eating heartily only on those occasions when he joined the Nobles over their generous table. He was a materialist at heart, one who pursued money as a shield and armor to protect himself from the world. He had left school even earlier than John, exclaiming:

"When you put all that book stuff together, it still don't

add up to a profit. What's the good of learnin' lessons before you know whether you're going to be able to eat?"

After dinner, in John's bedroom Marty studied the hundreds of sketches John laid out on the bed, his darting eyes jumping from paper to paper, seeking the solution to the enigma of his friend.

"Fine, you had a great summer, a wonderful vacation. But what does it all get you?"

John had been over this argument hundreds of times before. He was not distressed by Marty's seeming antagonism, for he perceived something which Marty himself did not dare acknowledge: that the little redhead, spending twelve hours a day on his laundry wagon and the other hours in a narrow airless rectangle off somebody's dark hallway, had a dull, gnawing hunger for the things that John talked about and worked at: the hundreds of books on the roughhewn shelves, the paintings pinned to the walls; rooted deep in the concealed passages of Marty Buckler's spirit was a respect for the fruits of the intellect. Love made Marty want to preserve John exactly as he was; but fear made Marty want to destroy him. Intuitively he sensed that any interest in art, literature or abstract ideas would lessen his drive toward money; a drive in which a man must be single-minded and fanatically dedicated.

"What are you going to do now?" he demanded in his thin, hurried voice.

"Well, there are a lot of pictures I'd like to develop, things I saw that are coming into perspective now."

"But, John, you can't waste a whole winter like you spent the summer, just drawing things. How are you going to turn it into a profit?"

John chuckled as he gazed at his friend's troubled face.

"It gives me pleasure to work with this stuff, Marty, and little by little I seem to catch hold of, well, a little understanding. What could be more profitable?"

"Now look, John, we're not kids any more. We're goin' to be twenty in a few months. We got to find a permanent place for ourselves. Then there'll be time for play." With an angular gesture of his bony arm he swept the room and its hundreds of fragmentary drawings, to indicate what he meant by play.

John smiled amusedly, but in his expression there was also a cross between resignation and despair.

"You should've been my father's son," he said. "You put into words the things he thinks when he looks at me."

"Holy Jehosophat!" exclaimed Marty, jumping up from his chair. "How I wish I was your father's son! We'd own the state of Kansas before we got through."

"Pa's doin' pretty well all by himself," replied John. "What are you doing in that direction?"

"All right, John, smile. I know I've come up with some lulus in the past, but this one is practical. I'm gonna open a laundry."

"For heaven's sake, Marty, I thought you were tired of carting other people's dirty wash all over town."

"Only because I'm carting it for somebody else. John, everybody on my route's complained to me about how many things are lost; they're gettin' bad service: that mangle is ripping the shirts, and you should see the collection of buttons we end up with every washday."

"And you're going to remedy all that?"

"You bet! I open an office on Main Street, say. I know an empty store right now that's going begging because it's so black inside, but boy, what you could do to it with a bucket of paint. People pass there every day of the week. We give 'em a reduction, ten per cent on every bundle, because they bring and pick up themselves. We give 'em receipted lists for everything they bring. We sew buttons back on, darn socks, repair rips and tears. What do you say, pal, do you think it will go?"

"You'd sure get all the work from the bachelors in town. But you're going to need a pile of money, Marty, to open that office and pay for lost clothing and hire women to sew."

Marty shook his head with a quick, eager denial.

"What do you think I've been doing in that laundry for three years? Old Swinden thought I was a fool; for my five bucks a week I not only drove his wagon, but bought his supplies and kept his books and repaired his machines when they broke down. John, I can tell you to a tenth of a penny how much soap it takes to wash a shirt. When I open my laundry it's goin' to be run efficient. All I need is a hundred dollars more. Why don't you come in with me?"

John shook his head in incredulity.

"Marty, after all these years you can't still think that I'd want to run a laundry?"

"Now wait a minute, you long-haired book reader," exclaimed Marty sharply. "The laundry isn't the end, it's only the beginning. I got big plans. I know a dozen ways we could branch out from there . . ."

John got up, stretched, yawned a prodigious muscular yawn.

"You say you're gonna run a laundry, you'll run a laundry. You say you're gonna expand from there, I'm convinced you'll expand. But there's just one way you're soft in the head, and that mistake could ruin a better hombre than you."

"What's the mistake?"

"Me," said John. "You keep trying to draw me into all your schemes when you know perfectly well I couldn't be anything but a liability."

Marty evaded John's eyes, replying sotto voce:

"I never said you were a genius with a dollar, it's only that, well, you know, I'm alone in the world, John. You been my best friend. It's no fun startin' out alone. I know we're awful different, extremes like, I guess. But that might be a good thing. You'd have plenty of smart ideas that I could never think up, and I'd have all the hard business sense the two of us'd need. We'd have good times, too. It wouldn't have to be just all business."

John had picked up a pencil and sketched rapidly while Marty talked, filling in the details of Marty's face: the short red hair like stubble of a cornfield after it has been burned over; the big, eager, pleading purple eyes; the hollow cheeks and the dry, fevered lips. Suddenly he stopped, tossed his pencil across the desk. He had caught only a few hours of sleep the night before on the way up from Coffeyville.

"Let's get some shut-eye, boy."

Marty walked to the door, then hesitated and turned, looking at John with his head cocked to one side, a half-nervous expression on his face:

"Look, John, I think I ought to tell you: this summer I took Frances to hear Sousa's band when it played at the Toler Theater. I got a couple of passes for tacking up their posters on the side of my laundry wagon."

John, who had slipped out of his shirt and trousers, stood gazing at Marty, wondering why his friend seemed so ill at ease.

"Why in hell are you tellin' me about it at three in the morning?"

Marty fidgeted in the doorway.

"Well, I . . . didn't want to hide anything from you . . . in case you wouldn't like it."

"Look, Marty, I haven't got my brand on that girl."

8

Like the Kansas prairies on which he had been raised, where the snow froze the winters and the sun seared the summers, he lived in a cyclical climate of extremes. He either wore the same soiled and wrinkled clothes for days on end, or dressed up like a dude; he either worked locked in his room for a week, drinking a glass of milk occasionally and throwing himself fully clothed on the bed for an hour of troubled sleep, or he pushed aside his drawing materials with the nausea of repletion, ate famishedly of his mother's food, took Frances to parties, practiced with the Wichita Maroons to get back his throwing arm and batting eye, boxed eight rounds in the town gymnasium and rode Wichita Bill out through the prairies, stopping overnight at the sod houses of the early settlers. He went for a month without a coin in his pocket or swaggered into the Eaton Bar with a wad of greenbacks and stood treat for the house.

When it rained he went up to the office of the *Eagle* to swap yarns with Dave Leahy and draw pictures to illustrate the tall tales which his friend was now signing with the by-line of The Kansas Liar. He frequently found young Victor Murdock in Dave's cubbyhole, arguing politics from Plato's *Republic* down to that morning's speech by Congressman Blowhard. Victor sopped up political history the way other Wichitans did schnapps: he was wise to the fraud, graft, pretense and hypocrisy of the politico, and endlessly amused by it. John had drawn a few cartoons to accompany Victor's editorials on state and national government.

"Why not come to work for us as a staff cartoonist?" urged Victor. "You've got the gift of plunging to the essence of a matter with a very few lines . . . hardly a tenth of the lines it takes me in cold print."

"Thanks, Victor, but I still want to keep my freedom."

"Freedom for what, John? You want to be an artist, we're offering you work as an artist . . ."

"I don't know, Vic," John broke in, but gently. "Just freedom."

This had been his pattern ever since his cousin, Anne Noble, traveling from the East to San Diego with her family, had spent the better part of the week in the Noble back yard making water-color scenes of Elizabeth Noble's beds of geraniums. Young Anne had taken some art courses at the University of Illinois, and ten-year-old John had been fascinated, asking endless questions on how she achieved her effects. By the third day he had sat himself next to her, his feet tucked under him in a big chair and a drawing board on his lap.

Until he was fifteen he had been able to fit his drawing into his spare hours. When he went with his family to St. John's Episcopal Church of a Sunday morning, and the congregation sat silently weighing the minister's words about sin and life eternal, John drew the congregation from the back, the expression in their shoulders and the angle of their heads, the minister gesticulating from the pulpit, the scrubbed faces of the choir boys behind him. When his schoolteacher told him about Lincoln at Gettysburg, and while the youngsters read the speech, John drew what he had heard of the troops and the fighting, and superimposed on this destruction tall cavernous-eyed Abraham Lincoln speaking from rough notes which had been tucked into his stovepipe hat.

He had a draftsman's eye and a draftsman's fist. He saw nature clear and true; once sketched on the swiftly changing film of his mind, nothing of the imprint was lost. Whenever he wanted an image he had only to press a button and the print that had been stored in the vaults of his memory slid out in front of his eyes, on an invisible easel for him to study and draw.

He had often asked himself, What makes a good draftsman? Some of the answers had emerged from experience: clarity of eye, courage to attempt difficult themes, the daring to eliminate the meaningless or obstructive, the discipline of hard work until the pencil became part of the hand, a natural extension of the arm as well as of the mind and temperament.

His big awkward figure hovered over his desk, setting down everything he had seen, heard and felt during the summer. Drawing was his way of understanding life, of coming to grips with it, extracting meaning and sense from it, achieving some tiny payment of fulfillment. He wanted to make a drawing in the same way that Marty Buckler wanted to make a dollar. In this work he was not arguing or proclaiming, he was seeking. Each man traveled his own road to wisdom; John knew no other road except possibly his few valued books, yet for him there was an essential difference between finding wisdom in a book and creating wisdom in a drawing. He was not searching for facts or information, for he had already learned that yesterday's fact became tomorrow's falsehood.

What was it he wanted to feel and understand? He did not know. He had the hunger; the ever-present food of work was at hand, yet he was never able to assuage his desire. At the outset of each new drawing he thought he was on the trail, that this time the mystery would be unraveled, the longing placated. He went to the fresh concept and the fresh drawing the way other men rushed out to a new love, yet drawings which had great meaning for him while he was in the middle of them went empty and meaningless after completion. The sense of inadequacy was painful, but the compulsion to try again was as natural and immediate as the impulse to breathe: they came together, interlocked.

It took two months of uninterrupted labor to put down everything that pressed for expression; then one day he tossed aside his drawing pencil with a feeling of disgust: all of these hundreds of drawings were fragments, and no matter how carefully fitted together they could not add up to anything whole or complete. For the first time he understood that, beautiful as some of the sketches might be, honest and authentic as he had tried to make them, they were little more than preparatory studies: a rehearsal arduously performed but nonetheless a rehearsal.

He awoke one morning with the knowledge that he wanted to start working in oils. He had never handled a tube of paint, a brush or a piece of canvas. Occasionally he had stumbled upon some clue, a chance remark in Vasari's *Lives of the Artists,* or Delacroix's *Journal.* But where did one begin? And how?

After breakfast he found himself walking excitedly to town. He went directly to Hyde and Humble's stationery store where the family had a charge account. There he bought a supply of prepared canvas, a set of brushes, a palette, some linseed oil and turpentine, and all the earth colors they had in stock: ocher and raw sienna of the yellows; Indian, Venetian, light sienna and alizarin crimson of the reds; terre-verte and chrome of the greens; ultramarine and cobalt of the blues; raw umber and burnt umber of the browns.

The moment he reached his room he began clumsily to transfer paint to his palette, arching from the highest lemon yellow nearest to hand, through the reds and blues to the darkest greens; in the center he put the neutral umbers and white. Without bothering to conjure up a picture in his mind or draw an outline on the canvas, he began dipping his brushes in the paints and running them across the blank surface before him. At first they were so thick he could not make them move across the canvas; after frequent wetting of his brush with linseed oil and turpentine they got so thin they would not cover a solid surface.

He spent days learning how to mix the pigments to approximate the colors he wanted, then, wiping his canvas clean with a rag, he put the primary colors next to each other in sharp thick lines or in thin washes to see how they affected each other and changed each other's tones. He was so possessed by his new adventure that he could not tear himself away for food or rest.

It was very late on the fourth night when he had an uncontrollable desire to paint an actual picture. He had given no thought to what his first painting would be; nor did he think of it now. He tacked a piece of canvas onto the flat desk and quickly set down an outline. He then began painting a wide green valley with Indian warriors riding either slope, a brown-black living carpet of buffalo pouring in through the mouth of the canyon, and at their head an exquisite and glowingly white buffalo, the brilliance of his hair caught up by the sun, the gleaming, golden rays between them forming an arched bridge.

Day had broken by the time he finished. His teeth chattering with cold and exhaustion, he dropped out of his clothes, climbed gingerly between the sheets and fell asleep at once. It was late afternoon when he was awakened by the sun streaming in the west window. He rose, slipped into his trousers and stood gazing at his effort of the night before, shaking his head in amused bewilderment. He had thought he understood the principles of perspective, yet he had failed to realize that the stronger the color the more it pulls the object in close, and that in order to put the far cliff in the back of the picture he had to deliberately weaken its color.

He had just finished wiping the paint off the canvas and was about to start afresh when his mother came into the room. She found him crouched over the desk.

"Why don't you go downstairs and use the parlor?" she asked. "You're much too crowded in here."

Shocked, John could only look up at his mother and say:

"The parlor! But, Mother, no one in Wichita uses the parlor; that's to be kept for the minister's visits, and for funerals."

"Both of which I try to discourage. That parlor has been useless ever since we moved into this house, and no one gets to see those beautiful cherrywood walls. But there's a good light, John. I saw it once, before we put on those heavy velours draperies."

"But, Mother, I'm sure to spill paint on your rug."

Elizabeth Noble set her mouth resolutely.

"Things are to be used."

He straighted up from the desk. He wanted to go to his mother and take her in his arms, tell her how kind and good she was. Yet he couldn't move, he could only stand awkwardly, feeling warm inside himself, with no words coming to his lips.

9

He saw himself walking on the prairie. It was dusk. There was no man, no tree, no house, no sun, no star. Just John alone. He had been walking for a very long time, yet there was no end in sight.

There was a pain around his heart. He began to run toward the dim horizon. Faster, faster. His breathing became heavy, labored. There was a weight on his chest, he could find no air around him to gulp. Now he knew what he was fleeing from: loneliness: being solitary on the face of the earth. Behind him were people, family, friends, passers-by on the city streets. But he had walked these streets, and no man's eyes had seen him. He had entered houses, intruded into intimate circles and conversations, yet no man's ear had heard him. He had shaken people by the shoulder but they had gone on calmly, uninterruptedly, just as though he were not there, not bulking physically before them, crying out:

"Notice me! Talk to me! Admit me! I'm lonely. Don't treat me as though I weren't here, as though I were dead!"

Dead?

Could that be it? Was that why no one knew he was there? Could a man die and not know it, could he walk the face of the earth, cry out to his friends and loved ones and never have them know he was there? Why else should a man feel this torture of loneliness, this tangible physical agony?

He began running again. Suddenly the terrain changed; he had come out of the endless prairie and into a spreading valley. Gone was the dull yellow-gray sea of buffalo grass; before him spread a vast carpet of white flowers. No, not flowers, cotton in bloom, extending endlessly in all directions.

The pain over his heart eased, and he went quickly down the slope into the gleaming white fields which lighted the crepuscular dusk like a lamp on the center table of a room.

Then all breathing stopped. Now his ribs and lungs and heart were crushed together in agonizing pain. For these were not white flowers, nor blooming cotton plants, these were the bleached bones of buffalo, millions upon millions of buffalo who had been slaughtered by the hunters, their hides cut off roughly, their carcasses left to the coyotes, the vultures, the ants, until nothing remained but this endless field of white bones, white extinction, brutal, wanton, meaningless death.

Terrorized, he tried to find his way back, but there was no longer a road to retreat. He bruised his feet and shins on the jagged white skulls. But no matter how far or fast he ran, his tongue swollen and parched, the stinging sweat pouring down into his eyes, he made no progress. This was an endless sea of death.

Death. Yes, he too was a part of this death. But how? Only a few hours before he had been alive, intensively alive. He had been standing before the easel in his mother's parlor, painting absorbedly. He was too young to die. He had not yet begun to live, to work, to understand. If he could only find a way out. He could not endure being dead in the midst of life, among people who did not know he was there; neither could he endure this being alive in an endless procession of white death.

His pace slowed. His eyes cleared. Ahead of him lay a green upland valley, walled in by gentle slopes. Far down the valley a living ceature was moving about. He walked quickly on springy turf down the draw, taking great gulps of cool moist air into his lungs.

Then he stopped. The living creature before him was a white buffalo, small, superbly sculpted, its coat the vibrant color of early morning clouds. All his days he had hungered for a sight of the white buffalo; he had searched across thousands of miles of barren desert and rock-crested mountains, hungering as a lover hungers for the image of his beloved. And now, here before him stood the white buffalo.

The White Buffalo was death. But hadn't he always known that, deep in the recesses of his mind? Hadn't he always felt that only in the glowing light of death could the meaning of life be grasped? If only at the instant a man was born he could for a moment die, then all the rest of his life would be endurable, nay, sweet: for weren't the uncertainties, the greeds, the brutalities of life caused by the fear of the unknown, of death? Life had been intolerable for him because he had had no knowledge of death.

He struggled long and hard to get his eyes open. When he succeeded he could see nothing. The room was black, airless. He fell onto the bed, his body burning with fever. He shivered just a little at first, then his teeth began rattling and his arms shaking in their sockets. Soon his whole body was convulsed. He doubled the blankets over him, but the added warmth only made him tremble the harder. When he was exhausted the chills lessened; and soon he was lying still, cold in his innards, his body covered with perspiration.

He threw the blankets aside and struggled up from the bed. His bones felt splintered upward through his skin. Curved around his brow and across the back of his skull were steel bands joined to each other by thongs and pulling ever tighter. He who found no darkness in the darkest night now found intolerable darkness inside his own head.

He beat around the room blindly, knocking over the chair by his desk, putting his hand through a windowpane while reaching for support where he thought the big bureau stood, then pitched headlong over the footstool onto the floor.

Here his mother found him. She soaked a bath towel in cold water and wiped down his face. He rolled his head from side to side.

"What is it, darling? What hurts you, Johnny?"

Fumbling he reached out, took her hand and held it against his cheek as though it were his only grip on life.

"I'm so lonely."

"Johnny, you know I love you, and your father and brother and sisters love you, and Frances and Marty and Dave and Victor all love you."

When he did not answer or even seem to hear her, but instead took her hand and brushed it over the bony structure of his face, she continued:

"Is there someone you love . . . that you haven't told us about?"

"It hurts to be so alone, like you're the last human being left in the world."

"Let me get you some coffee, John. It will make you feel better."

She ran quickly downstairs and heated the coffee. He lay quietly on the bed while she was gone, knowing that he had to get out of the house, that he couldn't stand any longer his room's four narrow walls. Then his mother was standing beside him, pressing the hot coffee between his lips.

"Drink this, darling. Then I'll bring some soup."

He nodded in agreement. A sigh of relief came to her lips. He waited until he heard her moving about in the kitchen below, then he rose, slipped into a woolen shirt and stumbled down the main stairs, trying to be quiet, but knocking against the banister.

Elizabeth Noble heard her son. She stopped in the midst of ladling out a dish of barley soup with its square-cut pieces of beef, and stood at the stove, her head down, her heart beating painfully, knowing that she must let him go.

She saw him make for the stable where he kept a supply of Sunnybrook hidden. Since the whiskey was never disturbed, John thought no one knew of his hiding place; the entire family knew. Wichita Bill turned around in his stall, watching him climb up to the rafters and take down a bottle, then throw back his head and drink long and hard. John shivered once, made a wry face as his stomach seemed to rise almost to his throat, then his body relaxed with a long soughing sound. Wichita Bill came over, nudging him with his head.

"No, not now, Bill. Later."

He took another quick gulp, corked the bottle, then tried to slip it into his back trouser pocket. The bottle was too large so he tore the pocket down on one side. He went out the rear door of the stable and found his way through the back alley to Frances' house. He took another long drink and hid the bourbon in the bushes. He heard Frances playing the piano and began to hum a tune; already he was feeling better, his ears had opened, external objects began to come into focus before him, the steel plates encasing his head had loosened.

He tried the knob on the Birchfields' front door and found it open. He tiptoed clumsily into the dining room, came up behind Frances, put his arms about her and kissed her on the cheek. She smelt the whiskey on his breath. Most of the men in Wichita drank heavily; she had no objection, except that John did not seem to know when to stop. But if he had not been drinking she knew he would not be here with her now, his arms locked about her, his lips rubbing roughly against her cheek.

"Don't stop, Frances; play the song I used to sing when I was riding circle on the herd at night."

She knew that the only time he had ridden herd was when he and the other boys of the neighborhood walked their family cow to the corner of Wichita and Second streets, where an old man drove them out to pasture for the day. But this was no time to contradict him. She played "Hell Among the Yearlings" while he sang in a voice more suited to keeping cattle quiet than to charming an audience.

"That was great, you were always my favorite piano player." He sat on the back arm of the piano, facing her, his eyes overly bright. "Play me 'The Dying Cowboy,' that's the best one to keep the longhorns from stampeding when the thunder's crashing."

She played for an hour the ballads he liked best, "When the Work's All Done Next Fall," "Dinah Had a Wooden Leg," talking to him quietly in the hope that she might divert him from further drinking. But as suddenly and inexplicably as he had come, he was gone; from the side window she saw him retrieve his bottle, drink down half the remaining content in a long shuddering pull.

It was now the supper hour; the only person who would not have his feet under a dinner table was Dave Leahy, who disliked solid food and succumbed to it only once a day, and then at some hour when it was difficult to procure. John found Dave in his *Eagle* office leaning back precariously in his swivel chair, his legs stretched the full width of the table and exhaling sheets of smoke that seemed to come from every pore of his body. Dave required only one quick glance at John.

"Well, m'boy, I see you're wetting your whistle tonight. What causes this celebration? Did you witness another great Western epic?"

"No, but I am sure you and I could conjure one up, Dave. How about a little bug juice?"

"Just what I was sitting here and contemplating."

Dave took a fog-encrusted water glass from the bottom drawer of his desk and poured about six ounces of bourbon into it.

"I want you to know this is an act of charity I'm performing for you, m'boy; it's just that much less pizen'll be poured into that chaste and beautiful young body of yours."

He quickly drank down most of the whiskey.

"Johnny, you and I are going to bring about a great religious revival throughout the country. Have you ever heard of the Wantafess Mountains? Well, there's a pioneer rancher away up in the pastures, a repentant sinner who is dying, and who sent out word that he wants a priest to administer final

42

unction. The sinner's practically dead right now, but he has vowed to remain alive, until a clergyman can reach him."

"And we send the priest out to him on horseback?"

"That's right. Here, take this paper and pencil and sketch this scene while I tell you about it. Thousands of Wichita folk are at the outskirts of town, wishing the priest good luck and joining in a prayer that he reach the unfortunate man in time. You got that one?"

"Sure, in a few minutes."

"The next day's story tells about the fires that are lit along the road by the ranchers and farmers so that the priest can ride at night. Got it?"

"Will have."

"The next day's story shows how every few miles the faithful are gathered with fresh horses for the priest, so that he can make the best possible time. Then we see the people crowding the churches of Wichita, praying every day that the rancher can hold out. There's more joy in heaven over one sinner who repenteth . . ."

"Does the priest reach the sinner on time?"

"That's something we don't find out for three weeks." Dave grinned. "I'll write the first release tonight. The East will swallow it hook, line and sinker." He reached into his desk and pulled out a check. "Here's a hundred bucks, m'boy, your share of the returns on the Dalton story. Now run along and get in trouble with it."

"Thanks. I know just where it'll do me the most harm."

When John reached the street he realized that he had left his bottle behind in Dave's office. Then he remembered why: Dave had helped him empty it. He walked quickly homeward, climbed up to the rafters of the barn and took a second bottle from its hiding place. The night had turned cold and so he put on an old leather jacket that hung on the tack-room wall, placed his bottle under the right half of the coat and went across the railroad tracks to Marty's boardinghouse. He threw open Marty's door without knocking. Marty's long skinny arms were wrapped around his account books like an octopus.

"You're just in the nick of time, John. I want to show you how we would set up our cost accounts."

"You're a materialist, Marty. Put away your accounting and bring forth two of your most beautiful cut-glass goblets."

"Oh," grunted Marty disgustedly, "you're hitting the bottle again. I thought you came over here because you wanted to be with me."

"Course I wanted to be with you, Marty. Never share my liquor with anybody but my best pals. C'mon, boy, get those glasses."

"You know I never touch the filthy stuff," replied Marty; "besides, you look drunk enough already. Why don't you go home and sleep it off?"

"Jes' been home, sleeping somethun' off. Never been so sick in my life, Marty." He patted the bottle of liquor. "This is medicine, boy. The best medicine to cure a man's troubles that's ever been caught and bottled."

Marty pushed away the papers and rose from his little table.

"Sick, my eye. That's what your mother tries to make us believe. She says you would never drink if you didn't get so sick. Personally, I think you make yourself sick as an excuse to get roarin' drunk."

John laughed and hit Marty such a terrific slap between the shoulder blades that his skinny frame collapsed onto the bed.

"Marty, I'm ashamed of you. Since when did a native Kansan need an excuse to get drunk? Ah, here are two glasses." He poured two drinks, thrust one into Marty's hand and took the other himself. "Here you are, partner, let's drink to the best damn laundry in the state of Kansas."

He fished Dave Leahy's crumpled check from his trouser pocket and tossed it on the bed. Marty read it several times before he gathered that John was giving him the money. Tears came to his eyes, he gulped, but no words came. John pressed the glass against his friend's lips. Marty took a series of deep breaths to put out the fire in his throat, then began talking fast.

"I'll catch a coach up to Kansas City Saturday night. There's a yard up there specializing in secondhand laundry machines. I'll load those machines on a freight myself by Sunday night and catch a coach that'll bring me back by Monday morning. Meanwhile you can give that store on Main Street a coat of paint."

By absorbing John, Marty felt he had at last conquered him; he had proved that all his years of interest in art, literature and philosophic ideas had been kid stuff. He need have no more fear, no hollow feeling of inadequacy: for with John as his partner, they were equals.

"I knew you'd grow up and get practical, John. Sure, all this drawing and reading, that's fine for your spare time.

Hobby, like. But, hell, you got to make the dough while the makin's good. And I'm the hombre to make it for you."

John bid Marty good night and slipped out the door. The town was dark, locked up, asleep. His feet guided him instinctively through the back roads to his stable, where he took down that third bottle of Sunnybrook. He then went into Wichita Bill's stall and, with the greatest of difficulty, climbed up on the horse's back. He turned him around with the pressure of his knee. Wichita Bill had been through this many times before. He walked slowly out into the prairie, following familiar trails. John took the cork out of the bottle, threw it away and gulped the whiskey at frequent intervals. He began talking to himself, reviewing everything that had happened since the beginning of his vision. His senses began fading, his speech became jarred and indistinct; the half-emptied bottle dropped from his hands and poured itself out into the earth. He fell forward onto the horse's neck, asleep.

Wichita Bill stood completely still for several moments, then, making sure the weight on his back was evenly distributed, gingerly retraced his steps homeward, stopping when the grip about his neck loosened, moving when he felt John's arms revive their hold. It took several hours for the horse to bring the man back safely, across the vast sea of the priairie and into port.

In his own stall, Wichita Bill sank down evenly onto his knees, then turned sufficiently on one side for John to slip off.

It was dawn. Elizabeth Noble, sitting at the back window of her kitchen, had seen the horse and the man return. She went into the stable, patted Wichita Bill gratefully on the neck, then got a bucket of cold water and dashed it into her son's face. She helped him lumber to his feet, got him into the house and up the stairs without waking her husband, and safely under the covers of his own bed.

10

From the books on his shelf he knew that Edgar Allan Poe had had visions, William Blake had had visions, and so had St. Francis of Assisi. But in Wichita people did not have visions. The only Kansan he had ever heard about who admitted to visions was a woman by the name of Carry A. Nation of Medicine Lodge. Mrs. Nation was a reformer who battled the evils of drinking, smoking, spooning, dancing and card playing, maintaining that she drew the inspiration for her crusades directly from God. Whenever she had a vision, which was frequently, she ran through the neighborhood pounding on doors and crying out:

"I have seen a heavenly light!"

John decided to visit Carry Nation and try to learn something of the nature of her visitations. How often did they come, and what stimulated them? Why was she so proud of her visions, eagerly seeking them and proclaiming them to the world, when he fled in terror from his, refusing to speak of them to a living soul?

The winter months had been bleak and cold, but the first of May brought warm sunshine. He rose early, saddled Wichita Bill and headed southwest for Medicine Lodge. The wild gaillardias and prairie anemones were out in broad patches, covering the bright green buffalo grass with russet, golden yellow, white and pink tints.

When he reached the little town of Medicine Lodge he stopped at a store to ask the whereabouts of Mrs. Nation's house. From a full block away John saw ahead of him a tall, fleshy, middle-aged woman, dressed in a curious sackcloth wrap-around, doing a kind of dance as she loudly chanted a triumphant hymn. As he came abreast of the woman a neighbor stopped her and asked:

"Why, Mrs. Nation, what has happened?"

"Hallelujah!" replied Mrs. Nation. "There is to be a change in my life."

By the time he had tied Wichita Bill to a fence post, Mrs. Nation had gone into her house. John knocked on the door, feeling a little uneasy. He was admitted by David Nation, a harassed-looking old gentleman with a white beard, whose preaching performance in the pulpit every Sunday morning was directed by his wife from the congregation.

"Mrs. Nation is in the kitchen," her husband said wearily, "if you're wanting to join her in prayer."

John went through an open arch to the kitchen. He found Mrs. Nation on her knees, pouring ashes on her head and crying:

"Oh, God, you see the treason in Kansas. They are going to break the mothers' hearts. They are going to send the boys to drunkards' graves. Oh, Lord, use me to save Kansas."

The woman's circular swaying movement stopped. She turned abruptly.

"Yes, what is it?"

"Mrs. Nation, I have come to you for help."

46

Carry Nation sprang up, her small feverish eyes boring into his.

"You've been a drunkard! But you're ready to be saved! Priase the Lord!"

"No . . . I . . . understand that you have . . . visions. I . . . thought you might explain . . ."

Carry Nation stood with her feet apart, her hands on her hips.

"Yes, my young friend, God has just sent me the greatest vision of all. Yesterday I stuck a pin into the Bible, and there, in the first verse of the sixtieth chapter of Isaiah, it said, 'Arise, shine; for thy light is come, and the glory of the Lord is risen upon thee.' Three times He said to me, 'Go to Kiowa!' Come with me to Kiowa tomorrow, young man, and you will receive all the help you need."

Early the next morning John saddled Wichita Bill and followed Carry Nation's buggy into Kiowa. When she stopped in front of Dobson's saloon and began filling her arms with the stones she had brought from her own back yard, he quickly tied his horse to the hitching post. The bar's swinging doors closed behind him just in time to hear her cry to the half-dozen early drinkers:

"Men, I have come to save you from a drunkard's fate!"

Dobson, the owner, came from behind the counter.

"Now, Mother Nation . . ."

"I told you last spring to close this place, Mr. Dobson. Now I have come here with another remonstrance."

While the men watched with unbelieving eyes, Carry Nation threw her first stone, smashing the high mirror behind the bar. Exultantly singing hymnal verses, she heaved the rest of her rocks at the collections of bottles and glasses. Her job done, she cried:

"Now, Mr. Dobson, God be with you!"

John followed her out of the saloon, hypnotized. Carry Nation was singing at the top of her voice:

> "Who hath sorrow? Who hath woe?
> They who dare not answer no,
> They whose feet to sin incline
> While they tarry at the wine."

The male population of the town crowded the street. Carry Nation announced:

"Men of Kiowa, I have destroyed one of your places of business. If I have broken a statute of Kansas, put me in jail.

If I am not a lawbreaker, your mayor and councilmen are. You must arrest one of us!"

He mingled with the crowd, listening to a hasty conference of the city officials. The marshal wanted to arrest her but the mayor groaned, "We can't. These joints are illegal." He turned to the sidewalk and called out, "Go home, Mrs. Nation."

Carry Nation raised her arm like a preacher over the assembly, a beatific smile on her face.

"Peace on earth, good will to men."

With that she climbed into her buggy, clucked the reins and went down the street, finally turning out of sight. John located a small saloon on a side street. Here he had two quick whiskeys. Then he mounted Wichita Bill, patted the horse's neck and murmured:

"Every man to his own vision."

11

The following week John rode northeast with his father to where the family owned a sheep ranch. They sat up on a mound chatting with the sheepherder.

"Just watch the flock now, Misters Noble. I'll tell them to come up this way to me, but I won't call them, I'll only tell them inside my head."

After a few moments John saw the lead sheep pick up their heads, look in the direction of the sheepherder and start moving toward him, the flock following.

"John, I could use a little of that telepathy," said John Noble, Sr., quietly. "I'd like to figure what makes you want to participate in that Cherokee Strip Run. Since when are you land-hungry?"

John gazed at the landscape below them, not meeting his father's eyes.

"I'm not hungry for anything, Pa. It's just that I know a site down in the Strip with an ever-runnin' stream on it where I've camped every time I went through the Nations. Wichita Bill can get me there ahead of all these rigs and covered wagons."

"Sure he can," agreed his father; "but what would you homestead after you got there? You're not cut out to be a farmer, and they won't let you stake out a piece big enough t∩ run a herd. If you really want to become a cattle rancher

48

bad, I'll lend you that ranch I bought down near Amarillo. Better yet, I'll give it to you and Frances for a wedding present. But I just can't figure out how you're going to make a living on that ever-running creek down on the Strip."

"I hadn't given much thought to that question, Pa. You raised me good, but you didn't raise me practical."

His father saw that the boy was pulling his leg.

"Just one bit of advice: don't try to brand your cattle with a paintbrush."

John and Dave Leahy reached Hunnewell on the Oklahoma border at sunset. The tiny town was already swollen by thousands of milling men. The starting line for the Run had been marked off by soldiers about a hundred yards into the Strip from the Kansas border. Here they found hundreds of covered wagons, buckboards, buggies, spring wagons, carts, surreys and two-wheel rigs, some of which had been in these vantage spots for weeks. A tent city had sprung up with signs advertising fruits and vegetables, cooked foods, tools. Men were lying on blankets around small campfires with the coffeepots boiling, telling how they had come from Wyoming with a span of mules, from Texas and Arkansas on cow ponies, from New Mexico in a covered wagon without a cover.

The two men moved from group to group through the long hot night, scribbling steadily in their notebooks, Dave jotting down the stories of people's lives, why they had come to Hunnewell, what had caused their land hunger, how they hoped to set up new and secure lives in the Strip; John trying in the half-dark to draw the hungers, the yearnings, the fears and trepidations, the hopes, the weaknesses and strengths of character, to capture the few simple lines revealing which of these men would move swiftly and surely to a working claim, and which be left hopelessly behind, or worse, staking a claim, live on it miserably for a number of months and then return in defeat and despair to the life from which they had fled.

Here were people with their basic natures on the tips of their tongues, revealing the long heartbreaking story of their struggles and ambitions, their failures, their anxieties, their movements from job to job, county to county, from hope to hope and disappointment to disappointment; the wanderers of the earth with no great skill or talent, no roots, no security, no gratification: the wind-swept, chance-swept bootless ones, always yearning, always hoping and trusting, always moving

49

and always failing; talking freely because these were strangers they had never seen before and would never see again; because this was a period cut out of time, this camp in the midst of a vast prairie like a ship in midocean, caught between the life that had been and the life which was to be.

When the registration books opened at dawn, John took his place in line. A hundred feverish discussions swirled around him: were the Sooners sneaking in in such large numbers that there would be no land for the legitimate claimants? What about those forty-two cattle cars of the Rock Island Railroad south of Caldwell, and the Santa Fe's cars at Arkansas City, Orlando and Kiowa? How was the official start on Saturday at noon to be given? What if the crowds stampeded ahead of time?

During the next days some ten thousand people poured into Hunnewell from every city and state in the Union. The restless throngs waited in the fierce Oklahoma sun and in the endless dust kicked up by the thousands of feet, frightened lest the booths close before they got their entry blanks. Few slept at night, only those men who had brought their wives and children and parents; the solitary men drank and gambled and swapped yarns; there were quarrels, fist fights and an occasional exchange of shots.

John met old friends from his trips down the herd trails; these men had the toughest cow ponies in the world, but they were being laughed at by more prosperous adventurers who had brought trained race horses to the scene. The old-timers worked feverishly on their wagons, greasing the wheels, testing the springs and poles, feeding their horses. Water was scarce and there was increasing hardship. As he went about among the family camps he saw young mothers nursing their infants, mothers out of the crowded tenements of Chicago and New York City; he talked to aged grandparents off the rolling, fertile farms of Ohio, visited with clerks out of offices and salesmen out of shoe stores, trying to answer their anxious questions about the nature of the land, where they should go and how they should stake their claims. He thrilled to their great blind courage, and was at the same time saddened by the knowledge that a large proportion of them would never get farther than a few miles past this dust-choked starting place.

It was at suppertime of the last day that he stumbled across a white-bearded old man from the Ozarks with his nine-year-old granddaughter. Their equipment was so pitifully inadequate that only an act of God could pull them through to a homesite. The girl, Olivia, was all skin and bones, but with unusually determined brown eyes. She kept questioning him about the best sites in the Strip and the best way to reach them. To John it became apparent that Olivia was leading the pilgrimage and so, in pity and admiration, he drew the nine-year-old child a carefully detailed map.

On Friday night, after the registration booths had closed, a hush fell over Hunnewell. The days of waiting and speculating were over. The Saturday sun rose naked, and within an hour it was blazing down mercilessly. A hot wind blew up from the south, moving the loose red dust in great squalls. Horses galloped up to the starting line and were put between the traces of the wagons, buggies, buckboards and carts, the reins held tight lest someone break through and start a stampede. Even the cowboys stood with their ponies on the dust-choked border.

John rode Wichita Bill up and down the long line. He felt the terrible tenseness now that the hour of decision had arrived, for the great game of something-for-nothing was no longer a game: it was a contest, a war against barren years, against closed lives, against the hopelessness of monotony and poverty.

He was almost the last to mount. He said good-by to Dave, who would be heading back for Wichita with the speed of the cow ponies in the Run, so that his stories would be the first to reach the Eastern papers.

Then, just before noon, a soldier rode out, pointed his carbine at the heavens and fired.

The men on horseback broke out of the line as though projected from a cannon. A dust storm was kicked up which enveloped horses and riders and behind them the wagon drivers whipping their teams forward. Over his shoulder John beheld covered wagons and surreys already broken or overturned, household goods spilled in the thick Oklahoma dust, men and women trapped and inconsolable by the side of their collapsed worlds.

He headed for the Cimarron. There were many riders ahead of him now, particularly those who had brought in highly trained race horses. He touched Wichita Bill with his heel. The horse leaped forward. Within an hour he found himself passing the prized race horses who had shot their bolt and could go no farther; their owners were thrashing about frenziedly trying to find a worth-while claim wherever they might have landed.

It took him until dark to reach his site. A good many

claims had been staked out. He made swiftly for the spot of his former camp, saw that no one had been there, and laid rocky mounds at the four corners. By the time he finished his job the night had grown cold. He had a pocketful of dried apricots for Wichita Bill.

"I hope you don't mind sharing your supper with me," he murmured as he alternately fed the horse a piece of fruit and slipped one into his own mouth.

Exhausted from the long hard ride, he built himself a fire, took a drink of water from the stream and went to sleep with his head on the saddle.

He wakened in the chilly dawn, cold and stiff; the North Star had almost faded. He heard Wichita Bill champing by the stream. Then he sat bolt upright: about thirty yards away, at the other end of a little rise, was a covered wagon. He pulled on his boots and stalked up to the intruders. There was no sign of life on the outside, so he opened the back curtain. There lay Olivia, and beside her, his eyes wide and frightened, her grandfather.

The old man rose and came to the rear of the wagon.

"We just got here a couple of hours ago. It was such a long ride, but Olivia kept reading your directions. When we reached here, she knew it was the spot you had been talking about."

"Sure, only I didn't tell you to come to my own campsite. Weren't there enough miles up and down the stream without stumbling onto the one claim that I had staked?"

The man's eyes filled with tears. "Oh, oh, we didn't know. We didn't see you in the dusk. What are we to do now?"

The girl had awakened. She came forward to the end of the wagon, looked out and saw it was John.

"What's the matter, Mr. Noble?" she asked, her eyes bigger than the rest of her face. "Have we done something wrong?"

"No," replied John, "just jumped my claim."

The girl turned to her grandfather. "What does that mean for us, Grandpa?"

"It means we can't stay here," replied the grandfather. "We have to see if we can't find another place."

There was a silence. Then John shook his head bemusedly.

"Look, you don't have to move on. I never intended to stay here anyhow. I just wanted to be part of the Run. The four corners are marked off, so fill out your registration claim and I'll file it for you on my way back home."

To Wichita Bill he said wryly, "I drew that map too well."

No one was greatly surprised when his solid tread was heard coming through the hall. He slipped into his chair at the dining table with a quiet smile.

His sister Belle exclaimed, "Was it exciting, John? Did you find your ranch?"

"Let him have his dinner first, Belle," said his mother.

"The only thing that annoys me," said his father, "was that advice I foolishly gave you. Why didn't you tell me you had no intention of staking out a site?"

John was making up for his week of lean rations. He paused long enough to murmur, "Oh, but, Pa, I did. That beautiful knoll I told you about."

"But somebody'll jump your claim if you don't stay on it long enough to put up a little shack."

"Alas! That's already happened: when I awoke the next morning there was an old gentleman and his nine-year-old granddaughter sleeping in a covered wagon. They almost ran over me during the night."

There was a moment of silence. His father pulled his head back deep into his shoulders. "How did an old gentleman and his granddaughter find your completely unknown site, and in a covered wagon, to boot?"

"I drew 'em a map."

"But you were there first," said his brother Arthur.

"That's true," replied John, wiping the blackberry pie from around his mouth with one of his mother's damask napkins. "But they had nowhere else to go." He turned to his father with a guileless smile and murmured, "I figured I could always come back here, Pa."

Oblique arguments made Mr. Noble uncomfortable. "If you didn't want that homesite, John, then why did you go to all that trouble?"

"I guess I wanted to see why thousands of people from all over the world would join the Run."

His younger sister Elizabeth exclaimed, "But, John, they wanted free land."

John tilted back in his chair, gazing at the portrait of Grandmother Noble which hung over the buffet, a stiff and stately woman in a black lace cap, with ribbon streamers hanging down either side of her neck.

"They wanted land, but that was the smallest part of it."

His father added, "They were all poor folk, or youngsters wanting a start in life, a chance to make a home."

John lowered his head while he thought for a few moments, bringing forth his visual memory of the faces of the people with whom he had talked at Hunnewell. When at last he lifted his eyes they admitted confusion.

"I don't know, Pa, but it didn't seem to me that they were thinking so much of land or plows or crops, or cows and chickens and pigs. These were the things they were talking about, all right, but I had the feeling that all this was on the surface. Underneath it I felt a bigger hunger, something stronger, something they couldn't express and I couldn't fathom."

Elizabeth Noble leaned across the table, asking, "Then what could it have been, Johnny?"

"Let me show you what they looked like, Ma, when they didn't know how they were looking."

He went into the front hall, took his sketchbooks out of the saddlebag and brought them back to the dining-room table. His mother, father, sisters and brother came and stood close to him, peering at the pages as he turned them over. Halfway through, he looked up at his family and said, "These were done too quickly. Let me make some fresh drawings and try to show you."

He went upstairs, returning immediately with several large sheets of paper. His mother and sisters had cleared the table. He began drawing rapidly with strong lines, bringing Hunnewell to life: the engulfed little village, the hundreds of surrounding tents, the wagons and carts lined up at the starting line, the heat, the dust, the broiling sun: and then the people in their regional garb, the excited children, the silent oldsters, the young married couples, the middle-aged ones arrived from many miles, many defeats and limitless shattered hopes. They came to life under his pencil, and on their faces, but very deep, deep behind the burning eyes, behind the clenched teeth, the tight lips, the furrowed cheeks and brows lay some universal longing, some hidden tragedy, some terrible hunger and fear and yearning.

Tired now, and having expressed everything he had felt, John threw his pencil onto the table and leaned back in his chair. His mother was the first to speak.

"They're lonely, John; is that what you mean?"

"Yes."

12

The next day at noon when John went into the Eaton Bar for a glass of beer he found his father waiting for him.

"Just had a talk with Dave Leahy, son, and told him about that big drawing of Hunnewell you made last night. He wants to have it to illustrate his story of the Run, says it should make you a hundred dollars just like the Dalton drawing did."

There was both affection and pride in the older man's voice, but John felt hollow inside.

"No, Pa."

"No, what?"

"That was just my way of talking confidential to you and Ma and the kids. I've been sorry I let him publish my drawing of the Dalton brothers, it's like I was violating their confidence."

"But, John, you can't turn down a chance to make some money, not money that's honestly earned . . ."

John's failure to answer was neither deliberate nor hostile; his father felt the boy thrashing about in his mind.

"John, how about a horse trade? I just rented those big rooms on the second floor of the Douglas Building to George Israel, the photographer. I offered him a deal: his rent free for a partnership for you. I won't prevail on you to sell the Run pictures, if you will go to work as a photographer. After all, what's the difference between taking pictures and making pictures?"

John tried to think, but nothing would come clear. The experience of the Cherokee Run had exhausted him emotionally. He didn't want to be a photographer, he didn't want to become a partner, and yet there didn't seem to be anything else he wanted to do at the moment. Maybe he ought to try a job, work like everybody else, fit himself into an accepted and normal pattern? In the midst of a drawing spree he wouldn't be able to think this way; later, if his oil painting clarified itself he might not be able to go along with his father. But just now he felt suspended; if it was easier to make his father happy, to conform for once . . . From some obscure corner of his mind he found himself pleading for a dread word, one he rarely used.

"All right, but could you give me . . . a little time? Just a little time?"

"Why, certainly, son. How much time?"

"Well, say . . ." he flailed about, trying to grasp something concrete, "say six months."

"Come now, John. That's the equivalent of forever. If you have got some loose ends you want to tie up, one month will surely do it."

He was feeling too weary to argue further; besides, his father's manner was terribly persuasive.

"All right, Pa, if you want it that way."

"Jerry, set 'em up for the house!" exclaimed the older man. "I just made me a horse trade." He turned to his son and added in an undertone, "Take three months, boy."

That afternoon he went back to the cherrywood parlor, scraped all the paint off the canvas on the stretcher and started anew. Somewhere he had read Rembrandt's wonderful advice to students:

"Take your brush in hand and begin."

He was thrilled with the luscious flow of the paint, its buttery and rich qualities, and how a whole mass of color could glow on a canvas. In the earlier years he had tried crayons and water colors only to find that he had no ability to make a statement with a line or a tone, to see forms or movements in terms of these delicate mediums. But ah, these oils with which one could draw, which he could push around and mass, which he could mix on the palette and on the canvas because they were flexible and stayed moist; here was the robustness, the solidity which matched his own temperament and the images in his mind.

Yet the problems inherent in oil were as great as the pleasures of the medium. How long it had taken him to discover that color had a perspective of its own; that hot colors like the yellows and oranges came forward, while the cool colors, the blues and violets, receded into space, that shadows were neither black nor gray, but made up of all the colors that surrounded them. If there had been good pictures to look at in Wichita he could have avoided much of the stumbling, the experimenting, nor need it have taken him so long to learn that blue is the horizon color of deep space and far away, for the old masters had discovered that centuries before.

He had not minded the failures, the waste, the fumbling efforts to master the medium, for he had never felt there was any rush. He had patience, infinite, unshatterable patience. What did it matter how long it took him to learn that as things go away from the eye they become neutral; that fore-ground colors must be intense; that one practically never saw a white in nature; that the problem of the overlapping of planes and the amount of space between objects had to be indicated by color rather than line; that highlights had to be determined by the source of the light and the color of the object the light shone upon; that the third dimension of depth could be created by the ingenious device of placing objects higher on the two-dimensional canvas? He had time. He had his entire life.

But now an uneasiness pervaded the atmosphere. He had never developed an accurate device for keeping time inside his own head. Suddenly a metronome within him started tick-ing, "Quick! Quick! Hurry! Hurry!"

It was Sunday and from the parlor he saw his mother and two sisters returning from church. Frances was with them, wearing a pale blue hat and gown which emphasized the shining blackness of her hair, the olive tint of her complex-ion. He threw open the door and bellowed her name.

Frances had been greatly pleased when John's father had told her about his pact with his son, but now she found John's face twisted into lines of conflict, his eyes sunk deep into their sockets. She walked quickly to the easel to see what he had been working on. The canvas was a mess: dark and muddy.

He sank down wearily on the mohair love seat. She sat be-side him and took his heavy hand, with its powerful fingers, between hers.

"What's wrong, John?"

"I . . . I'm rudderless on this confounded sea of time. I don't know how long it is since . . . for all I know, Father might throw open that door right now and yell, 'Time's up!' "

"But, John, it's only a week since you made your agree-ment. You have almost the full three months left. Why are you worrying so soon?"

He gazed at her in blank astonishment, then took a hand-kerchief from his trouser pocket and wiped the perspiration from his face.

"Only a week? My God, I thought it was all over. Frances, have you ever stood in the middle of a room with every mus-cle in your body knotted, waiting for somebody to exclaim, 'Time's up!' Surely those must be the most terrifying words in the English language? Art is timeless. It can exist only outside the realm and control of calendars. It can't be pushed, shoved, hustled, hurried."

An inner gray smoke seemed to cover the blue of his eyes. Frances' heart went out to him as his expression became confused, unhappy, a little frightened.

"Your father said he didn't force you into this, John. He said you seemed content to make the deal with him. But if it's making you ill, he wouldn't want you to go through with it."

A tremendous sigh came out of him; his shoulders and arms unclenched as he slowly relaxed beside her. The focus of his eyes passed from their intense inner gaze, and rested upon Frances, looking so concerned about him. He put his arms about her.

"Thanks, Frances. I understand now that what I asked Father for was a reprieve. A reprieve's no good. You die every minute in the death house. I'm going to shave and go down to George Israel's studio right now."

She chuckled gaily, happy for the first time.

"Now I really believe you don't know what time it is: today is Sunday, darling, the photographic parlor is closed, and the *Eagle* announced you were going to play left field for the Maroons this afternoon."

He jumped up from the seat. "But say, I forgot, this is the big game of the season against Topeka. I haven't seen a baseball since Dave and I went up to Hunnewell; I won't be able to hit the side of a barn."

"You'd better hit something," she replied, "or this town will be broke tomorrow morning. Even Marty bet a dollar on the Maroons. By the way, he's taking me to the game: he talked about the three of us having supper together afterwards, seems that he's got something terribly important that he wants to tell us."

The Wichita Maroons squeezed out a ninth-inning victory, thanks to John's double through center field.

"You almost disgraced the whole town with those first two strike-outs," exclaimed Marty, when they were sitting in a booth in the Occidental Restaurant. "How did you finally get ahold of that last one?"

"Search me," replied John with a grin, "the first two times up I tried to follow the ball. On that last one I just closed my eyes and swung."

He and Frances were sitting on one side of the table, their bodies pressed together from knee to shoulder. Seated opposite them, Marty seemed skinnier and more alone than ever,

58

yet it was Marty who was the most jubilant of the three; this was his twenty-first birthday party. These were also the happiest days of his life, for his laundry had been an instantaneous success. The sudden prosperity had not persuaded him to change his way of life: he still occupied the same rectangular hall bedroom and was wearing the threadbare serge suit he had bought many years before. But his flying red hair and his flying hot words gave him the appearance of a dervish as he stretched across the table, excitedly drawing designs into the white cloth with the prongs of his fork. His eyes were beautiful: deep purple, intensely alive and filled with love for this couple, so close to him now as they leaned over the table, their heads touching, and yet so far, so infinitely far away.

"John, there's no future in being a photographer, you can't make big dough keeping your eyes glued to a camera. Why not close your eyes and put one out into the buffalo grass?"

"Meaning what?"

"Meaning money. Why should you go in with George Israel when you've already got a partner? All right, you don't want to be in the laundry business, but I got plans. You know that store next to me? We tear down the wall . . ."

"Don't serve them over the plate so fast, Marty. What are you tearing down the wall for?"

"Because you gotta spend, you always gotta keep spending. Look, John, it's a perfectly natural development. People like to do all their business in one place. Why should we let our customers take their cleaning and dyeing work to that Nonpareil? And their hats, too; there's a lot of money to be made in cleaning men's hats, John. I bet you didn't know that."

"Marty, you can see a profit where another man can only see a coffee stain on a vest."

"You know what else I'm going to put in there?" replied Marty, ignoring him. "A shoe repair shop; it's just as easy for people to bring us their shoes while they're bringing their laundry and suits and hats. What do you say, John, do you think it's a good idea?"

"Sure, but what's it got to do with me?"

He hadn't meant to hurt Marty; but now he saw the excitement and happiness draining out of his friend's face.

"It's because you don't have faith in me," said Marty quietly. He shifted his gaze to Frances. "Frances, tell him about the profits from the laundry."

"What would Frances know about it?"

"Well, she's . . . she's been helping me . . . keep the account books."

There was a moment of strained silence; in some numb and inarticulate way it was now John's turn to be hurt. There was the tacit understanding that Frances was his girl; but Marty had never tried to conceal the wholly unconcealable fact that he was in love with her. It wasn't that he tried to compete with John or to insinuate himself into Frances' affections; he knew that Frances loved John completely and that in his own peculiar fashion John was devoted to Frances; yet he also had an intuitive conviction that these two would never marry. And if Frances wasn't going to marry John, why should she not marry him?

Frances was the first to speak. Her voice was quiet, but the tempo of her words was a little faster than usual.

"We didn't mean to keep it from you, John. It's just that you weren't around."

"Perfectly all right," he replied, but he could hear his voice echoing hollowly against the back wall of the restaurant and rebounding to their booth.

"I have the spare time," she explained tentatively, then gave her head a quick toss as though to shed this moment of unpleasantness and continued in her normal manner. "Look, John. Marty is going to make it. The laundry is earning a wonderful profit each week; and this cleaning business will too. He has other good ideas."

This was a double triumph for Marty. He flushed with pleasure.

"John, I can make you a millionaire. I'm going to make Frances one too. We'll make this a three-way partnership: Frances, you throw in that block of land your mother left you out on Douglas Avenue. We'll put up a store and office building, use as much space for ourselves as we need now and rent out the balance. Your father said he'd sign for our loan, John. We'd really be in big business then."

John heard the excitement in Marty's voice, saw the flush of color rise high on Frances' cheeks. He gazed at them, disturbed.

13

On Monday morning he had breakfast with the family at seven o'clock. At a few minutes before eight he was standing before his father's L-shaped brick building on the corner of Douglas and Main, occupied by Ed Vail's jewelry store and the Rock Island Railroad office. On the sidewalk was a show-case which had *Israel and Company* printed on the bottom and number 106 brushed in over each of the three gables. Inside were chicken wires on which George Israel's photographs were displayed.

In Ed Vail's window he saw a thick gold watch, its front and back covers open so that its works as well as its time could be seen by a prospective buyer. The price tag read forty dollars. He searched in his trouser pockets and came forth with the twenty-five dollars he had been paid for playing with the Maroons on a winner-take-all basis. He walked into the jewelry store. Ed Vail was dusting the showcases; he was a small man with an immense soup-strainer moustache.

"Ed, I'd like that gold watch in the window, and the heaviest chain you've got in the store."

"Why, sure, John, I've got a solid gold interlink here, just the thing to go with it."

He took the watch out of the window, wound it, set its hands by the big clock on the wall, handed it to John and then took his own timepiece out of his pocket. Each man consulted his watch with a long somber face, looking up intermittently at the master clock; the three timepieces now matching, the men shook their heads approvingly and snapped the cases shut. John dropped his watch in his right shirt pocket, draped the heavy chain as low as it would reach across his stomach and anchored the knot in his left shirt pocket.

"It's wonderful, Ed," he said as he laid his greenbacks on the glass case. "All over the world millions of people pull their watches out every few minutes, glance up at a wall clock and nod wisely, the guardians of time. Up to this morning, Ed, time was a free and kicking thing, independent of me; now I've got it jailed in solid gold and imprisoned on my chest by this heavy chain. As long as I can feel it ticking against me, Ed, I'm the boss of time."

"Sure, you'll find that a right good clock, John. Now if you'll just sign this sales slip, you'll owe me fifteen dollars more for the watch and twenty-five dollars for the chain."

John walked up a flight of stairs from the street and entered a big reception room with red carpet on the floor, gold fleur-de-lis-patterned wallpaper and glass showcases on either side displaying artistic portraits and group photographs. On the walls were elaborately framed oval pictures. The room was filled with ornate wicker chairs, no two of them alike, some tall and thin, others squat and potbellied, ranging in color from darkest brown to silvery gray, all with manifold curlicues.

Stepping through a painted acorn curtain, he found himself in the workroom. Unlike the reception room the workshop was bare and austere, with a skylight facing north. An accordion Anthony camera stood on a table tripod. The only two adornments were functional: a three-paneled screen with flowers and one plush chair before it.

George Israel was adjusting his camera when John stepped into the studio. The two young men stared at each other; neither had really wanted this arrangement. Israel was a spunky little chap with brown eyes, brown hair and a savage sense of humor.

"That was quite a contract your father drew up for me," he commented hostilely.

"Oh . . . contract? I didn't know about that."

"I'm not complaining, mind you: I get my rent free, and some new equipment, but there was one clause I finally got into that contract too."

John looked at the photographer with blank inquiry.

"It says this partnership is dissolved if you ever go back to your boozing."

"Oh, that," replied John, feeling unhappy and desperately sorry that he had listened to his father's persuasive arguments. How could he explain to this stranger all of the agony and terrifying realms he traversed before he fled for escape into what practical-minded George Israel called boozing?

When he lifted his eyes to his new partner he saw there was no need for an explanation: Israel had made his one stipulation and then put it out of his mind.

"I understand you want to become a first-class photographer," said Israel. "I'll teach you to develop, print and retouch, but let me warn you that you don't learn this craft over a week end. Come on in the darkroom. I don't have an appointment until nine o'clock, and I'll show you how we run the collodionized paper through the nitrate silver baths."

"That's fine," replied John, who hadn't the slightest desire to run collodionized paper through a nitrate silver bath.

George Israel had spent several years as an apprentice photographer, visiting the raw settlements of Kansas, Oklahoma and Texas, setting up headquarters in hastily erected tents or just-completed stores. He was generally the first photographer to come into these outland settlements, and practically everybody had his picture taken to send back to the folks at home. Working under physical difficulties and with almost no competition, George Israel could have succeeded as well with poor photography, but his professional pride matched his technical skill, and his pictures were clear, light and expertly printed.

He took John into the developing room where he showed him how to pour the nitrate silver bath into the twenty-by-twenty trays, then take dry collodionized paper and tape the paper down flat in the tray, seeing that the solution was spread evenly so that there would be no air bubbles to leave white spots. He then showed him how to hang up the sensitized paper in the fuming room until it curled and was drawn.

After a few days John became enchanted with the anesthetic of routine. The more rigidly disciplined he kept that routine, the more duties and obligations he piled into it, the more completely did it serve the purpose of absorption. Since his graduation from grammar school he had lived according to inclination: when he was hungry he ate, whether it was mealtime or cold-kitchen time; when he was tired he slept, whether it was midday or midnight; when he was able to work he worked for as long as he was able; when he wanted company he sought out company regardless of whom it might contain. He had been as wide open as the Kansas prairie for every wind that might arise; winds of doubt, skepticism, despair, and that worst of all enemies, the sense of meaninglessness.

But, ah, the difference when you had to be up at six, put a tub of water on the stove for a bath, sit down with the family for breakfast at seven and walk briskly into town in order to be at the studio before eight so that you were actually working when the church chimes announced the workday; to have so many little duties on hand that it was impossible to think about yourself, the world, its spirit or its meaning because the first thing you knew it was twelve o'clock and time for lunch because there were a series of appointments starting at one . . . In the late afternoon there were the hours of retouching, crouched over pictures of odd-looking strangers, trying to make them look beautiful or charming so that they would order a quantity of the reproductions. The day's work over, one walked home quickly in order to sit down to supper, and the family fun of argument and debate that went on during the meal. The evening was short and fairly easy to get over with: a visit, a game of chess, an hour of music with Frances, and it was time to go to bed: for one had to be up at six in order to bathe, breakfast, walk to town and stand before Ed Vail's jewelry window, gold watch in hand, making time co-ordinate itself.

Ah, blessed anodyne! How wonderful to be free! Those who claimed that rigid routine chained a man were foolish: routine was not a chain, it was a velvet tieback.

Business at Israel and Company was very good: the Wichita Maroons came in to have their pictures taken in their uniforms, also a number of business groups and the Chess and Checker Club to which John's father belonged, as well as other friends who knew how important it was to the Noble family to have John succeed in this venture. This rush of business added to George Israel's already established practice made the studio quite prosperous. At first Israel gave John half of the substantial profits at the end of each week, but he soon learned that it was impossible to get a receipt from his partner and that by Monday morning John hadn't the faintest conception of how much cash had been put into his hand on Saturday night. From then on Israel paid the money to John's father once a month, John Noble, Sr., turned it over to his wife, and Elizabeth Noble put it in the little drawer at the top of John's bureau where she had kept his supply of cash all these years.

At the shop it became part of John's duty to help George adjust the curtains over the skylight and to set the three-paneled screen with its cobweb effect of flowers so that the light was suitable to the subject. He never got over being amazed at the gyrations the sitters went through while preparing to have their pictures taken: their heroic effort to appear externally, to the camera, like an amorphous and pleasant image they had of themselves, the starry-eyed wish to look like some early and unfulfilled dream of youth, to conceal not only the part of the face but of the character which they knew was unattractive; the manipulations to appear warm, bright, kind, generous, affectionate, to be transfixed for eternity as an ideal and worthy creature, concealing the greed, cruelty, egoism, pettiness, narrowness, ignorance which dominated their lives. He saw how frightened they were when they sat before the camera, as though it were judgment day and they had come before God. How good they wanted to look to God!

But all of this squirming, posing and posturing was as nothing compared to the gyrations they went through when looking at the trial proofs, for despite their craftiest efforts nothing could be completely concealed from the relentless eye of the camera. He found that the subjects not only wanted to be retouched, they wanted to be recreated: their blemishes erased with a Faber pencil, the hardness softened, the crooked lines straightened, the sour made sweet and the evil made pure, categorically refusing to buy the true and naked photographs but ordering in dozen lots and in varying sizes when the image had been remodeled to what they had dreamed of being, or what they still pretended to themselves they really were.

At six o'clock when George Israel had closed the office and gone home, John remained behind sitting at a little table in the bare studio under the fading skylight, sketching the day's sitters as they knew themselves to be and as they appeared before the world. These were pitiless portraits that grew beneath his hand, not in terms of moral judgment but because he probed deep with the scalpel of his mind, baring layer after layer of disillusion, frustration, confusion, fear, to get at the core. Always behind his work was the desire to understand what had made them as they were: not just the truth, which is so often meaningless, but what had created that truth.

"The youngsters and the old people are really wonderful," he told Frances. "They're the only ones content to appear as they are; they even seem to be proud and happy about being human. But those dreadful middle years, between sixteen and sixty . . ."

She replied, "Because that's when people suffer. I know that my mother did, terribly, yet she often told me of her happy childhood."

Frances was right. He was not free to judge people, particularly since he had never come to grips with himself, never tried to probe to the real truth. What was he, basically, and what had caused him to be what he was? What was the romance he had built up about himself that he tried to palm off as the truth, both to himself and other people?

He rose abruptly and went to the wall mirror that was used by the women to put the finishing touches to their hair and simple make-up.

"Look at the mask I present to the world! Watch me simper and pose. See how I posture and throw out my chest before the camera so that the world will think I'm a wild West character, when I've never lassoed a steer in my life or ridden the range or done anything but talk about the West. This mirror knows that I'm a fraud and a hypocrite. I strip other people bare; innocent and unsuspecting folks who come up here to get their pictures took. Very well, then, let's see how I look after all the veils of pretense and illusion are stripped away.

"Nothing my parents could say or do would persuade me to attend high school; I wanted to roam the streets and fields like a woods colt. My mother loves me, she backs me to the bitter end against all opposition and all logic, and in return I give her heartbreak. I love Frances, I know that; then why don't I marry her and put an end to her uncertainty, to the waste of her good years? Because I'm a coward, a miserable squirming coward who is afraid of love and marriage. I keep my hold on her because I need her, but I have never intended to marry her, and at this moment I am determined that I never shall.

"I pretend to drink to blot out the terrible things that go on inside my head, but that's not the truth. I like to drink, I find excuses to drink because only then can I lift myself out of this humdrum meaningless world and catch on to something, a spirit, a substance that enables me to justify life.

"Inside myself I think gently, I'm really as soft as a marshmallow, but when I talk to others I'm loud and harsh and tough and opinionated. Why? What's wrong with me? Why can't I be natural? Why do I have to strike phony attitudes? Why do I hurt the people I love? Other people want to look better than they really are. I want to look worse. Why?"

He burned all his drawings each night before he left the studio . . . including the ones he made of himself.

He worked faithfully all winter at the photographic parlor, making his way up the flight of stairs before eight in the morning and continuing straight through to six at the endless tasks of retouching and finishing. His family and friends were delighted. For his own part he was happy enough: he could feel a process of slow change going on inside himself, even though he could not decipher the change. He was content to let the strange organism which was John Noble work its way through the next phase.

After a few months of training George Israel let him begin handling the camera. George was not seeking self-expression in a beautiful or artistic creation on film; he wanted to get the best possible picture the subject could induce and then sell as many replicas as the subject could afford. John attempted to treat photography as an art form, to make each picture revealing and universal, even as he tried to do with his drawings. It had never been his concept that the function

66

of a painter was to hold a mirror up to nature, nor did he believe that the total of the component parts of a picture made a whole picture: for him there had to be an added element, a mysterious essence which was the artist himself: the meaning of a canvas must extend beyond its frame to a point of infinity. The more he broadened the camera's range by an experimental use of lights and the juxtaposition of objects, the more clearly he realized its limitations. By contrast he had a growing sense of the unlimited medium of painting, its power to bring into a canvas that which did not exist and yet without which all existence was meaningless.

When he tried to explain this to Frances, she asked, "Aren't you painting at all, John?"

"Only in my head. I'm beginning to figure out what should be in a painting and what can be left out."

She studied his face, the serious, opaque blue eyes, the strong though sensual mouth, reassured at his calm tone yet anxious too, because she realized that once he resolved the problems that had been bothering him about painting there would be an end to this sojourn in photography. Yet she had no desire to hold him prisoner in this studio if it were just a way point for him.

She was awakened at two o'clock one morning by noises beneath her window. Down below was John on Wichita Bill, holding a second of the family's horses by the reins. He had taken off his good suit and was in cowboy chaps, heavy shirt and sombrero. She slipped into her riding clothes, going down the stairs quietly so as not to awaken her brother. John helped her up into the saddle and they rode quickly out of town, skirting the edges of freshly planted fields.

He had not uttered a single word, but led them down into ravines, along creek beds and far out over the trackless ranches. The night air was cool and nascent with spring; even the horses felt a sense of life awakening and renewing itself. An ash-gray dawn was seeping upward in the east when he turned for home. He helped her dismount and accompanied her to the front door, waiting until she had admitted herself. She stood in the dark living room and watched him ride away, tired and sagging over his saddle.

This was the beginning of his night rides. He rigged up a drawing board which he bound to the pommel of the saddle, and although it rocked before him like the prow of a ship in heavy weather, he soon learned to compensate for its movements. The lack of light hindered him not at all; in part he was drawing what he saw about him in the night's stillness,

67

but in greater part he was drawing what he saw in his own head: there was daylight in his head illuminating everything he wanted to put down.

Frequently he brought Lady along and called for Frances; she enjoyed these rides, the sense of being alone with the man she loved, feeling close and intimate under the vast night sky, and because she knew that he would have taken no one else on these journeys. After a time she perceived that he was not aware of her presence, any more than he was aware of his own. She never refused to go with him, no matter how tired she might be or how impossibly late the hour, and yet her feeling grew that she was riding alone on the prairie, that this wasn't a man beside her, a sweetheart, a lover or a husband, but a demoniacal force which compressed itself into a tiny area the size of a sheet of drawing paper tacked to a board that was lashed to a saddle, trying to capture a fragment of a lopsided moon behind a jagged cloud, a tree alone on the white bosom of the earth, a man riding a horse across the curve of the universe.

14

Business at George Israel's fell off during the heat and harvest. John now had long afternoons to himself. He went back to painting with a calm he had not known before, and an assurance that was born not of any improved technique or craftsman's skill but of a basic concept of the scope of his medium. During his novitiate with the oils he had been fumbling and awkward; during the second period he had been nervous and upset by the pressure of time. But the many months away from painting, the freedom gained by the rigid adherence to a business routine, his months of utter stillness on the night prairies had resolved many things. He knew that the Israel and Company episode was at an end. There was no need to break off abruptly; the time would come, next month or next year, when the moment would be ripe.

Israel did not disapprove of his painting in the back room of the studios when there was nothing else to do, yet he was not comfortable there. At any moment a customer might walk in. Nor could he leave the studio in the middle of an afternoon and go home to his easel in his mother's parlor.

One evening as he rode with his father to the Toler Theater where a traveling troupe of prize fighters were giving exhibition bouts, John, Sr., mentioned a vacant office just across the street from Israel's.

John asked eagerly, "Father, do you think you might let me have that office for a while? I mean if there's nobody after it already?"

"What did you want it for, John?"

"Well, I . . . business is slow at the studio just now. I have considerable time for painting, but I can't work up there. . . ."

"Now, son, don't tell me you're going back to that arty stuff. After all, you and George have been making yourselves a nice profit and George tells me you're learning fine."

"But I wasn't planning to leave George, Father, I just wanted a place close by to work sometimes . . ."

John, Sr., began to speak, checked his words, then studied his son for several moments.

"Look, boy, it's not the loss of the rent I care about; if you wanted that office for any business on God's green earth, I'd be delighted to give it to you. Even if you wanted it for monkey business, to have a place to drink and play poker with your friends . . . But I am not going to contribute to your becoming less a man because you are doing more of that feminine painting."

John was more amused than hurt. He left his father just inside the theater to join Frances and Marty, whom he had invited to see the matches, the climax of which was to be the appearance of an alleged champion called the California Crusher. Most of Wichita turned out, and the Toler Theater was jammed. A smoke haze puffed slowly upward. The bouts were rough, with first one fighter being knocked down and then his opponent dropping to the canvas.

"That's funny," said John, "they're not getting hit hard enough to go down."

"It looks hard to me," said Marty.

The California Crusher was brought before the curtain and introduced as the champion of the Pacific Coast. The two-hundred-pound figure exposed on either end of the green trunks was a powerful one.

". . . ten-dollar gold piece to any local pride who can stay three rounds with the California Crusher," the manager was saying.

He was a chipper little fellow with a derby hat and spats. He was holding a ten-dollar gold piece in the circle of his left forefinger and thumb. Then from the inside pocket of his checked sport coat he took out a black oblong jeweler's box, the kind used for displaying pearl necklaces.

"And to anyone who can knock out the Crusher, these five twenty-dollar gold pieces. One hundred dollars in cash to the local champ. All he had to do is put the Crusher down for a count of ten!"

A big blond farm lad pushed his way up to the stage. He had friends in the audience.

"That's it, Swede! You can buy a lot of acres for a hundred bucks!"

Swede was fitted with shoes and gloves. After considerable fanfare the portable bell was rung, and Swede went flailing like a windmill at the Crusher while the crowd roared its approval.

"Swede's not hitting him," murmured John, who was watching closely. "As soon as he begins to tire . . ."

"He won't tire," cried Marty.

But in the middle of the second round Swede suddenly stopped, out of breath. The Crusher feinted once with his left and threw a knockout right.

The next challenger was a tall lean cowboy with whom John had boxed in the gymnasium. The Crusher took a few left jabs on the face, to the intense joy of the audience, and then toward the end of the second round dumped the cowboy with a low, loping right to the belly.

"He telegraphs that right at least five seconds before he swings it," said John. "Why can't they see it coming?"

"Maybe they're closer to him than you are," observed Frances, not meaning to be sarcastic.

"His left is completely muscle-bound; he hasn't hit once with it. If a fellow could keep moving fast, always on his left side . . ."

"Step up, step up!" cried the manager of the stage. "Where is the pride of Wichita, the future Kansas Crusher? Where is the Prairie Champ who will take home this velvet box of gold?"

"Right here!"

John rose, pushed past Frances and Marty to the aisle. There was a short silence, then he heard Dave Leahy's voice, and Vic Murdock's, shouting encouragement.

His right was faster and easier for him than his left, but he made no effort to use it, content to keep circling the Crusher, always on his left, getting in with his own straight left jabs. The Crusher was content to let John box himself out during the first round and give the cheering crowd a show for its

70

money. By the middle of the second round the Crusher began tying him up in a clinch as he came in. When the troupe's referee separated them, he pushed John off balance just long enough for the Crusher to bring over a haymaking right. The blow grazed John's jaw; he was able to get up at the count of five. He knew now that he had to keep out of clinches, or the referee would set him up again.

After a minute of the third round the Crusher got reckless. He stalked John with his fists low, his face exposed, unafraid of John's right because it had not yet been used. In a flash John saw the opening for which he had been waiting. He stepped in, swung his right with all his strength for the Crusher's jaw. He felt his fist meet its target; then, for an instant, he lost consciousness.

When he opened his eyes there was a strange hush in the auditorium. The Crusher lay flat on his back, arms and legs spread out wide.

"The count!" John yelled at the referee. "Start your count."

But the referee was standing over the prostrate champion of the Pacific Coast, too astonished to say a word. John began waving his arm, shouting numbers.

"One—two—three——"

By the time he reached ten, threw up his arm and yelled, "You're out!" the audience was in an uproar. John helped pick up the Crusher and set him on his stool. The subdued manager dumped a bucket of water over his main attraction, then held out his arms for silence.

"Ladies and gentlemen, we have a new champion in Wichita. The old champ wants to present him with the prize himself, personally. There will be a short intermission while the Crusher gets ready for the presentation ceremony."

People crowded around John, pounding him on the back. From across the aisle he saw his father looking at him, a strange glitter in his eyes. After a spell of handshaking, Marty exclaimed:

"Say, it's taking them a powerful long time."

"They're still trying to bring the 'Nutcracker' to!" someone laughed.

But after a half hour had passed, John made for the dressing rooms. They were deserted. The jeweler's box with its five gold coins was already several miles on the road to Hutchinson. He ran back to the stage, held up his hands for silence.

"They've flown the coop! Who'll come with me? We'll get horses from Doc Saug and overtake them!"

Within minutes some twenty men were pounding at the dark road. It took them less than an hour to catch up with the troupe's two wagons. Riding the dark fields on either side, they reached the road ahead. The cowboy and several of his friends had revolvers cocked.

The manager emerged from the lead wagon.

"What's the meaning of this outrage!" he spluttered. "I'll have the law . . ."

"We'll take that hundred dollars in gold," announced John. "And a dollar a head for these horses we rented."

The cowboy fired twice, over the top of the wagon.

"All right, don't get excited," pleaded the manager. "I was just going after my money box."

The greater part of the fight audience was in the Eaton saloon when John pushed through the swinging doors. He opened the jeweler's box, letting the five gold coins ring on the polished wood surface of the bar. His eyes sought out his father at his permanent table. The older man laughed and nodded his head.

"Jerry, set 'em up for the house!" called John, imitating his father's deep voice and half-swagger smile. "I just made me a horse trade."

The office was in the rear of the building, looking westward over the roofs of Wichita to the juncture of the Big and Little Arkansas rivers and beyond to the cornfields which stretched to the horizon, fields which had been solid buffalo grass when he first rode Wichita Bill across them. He kept the room bare except for his easel and a table of long pine planks laid across wooden horses, on which were his books, piles of magazines, tobacco jars and emptied paint tubes. Sometimes he became so engrossed that he forgot to go back to the photography parlor, or worked all night under the glaring electric light bulb suspended on a wire from the center of the ceiling. By ten o'clock the downtown district was dark; few sounds came through the night hours to distract him. Toward dawn he would fall asleep in his chair, waking in time to rush up the stairs to George Israel's washroom where he would shave and comb his hair before his partner arrived.

One day his mother sent him a huge couch.

"But that's exactly the wrong way to get him home nights," her husband complained. "The more you make it convenient for him to sleep down there, the more he'll stay away."

"He's going to stay anyhow, when he wants to work," she

replied, "and he should have a place to lie down when he needs to rest."

By tacit agreement the Noble family never visited the office. Dave Leahy or Victor Murdock came in of an evening to smoke, drink and discuss the newest books, politics and frontier talk out of the Southwest, but they were the only steady visitors. The first time he brought Frances up to show her his workshop, she stood aghast at the confusion and dirt. The room had not been swept for weeks, nor had anything been dusted; standing in every conceivable position on the table, the floor, the window sills, stuck between the cushions of the couch were dishes and bottles all filled with ashes, matches and cigarette stubs.

She cried, "John Noble, you're such a sensitive person, you're so aware of beauty around you, how can you even think of trying to put beautiful things down on canvas when you're surrounded by all this clutter and dirt?"

"That's just the external world, Frances; I don't see it."

She took off her jacket and began gathering together the ash trays and wiping down the debris from the long table with a stiffened paint rag. He handed her the last of the empty bottles from behind the cushions of the couch, then stretched out full length, his hands locked beneath his head, joyfully watching the effortless movements of her tall lithe young body under the white organdy waist and black velvet skirt.

"It's a funny thing, Frances," he mused. "My father has always said I was undisciplined. Yet I accept unquestioningly all the disciplines of painting, even when I have a hard time measuring up. Why should I have refused to follow anybody else's orders, or any one else's scheme of life, and now make myself a slave to a set of brushes and some colors squeezed out onto a palette?"

She straightened up from scouring the washbowl; her eyes were sympathetic and serious.

"That does not seem difficult to answer, John; you've at last found an adversary you consider worthy of your mettle. Do you know where the broom closet is in this building? And do they have a bucket and running water in it?"

An hour later when she had finished sweeping and scrubbing out the room, she stood before the easel over which he had thrown a rough piece of cloth.

"I know it is asking a very high wage, but in return for getting you all neat and tidy again, could I see what you've been painting?"

She could feel him stiffen, then he rose, came to her side.

"There is nothing to see," he said quietly as he slipped the cloth off the canvas. "I've started three or four separate pictures on this one canvas, but they don't come to anything."

She gazed in silence for a long while. There were indeed several pictures on the big canvas: in the center a white buffalo coming down the draw of an upland valley; in the upper righthand corner a man without a face, standing alone in the middle of a vast plane, the top half the beaten blue sky of mid-July heat, the bottom half the yellow monotone of corn on the earth; the left half of the canvas the Kansas prairie before it had been broken under foot or plow, a sea of high red buffalo grass but on it no man, no ship, no sail.

"What are they about, John?"

"You mean what was I trying to say?"

He took a palette knife and with swift vigorous movements scraped the paint off the canvas.

"I don't know. I have the feeling that something is trying to break through the tough outer crust of my mind . . ."

He broke off, embarrassed by Frances' strange look.

The next few days he avoided his workroom and the photographic parlor, talking earnestly with his friends in Wichita, leading them to pour out their interests and excitements: Doc Saug loved breeding and caring for fine animals; Marty loved business and money; his mother loved her home and family; Victor Murdock loved politics; the Episcopalian minister loved morality; his father loved horse trades; Dave Leahy loved tall tales; young Sidney Toler, whose father owned the Toler Theater, loved dramatics. As far as he could tell, none of these people was tortured to live something beyond his own manifest pattern; nor was there any mysterious element beating against their waking hours, crying to be admitted. Yet might not they be concealing, knowingly or unknowingly, just as he would conceal if anyone had tried to pump him? Wouldn't he talk about the old West, tell of how he helped drive the first herd of cattle across the Staked Plains with Goodnight and Loving, or how he shot buffalo and skinned them and shipped their hides East?

Did any man reveal what he truly was?

15

He was cleaning his brushes when two men walked in without knocking. He recognized them as Thomas and John

Mahan, owners of the elaborate bar in the basement of the Hotel Carey, one of the best-known drinking establishments west of the Mississippi. Its beautifully carved and highly gleaming walnut counter ran the entire length of the room, which was finished with the startling gray stucco blocks the Mahan brothers had bought when the 1893 Chicago World's Fair buildings were torn down. The older of the two brothers, a distinguished-looking gray-haired man, opened the conversation.

"Mr. Noble, we understand that you are a painter."

"An interesting accusation," replied John, "but one I would have a hard time proving."

"But do you paint pictures?" broke in the younger man brusquely. "We need a man as can paint a picture. We've been all over town and all we can find is spinster ladies that paint china dishes."

John winced as he heard his father's voice on the subject of spinsters and china dishes.

"Very well, gentlemen, I'm the only painter in town. That doesn't make me good but it makes me unique. What can I do for you?"

"You know that big empty space behind the Carey bar?"

"Yes. I have spent some of the worst hours of my life staring at it."

"That's what's the matter with it," exclaimed the younger of the brothers. He took out a handkerchief, carefully spread it on John's sofa, and gingerly sat down on the protected area. "We want something on that wall so men don't have to stare at it blank-like."

"What kind of a picture do you want, gentlemen? Something out of Peter Breughel: peasants drinking in the field when the harvest is in?"

"Not exactly, Mr. Noble." The older and more cultivated of the brothers smiled tolerantly. "From years of watching men drink at bars all over this country we have come to the conclusion that the more they think about women and love-making, the more they drink."

"A profound conclusion, Mr. Mahan."

"We want you to make us a painting that can be seen from every corner of the Carey bar. Nude women, shall we say? Not harlots, you understand, but respectable women, caught unawares . . ."

"Are there any women you have in mind? Say, Lillian Russell or Lily Langtry?"

The younger brother took him seriously, springing up from

his seat. "No, no. We couldn't get away with that, they'd sue us into bankruptcy. It should be well-known women, like you say, but ones that lived a long time ago."

"Like Cleopatra, for example?"

"Bull's-eye, Mr. Noble," cried the older brother. "Cleopatra at the bath. Surround her with beautiful young handmaidens, plump women—skinny women make men morose—and perhaps a couple of eunuchs to serve them."

"Also nude?"

"No, no," expostulated the younger man, "That wouldn't be decent."

"What would be your charge for such a picture, Mr. Noble?"

John's head whirled from the suddenness of the entire conversation. This was how painters had lived during the centuries, getting commissions from the state, the church, or from wealthy patrons who wanted their walls decorated. But nude women over a bar in the Carey Hotel . . . so that lonely men could gaze up at them hungrily, drinking themselves into unconsciousness? Still, it wasn't up to him to make moral judgments; a painter was a craftsman who ought to do the jobs that were wanted. He cast about in his mind for a figure, any figure, so that it would not be apparent that he didn't know that paintings had a value. The only sum he could think of was the amount Dave had paid him for the Dalton drawing.

"One hundred dollars!" he exclaimed in too loud a voice.

The Mahans exchanged an amused smile. The older said quickly, "Agreed! How long will it take you?"

"I don't really know. How large do you want it?"

"Big!" exclaimed the younger brother, stretching his arms as though to embrace the world.

"All right," said John, "I'll start right away."

The younger Mahan took a roll of greenbacks from his trouser pocket, removed two thick rubber bands and peeled off ten ten-dollar bills, dropping them into the collection of wet brushes on the table. "The Mahans always pay in advance. C'mon over later, have a drink with us and measure that space behind the bar."

The Mahans departed. John threw himself face down on the divan, laughing hysterically for a couple of minutes, and then, to his amazement, found himself crying. The whole scene had been so vulgar; but surely no more vulgar than his own delight at being called a painter, and his eagerness to get the commission?

He heard heavy footsteps coming down the hall. For a moment he thought it was the brothers. Bitterly as he had been hating himself the instant before, his heart now began racing for fear the barkeeps were returning to cancel the order. He sprang up and was halfway across the room when Dave Leahy threw open the door and entered.

"What's happened to you, m'boy? You've got stars in those lovely blue eyes of yours, or would they be tears, now?"

He stood a bottle on the table, roundly wrapped in brown paper. "And what's all this green stuff doing here?" he exclaimed, as he jostled the Mahans' ten-dollar bills. "Looks like you ransacked the First Natonal Bank."

"Take that cowardly concealing paper off your bottle," laughed John, "I've just been awarded the Prix de Rome."

"The roof of whose chapel will you be decorating?"

"The Mahans'. Behind the bar. Cleopatra at the bath. With lush handmaidens. And eunuchs in loincloths."

Dave inserted the corkscrew blade of his knife into the bottle of whiskey.

"Break out the goblets," he said, "and let us drink to Michelangelo Noble, the pride of Wichita. Look at the quantity of this prize money. Two thousand, three thousand, four, five, six, seven thousand, eight, nine, ten thousand dollars of prize money!"

The men clinked their glasses.

The next day John found himself on the front page of the *Eagle,* with streamers across a two-column spread.

JOHN NOBLE WINS PRIX D'WICHITA

Local Boy Defeats All Comers in World Competition

by Dave Leahy

Thomas and John Mahan, proprietors of the Hotel Carey bar, announced that the winner of their ten-thousand-dollar Prix d'Wichita is John Noble, Kansas' most outstanding painter. From among the hundreds of sketches and drawings that were submitted from all over Europe, and as far as Mongolia, John Noble's study, entitled "Cleopatra at the Bath" was judged by an outstanding group of art experts to be the finest.

Interviewed yesterday in his painting studio, John Noble denied that he was going to accept any of the fabulous offers to paint his murals in Paris, Berlin or Rome.

Mr. Noble told your reporter yesterday, "I intend to remain here in Wichita until the commission is completed." This is the first time that a native Kansas artist has won an international art contest. The studio was thronged with his admirers wishing him well.

John walked up to the *Eagle* offices with the paper stuffed into his coat pocket.

"You've outdone yourself this time, Dave. This yarn makes all your others look like the census reports. Everybody in town knows there isn't a word of truth in it."

"Nonsense, m'boy: what people read in a newspaper they believe is true even when they know better. Who's going to deny the story? The Mahan brothers? They're so delighted with the free advertising they sent me over a complimentary case of bourbon this morning."

His family was indeed delighted with the newspaper story, and with the commission. He found that, despite the obvious nonsense of Dave's article, the townspeople evinced a new regard for him: he was no longer an idler or a dilettante; he was a man with a trade to whom people went when they wanted merchandise. True, it was a strange and perishable commodity in which he dealt, nevertheless he could earn a living at it. That made him respectable.

He settled down in his workroom and found that he hadn't the faintest notion of how to paint Cleopatra at the bath. What did she look like? Was her face Egyptian, or did it look like any other female face in Wichita? How did the Egyptian women comb their hair, and just where would they be taking this historic bath? On the banks of the Nile? On the royal barge, in the palace, or somewhere deep in the Egyptian woods? Were there any woods in Egypt?

Most disconcerting of all, what did a group of nude women look like? Except for fleeting moments several years before when he had gone to what was left of Wichita's sporting houses, hoping to meet a modern-day Dora Hand of the Alhambra saloon or the equivalent of Alice Chambers, who had reigned over Dodge City, he had never seen a naked woman. Like the rest of the wild West into which he had been born too late, the girls had lost their color and romance: they were drab, joyless creatures trying to earn a living; he had escaped as fast as he could.

Ridiculous as the project appeared to him now, he knew that he could not multiply the crime by making himself ridiculous as well. He ransacked the public library in Wichita, searching for pictures of Egyptian and Roman women, wrote to Chicago and New York for books which contained reproductions of Egyptian costumes, jewelry, landscapes. By the end of the first month, at which time he was supposed to deliver the canvas to the Hotel Carey bar, he had filled his room with hundreds of rough sketches, attempting to lay out a composition. He could now draw with his eyes closed an Egyptian ring or hair style, but he was no farther along with his concept of the female nude than he had been a month before. There were no models in Wichita, and no woman he knew well enough to ask to pose. Word had only to circulate that he was posing naked women in his room, and the church ladies would ride him out of town. His only alternative was to copy the pencil drawings of nudes out of the art books he had received from New York. To his surprise, he found that the lines which artists for centuries had considered the most exciting in nature, the upward tilt of a woman's breast, the rolling swell of a thigh, the arch of a sensuous back, were less interesting to him than the undulating planes of a mountain range.

He worked hard and thought of little else, essaying canvas after canvas, running up a bill at the supply store, and knowing now that his rough guess of a month in which to finish the picture could easily run into a year. Nor was there any escape from the impracticality of the whole deal, for Marty Buckler was keeping an accurate set of books on the venture.

"Look, Prix d'Wichita," he said, "you've been on the job for four months now. You're in hock to the supply store for two hundred and eighty dollars, and you've spent another three hundred on books and pictures to copy from. Let's add to that what you were earning with George Israel, that was about two hundred dollars a month. You've already laid out fourteen hundred dollars for a hundred-dollar job, and according to your own guess you have another six months of work left. Tell me, John, how do you make these figures add up to good common sense?"

"I don't try."

"All right, let me give you the other half of the story: four months ago, when you started this painting, I advertised in the Wichita *Eagle* announcing the sale of all laundry, clothing, shoes and hats which were left unclaimed. The sale cleaned out the leftovers, but during the following days people kept coming into the place thinking it was a secondhand store or pawnshop, wanting to buy guns, tools or jewelry, or make loans. We opened a secondhand store and pawnshop next door to the laundry. In the last four months that outfit had earned, in cold cash, five thousand dollars. For her third interest Frances put in a thousand dollars, and already has half again that much in profit. Why couldn't you have been sensible and taken the other third? Instead of being down the drain for thirteen hundred dollars, you'd have had a couple of thousand in your jeans."

"I might have had two thousand dollars, Marty, but never in cash: you would have had it sunk in another venture by now. According to my way of figuring, you're going to die the richest poor man in Kansas."

Marty flushed. "I have got a new idea, and this one will make us more money than all the others put together. You'd be surprised how many people come in who want to borrow money, but without collateral."

"What in hell is collateral?"

"Security. Something they leave behind, like a camera or a violin. Do you know how much those loan companies charge up in Kansas City and Chicago? Twelve per cent. Fifteen per cent by the time they add the paper charges. We could bring it down to a flat ten, and that would be the best rate in the country."

John turned from his canvas, laid down his brushes. "Now, Marty, don't tell me you're going to become a usurer. If you must make more money, open that junk yard I sneered at last year."

The red flush on Marty's face settled to a purplish color matching his eyes.

"Don't let's be sentimental, John. Usury is just another word for high interest rates. High interest has to be charged when the risk is great. Sometimes people need money under circumstances where the banks won't loan. A quick five hundred or a thousand dollars could save a man's home or his business, maybe even his life. I'm not trying to make out I'm a philanthropist, I'm only saying that a loan is worth ten per cent when you need it. Any businessman will tell you that."

John dropped onto his couch; his body sagged with fatigue. He hadn't slept much of late, catching only an occasional nap when he could no longer keep his eyes open.

"Marty, it's all come clear to me: you're on your way to becoming a banker. Marty Buckler's Second National Bank."

"That's right, John. We are going to put up that building we planned on Douglas Avenue. Only we're not going to call it a bank . . . yet. We are calling it the Wichita Finance and Credit Corporation."

John swung his legs around and sat up, his eyes wide open. "Who is this 'we,' Marty? Would it be the editorial 'we' that Victor Murdock is always using in the *Eagle?*"

"No, it wouldn't be the editorial 'we.' " Marty stuck out his chin belligerently. "It's Frances and me. She's my partner now, and as soon as the papers are drawn for the building we are putting up on her land . . ." He broke off, stared guiltily at the floor for a few moments, then came and sat beside John, dropping down so close that he bruised John's hip with his heavy leather belt. His voice was pleading. "I've never done anything behind your back, boy. You know that I've always loved Frances, just as I've always known that she loved you. But you see so little of her, and so many years have passed. You don't ever intend to marry her, do you, John? Then why shouldn't I have her? She has to marry someone. She can't wait her whole life for you and then get left out in the cold. That's not fair, John. If you'd only tell her the truth, let go of her altogether. We have been working awfully close together these last couple of years. I know she likes me, and I know she'd have me if only you . . ."

John interrupted Marty's impassioned appeal by rising, going back to his easel and blindly slashing color onto the canvas. Marty rose wearily, stared at John's back for a few moments and then went out. John locked the door behind him, reached for a bottle of Sunnybrook from under the divan, opened it and took half a dozen long swigs. Only then did he stop trembling.

16

The night that *Cleopatra at the Bath* was unveiled, the Mahan brothers and John Noble, Sr., combined to throw a monumental party. The Carey bar was jammed with all the men who had helped the older Noble transform Wichita from a mud-packed prairie settlement to a thriving metropolis. At a signal the bartender pulled a cord and the big white sheet concealing the painting fell to the floor.

There were gasps of surprise and pleasure, much handclapping and calling out of congratulations. But John heard nothing: there was a roaring in his ears, and his eyes were transfixed to the canvas.

Cleopatra had come alive! She was actually breathing up on that canvas, her ample bosom rising and falling rhythmically.

Someone thrust a glass into his hand. He drank gulpingly. When he opened his eyes again surely Cleopatra would be just as lifeless and wooden as he had painted her? But when he looked up he saw that she was not only still breathing, her bosom seemed also to be lighted from within by an incandescent glow.

He dug his nails into the walnut bar to keep from crying out. Then his head cleared. He pushed himself out of the crowd and made his way to the storeroom behind. Looking up, he saw an electric wire tacked along the wall, and at the end of it a muffled pink electric bulb, flashing on and off, automatically.

". . . lollapalooza of an idea, ain't it, John?"

John turned. It was the younger of the Mahan brothers, his face beaming in a self-congratulatory smile.

"We're going to have 'em hanging over that bar, John. It'll be like looking at a real live naked woman up there."

Now that the shock had passed he could not even feel anger. This last touch of vulgarization was little more than simple justice. To whom could he complain? To the excited little man beside him, already counting his profits from the lonely and famished men who would drink themselves into unconsciousness while dreaming of a distant love? Hadn't he made this painting for money? What was there to choose between the giver of the bribe and the taker?

He made his way out the rear delivery entrance and walked down the back streets to his office. Once in his workroom he locked the door, pulled the blinds so far below the window sill that he almost tore them from the rollers, and gathered up the preparatory sketches and studies for Cleopatra. His strong fingers ripped apart hundreds of the drawings, the others he burned scrap by scrap in his washbowl.

Then he took from against the wall the painting to which he had turned for solace when he became surfeited with the artificial Cleopatra. He set the canvas up on the easel; as he looked at it the outside world fell away: the jostling, shouting crowd in the Carey bar, the grinning face of Mahan as he gazed adoringly at his pulsating electric light.

Before him stood *The Run,* a big canvas extending from a covered wagon in the right foreground with a white-bearded patriarch holding the reins, on across the plains of Oklahoma to the infinity of the horizon; and in between all the hundreds

82

of pilgrims with whom he had lived in Hunnewell, caught in the moment just after the starting gun had been fired, the trail herders shouting at their cow ponies, the city men booting their race horses, the women and children clinging to the sides of the frail rigs and surreys, wide-eyed with excitement and fear; behind them the wrecks of broken axles, collapsed wagons and collapsed plans.

He knew that the work lacked years of hard-bitten craftsmanship; yet it made him feel clean and whole inside because every touch of the brush was honest and true. He pulled up a wooden chair, then turned out the light and sat before his canvas in a deeply reflective mood.

He knew that he had a completed picture before him. Everything was there: the packed prairie, the clouds of dust, the sky, the sun, the buffalo grass, the horses, the men, and yet when they were all put together, they added up to no total, no whole. They were scattered fragments. Something else was needed to give the various parts a harmony, a meaning, a unity.

What can it be? he asked himself. Have I left out something important? Failed to perceive it, get it down on the canvas? What is missing, that without which all the rest is a dry river?

God.

He raised his head sharply, as though there were someone in the room who might have spoken. There was a steady hum of silence about him. Except for distant animal sounds the night was quiet. He thought back to the sound; had he uttered it?

He got up from his chair, paced the room. Suddenly he felt faint. For he knew where he had heard the word: inside his own head. Was that possible? Could he have told it to himself, uttered aloud a concept that had been buried deep in his consciousness?

He did not feel that the source really mattered. As he gazed at his canvas in the darkness he knew that he had the answer for which he had been so blindly yet ardently searching: to expect a canvas to glow, to have a meaning beyond its narrow borders without God shining through, was like expecting a candle to lighten a black room before a match had been set to its wick.

He sat down abruptly on the hard chair. For an unbeliever, an agnostic, a pagan like himself to have been hungering for God all the time without knowing it: there was something sacrilegious in the idea! He found his discovery wonderful and terrible.

He knew only too well the concept of God that was abroad in Wichita. Mostly He was a stern old committeeman who spent His time fighting for prohibition and opposing sin; tight-lipped, avengeful, a God of repression, negation and hate. He had His inning with the local clergy between eleven and twelve on Sunday mornings; for the rest of the week He was laid away in moth balls.

If this concept of God were true, then John knew he must be thinking of something else: essence, meaning, illumination, the whole affirmative serenity and beauty of creation. He had never heard any such description of God in all his years in Wichita; could that perhaps be the reason why it had taken him so long to discover the object of his hunger? Among the cowboys and settlers there was rarely any talk of God or religion; during the enforced idleness of winter the ranch hands and farm families would ride for miles to hear a spell of good preaching but it was the quality of the minister's performance they came to judge, and not the wonder or beauty of God.

He threw back his head and laughed loudly in embarrassment, as though he were a small boy who had been caught on a high kitchen stool, his fingers in the jam jar. Then he became still, frightened: suppose people should find out and jeer at him? He must never let it show on his face, in his gesture, or his speech; he must not change his ways lest someone spread the word and he become the butt of ridicule. What if, every time he walked down the street, a crowd gathered about, shouting:

"Jump! Jump!"

Where would he jump from this high, dizzy span? Into the shallow waters? Into the arms of death?

No, he had been mistaken, terribly mistaken. The White Buffalo he had been pursuing was not death, as he had imagined. The White Buffalo was, and always had been, God.

He began walking about the room, bumping into the rough-edged furniture, pounding his right fist painfully into the palm of his left hand. Miles of canvas had to be covered with tons of paint before one tiny picture achieved any beauty or meaning. Wasn't the whole craft difficult enough without adding this extra burden? How could he, an ignorant, untrained, confused young man, transfer any semblance of God onto a canvas? For that matter, what was God? Where did one find Him? How did one persuade Him to pose on a model's stand?

In his mind he reviewed the line of men stemming from Giotto and Cimabue who had painted in and for churches: the Madonna with Child, Christ on the Cross, the Last Supper. To him these frescoes and paintings were more in the nature of beautiful illustrations of the stories of religion; they did not seem to be directly concerned with God, or the search and hunger for God, but rather with the effort to compress an elemental concept of God into simple folk myth. Churches were full of religious paintings, as though this worship of outward forms would somehow placate a mysterious and unapproachable Deity.

By temperament he could accept no middleman. If his yearning all these years had been for God, and he no longer could doubt this, then he must conduct his search alone, unguided, the secret held securely between himself and his Maker. Such a deep-seated hunger could not amble amiably beside serene cathedrals nor walk nostalgically through sunlit church cemeteries. He remembered that he had told Frances: "My white buffalo is running free over rugged mountains and through green valleys; it is alive and strong and beautiful, so beautiful that a man's eyes are hardly capable of seeing it!"

In sudden terror he asked himself, Where will I search for God in Wichita? This was a most unlikely place, for barriers had been erected against His appearing which might seem insuperable even to Him. Was this true in all towns where people congregated for worship: a little organ music, the singing of a hymn, the admonitions of the preacher against greed and lust; another hymn, a little more music, and then the social chitchat on the front steps?

Where was God in all this?

He believed that God was a solitary creature, that He would reveal Himself to only one man at any one time; that it was impossible that He should give manifestation to baptismal crowds being immersed in rivers, to a milling mob, baking under the tent of a July revival, to businessmen's luncheon clubs falling on their knees to pray under the exhortations of the visiting evangelist.

No, he thought, a man must be alone to see God, to feel God, to understand God, to walk with his hand in God's. To the cowboy riding the distant range, the sheepherder watching over his flock in some hard-won clearing, the wandering mountain man or trapper, the sod house settler alone on the vast prairie, to all of these God might appear, probably did appear in His own particular fashion: for these lonely folk seemed to have more wisdom and repose, to see deeper and feel clearer, to know more about the naked form of truth.

God just couldn't get down into cities; there was so much smoke from factory chimneys, so much noise and clangor, so many voices raised in anger and protest; people were so busy gesticulating, arranging swaps, making deals. If God should be so indiscreet as to show himself in a crowded city, people would say without looking up, "This is my busy day! Come back later."

This feeling that God could reveal Himself only to those who were lonely, desperately lonely, so lonely they could hardly endure life any longer: this clarified for him his own dread-filled and horrible loneliness, his desperate bouts of illness, the seizures, when he reached out to embrace what he had thought was death. Only when one reached this low estate, this need that was greater than the need for life itself, would God reveal Himself; for only then could He be seen, clearly, sharply; only then would a man rush forth with open arms and loving heart; only then would God be fully wanted, for there would be nothing else in the mind or heart of that man, save love of God.

It was incomprehensible to him now that people could wander blithely on their way, no more concerned about God than they were about the Hottentots. Or were they equally hungry, searching just as ardently for God but without knowing or acknowledging it, and calling God by vastly different names? Could Marty Buckler be calling God money; could his father be calling Him land; could his mother be calling Him family, Vic Murdock calling Him politics, Dave Leahy calling Him tall tales, and Doc Saug calling Him animals? For no man to whom God had revealed Himself ever could tell of that meeting: those who cried out in the market place, who protested their intimacy with their Maker and His will, they were the noisy ones, the self-seekers, the deluded.

He had come but the first stumbling step on his journey; to know for what one searches is already a great deal, but ah! to find it! Where did he look? What divining rod did he use? To whom did he speak? With whom did he search?

Himself.

He did not know what changes he must make in himself, or how he must alter his thinking, feeling and doing. He knew only that he must never lose this knowledge of his own nature, nor let the edges of his desire become blunted. If he ever were to find God, he would not be the one to set the time, the place or the circumstances. All that would happen in God's own way and in God's good time. For a man did not go out on the dusty roads of the world like a mendicant, crying, "Oh, Lord, where art Thou?" A man continued his work, hoping that through the quality of his devotion and skill the path to God might somehow be found.

He would continue his painting; it was the only road he knew.

17

Late one night when he went out to the barn he found Wichita Bill lying quietly in his stall, unable to raise himself. His breathing was quick and shallow. He put a hand on Wichita's neck; it felt as though a fire were burning beneath his touch. He saddled one of his father's horses and rode downtown for Doc Saug. Doc jumped into his work clothes, packed a bag of medicines and instruments, and swung up behind John.

The veterinarian worked over Wichita Bill, felt the dryness of his mouth and lips. When he looked up his weather-beaten face was lined with anxiety.

"He's an awful sick horse, John. Pneumonia, I'm afraid. See how clouded his eyes are. Probably a heart complication, too. Looks like we're going to lose him."

John had known this the moment he saw Wichita Bill lying on the floor of his stall.

"There must be something we can do, Doc."

"I'll try, boy. But when a horse gets to be this old . . ."

John sat in a corner of the stall, his knees clenched under his chin. Across his mind flashed a series of pictures: his first sight of the little bay a few hours after it had been dropped; the patient days he had spent in training the young colt; their long summer trips into the mountains of Colorado and across the open ranges of Texas and Oklahoma; the wonderful nights of comradely riding over the prairies with only the sea of earth beneath them and the sea of sky above them; and those moments, bitter to remember, when he had been ill and frightened and drunk, and Wichita Bill had brought him home safely to this very stall. He knew that he would never replace Wichita Bill.

In the dark hours before dawn he walked out Douglas Avenue to where Marty's and Frances' new building was going up. He had watched the progress of the steel girders and the wooden framework. By now the windows had been glassed in, the floors laid. He saw that the building was going to be beautiful, with clean utilitarian lines, free of the gingerbread ornamentation common in Wichita. Frances and Marty had worked together for months over the plans; and he had to admit that they worked together very well indeed.

Yet when the news of their engagement reached him, he found himself emotionally unprepared. One of his sisters mentioned it first at the Sunday dinner table. John dropped his fork, stared at her blindly, then rose and walked heavily from the room.

Many hours later he found himself standing in front of Frances' house. He walked up the front steps and bruised his knuckles knocking on the wooden panel of the door.

Frances stiffened a little when she saw him standing on the porch. Then she extended her hand.

"John, it's good to see you. Come in."

She led him into the dining room where she and Marty were working out the finish details for the Douglas Avenue stores. In the center of the table was a plate of sandwiches and a pitcher of hot chocolate. Marty was the only one of the three who was not embarrassed.

"Welcome, partner. You're just in time to tell us what color to paint the walls of our stores. Pretty soon we will be ready for the formal opening. We're making it on a Sunday afternoon. There'll be food and drink and an orchestra for dancing . . ."

"Sounds more like a wedding than a dedication, Marty."

There was a strained silence. John hadn't known that the words were coming out. He felt awkward and unhappy. After a moment he rose and left as confusedly as he had come in.

That night, while he sat dejectedly on the old couch in his office, his fingers interlocked on the back of his neck, forcing his head ever lower, he thought he heard a noise in the hall outside. He straightened up, his eyes intent; but there was only silence. He slumped forward again, but this time there could be no mistake: there was a faint, almost imperceptible knocking. He bounded up, reached the door in a few swift strides, and flung it open. There in the darkness stood Frances, her eyes large and frightened.

Their arms reached out for each other, their lips pressed tightly together. Then, when the breath was gone out of them, they clung tremblingly, unashamed of the pain and the longing and the tears in their eyes.

"John . . . when I saw how hurt you were this evening . . . I thought you had forgotten me . . . that you didn't care . . ."

"It isn't true!" The words were torn from him. "I've always loved you. You must know that."

"Why must I, John? This is the first time in all these years that you've told me."

"Oh . . . words . . ."

"Only a very few, John, spoken once . . ."

"But you've known . . ."

"Only that I love you. What kind of love is it that cuts a woman out of its life, lets her believe that she is unwanted, lets her spend her days with another man . . . until it seems she has nothing left to do . . . but marry him. You have to go where you're wanted in this world, John."

She hadn't meant to be unkind, but he felt as though he had been beaten severely about the head. The low vibrancy of her voice pierced his insides:

"It's not too late, John . . ."

He left her side and walked to the window at the back of the room, rolling a cigarette from the tobacco jar on the sill.

"It has nothing to do with you, or . . . our . . . love. Only with me. I can't find any place for myself, Frances. The months and the years go by, and I get no closer. I should be able to accept responsibility, set a pattern for myself . . ."

"You want to be a painter," she said softly, glancing at the canvas on the easel. "That's your job in life, your responsibility . . ."

"But there's no place for me here." His voice carried the anguish of indecision. "In Wichita an artist is a dilettante . . . good for painting china dishes."

"What do you want to paint?"

"There's something I must get down on canvas . . . but whether I can ever capture the least corner of it . . ."

"You can try, darling. No man is bound to succeed, only to try."

He held out his arms to her. "Frances, come here."

She went to him. He was half seated on the window sill. He held her close to him.

"Darling, believe me," he whispered hoarsely, "there is no possible life for us. I could never bring you anything but misery. . . . What else have I ever brought anyone?"

"I'm not afraid of misery, if it's part of love. We could go away from Wichita. We could go a thousand miles west the way your parents did."

"The old West is gone, Frances. There is no more frontier."

"It isn't gone, John, just moved on. To Wyoming, or Arizona . . . there is still open, wild . . ."

He put a finger over her lips. She kissed it, softly: he didn't really want the life of the old West, but only its romance, its tradition, its pictures. He admired it in retrospect; he would never consent to live it. He was not really a participant in life. Even in love he was only a spectator.

He held her against him so tightly that he hurt her at every point of contact.

"Go home to Marty, put your arm through his, and never look back over your shoulder. Something's hanging over me, Frances. I don't know what it is. I try to find my way. I fight, I run . . . It's why I drink so much, and am so confused. Happiness just isn't in me. . . ."

She took a lace handkerchief from the pocket of her wool coat and wiped the perspiration from his forehead. She knew that he was lost to her forever. Yet she could accept that judgment now with a kind of resignation. For she could see, looking at his troubled eyes, his quivering, parted lips, that he loved her.

She stroked his cheek gently to quiet him. The terror receded from his face.

"It's all right, John. You needn't worry about me ever again."

An involuntary cry was wrenched from them, and they were again locked in a passionate embrace, their lonely mouths crushed in the bittersweet of good-by. Then he felt rather than saw her pull down the dark green shade. He picked her up, placed her on the couch, turned out the naked bulb.

Later, when he moved the blind a trifle, and stood in the dark room gazing down, he saw her come out from the building's entrance and walked quickly down the street. She didn't look back.

18

He drank steadily, worked not at all. He was at a trail's end, with a chasm in front of him and no desire to turn around and retrace his steps. He hungered to cut the strangulating umbilical cord which bound him to Wichita, to travel for thousands of miles away from everyone he knew and loved, away from his childhood, his background, his anchorage, just as his father had when, with fewer valid reasons, he picked himself up from the familiar security of his Illinois home and came out to these few transitory shacks pasted against the buffalo grass of a Kansas prairie. But where did one go, and how, and when?

He was standing idly at the Hotel Carey bar when Carry Nation, wearing a long black dress with a black cowl draped over her head and shoulders, entered the saloon. She stalked up to the bar, her eyes focused on Cleopatra on the wall. Horror and repugnance swept over her face. She pointed a finger at the bartender and exclaimed:

"What is that naked woman doing up there?"

"That's only a picture, madam. There's the artist standing right beside you, the man who painted it."

Having thus shucked his responsibility, the bartender picked up a glass and began to polish it. Carry Nation turned on John.

"It's disgraceful," she cried. "You're insulting your mother by having her form stripped naked and hung up in a place where it isn't even decent for a woman to be when she has her clothes on."

John remembered what had happened to the saloon in Kiowa and shrank several feet down the bar.

Carry Nation turned to the bartender. "You're a rummy and a lawbreaker! Take that filthy painting down and close this murder mill." She glared at the other drinkers, picked up the bottle of Sunnybrook from which John had been drinking, smashed it on the brass rail, then ran up the steps and out.

The bartender shook his head and took a short beer to settle his nerves. One of the drinkers exclaimed, "You handled her fine, Eddie. She'll never come back to this joint."

"Don't be too sure," said John. "She's harder on a saloon than a Kansas cyclone."

He had no sooner pronounced the word "cyclone" than Carry Nation was back, carrying a newspaper package in which there were jagged outlines that he recognized. She wasted no words but threw a large stone at *Cleopatra at the Bath*. It tore a long hole in the canvas. When the bartender reached out a hand to protest, she shouted:

"Glory to God! Peace on earth, good will to men!"

She took another stone from her package and smashed a huge wall mirror. She then drew out a cane to which an iron rod had been fastened, and ran behind the bar swinging her weapon over her head, smashing every bottle, decanter, glass and remaining mirror in sight.

Spectators started coming down the stairs to watch the show, and finally a detective whom John recognized as Park Massey came to her side, ducked a circular blow of the cane and clutched the lady by the arm.

"Madam, I must place you under arrest."

"Arrest me!" cried Carry Nation. "Why don't you arrest the man that runs this hellhole? Can't you smell the rotten poison?"

"You are destroying property, madam," the detective said. "I must arrest you."

He took the cane away from her and led her up the steps. The crowd followed. John stood alone amidst the debris. He looked up at *Cleopatra at the Bath*. One of the eunuchs had been put out of business for a second time, and half of Cleopatra's figure was lying somewhere behind the bar, amidst the fumes of spilled whiskey. He decided that it was a fitting and proper demise for his painting. It was a ridiculous idea to begin with; that it should now be destroyed by the equally ridiculous Carry Nation seemed to constitute a poetic justice.

He was about to muse that his life was in a similar state of chaos, consisting of shattered fragments and reeking whiskey, when the younger of the Mahan brothers walked dolefully through the door.

"I'm going to prosecute that crazy woman," he vowed. "They got her locked up in jail right now."

"You mean you're going to tell the judge you run a saloon in dry Kansas?" commented John wryly.

Mahan wasn't listening. "And you're going into court and testify that she wantonly and willfully destroyed your great work of art."

"I wish I could," replied John. "I mean I wish it were a great work of art she threw that rock through. But it was only a bad chromo. She may be terrible as a reformer, but Mrs. Nation has the makings of a great art critic."

When he got back to his workroom he saw that Dave Leahy had been up to see him, for a copy of Frank Berkeley Smith's *The Real Latin Quarter* had been tossed through the transom. John picked it up, stretched out on his couch and began to read.

By the end of the first chapter he knew he would leave Wichita the following day. Paris was the art center and painting capital of the world. Into that city poured painters of every age and creed, from every distant land and remote degree of talent. Parisians knew that painters and poets were important, that the arts were urgent to civilization. In Paris a painter was a man; his craft was respected, his product purchased, he could breathe free air, live with men like himself, work in an aura of sympathy, experimentation and artistic striving. It took money to travel abroad, money to live in a strange land. Yet he knew that he must get to Paris or he would slowly drink himself to death in this dirty and littered workroom.

There was a fragment of mirror lying on his worktable. He looked into it and saw that he had a four days' stubble on his chin, his hair was unkempt, his suit badly bedraggled. He had long since stopped winding his own watch: when he got down to the street he peered into Ed Vail's show window and saw by the dozen wall clocks that it was four o'clock. He went into the New York Store where he bought a pair of socks, some underwear and a fresh white shirt, then walked over to the barbershop where he had a bath in an iron tub in the rear room, put on his clean clothes, had his face shaved and his hair cut. His next stop was at Marty Buckler's new building, where he found Marty in his private office examining applications for loans.

"Marty, could you do me a favor? Would you take this suit of mine down to your shop for a press, and have these shoes shined?"

Marty blinked. "Sure, John, but why?"

"I'm leaving for Paris on the night train."

Marty half rose, arching his fingers as he leaned forward, the anger flooding to his face.

"What do you want to go to Paris for? What have they got that Wichita hasn't got, except maybe a lot of loose women?" His voice was rising and had become shrill. "What right have you got to run away from us? To insult every man and woman in Wichita by saying that this town's not good enough for you. You think you can look down your nose at us, John, just because you can make meaningless daubs of color on canvas. Anybody who wants to spend the money for supplies can do as good! Why are you better than we are? What gives you the right to feel superior, to think that you got to go to Paris?"

John stared wide-eyed at his friend. Poor Marty, he thought, while I stayed here doing nothing, accomplishing nothing, being the town idler and the town drunk, he was secure. He had defeated me. He had proved that it is a man's job to make money, and that anybody who fools with other things, ideas or books or pictures, ends up in a ditch. But once I leave here, go to Paris, his victory vanishes. He'll have to spend his whole life accumulating more buildings, more businesses and more dollars to convince himself that he was right and I was wrong.

Aloud he said, "It's just that I think I'll be happier there, Marty. There's no criticism of Witchita involved. It's no use being the only one of a species in a town. Paris is full of painters, good and bad, and one more won't make any difference to them. Maybe I can learn something over there; certainly I'm not learning anything here; I've come up against the cliff at the end of a dry gulch. If I don't move in some direction, the vultures and prairie dogs will be feasting on my carcass. Now would you mind taking this suit down and getting it pressed for me?"

Twenty minutes later he rushed over to the *Eagle*. Dave Leahy and Victor Murdock were still at work.

"I want you both to come out to the house with me," he said. "It's terribly important."

The Noble family was about to begin its supper. Elizabeth Noble invited Dave and Victor to sit down with them. John insisted that they accept. Though he had not eaten for several days, he was too excited to do more than toy with the food on his plate. His eyes were sparkling, and his whole face had come intensely alive, his usually pale skin now high with color. His mother thought, He looks younger and happier than he has for years . . . since he came back from that summer trip through the Nations.

"I haven't seen you shaved and clean for several weeks; in fact I haven't seen you for several weeks," commented his father acidly. "Looks like a festive occasion."

"I hope it will be, Pa. I want to go to Paris and study painting there. I know you don't think there is any future in painting, and even if there was, you're not sure I've got any ability. That's why I asked Dave and Vic to come here tonight. If they think I can become a good painter and justify all of the expense, then I'm going to ask you to send me to Paris and give me an allowance so I can live. However, if Vic and Dave don't think so, I just won't bother you any more."

Everybody started talking at once. John, who was watching his father's face intently, heard random words: "Paris . . . Latin Quarter . . . artists . . . steamship . . . strange language." John said softly, so that only his father could hear him:

"I think I could be happy there, Pa. I think I could work and learn. I think I'd find a place for myself. Then I wouldn't be so lost, drink so much . . ."

"I can understand a young man wanting to break away clean and start a new life for himself. I did that myself. Why not go West, the way I did, New Mexico, maybe . . ."

"The West isn't a matter of geography, Pa; it's a state of mind."

He looked across the table at his mother; her eyes were big, and all the color had drained out of her cheeks. She was trying to smile at him, to tell him that she would help him; but only he would know what a severe wrench it was for Elizabeth Noble to let go of her son, the son she loved above all the others because he needed her most.

"All right, John," said his father in a low voice. "I'll take that deal. God knows we got to do something with you." He turned to Victor. "What do you say, Victor? Has this boy any talent? Can he get anywhere? Can he sell his painting?"

"I don't know about selling, Mr. Noble," replied Victor. The entire family listened carefully, for they respected his judgment; all the Murdocks were respected in Wichita. "But I would bet my bottom dollar that John has the makings of a good artist. I also think he's got a first-rate mind. Once he develops his technique, finds a way of getting onto canvas what he's thinking and feeling, you're going to discover that you have a great painter in the family."

Elizabeth Noble sighed. Her shoulders relaxed and the color came back into her cheeks. She leaned across the table toward Dave Leahy.

"What do you say, Dave? Don't let your friendship for John sway you. We want an honest opinion. Do you think John has the makings of a good painter?"

Dave sorted his thoughts for a moment and then spoke quietly.

"Let's put it this way, Mrs. Noble. Some men spend their lives on the surface of the water, skimming over it like skeet bugs. Others have some kind of need in them to plunge down into the depths. John has that need. We know that his drawings are good; the Eastern papers paid hard cash for them. We also know that it takes time to convert a good draftsman into a good painter. If you'll forgive my taking the privilege, folks, you don't need John's earnings, and you can spare him the money for his expenses abroad." He paused for a moment and then turned to John's father. "Invest in him, Mr. Noble. You won't get the same kind of financial return you would out of those lots you bought on Douglas and Main, but maybe you'll get an even more important kind."

There was a strained pause while the elder Noble chewed the cud of his thoughts. John whispered boyishly, "I didn't ask Vic and Dave to say these things, Pa. I didn't even tell them why I was bringing them home."

The elder Noble kept his head lowered for a long time, his unspoken thoughts ricocheting about the four walls. When he looked up he studied the faces of his family: his wife praying for her son, his two daughters and his younger boy rooting for their brother, and then at his son's two friends, who trusted and respected the younger John Noble.

"All right, I can hear you all," he said. "I'm not deaf. Besides, who wants to be a minority of one in his own family? John, if it's Paris you want, Paris it is."

John bolted from his chair, threw his arms around his father, hugging and kissing him. The whole family laughed . . . and then wept in relief.

Out on the porch, when he was thanking Dave and Victor, Dave asked, "Happy, m'boy?"

"Sure, Dave, but scared too."

"At what, in the name of all the blessed saints?"

"Going into a strange world, where I won't know anybody, and nobody knows me."

"Ah, but they will, Johnny m'boy. You just take your white Stetson and your cowboy boots and chaps and six-shooter, and that rattlesnake vest of yours with its elk's-tooth buttons. Create a character for yourself, Johnny, a rootin' shootin' wild Indian killer, the same way Buffalo Bill did."

"Call yourself Buffalo John," said Victor with a chuckle.

"That's it, Buffalo John, and spin 'em tall tales the way Dave taught you. The bigger they are, the easier they're believed, you saw that on the *Eagle*. The people in Europe are awful ignorant about conditions out here, Johnny, they think we're still primitives who spend our time stalking red men and pushing buffalo off our front porches. Make yourself into a ripsnortin' cowboy and two-gun desperado who kills an Indian every morning before breakfast just for the fun of it. . . . First thing you know, m'boy, you'll be famous from one end of Europe to the other."

The next day, just before the family was to leave for the railroad station, Elizabeth Noble called her son into the kitchen. She was holding a small white box in her hand.

"Why, Ma, did you get me a going-away present?"

"Not exactly, son; it's something to help keep your heart at home."

He opened the lid of the box.

"The North Star!"

"A silver replica, John."

There were so many things she wanted to tell him in this last instant of confidence: don't be unhappy, don't drink too much, see that you eat regularly, and sleep at nights, take pleasure from your work, keep away from temptation and evil companions; and write to me, my son, write every day, so I'll know what's happening to you. And always remember, no matter how the outside world may treat you, we love you and want you back home.

But all she could say was, "Always carry it with you, John. Then no matter how far you wander, you'll have the North Star for guidance."

"I will, Ma."

"I had no time to get a silver chain for it, darling, but you can buy one in New York before your ship sails."

He went to the drawer where Elizabeth kept her kitchen cutlery, cut off a piece of butcher's string and slipped one end through the eye of the silver star.

"Tie it on me, Ma, with a good strong knot."

Book Two

PARIS

The Search

HE EMERGED from the glass- and smoke-covered dimness of the Gare St. Lazare into the sparkling autumnal air of Paris, located a small hotel at the Place de la Trinité but did not bother to go up to the room with his bags, stepping out again into the brisk sunlight.

Paris was his first big city, for in New York he had walked from the railroad station, a heavy suitcase in each hand, through the dark streets to the pier, boarding his ship several hours early for fear he might miss the sailing. His first impression was the staggering contrast between Paris and Wichita, where everything was new, raw, sudden, hasty. As he walked half a dozen blocks south toward the dome of the Opera House, which served as a magnet, he realized for the first time that architecture too was a deeply moving art form, as emotionally gripping as painting or literature: the stone buildings, some of them obviously hundreds of years old had solidity and structural grace. He circled the majestic block-square Opera House with wide-eyed admiration for its opulence, continued onward to the broad Boulevard des Capucines, with its expensive-looking shops and smartly groomed Frenchwomen going in and out, then stepped for a moment into the quiet darkness of the Madeleine church, which he felt must have been patterned after a Roman temple. As he stood by the fountains of the Place de la Concorde, gazing at the magnificent buildings which swept up the Champs Elysées, he understood that here in Paris, the art and cultural center of the occidental world, age signified all the heartening symmetries of tradition, of a word which he would not have dared to use in Wichita: sophistication. He felt warm and good and happy inside himself, happy because, a complete stranger in a foreign city, jostled by passing crowds of whose language he could not understand a single syllable, he nonetheless felt utterly at home.

He crossed the Seine at the Pont de la Concorde, and on a corner of the Boulevard St. Germain came upon a sidewalk café called Les Deux Magots. When the waiter appeared, John pointed to the table next to him where two young French students were drinking a purplish liquor, pouring water into it constantly, fading the color but keeping the quantity steady. He also raised his hand to his lips and went through the motion of chewing; the amused garçon brought him a dish of hard-boiled eggs. John ate three of them as he sipped his apéritif.

Refreshed, he rose and walked back to the river, sauntered slowly along the Quai d'Orsay, then recrossed the Seine and made his way down the slight grade of the Avenue du Bois de Boulogne to the deep green woods. Here he found a bench on a pathway frequented by crisp, gray-clad nursemaids pushing perambulators. Pleasantly fatigued, his mind went back lazily over all that had happened to him in the past week; the quick change in the railway station at Chicago, the few disjointed hours in New York until his ship sailed at midnight, the long smooth voyage on an ocean which made him feel that he was riding the open, endless prairies of Kansas.

The sun went down beyond the treetops. The air turned cool. He hailed the driver of an open carriage headed toward town. Back in the city the lamps were lighted. He passed a restaurant and told the driver to stop.

The main salon of the Brasserie Universelle was upstairs above the café. The maître d'hôtel seated him at a small table in the corner, then brought a blackboard mounted on an easel. He could read a little printed French but the chalk handscript baffled him completely. With a sweeping gesture he indicated everything on the blackboard. The waiter served him a chopped-herb omelet, a thin soup which he did not recognize, a filet mignon with hot butter sauce and small

99

puffed-up potatoes. For desert there was a deep glass of fruit and sherbet covered with champagne.

John sat back in his corner, sipping a brandy and watching the restaurant fill, enjoying the sight of the elegantly gowned women. He listened to the hum of French about him, and he knew that he would never speak nor learn this language no matter how many years he remained in France. Yet he felt no need to understand the words; as his eyes went from table to table he knew what these people were saying, knew as a draftsman knows: by the pitch of a shoulder, the gesture of a hand, the curve of a back, the fullness of the lips, the luster of the eyes.

He wandered around Paris for the rest of the night, walking along narrow quiet streets and sitting in obscure cafés, listening to a dozen different dialects, studying the faces of the men and women as they sat morosely over their drinks or engaged in sharp, spirited conversation. Shortly before dawn he found himself on a cobblestoned street with many carts and rough farm wagons loaded high with flowers, vegetables and fruits. His pace quickened, soon he entered the vast market place into which the choice produce of France was poured each night: huge piles of scrubbed carrots and green beans, bins of flowers in a riotous display of color. He took a pencil and paper from his pocket and began sketching a young boy unloading a family cart. The boy's father asked if he might keep the sketch. John suggested that the three of them have a drink together. The father led him to a hole in the wall where they ordered hot onion soup.

The sun was rising when he bade his companions adieu. While fumbling to put the change into his wallet he caught a glimpse of his railroad ticket with Gare St. Lazare stamped on it. He found a cabby, showed him the name on the ticket, and after a considerable journey came once again to the railroad station. He located the gate from which he had emerged the morning before, walked down the Place de la Trinité and at last was in his hotel.

Starved for the sight of good pictures, he slept for only a few hours, then dressed hurriedly and made his way to the Louvre, where were hung some three thousand of the world's most important paintings, representing every age, country and technique. Wanting to start chronologically, he sought out the Italian School, standing almost numb before Giotto's brilliantly colored and deeply spiritual *St. Francis Receiving the Stigmata from Christ,* and Fra Angelico's tender *Corona-*

100

tion of the Virgin. He had never before been impressed by religious subjects, but Bellini's *The Saviour Blessing* and Leonardo da Vinci's *Annunciation* communicated a feeling of religious ecstasy through the sheer brilliance of craftsmanship alone.

The following morning he was back at the Louvre when the guards opened the heavy doors, going directly to the big room which housed the Spanish School. Here he saw Velasquez' paintings of the Infanta Margarita and Queen Maria Anna, so vividly and humanly alive they looked as though they could step down from their frames and go about their daily affairs. But as long as he had stood before Velasquez, he was even less able to tear himself away from the El Greco canvases: for here he heard a voice calling out to him, not only because of the long, lean, penetrating realism of the portraits, but because he felt that El Greco was an artist who was trying to say something beyond what could be read in the human face and human heart, no matter how eloquently they might be portrayed.

After the richness of the dark Spanish colorings and the overly bright flesh tones of the Flemish School, in particular Rubens, it was with excited amusement that he came into the Dutch School and found Jan Steen's tavern interiors, with ordinary workaday mortals considered worthy of being painted, even when they were ugly; and the full dozen Rembrandt canvases, with their dark, somber backgrounds, and the subjects lighted as fiercely as though the summer sun were upon them. The only major disappointment he suffered was in the French School where he found dull, lifeless academic canvases hanging alongside the volcanic and dramatic Delacroix.

Having had considerably more than he could absorb of some seven centuries of the best art, he now developed an eagerness to see where the newer French painters had lived and worked.

The manager at the hotel spoke a little English and was able to direct him to the forest of Fontainebleau where Daubigny, Rousseau, Corot, Millet, Dupré and Diaz had created the great landscape school. He also visited Auvers sur Oise where Vincent Van Gogh had painted his last powerful canvases, and Eragny, the little village where Camille Pissarro raised his family, fought bitterly for the few elusive francs with which to maintain his home and created what to John seemed the most lyrically beautiful of all the newer paintings.

He wandered the countryside in the shade of hundred-year-old trees, thinking back to the flat, treeless prairie of

Wichita, recalling all the wonderful pictures he had studied since he left home. He had seen master technique, perspective, color, new approaches in sentiment, new attitudes toward light and shadow, form and subject. But in all of these pictures he knew that he had been looking for something above and beyond form, color, design. He had asked himself as he stood before each canvas:

Does this picture extend beyond its frame to the point of infinity? Does it glow and vibrate with a spirit and essence beyond its immediate detail?

2

He had talked to no one, far too excited to feel any need for company. Nor did he have any idea of the passage of time. He was surprised when the manager handed him a bill with his key one afternoon, remarking:

"It has now been a month since Monsieur has been with us. Doubtless he would like to pay his account."

"A month! You don't say. Have I really been here that long?"

"Oui, monsieur. And tonight at the Bal Bullier is the Quatz' Arts ball. Monsieur should go, since he too is a painter."

He paid his bill, went up to his room and stretched out full length on the bed, his hands under his head, staring at the ceiling. The element of time having been unwontedly thrust upon him, he began to review his situation in Paris.

During the past weeks he had seen men painting in the streets, in the Louvre, by the quais along the Seine, and in the forests at Fontainebleau. In the evenings he had passed sidewalk cafés where men in corduroy coats and flowing black ties bore all the outward signs of the painter. Yet he had not talked to them, for he would not have known what to say. Could he just go up to a man painting the Sacré-Coeur and ask:

"Look, pard, I'm an artist too. How's chances of running herd with you hombres?"

He could not bring himself to speak to these strangers, even if he could have made himself understood in their language. He did not know where the ateliers were located so that he could get good instruction. Unless he made some kind of conscious effort he might live in Paris for years without establishing himself in a painters' colony. More important, he must begin to paint, start to work again, give himself to the task with the whole creative and passionate vitality of his being.

He stoppped thinking and lay still on the bed. The room was warm and silent. Loneliness overcame him like a suffocating quilt. He was no longer in Paris, but on some vast ocean, the only man on a small vessel with one white sail, wandering the face of the endless water, not knowing where the ship was going, having no wheel or map or compass and no knowledge of how to use them if they had been present. From the frayed look of the sail he saw that he had been on this ship a very long time, wandering directionless, seeing no other ship, no land, no human face, hearing no human voice.

He began to tremble. Then he stretched out his arm, locked the door, and flung the key blindly into a corner. Braced to endure whatever might come within the confines and privacy of this room, the pressure began to ease, his tense body relaxed.

He must not remain alone in Paris. He had come here to find friends and take his place among other painters, to plunge into the caldron of art.

He sprang off the bed, went to the big wooden wardrobe which stood against the red and yellow striped wallpaper, and flung open the two heavy doors. There were his cowboy chaps, his rattlesnake vest with the elk's-tooth buttons, the high boots and wide-brimmed Stetson and two six-shooters.

Because he could think of no one else to help him he went to the American Embassy where he was turned over to the Third Secretary, a pleasant and handsomely groomed young man from San Francisco.

"I need some help, Ambassador," said John. "I want to rent or buy the largest white horse in Paris. I also need a supply of rock salt and bacon rind. It would take me at least ten years to find these things by myself in Paris."

"Always happy to help a fellow Westerner," said the young Secretary; "but would you mind telling me what you are going to do with a combination of a white horse, rock salt and bacon rind?"

"I intend you should know," replied John with a broad grin.

At dinnertime an enormous and ancient white horse was delivered to his hotel. The Third Secretary had bought him from the stockyards. John ran his hand over the animal's protruding bones.

"You're gonna have one last fling before you join your ancestors," he told the horse.

The Quatz' Arts ball was reaching its climax when he pulled up at the front door. The motif was the Pompeian era, and the walls of the huge wooden structure were hung with paper frescoes picturing the village of Pompeii at the moment the volcano erupted. The ceiling was covered with a painted cloth draped low and gathered in the center to represent the flaming volcano; streamers of hot lava simmered downward toward the dancers. The artists had created their own costumes from inexpensive sackcloth.

The costume prizes had just been awarded and the evening's first champagne served to the ring of tables around the sides of the hall when John kicked his heels into the old white horse; the horse leapt a dozen feet through the doors, landing on the dance floor. John caught a quick impression of the dimly lighted scene before he gave a bloodcurdling Indian war yell, pulled out his two pistols and fired the rock salt and bacon rind.

Women began to scream, men to shout as he galloped around the hall, shooting out each light as he passed it. The dancers ran wildly across the floor and the people at the tables rushed out the wide doors.

He circled the hall twice. Now there was only one light left burning which threw a macabre shadow over the houses, temples and volcano of Pompeii. He looked around the vast dark room. He was alone. He pulled in the horse at the bandstand, dismounted and found himself standing by a table with an unopened bottle of wine.

"Pull up a chair, Whitey," he said to the horse. "It looks like you and I are the only ones left at this party."

"Not quite the only ones," said a soft voice behind him.

A girl emerged from the shadows. She was tiny, surely no more than five feet, thought John. He could see her face well enough in the dim light to perceive that her features too were small, her skin luminously white, and the hair woven on top of her head, Pompeian style, a pale blond. Though her costume was scanty, it was quite ample compared to that of most of the girls he had seen running for the doors.

"It was an enchanting performance, monsieur. I could not tear myself away."

She spoke English with a piquant accent. John rose, took off his Stetson and gave her a sweeping bow.

"How nice to have company. Won't you sit down? Someone left this bottle of wine for us."

"My escort."

"Then it seems only fair that you should share it with me, mademoiselle. What might your name be?"

"Maud. What might yours be?"

"It might be Buffalo Bill, it might even be Charles Goodnight, and I frequently wish it were. But actually it is John Noble."

"Now that we have been formally introduced," she said, "perhaps you had better pour. The gendarmerie will not give you too much time to sip your wine."

He pulled the cork on the champagne bottle; it shot ceilingward with as much noise as the firing of his pistols.

"What shall we drink to, mademoiselle?"

"*A tous les deux?*"

"*Tous les deux?* That means both of us, doesn't it? A nice idea."

They leaned across the table to each other and clinked glasses. Inside Maud's low-cut blouse he saw nestled two white doves with shell-pink beaks; they fluttered softly as she raised her glass to her lips. John chuckled low in his throat.

"How does it happen that you were not frightened like the rest of them, Maud?" he asked.

"I was fascinated by your white horse," she replied, mocking him.

"It's too bad I upset the orchestra, or you and I could dance."

"I will sing."

He rose and held out his arms. She came close to him, running her fingers lightly over his powerful shoulders and chest, her eyes unabashedly speaking their admiration.

"Surely Monsieur did not develop these formidable muscles by holding a paintbrush?"

She slid into his arms. He whirled her about on the huge floor. Maud was finishing her song when they found themselves surrounded by a ring of gendarmes.

"We regret to disturb this charming mise en scène, monsieur," the one in charge said, "but it is my sad duty to inform you that you are under arrest."

"That is not altogether unexpected, Sheriff," replied John. "Will you join us in a drink before we go to the Bastille?"

3

He awakened to see a patch of sunlight moving across the lead-gray wall of the cell. He rose from the straw pallet, massaging the soreness out of his bones. In the chilly light of morning he appeared to himself as an utter fool. What had he gained from his ridiculous piece of buffoonery? He wouldn't have minded so much if he had caused a small riot while drunk; but to have put on this display while sober . . .

He heard footsteps coming down the stone corridor. He brushed the straw off his clothes and ran the open fingers of his hand combwise through his hair. The Third Secretary of the American Embassy looked as though he had been wakened too early, but he was dressed most impeccably. He stood for a moment gazing through the bars at John.

"Tell me, Mr. Noble, why do all the crazy Americans come to Paris and all the sane ones stay home?"

A guard unlocked the door. John stepped into the corridor. He picked up his two revolvers at the property desk. Outside the jail he fumbled in his pockets and brought forth a roll of bills, repaying the Secretary the amount of the fine. The streets were still deserted at this early hour, the metal shutters rolled down in front of the stores, the venetian blinds pulled tight in the houses.

"I know an American woman who runs a little restaurant in the Rue Jacob," said the Secretary. "It's the only place in Paris where you can get ham and eggs fried Western style. It's a good thing I'm a Californian and understand you Southwesterners; if the Third Secretary had been from New England, he would have let you cool your heels in that jail for a week."

It was one o'clock when he wandered back to the Bal Bullier to find the owner and pay for the damage. At the adjacent café the sidewalk tables were crowded with Parisians taking their midday apéritif. Since he had not gone to his hotel to change he was still wearing his cowboy outfit, the two guns in their holsters, the white Stetson set rakishly on his long blond hair. While a considerable distance from the café he heard the beginnings of a hubbub; by the time he reached the tables everyone was talking excitedly. A man rushed toward him, clutched him by the arm and shot a stream of highly voluble French at him.

"Don't get excited, partner," exclaimed John. "I'll leave. But first I want to pay for the lamps and whatever else I broke."

A tall thin chap stepped forward; he had close-cropped brown hair and wore silver-rimmed spectacles astride the hump of his long nose.

"He's not trying to chase you away, friend. He just wants you to work for him."

"Oh, you're an American," said John gratefully. "Lucky for me. Would you mind telling this chap I don't have to work for him, that I can pay off in cash."

The proprietor spoke now in soft but urgent tones. The American interpreted.

"He says he's never had such a crowd on a Sunday morning: that midnight ride has made you the talk of Paris. He's been saving this front table for you; you can have all you want to eat and drink, all you have to do is sit here in that Buffalo Bill costume."

John threw back his head and laughed, then sat down at the little table that had been reserved for him and placed his six-shooters on its marble top. Before long reporters began to arrive. John's new friend interpreted for him. When the newspapermen wanted to know who he was he told them tales of how he had driven herds of cattle from Texas to New Orleans during the Civil War to feed the Confederate Army; of how he had fought beside Custer against the Indians and been the only white man to escape; of how he had been a United States marshal rounding up desperadoes until he had grown weary of being on the side of the law, joined the Dalton gang and robbed railway express cars. Each reporter and each newspaper was provided with a different adventure. When the last of the men had disappeared, he had pretty well covered the history of the Southwest.

His new friend murmured, "Just who are you and what do you do?"

John shook his head sadly. "This is going to be something of a disappointment to you; I'm that most unsensational thing in all Paris: a painter."

"Well, welcome home!" exclaimed the American, putting out his hand. "I'm a painter too. Name is Gerald Addams. From Boston." He turned to four men sitting at an adjoining table, and introduced each of them formally:

"May I have the pleasure of presenting Marcel Charbert, who aspires to be another Gustave Courbet. Got a good chance, at that."

Charbert was a squat, powerfully built man of about forty, with an enormous, close-shaved head which seemed sunk into his huge shoulders: his smile was friendly and a little naïve. Angelo Verdinni from Fiesole was a thin Italian boy whose blue-black beard and long blue-black hair contrasted strangely with the pallor of his skin. Angelo murmured his pleasure in the softest, most musical tongue John had ever heard. Anton Van der Meetch from Leiden in Holland was a strawberry blond with deep blue eyes and strong yellow teeth; and Ichiro Kunogi, a young Japanese of not more than twenty, as tiny and graceful in his movements as a bright black kitten.

John shook hands with each of the men, said, "I am John Noble, out of Wichita, Kansas," and invited them to have a drink with him. A garçon pushed the two tables together and the six painters sat in a semicircle facing the street. His acquaintances all began talking at once.

"They're inviting you to come over to the Ruche to live," said Gerald. "It's a huge barn near the fortifications that was left over from the Paris World's Fair, and remodeled by Boucher, the French sculptor. He rents the rooms to artists for a few francs a year. There are almost a hundred painters living there. We call it the Beehive, though actually it's more like a Tower of Babel."

A deep slow, involuntary sigh came out of John, carrying with it all his uncertainties. Only a few hours before he had cursed himself for an idiotic performance, for thinking that he could make a place for himself in the most civilized city in the world by shooting out lights with a revolver. Now he would live with painters, learn everything that was being painted in Paris, see hundreds of canvases with the paint still wet on them, participate in exhilarating discussions about new and exciting theories of light and color and composition, discover what motivated contemporary art.

"Count me in," he murmured gratefully.

4

The Ruche was a circular building at 2 Passage de Dantzig, built around an enclosed courtyard in which there were shade trees and a model's stand. On the main floor were lounging and dining rooms and work studios. The two upstairs floors, both of which had circular balconies overlooking the open court, consisted of about a hundred bedrooms each fitting into the circular pattern like spokes of a wheel, being wider at the outside street wall than the inside balcony wall. The bedrooms had originally been unfurnished but the tradition had grown of leaving behind whatever furniture each occupant brought, and so there was now an adequately though austerely simple supply of kerosene lamps, narrow cots, roughhewn tables, chairs, bureaus, washbasins and pitchers.

It was late afternoon and a number of the Ruche's bees were sunning themselves in the warm enclosed courtyard, some smoking and chatting, a few reading the papers, others sketching from the model up on the stand. Apparently most of them had been at the Bal Bullier the night before; they grinned broadly as they wrung his hand and told him in French, Russian, Norwegian, German, Dutch, Magyar, Italian and Spanish that he was welcome. He was introduced to Karl Leipsche, a fiery redhead from Heidelberg, a Slav by the name of Oscar Magozanovic, with huge black eyes and a diffident smile; a beautiful Piedmontese Italian called Giuseppe Donello who towered over the courtyard to some six feet four in height and had light blue eyes and corn-colored hair; to a Turk by the name of Nejat to whom nobody could talk because no one in the Beehive understood his language: to an American Negro by the name of Tanner, with eyes and manner as gentle as a lamb; an Englishman, George Turnhouse, in an incredibly wrinkled suit of once good tweeds; a Belgian from Brussels, a young Russian named Alexei, who could not have been more than twenty-one and yet had an enormous beard covering all of his face; and a dozen Frenchmen from practically every arrondissement: a sailor from Marseilles, a postal clerk from St. Brieuc, a former art teacher from Grenoble, an ex-monk from Reims.

The obvious leader of the Ruche was Charbert, whom he had met at the café. He ran the office of the Ruche, collecting funds, paying bills, trying to establish a sales gallery and an artists' supply shop, writing and setting into type a four-page weekly pamphlet for the members and scouring Paris to secure for the less fortunate of the Ruche a warm suit, a stout-soled pair of boots, medical care and medicines in exchange for canvases.

Gerald Addams led John to a third-floor cubicle.

"Here's a room for you. It was occupied by a wild-haired Bulgarian who upped and disappeared last week; the poor fellow lived on one egg a day, which he cooked by holding a lighted newspaper under it."

John dropped his suitcases onto the bare floor. The two men sat down on the bed, and John offered Addams a cigarette. They puffed for a moment in comradely silence. Then John turned to Gerald and said, "Tell me what's going on in Paris now, among the art groups, I mean. What kind of work are they doing? Who are the most impressive of the painters?"

Addams took a deep breath.

"Well, there's the American Art Association on the corner of the Notre Dame des Champs; it was set up by an American millionaire and has a good restaurant and comfortable rooms for students of painting, architecture and writing. They have some pretty good painters coming in and out: Alexander Harrison from Philadelphia, the French call him Le Grand Harrison because of his poise and beautiful white hair, is the leader; then there's George Luks, a former newspaper cartoonist from Williamsport, Pennsylvania, Charles Hawthorne, Fred Waugh from New Jersey, who is a fine seascape man. Then there's the group of young Frenchmen and Spaniards who live up on the winding streets of Montmartre. The best of them is Henri Matisse, who first studied under Bouguereau but revolted against the brown-gravy painting; Pablo Picasso, a vigorous and irrepressible young Spaniard; and a number of good young French painters like Georges Rouault, who does religious subjects, Raoul Dufy, who paints gay outdoor scenes of the race tracks and yachting harbors, and Georges Braque, who does still lifes, mostly homely objects thrown onto a kitchen table . . ."

Addams sprang off the bed, snapped his spectacles into a black oblong box which he then thrust into his trouser pocket. He walked about the small, triangular-shaped room agitatedly for a few seconds.

". . . the age of giants is gone," he exclaimed. "Toulouse-Lautrec is dying here in Paris, Cézanne is a hermit in Aix-en-Provence, Gauguin will never come back from Tahiti. All of us here in Paris are in a kind of vacuum; we don't know in what direction to go, or why. We don't want to imitate or repeat, and yet innovation for its own sake is the worst of all impasses. There will be years of seeking and experiment . . . for we somehow have to begin a new era, start a school of painting of our own, with a technique which belongs in the twentieth century. I don't mean to frighten you . . ."

"On the contrary," replied John. "I know that I have many years of groping ahead of me, and now I see that I won't be alone."

110

"Alone? Indeed not! Here in Paris we believe that all painters are brothers."

John gazed up at Gerald, his eyes shining like summer stars seen from the top of the Rockies.

"Could I throw a party tonight for the men? A sort of initiation?"

Gerald passed the word in French, then advised John, "Give whatever money you wish to spend to Jacques and Etienne. They know where to get the best food in Paris for the least cost."

That evening long planks were set up on wooden horses in the dining room. The dishware and cutlery consisted of what each man had brought to the feast. The bottles of cheap but strong red wine stood at attention down the long table like a company of soldiers, while at frequent intervals were big platters of beefsteak, french-fried potatoes, endive salad with tomatoes and cauliflower, and long, hard-crusted French breads. John found himself sitting at the head of the banquet table with some forty to fifty painters stretching below him on either side. Gazing down at the infinite variety of faces, he remarked to himself how resourceful an artist God was, to have so little raw material to work with; a few teeth, a pair of eyes, a nose, mouth and chin: and to be able to make each face so distinct and different. He thought back to Wichita where he had been only a few weeks before, to Wichita where he was the lone painter of the town, where painting was thought to bear no possible relation to life; yet here in one room were men who believed that painting was the most important thing in life, that nothing much else really mattered.

The last of the food had been dispatched, the last drops of the wine pounded from the bottles, the last echoes of the animated discussions about the application of paint, the strangle hold of prettiness and sentimentality on the Royal Academies and official salons, had drifted from the air. John saw that the painters of the Ruche took courage from the fact that everything which had constituted an advance in their art or involved change had been fought ferociously by the critics as something not only unworthy but indecent. Knowing about the vilification of the men who had gone before them, they were nonetheless determined to carry forward and extend their craft.

Now he felt a strong need to see their work; if their painting was as penetrating or wise as their analyses of other men's art . . . He asked Gerald if it would be possible.

"Don't be so hesitant," laughed Gerald; "there's nothing these men like more than to show their canvases."

He spent the night going from room to room. Not only was every nationality, religion and temperament represented in the Beehive, but every degree of intelligence and ability as well: the best talents were at the hub of the wheel, the less talents fanning out toward the rim until at last there were only those upon whom the wheel turned, a flat surface that took the bumps and punishment. The test at the Beehive was not, "Can he paint?" but rather "Does he paint?" No judgment was passed on the quality of a man's work, only on the quality of his sincerity. Most of the men had been painting for years, but few of them yet knew what they wanted to say or how to articulate in paint the things they felt. They could not stand still, become little Cézannes or Van Goghs. The road ahead would be uncharted for them as it had been for all the others who had spent a lifetime of unrelenting labor to find out how best they could express themselves.

It was dawn when he finally took off his clothes, threw himself down on the rough blanket spread over the cot and covered himself with his buffalo robe. He was filled with a sense of pleasant fatigue, exhilaration . . . and a kind of graspable despair: for although he had seen what he believed to be all degrees of talent and experience during his night's travel through the Beehive, he felt that no one of these men was as yet doing mature work.

What, then, were the chances for him? Through how many years and how many stages and how many dark labyrinths must he stumble and blindly grope before he could reach the fullness of expression, the excellence of technique which he saw nowhere around him in the Beehive, and yet for which his companions were working with what he perceived to be an almost fanatical devotion? Would any of these men whose paintings he had gazed at during the night become great painters? Would he, John Noble, ever achieve anything worth setting down on canvas? Was there even the slightest chance that he might find that which he was seeking, and the technical skill with which to create it?

Suddenly he understood that no man had the right to ask himself that question. The only question he could ask was: Can I persevere?

5

He dreamt that someone was boiling coffee and the aroma made him run his tongue over his wine-parched lips. He had not awakened to the smell of fresh coffee since he left Wichita; for a moment he almost believed he was home again.

Then his eyes shot open: this coffee was far too real to be cooking in his dreams. Across the narrow room he saw a woman leaning over a little stove. He sat up on his cot. The woman heard his movements, turned her head and smiled.

"Maud!" he exclaimed. "From Pompeii. How in the world did you find me?"

"It was not difficult," she replied, her eyes sparkling. "I asked a few questions at the Café Bullier . . . described your snakeskin vest . . ."

She picked up several of the Parisian newspapers which she had dropped on the wooden table.

"The papers say that among other things erupted by the Bal Bullier volcano was a wild Westerner by the name of Buffalo John. Would you like me to translate these stories for you?"

"No thanks," he grimaced, his blue eyes smoky. "I know what's in them. But if I could have a cup of that coffee, instead?"

She poured the coffee with quick, deft movements. It was black and strong, and he drank it gratefully.

He threw the buffalo robe aside and sat on the edge of the bed watching her as she set some breakfast buns onto a chipped plate. Though she was tiny her figure in the simple brown cotton dress seemed robust enough, and nicely proportioned. He took some American greenbacks out of his pocket.

"Here, you'd better take this money to pay for the stove and the food."

"The stove didn't cost anything . . . and the brioches were only a few centimes. Have you paid your rent yet?"

"No."

"Then suppose I take twenty-five dollars and give it to Charbert? That will pay you up for a year."

There was only one chair in the room. She pulled it up to the table for him. Then she poured another cup of coffee and seated herself on the edge of the table, facing him. He spread jam onto a brioche while he studied her face. No one of her features alone would have been good enough to be considered pretty; her nose was a little too short and too thin, her lower teeth were irregular and her skin a touch on the sallow side. Yet her eyes were good, well spaced and with a curious milk-gray color. He decided that she was pretty.

"How do you happen to speak English, Maud?"

She smiled fleetingly. "In your country you would call me a specialist. When I was fifteen I had a chance to pose for a young American who had just arrived in Paris. From him I learned a little English. Whenever an American or an Englishman wanted a model people would say, 'Get Maud; she can speak your language.'"

John wondered how many Americans had contributed to Maud's knowledge of the language; but that was hardly his affair. They chatted animatedly while they finished their coffee and smoked their cigarettes. There was neither accusation nor bitterness in her voice as she told how her father had abandoned her mother, how she had lived in various orphanages until she had been apprenticed at the age of eleven as a slavey to a dressmaker. After four years she had stumbled onto the American painter, who had taken her in with him.

"Would you like me to pose for you?" she asked.

"Not particularly."

"All the others have."

"I'm just not interested in figure drawing."

"Tiens! You don't like the nude female? A man who wears rattlesnakes on his chest and has killed whole tribes of Indians?"

"I'd much rather draw a nude horse."

Maud laughed delightedly.

"You make the strangest jokes." Then a hurt tone crept into her voice. "Is it that you don't like my shape? You do not think it would look beautiful on canvas?"

She quickly took off her dress, slipped out of her shoes and peeled the stockings off her slim white legs. She then stretched her arms upward and gracefully arched her back, bringing into relief the line of her breasts. Into his mind flashed the picture of the two white doves with their flesh-pink beaks as they had moved softly under her Pompeian gauze.

"Would you still prefer a naked horse?"

"Only for certain purposes."

He picked her up and laid her none too gently on the buffalo robe.

When she had slipped into her clothes again, he said, "Sometime you shall pose for me. I don't intend to paint undraped women, that's a lifetime job in itself. But didn't Vincent Van Gogh say that figure drawing is the basis of all good craftsmanship, even in landscapes? Why are you laughing?"

6

Each morning the Beehive emptied as though someone had rung a bell, the individual bees scurrying forth with canvas and easel and paints under their arms, their heads stuck out ahead of them with eager expectancy. He found that his companions at the Ruche were driven by a terrifying urgency: paint, and paint some more; never mind what the subject or how well you understand it, just get something down on canvas, for everything you get down gives you more experience, more grasp, more insight, more power. Some were painting street scenes, others going to the markets or railroad stations or the surrounding woods, still others specializing in houses, churches, open squares or passers-by who could be persuaded to stand still in return for a few centimes. He watched them painting avidly every scene, every detail, every idea they could lay eyes or mind or brush on.

"Come and paint with us today," each group urged him. "We can show you a view over the roofs of Paris . . . a little section where the streets and the houses merge into the horizon . . . a fish market where the shadows are the deepest of silver and blue . . ."

On the fifth morning Gerald Addams took him down to the shop of the color merchant, Lefèbre Foinet, where a large portion of the young painters traded and met to discuss the newest processes of grinding colors. John opened a charge account, bought a new palette, easel, brushes and supply of paints.

Each day he went out to paint with another of the men, for he too caught the fever of sheer activity, painting all day, every day, the pretty, the obvious, the banal, the obscure, the meaningless . . . as well as all of the wonderfully paintable vignettes which Paris offered so profusely. Like his comrades, he became a painting machine, dashing the oils against canvas on the quantitative theory that two paintings were twice as

115

valuable as one. When the weather was too cold or rainy to work in the streets he accompanied Gerald Addams to the Louvre or the Luxembourg to copy old masterpieces. He never stopped to ask himself whether he was doing good work or bad, but indulged in an orgasm of expression for its own sake, painting dozens of canvases about subjects in which he had never been interested and for which he had no real emotion.

Late every afternoon he dressed in his cowboy outfit, strapped on his pistols and went to the Café Bullier. The same table was reserved for him at the apéritif hour, the café was always jammed with people who had come to see Buffalo John, the fabulous Indian fighter and two-gun desperado. Admiring crowds gathered around his table while he spun his yarns. Dave Leahy had taught him:

"Stories must be as big as the country and the people they are told about."

He always took a couple of the painters from the Beehive with him, the ones he thought were the most starved at the moment, ordering the biggest dinner the café could serve, then making his tale last as long as his companions needed to devour the food.

"When I was only a month old my family was massacred by the Unkpapas. The Indians named me Crazy Horse, and Sitting Bull trained me to become a great warrior. Sitting Bull and I moved into Little Big Horn Valley with twelve thousand tribesmen from the Minneconjous and Cheyennes. First we drove General Reno and his troops across the Little Big Horn and killed half their men. Then General Custer and his famous Seventh Cavalry attacked us from the other end of the valley, and we annihilated them. Yes, sir, with my lieutenants Dull Knife, Two Moons and Little Wolf we wiped out the entire United States Army."

There was a gasp of amazement from the spectators.

"More, tell us more . . ."

"The following year I entered West Point. I learned that I was a white man and that the Indians had massacred my family. So I pursued Sitting Bull and the Unkpapas all the way up to the black pines of Canada, where they could never fight again. When I finally conquered Geronimo and the Apaches, that was the end of the Indian wars in America."

During the cold evenings the men of the Ruche gathered in the downstairs studio around a blazing fire, with each of the models posing in turn. The crackling of the logs in the fireplace induced the men to talk nostalgically about their homes, their families and childhood and the strange, complicated paths which had led them to this hub of the art world.

The letters he started to his mother were never finished, for the things that were important to him he could not bring himself to write about. Whenever he had a drawing or sketch that he thought was well done, he mailed it to the family in Wichita. His mother answered these drawings as though they were long and detailed letters.

Sometimes when he walked the streets alone at night, moved by nostalgia for Wichita, he looked for the North Star but he never could find it. Apparently it was not a city star. Then he would pull his mother's silver star from inside his shirt and grip it firmly in his hand, the points cutting into his palm with pleasurable pain.

"Why don't you let me wash that string for you?" Maud asked in his room at the Ruche one night. "It's turning black."

"No, thank you."

"If you don't wash it soon, it will dissolve into thin air, no string, only dirt."

"It's never been off my neck. I'd be afraid I'd lose it."

His attachment to the ornament piqued her. When he asked her what she would like for Christmas, she replied: "How about the star you wear around your neck on that filthy string?"

"No, Maud."

"But you said I could have anything I wanted?"

"Why are you so anxious for that little star? It really has no value."

"Except that you protect it so strongly. It's funny about painters: you always leave somebody behind that you can't forget. And you always go home to marry them."

"Not this time, Maud. It's my mother. She gave me this as a going-away present. A good-luck talisman . . . to watch over me . . . when I haven't enough sense to watch over myself. But I'll get you a necklace for Christmas."

He had grown fond of Maud, in a casual way; when he wanted feminine company, instead of taking the nearest girl at hand he would send word to Maud or set out to find her. She had an apartment in the Impasse du Maine, at the top of several flights of narrow wooden stairs, and when they attended a late party on her side of town, he stayed the night there.

There was a big wooden bed on the dark end of the one room, and a pair of comfortable chairs under the windows which gave a magnificent view of Paris. Off the room were two alcoves, one serving as a kitchen, which she rarely used for anything more than coffee, the other as a bedroom. There were no feminine touches, no gaily colored curtains on the windows or soft rugs on the floor, no decorations, no table of perfumes or personal treasures. Maud had lived here for five years; for all the impression she had made on the place, it could have been rented only the hour before. When on occasion he offered her money she replied, "I don't need any. I work at the dress shop, and I am doing their difficult beading now. They pay me well."

He had given little thought to her personal life, and so he was mildly surprised to learn that she was faithful to him.

"It's the only kind of monogamy permitted to me," she retorted, her milk-gray eyes deepening with anger. "One man at a time, and not much of that one man, either: little more than the dregs, really."

It was the first time he had seen her emotionally upset. He lowered his head, unable to meet her eyes, for he knew that she was right. Like the other painters in the Beehive he was functioning almost completely outside the realm of love. Each man had his model and girl, but these relationships were rudimentary. Painters, working in a group, were like cowboys or sailors: they went on long, hard-driven and abstemious voyages on canvas, leading monastic lives, taking their joy from the work's progress and the companionship of the painters about them. Then, when the voyage was terminated, the ship brought home safely, the herd delivered to the railhead, the group of paintings completed, they turned their backs on their work in satiation, bellowed loudly for their girls, took them to the cafés for food and drink, danced through the night and returned to their cells for the climax of their carousal. But they fooled neither themselves nor their girls: no matter how much passionate abandon they might pour into these few hours or days of rebellion, they know that very soon they would clumsily wash out their neglected brushes, select a fresh piece of canvas, begin the first stumbling steps of the new journey: a journey alone.

7

On the first of December he received an extra check from his father for the holidays. He turned it over to Charbert, for

Christmas did not promise to be a hearty season at the Beehive. Charbert summoned the men to a meeting in the big dining room.

"We've got to sell some canvases, and sell them fast. That's why we're going to stage a new kind of exhibition. It should earn us a *succès fou*."

The men blew smoke into the room and waited anxiously for him to continue.

"Each of us will hang what we consider to be our best canvas, and under it we will write the legend of what we were attempting to do and what we conceive to be our derivations: whether we think our landscapes derive from Breughel, our portraits of lined old faces from Rembrandt, our pointillism from Seurat."

The painters chewed on this for a moment.

"I don't like people coming here to view an idea," exclaimed Karl Leipsche, the red-haired German. "If they want a history of art let them go to the Sorbonne."

"What do you care what method is used to get the critics and buyers in here?" shouted Charbert. "Haven't we tried endless times to attract dealers? They say we are amateurs, beginners."

"It won't work," said Giuseppe Donello in his soft, placating voice. "Painting, like music, cannot be described in terms of words."

But Marcel Charbert was a stubborn man.

That night the Beehive was rocked by considerable soul searching. As John went from room to room he found the painters going over their stacks of canvases, their eyes serious and troubled.

"They're not good enough . . . I thought at least this one . . . up to now I had imagined that I had captured something. . . . How can I show this when I know it is not right, when I have come so far during the past weeks . . . ?"

Deep in the night he at last came to Charbert's room. Marcel was leaning over his table writing furiously, invitations, advance notices for the newspapers.

"Look, Marcel, I think this is a great idea, but you will just have to count me out. I am not good enough to exhibit . . . I'll disgrace you."

Charbert's powerful body set as though coiled to spring.

"You're not the best painter in La Ruche, nor are you the worst. We have seen only too well that the most mediocre painters of France get the highest honors, the Bougereaus, Delaroches and Greuzes. And who do you think were the members of the Salon des Refusés in 1863, and men not considered good enough by the official judges of the Salon even to have their canvases hung in the great state show? Shall I tell your their names? Fantin-Latour, Legros, Manet, Whistler, Jongkind, Laurens, Harpignies . . ."

"I know that, Marcel, but just at this moment everything I do is so confused, I'm like a composite picture worked on by thirty men. You can take any square inch at random and say who I copied it from."

Charbert picked up his drafting pencil and continued writing on one of his articles. "Then stop wasting your breath and go to work. You have a month." He looked up, and when he spoke it was with a whimsical smile. "There probably isn't a canvas in the Ruche tonight which will hang on the walls of the show."

He began work on a project which had been haunting him: a ship upon a sea, an endless sea which had no shores or harbors or piers; overhead on the right there would be a molten, fiery sun, while to the left there would be a single pure white cloud. He did not want to paint any particular ocean, nor was the ship to be any definitely recognizable one; nor yet was this lopsided sun nor even this rhythmically shaped cloud to be a sun or a cloud which one had seen on a specific day and remembered for its color or shape or form. No, these objects were to be rather the essence of the things they represented: a vast shoreless ocean which was all oceans, a ship which was the spirit and embodiment of all ships which plied all seas; a sun and a cloud which would convey the inner reality and significance of all suns and all clouds seen through a man's lifetime.

The month passed in a fever of concentrated work. He never went near the Café Bullier nor visited with Maud. All social activity was suspended and when the girls came in to the Beehive they came in as models, posing for long hard hours.

As he went about to the other workrooms he realized that every painting was a self-portrait even when it was a still life or a scene over the roofs of Paris; for no man ever pictured anything but himself, his core, the things that he was basically. With every brush stroke the artist was mercilessly exposed: he could conceal nothing, he could pretend to be another person, to believe in other values, but in the end he would fool no one. Only now, years after having read through the works of Shakespeare, Dickens, Scott, Poe, Balzac did he realize that even the most prolific writer created only one novel; throw away the individual bindings and the whole of each man's writing constituted one book: the true and complete portrait of himself. An artist had one thing to say, and one only; he might flail about, seek new techniques, forms, color combinations, subjects, but intrinsically he would always paint the same canvas, write the same book.

Yes, each of his painter friends here in the Ruche had his own White Buffalo: Angelo Verdinni painted over and over again a pale young girl's face which showed the line of her nose curved away from the light; the Pole from Bydgoszcz painted the suffering of his people, shown eating a hard crust of bread, or being whipped by overseers; Jacques, from Lyon, was trying to prove that the earth, rocks and trees beat with an inner pulsation of their own; Karl Leipsche sought the ultimate meaning of life in broad-bosomed, thick-buttocked nude women, never bothering to finish their heads or their feet; Pablo Anza scorned the idea that there could be any spiritual or literary content to a canvas, and attempted to capture pure emotion by the delights of color alone; Alexei, the Russian, went looking for the corrupt, the diseased, the sordid, revenging himself in canvas after canvas on someone who had crushed all goodness and beauty out of his youth; Kunogi, the young Japanese, believed that all of art could be expressed by the grace and charm of the delicate line; Marcel Charbert, who had painted over half of Europe, pictured only house-lined streets, forever seeking a home and never finding it; Anton Van der Meetch painted only men at work, digging, hammering, cleaning fish, compensating his troubled conscience because he himself was not engaged in manual labor; the fisherman from Brittany painted wave after wave pounding against the rocks and throwing sheets of spray into the air; Tanner, the American Negro, painted only religious scenes, laid in a whimsical heaven; Gerald Addams only copied masterpieces in the museums, forever pursuing some mythical concept of perfection as attained by other men.

And what about himself?

The thing he loved most about the West was the vast, horizonless prairie. Did he not have to admit then that the prairie was synonymous with heaven in his mind, just as the sea was synonymous with the prairie; and the vast dome of the sky synonymous with the prairie and the sea? These were the three scenes which interested him most; in them he always painted the three symbols that were synonymous with God in his mind: the white buffalo on the prairie, the white ship on the sea; the white sun in the sky.

Some people were born with a hunger for power, some with an unquenchable thirst for adventure, for movement, for learning, for sexual passion. There was no man born without his hunger, even if it was only the hunger for a shell to crawl into or the hunger to be let alone, to have no hunger. Yet there could be no man without the hunger, for that was the driving force of life.

Some few, like himself, had a hunger to know God; and this hunger too became a relentless preoccupation which fed on itself, recreating its own needs.

He returned to his slice-of-the-pie-shaped cubbyhole and studied the painting on the easel. He perceived that his own desire to capture the ocean of oceans, the sun of suns, the ship of ships, was in reality his effort to paint a portrait of God. He took out the piece of scratch paper which would be tacked under his painting at the exhibition and wrote:

"All forms of art are a seeking after truth. Yet it is not the finding of this truth which determines the worth of the work, but rather the intensity and faithfulness of the search."

8

The painters were dressed in their Sunday best, scrubbed and pressed, and waiting with the terrible fear and expectancy of the creative artist whose efforts are to be exposed to the frequently rude and disinterested eyes of strangers.

John did not know the language well enough to understand the discussions that took place before each of the canvases, but when he stood in front of his own painting and watched the expressions of the passers-by he learned quickly that indifference sounds the same in any tongue.

When the last of the guests had gone the men gathered about the fire in the studio, anger banked deep in their eyes.

"Didn't we sell anything?" asked John.

"No one even came to Charbert at the desk to ask the price of a canvas," replied Gerald.

"But what hurts most," growled Charbert, "is that not one of the major critics bothered to come."

Not a single line, not even a bad or contemptuous notice, appeared in the Parisian press. The gloom at the Beehive could be cut with a dull palette knife.

John was working in his studio when he heard a tentative knock on the door and threw a mumbled *"Entrez"* over his shoulder. After a few moments he felt someone standing behind him. He turned, irritably, then gasped in astonishment.

"Marty! Marty Buckler!"

"It's me, all right. But for a minute there I wasn't sure it was you."

John sprang up, warmly pumping Marty's hand.

"Marty, let me look at you, you old cay-utte. Will you look at that brand-new suit, all fresh-pressed, and that beautiful shirt and tie."

"That's more than I can say for you, John! You still look like a bundle of soiled linen that's been dumped at Buckler's Laundry. But it's good to see that homely old phiz of yours, even if it is unshaved."

"Here, sit down, boy," urged John, running his hands quickly over the bed to flatten out a space. "How is Frances?"

"All right . . . I guess."

"What do you mean, you guess? Don't you know?"

"Can anyone ever know, with Frances? She keeps her thoughts and her feelings to herself."

Uneasy, not wanting to learn more, John asked about his family back home, and then about Marty's businesses. Marty's body had filled out considerably, but his face was just as bony as ever. His purple eyes, which had been troubled, now flashed happily.

"That's the big news, boy. We're going to open Buckler's National Bank in the spring. The builder broke ground just before I left Wichita."

"Marty, you're going to be a banker! Well, I'll be a ringtailed Texas steer! Marty Buckler, Banker! And a National Banker, to boot. If only your mother could see you now, eh, Marty? Say, how about staying with me while you're in Paris? We'll move another cot in here."

Marty gazed at the disheveled cell, his mouth slightly awry.

"Thanks, John, but Cook's Tours booked me into the Crillon."

"The Crillon! Where all the visiting royalty stays! If you're not careful, you're going to be President of the United States! I can see the title on the cover of the book right now. *From Sod House to White House,* by Horatio Alger Buckler."

Marty squirmed, not unpleased.

"What do you say, Marty, we throw a barbecue for all the

painters here at the Beehive? To celebrate your arrival and the Buckler National Bank."

"I was hoping you'd suggest that, John. I'd like to meet your friends, get to know Paris . . ."

"Great. We'll have plenty of food and drink . . ."

". . . and girls, John?"

Marty's lips had gone dry. He stood licking them, nervously.

"Girls? Why sure, Marty, if you want them. Why don't we hire some musicians, then we can clear away the tables afterwards and have dancing."

"That's swell, boy."

John measured his old friend with a glint in his eye.

"Got some money? I'll give it to the boys who stage these roundups."

"Sure." Marty took a clip of crisp French bank notes from his wallet. "Here, take what you need."

John lifted the entire packet.

"Might as well use it all, Marty. That's what money is for, to spend."

John spread word over the Latin Quarter that all painters and their models were welcome. Many of the girls came in the Pompeian costumes they had worn to the Bal Bullier, and by midnight Marty Buckler, of Wichita, Kansas, was having his own private Quatz' Arts ball.

The party was the most lavish the Beehive had seen since the day Boucher opened its doors. There were enormous tureens of *panade*, a bread soup; large quantities of *charcuterie*, assorted cold meats; salamis and cheeses; liver loaf on toasted French bread; platters of sardines and *saumon*; red caviar on buns; big brass bowls filled with raisins, apples, green almonds; hundreds of petits fours; buckets of Reims champagne.

The dining room grew hot with the dancing, smoking and drinking. Maud, noticing John search the room for Marty, explained:

"He went with Yvette . . . in the middle of the last dance."

Marty disappeared four times in all before daybreak, and on each occasion with a different girl. He had been drinking champagne steadily; just before dawn, with a half-finished glass in his hand, he suddenly slumped forward on the bench where he was talking to a scantily clad model by the name of Mercedes. John caught him before he hit the floor, carried him to his room, took off his suit, wrapped him in the buffalo robe and settled him on the floor. Maud put a pillow under his head.

Marty awoke at dusk. He had a cup of the coffee which Maud had brewed before she left, then washed and shaved in the cold water of the communal bathroom, and was eager for another celebration.

"All right, Marty, but you'd better stop off at that Cook's Tour of yours and get some more of those pretty bank notes."

John bought himself a new suit so that he wouldn't disgrace Marty, then suggested they have dinner at the Brasserie Universelle, where he had dined on his own first night in Paris. Afterward they went to the Moulin Rouge. Marty was fascinated by the show, but it was not until the entr'acte when they went out into the foyer to have a drink at the bar, surrounded by flashy women in low-cut evening gowns, that he really became excited.

"Say, these ladies are wonderful, John. Look at those hair styles . . . and those slit dresses. They've got more class than those little models last night, haven't they?"

"Oh, sure," replied John.

He didn't see any use in telling Marty that these were prostitutes, while the models who had been kind to him at the Beehive had done so out of a sense of gratitude and camaraderie, without thought of personal gain.

"There's a stunner, John, that tall brunette talking to the little guy in the black suit. Do you think I could meet her?"

"Oh, I imagine so, if we play our cards right."

He gave the brunette the eye. She came to the bar with a too bright smile, holding up the train of a slightly threadbare gown. John ordered a drink for her, then slipped a ten-franc note into her hand, murmuring in bad French:

"Make my friend think you are doing it for love."

"Oui, monsieur, je comprends parfaitement."

"What's she saying, John?"

"She says she finds you very exciting."

"Swell. How about you getting one of these girls?"

"That was last night. I'll wait here at the bar."

Marty was back in less than an hour, but his eyes were dancing and he seemed highly pleased with himself.

"Where do we go next, John? It's just the shank of the evening. Let's find another café . . . and another girl."

The following weeks were a blurred kaleidoscope for John, trying to satisfy Marty's insatiable appetites for noise, music,

125

excitement and, above all, women. Early one evening, pacing Marty's room at the Crillon while Marty bathed and dressed, he noticed a little diary propped open on the desk against an inkwell. Glancing down idly, he saw that the page contained Marty's entries for the night before: the names and descriptions of the women he had had, and a brief comment on the anatomical character and performance of each. Intrigued, John slipped into the chair and began reading; to his amazement he found that Marty had each of the girls numbered, and the ones of the night before brought the total up in the seventies.

"What are you planning to do with these souvenirs of Paris, Marty? Take the little book home and save it for your grandchildren?"

Marty flushed, but only a little.

"You know I have a systematic mind, John. I promised myself when I left Wichita that if it was possible I would have me a hundred women."

"But, Marty, this bookkeeping system makes it sound as though these girls were units of something you wanted to accumulate . . . dollars, maybe. You remind me of a painter who thinks that when he's painted fifty canvases he'll be twice as good an artist as he was when he had painted twenty-five. Never mind the quality of the work, forget about its emotion, it's only quantity that counts. That's one of the things wrong with this world, Marty: the quantitative theory."

"Aw, cut out the morbid stuff, John. You know I don't understand all those hifalutin theories. Come on, let's paint the town."

But Marty's fun was spoiled. He ordered a bottle of whiskey to be put on the table, and then refused to touch it.

"John . . . was she . . . cold . . . to you?"

"Cold? Who?"

"You can be honest with me, boy. It doesn't matter any more . . . particularly since I've had all these girls in Paris." He leaned halfway across the table, his eyes holding John's. "Was Frances cold to you? I've got to know."

John gulped, and at the core of that gulp was a picture: Frances in his arms while they lay on the sofa in his darkened studio; so sweet of lips, so warm of embrace. He thought, There's no substitute for love. Aloud he said:

". . . we had only . . . childhood kisses . . ."

Marty brushed aside the evasion as though it were smoke blown at him from the next table.

126

"John, sometimes I think Frances despises me . . . sometimes I seem to catch an expression in her eyes . . ."

"You're imagining things, Marty. Frances loves you."

"As a . . . business partner. That's how I got her interested in me, by involving her more and more in my deals . . . my money-making schemes . . ."

He was silent for a moment, his face averted. John watched him wretchedly. Marty's food had grown cold; he pushed the plate aside in revulsion.

"John, you know I've always had an itch for the things that came to you so natural: books, ideas, painting. But I never had time when I was growing up, nor money either. And now that I got the time and money . . . I don't use 'em. I haven't read a book from cover to cover since you left Wichita. I'm lucky I can get through the paper at night, I'm so tired . . . on edge . . . with the day's figures spinning through my head. That's why Frances will never love me the way I want her to: I only got one string to my fiddle: business. She's bored with me, John, as bored as I am with myself."

John lighted a cigarette; he held the match aloft until it burnt his finger.

"That's a startling admission, Marty."

Marty leaned across the table, impetuously.

"John, let me stay here in Paris with you for a year. Oh, I'll cut out all the boozin' and whorin', that was just a spree. I'd like to read all the books you had on your shelves back in Wichita: Dickens, Voltaire, Shakespeare, and then chew over the stories with you to make sure I've got 'em straight. I'd like to buy tickets for the opera, listen to all that music and singing until it sounded like something more than a lot of cats screeching on the back fence. I'd like you to teach me about painting, oh, not to make those daubs myself, but to know why people get so excited about that kid stuff. I'd like to travel all over Europe so I'd know where Switzerland was when people talked about it. John, I want to become educated. It's not too late, is it?"

"You're the only one who knows the answer to that, Marty. What would you do about your bank, and all your other affairs?"

Marty's voice had raised to a high-pitched entreaty. Now all the timbre collapsed, and it sank to a whisper.

"You're right. I can't stop now. I've got to make the bank a success." He looked up, his face animated once again. "But it shouldn't take too long, John, five years maybe, ten at the most. Then I'll be rich . . . secure . . . and I'll have all my time to study . . . get educated. It won't be too late, will it, John?"

9

The day before he was to leave for Wichita, Marty asked if he couldn't throw a farewell party for the painters. John was thoughtful for a moment.

"Since you want to understand art, Marty, I suggest that for your farewell party you sponsor a Marty Buckler Exhibition at the Beehive . . ."

"Say, wouldn't Frances be impressed!"

"And make it a real buying exhibition."

"Fine, but who's going to buy?"

"You are."

"Me? You're plumb loco."

"There isn't a canvas at the Beehive that can't be bought for a few francs."

"Why should I waste my hard-earned money on that useless stuff?"

John asked guilelessly, "Marty, how much does my half of the Buckler enterprises amount to by now?"

"Your . . . what do you mean, John?"

"The hundred dollars I earned from the drawing of the Dalton gang was invested in your laundry. That just about matched your savings, didn't it? Everything you built since then stemmed from the laundry."

The high red color passed out of Marty's face and then returned as a seasick green. Though he never took his eyes from John their gaze became unfocused.

". . . you mean . . . you need money? Anything . . . you want . . ."

"Stop stumbling, Marty, I'm not asking for an accounting. It's just that I invested in you when it looked like I was drawing to a middle straight; I'm asking you to do the same for my friends."

"Why, of course, John. I just didn't realize how keen you were about this whole thing. . . ."

Marty could hardly recognize the men at the Beehive the following evening. "What are they so quiet about?" he asked. "And why are they staring at me bug-eyed?"

"Most of these people have never sold a canvas in their

128

lives. They've been told that you are going to buy fifty paintings, but they find this idea so incredible that they think we are playing some kind of joke on them."

Marty let his eyes wander over the wall slowly, looking at each of the canvases in turn.

"John, they're terrible. I don't like any of them. Couldn't I just give each man a few francs and tell him to keep his canvas?"

"No, no, the few francs is not what's important. It's that you perceive in their pictures something beautiful, true and important. They'll live on that faith, Marty, for months." He turned to Gerald Addams. "Gerald, tell the men that Mr. Buckler is eager to see which fifty canvases Charbert's purchasing committee has selected, so that he can pack them and take them home with him to the United States."

Marty muttered, "John, for heaven's sake, you're carrying this too far. Don't make me take them home, somebody's liable to find out I've got them."

As each winning painter was indicated, the artist rose, took his picture off the wall, carried it to Marty and thanked him in his native tongue.

Riding down to the Crillon in a fiacre, John noticed Marty's crestfallen expression. Suddenly he felt conscience-stricken.

"Look, Marty, I'll admit I took advantage of you. Those paintings aren't worth even the few francs you paid for them, in particular not the John Noble. But if it so happened that you bought a lot of weak shares on the stock market and wanted to recoup your losses, what would you do?"

"Why, I'd buy some strong stocks, obviously."

"Then that's exactly what we're going to do: we are going to buy some strong paintings to offset the ones you acquired tonight."

Marty let out a cry of anguish. "Oh, John, not still more!"

"Tomorrow I'm going to take you around to the important galleries and to the little hole-in-the-wall rooms where the dealers can hardly pay their rent. From these places I can give you a start on one of the finest collections of modern paintings that anybody in America will own."

"But, John, I don't want any pictures," wailed Marty. "I don't want what you call the good ones any more than I want the bad ones."

But John was not listening. "The Martin Buckler Collection!" he said. "Just think of it, Marty, in addition to being a banker you're now becoming a patron of the arts."

They spent the day buying a Pissarro, a Degas and a Renoir at Durand-Ruel's, a Delacroix, an Edouard Manet and a Van Gogh at Goupil's, a Cézanne, a Gauguin and a Matisse at Vollard's, a Seurat and a Toulouse-Lautrec in a furniture store in Montmartre, and an Henri Rousseau in a little teashop in Montparnasse.

"Look, John, do me one small favor, will you?" Marty begged as they were saying good-by at the Gare St. Lazare. "Ship these pictures to my warehouse, instead of to my home . . . they'll be safer that way . . . or at least I will!"

From the station John turned in the direction of the Rue de Fleurus, for the buying expedition had brought him an invitation to visit Gertrude Stein, patron of many of the artists whose canvases he had selected for Marty. At number 27 he found a small pavilion of two stories and behind it a large study. He knocked at the door and after a moment it was opened by the strangest-looking woman he had ever seen: roughhewn, like primitive sculpture, with a powerful jutting nose and chin and overhanging black eyebrows, so that one could not know, except for looking at the long black monkish gown and the string of beads hanging almost to the waist, whether this were a man or a woman.

"So you're John Noble! But where is your cowboy horse and the six-shooters?"

"It is not a role I enjoy playing before Americans."

He walked into the big studio room which was lighted by gas lamps high up near the ceiling. Heavy Italian Renaissance furniture stood against the whitewashed walls, and in the center was a massive Renaissance table looking as solid and hand-hewn as Miss Stein herself. But the most amazing part of the atelier was that the high and spacious walls were covered almost solid with hundreds of paintings and drawings, some framed, some unframed, bearing no relationship to each other in style, age, mood or content.

"Then the wild Westerner is a part you improvise, Mr. Noble? I'm disappointed."

"But why, Miss Stein? Everyone wears a mask in public. Look at yourself, acting as hostess to the poor, unknown artists of Paris. What would you be without it?"

"The greatest writer in the world."

"Perhaps, but who would believe it if you were hidden away somewhere quietly? As the patroness of modern art you have made yourself famous throughout Europe."

"Like all Westerners, you have a streak of brutality in you, Mr. Noble; but you speak honestly."

John smiled, a crooked, tentative smile. "Only sometimes."

He began an inspection tour of the room, walking slowly past Matisse's *La Femme au Chapeau,* a group of Cézanne landscapes, a powerfully etched head of an old woman by Daumier, two riotous Gauguins from Tahiti, several enormous Picasso Harlequins, a tiny Delacroix, many narrowly framed Japanese prints, a Toulouse-Lautrec drawing, pictures by Valloton, Duran and Braque, the pale face and bosom of a delicate French girl by Marie Laurencin.

The room began to fill now. Pablo Picasso came in, a short stumpy man dressed in an incredibly wrinkled suit that looked like burlap, whose eyes were brilliantly alive and all-consuming. With him was his mistress Fernande, with a beautiful face and large dull eyes. Next he was introduced to Alfred Maurer, who arrived with Alice B. Toklas, Miss Stein's companion; then to Mildred Aldrich, an American who had brought a group of German painters who called themselves by a new name, Expressionists; then to Alice Princet with André Derain, whose paintings John had seen and admired.

By now the atelier had become crowded. Looking down toward the end of the room, he saw Gertrude Stein sitting in a high-backed chair, her hands folded monastically in her lap, smiling benignly over her salon as the artists came to her to inquire over the progress of her new work, a long book called *Three Lives.*

Completing his tour of the big atelier, John at last came to a group of adoring young men who surrounded Picasso. A fluffy-haired blond was asking obsequiously:

"When one does not know how or what to draw, should one go to a master or a school?"

"Neither, you should found your own school," replied Picasso.

John's stomach rose, but even as he turned toward the door he saw Picasso's tiny hidden smile and realized that the man was merely entertaining himself at the expense of bores.

Gertrude Stein made her way quickly through the throng.

"Are you leaving so soon, Mr. Noble? Don't we amuse you?"

"I guess I'm just not the salon type, Miss Stein."

"You don't like to run with the herd?" Her voice was faintly mocking.

10

He was walking the streets of Paris in a high wind. It was night. The city was dark. The wind grew stronger and stronger, hurling papers about, sweeping objects up and down the deserted streets. He plunged headstrongly forward though he had no idea of where he was going, feeling only that he must somehow move onward.

The air began to fill with snow, small white flakes drifting lazily downward. He turned his face up toward the sky; the countless white particles now felt round and hard and metallic. They rained on his upturned face and his shoulders and chest, lacerating the skin. He picked up a handful of the flakes. They were dollars, small white dollars, millions of them piling around him, and all of them with Marty's face stamped on both sides, his features etched in silver like the negative plate of one of the photographs he remembered from George Israel's studio in Wichita.

The Marty Buckler dollars beat against him like the big rocks of a hailstorm against a windowpane, bruising every part of his body. He was too tired and hurt and confused to move, but he was not frightened for he knew that he could not be destroyed by these metallic images. He closed his eyes to rest for a few moments. When he opened them the dollars had turned into female dolls, all undressed, all with a fixed smile painted on their faces, and all exactly alike. He rose to his feet; the dolls vanished.

He moved down the dark streets; once again the snow began to fall. This time the flakes were tinted with every color that he had essayed on his canvases; they were of every shape: squares, rectangles, cubes, all the drifting forms to which he had tried to give body. The first one touched the earth. He perceived that it was a painting: line, color, delineated object. Hundreds of canvases began to pile up at his feet, canvases of all sizes, styles, degrees of skill. They covered the streets like the bleached bones of buffalo on the Kansas prairie. He looked upward and saw that the air was thick with paintings, filled so solid there was no oxygen. He tried to move down the street, but he was knee-deep in pictures.

For the first time he felt fear; he started to run, wildly,

bringing his legs high into the air. He fell, and when he rose, painfully, he saw that flight was hopeless. He was trapped.

The pictures were falling ever faster; when they beat about his head he saw that these were his own canvases, the tens, the fifties, the hundreds of canvases that he had poured out during the wild months. Had he created a monstrous delusion which was now returning to drown him? Must he perish so ignominiously, buried under his own creations?

No! He would fight his way clear.

Above him he discovered a latticework grill on a stone building. With a mighty effort he pulled himself up, pulled his aching legs free of their encumbrances even as a new gust of wind filled the streets and the buildings, the air and the sky with more and more paintings, thousands of canvases by Charbert, Turnhouse, Leipsche, Giuseppe Donello, Gerald Addams, Tanner, Durchamp, Alexei, all the men of the Beehive.

The slow dying sounds of Paris had whispered into silence. The city about him was lifeless.

Gasping hard, he pulled himself onto the roof of the building. Here too was an endless prairie of paintings over which he had to crawl on his hands and knees. The paint was still fresh; he could smell it in his nostrils, feel its stickiness on his fingers.

Stumblingly he made his way over the roofs of Paris; there were no more streets and no more houses; all crevices and canyons were filled solid with hard-packed pictures and their frames, soldered into one vast leaden indistinguishable lump.

Then he knew what he must do: he must get clear of this city, of this Paris which was buried and dead like Pompeii under the hot sticky lava of Vesuvius. Once out in the country, alone, in the clear free air amidst the wide fields, he would be safe. His body aching, his eyes locked tight, he began to run.

In the distance he saw a great open field. He increased his speed, tearing the skin of his legs and feet, but the more ground he covered the farther away the clearing receded. Panting, exhausted, he sank down on the rough-edged solidity beneath him. This was the end for him.

With a feverish gesture he put his hand inside his shirt and grasped the North Star, took it out on its long string to gaze at it. He saw the face of his mother before him, smiling, loving, infinitely sad. He struggled to his feet, clasping the North Star tightly in his hand.

The air became cool and abundant; his lungs filled with it

133

and his heart began pumping agitatedly. His body began to shake with chills, his teeth chattered so loudly they filled the cavern of his head with the sound of thunder. He rolled from side to side under the buffalo robe, his flesh cold and clammy.

He felt someone leaning over him, brushing the perspiration from his brow with soft finger tips. Painfully, as though he were coming up the path of a steep black cavern, he forced his eyelids open. It was Maud.

"John, what's the matter? Are you ill? I'll go get Gerald; he will call an American doctor."

He reached out, took her hand, crushed her small fingers in his grasp.

"I'm so alone. I'm so lonely."

Maud sat on the edge of the bed, put her cheek on his.

"No, *chère*, you are not alone. I'm here, I'm with you."

"It hurts to be so alone, it hurts up here inside your skull."

"I will get Gerald."

He could hear Maud's high heels tapping down the flights of steps. He stumbled out of the bed, found his way around the balcony to the opposite side of the stairs and made his way to the street. In the next block he bought two bottles of whiskey, drinking one halfway down while the proprietor returned his change. He stood motionless for a moment, gratefully, as the alcohol-laden blood reached his head and began eating away at the edges of the vast pain.

After a time he found his way to the stockyards. He sought out a butcher, shoved a wad of crumbled franc notes into his hand and repeated, *"Cheval, cheval, horse, horse!"*

They brought him an old bay and a discarded bit which he fitted into the horse's mouth. Then he headed for the fields behind the abattoir, alternately taking a long drink, talking to his horse, recounting the earlier years on the plains, the trip up the Rocky Mountains in Colorado and down south to Texas and New Mexico. He was happy to be home in Kansas again, to feel the buffalo grass beneath him. How wrong he had been about Paris and France, for that matter all of Europe! He hated it: the strange people, the strange language, the different customs, the oldness of the houses, the streets . . . why had he ever thought it was beautiful and exciting?

All of this he explained to Wichita Bill, telling the swayback horse that he was smart never to have left Kansas, that he, John, was glad to be back home again. When the second bottle of whiskey was exhausted his speech became mumbled

134

and incoherent; he fell forward, his arms thrown loosely about the horse's neck.

The old bay stood still for a long time, then slowly stumbled its way back to the slaughterhouse.

11

He packed his two bags, gathered up his paints, dismantled his easel and prepared to leave the Ruche, for it had become abundantly clear that he too had fallen victim to the quantitative theory, the slam-bang method of painting first and thinking afterward. He would have to reflect the immensely beautiful but equally private world which he alone knew and he alone could transcribe to canvas.

He glanced about the room with an amused nostalgia, remembering the excitement with which he had entered it the first time; if Wichita had been his infancy, the Beehive had been his irrepressible adolescence. His eyes swept the stacks of canvases against the wall. He had made a thousand errors, traversed fields where he did not belong, only to learn that none of the going techniques or theories were for him. He could not copy, join, absorb, fall in line. What he finally put on canvas would be pure John Noble, recognizable across a sea of buffalo grass. His would be a lonely art, not tied up with any age, school or theory; but how could it be otherwise: was he not a lonely man?

With a quick gesture he took his penknife from his pocket and set to work destroying the paintings, even as he had his hundreds of sketches for Cleopatra back in Wichita.

After considerable searching he found a studio which occupied the entire top floor at 7 Rue Belloni. It had had many users before him, but he managed to conceal most of the past with a quick coat of paint. There was a good-sized skylight facing north, but this north light was both dark and cold. He thought, A north light like this can set a man back fifty years in painting.

He had told no one about his studio, not even Gerald Addams or Charbert, his closest friends at the Beehive. He was therefore all the more astonished when the door opened while he was painting the ceiling, and he heard a soft voice say:

"*Tiens, tiens,* what a big empty barn."

He gazed down at Maud from the top rung of the ladder,

135

his broad brush dripping paint onto the floor. She stared back at him boldly, then shrugged her shoulders and laughed.

"If you don't want me to know where you live, you'll have to go back to Wichita."

"See here," he exclaimed, "I want this kept absolutely quiet."

She ignored his spluttering as unworthy of answer, then began looking about the studio and the small adjoining kitchen. He climbed down the ladder and followed her around hostilely.

"Now just get that light out of your eye, Maud. Nobody's going to set up any housekeeping. This is just a workroom. Savvy?"

"You want to sleep on the floor all winter and get pneumonia?"

"Well, no, I've got to have a bed."

"You don't want a stove in that kitchen to make hot coffee for cold mornings?"

"A stove . . . yes . . . I will need coffee."

"You want to eat your food standing up? You don't want a little table and a couple of chairs?"

Defeated, he thrust a roll of bills at her.

"All right. Go buy me a cot and a stove, a kitchen table and a couple of wooden chairs. Nothing else, mind you."

"Not even one comfortable chair, and a little piece of rug for this floor? And what about a pan to fry a beefsteak, and a spoon to stir the sugar?"

"You win, Maud. Go buy what I need, but if you tell one living soul in Paris where I live, I'll move out and leave all your furniture behind."

Aside from keeping his address secret, Maud did none of the things she was instructed. She bought a big double bed with a warm blanket and feather comforter, a good cookstove, a couple of lamps, and two chairs for reading and sitting about in a spare hour. She also bought a wardrobe for his clothes and some secondhand draperies which she hung on pulleys so they could close out the night beyond the skylight. The atelier had rather a cozy air when she had finished, and John could find little to complain about, since she had ransacked Paris and furnished it on half of what it would have cost him for the barest necessities.

"You did a fine job, Maud. Remind me to be grateful to you, sometime."

"*Merci,* no! The minute you Americans begin to feel indebted you find yourselves another girl."

136

The problem of the darkness or coldness of the north light over his skylight never disturbed him because he now slept during the day and worked all night, rarely bothering to turn on the lamps in the studio but using instead the powerful lights which he felt shining behind his own eyes and his own brow. He mounted a fresh canvas on the easel in the center of the big studio, drew up one of the chairs and sat in the rapidly falling dusk gazing at the blank space; darkness enveloped the studio while he slowly, painfully, still sitting in his chair, shaped in his mind the picture he wanted to paint: thought through to its ultimate conclusion every aspect of the design, the plastic forms, the line and shadow, the juxtaposition of colors to create the mood; then, when the picture had been completely painted inside his head, he rose from the deep chair, lighted a lamp, squeezed the paints out onto the palette, picked up his brushes and transferred it to the canvas with sure swift strokes.

He had no idea how much time elapsed, weeks, months, while he worked this way. He avoided the Beehive and the Café Bullier, went to a remote café on those rare occasions when he left the studio. When he could no longer contain himself within walls, when he felt a need to move his body through space he would set out about two o'clock in the morning and walk the streets alone, almost running, pumping his powerful arms and clenched fists ahead of him like a boxer doing road work.

He started a series of still lifes: the sea at dawn; a crescent moon over a frozen mountain lake; a boat drawn up on a beach with a white horse and a fisherman standing alongside; a single tree on a horizon against a motionless moon. He eschewed action pictures in which something was happening, for he reasoned that whatever was in motion was also in transit, and tried instead to capture scenes in which everything had been resolved, completed, its permanent place taken in an over-all design. On the back of one canvas, a vast buffalo herd against a vaster prairie sky, he wrote, "To see only one part of nature at a time is fractional vision; the universe must be seen and felt whole in order to be understood whole."

For relaxation he pored over the new chemical formulas for making paint and preparing canvas, using German colors and mediums instead of the oil or turpentine which he had been buying at Lefèbre Foinet's ever since Gerald Addams had taken him there. One formula in particular called Feigenmilch called for considerable cooking and so he spent hours over the pots on his kitchen stove, heating, stirring, adding chemicals from little paper bags, looking like a medieval alchemist, his shirt and trousers covered with paint, his skin pale from lack of sunlight, his long, corn-white hair falling over his face and his smoky blue eyes happy, excited, absorbed. Sleep was not in him, and while he waited for the brew to boil he played solitaire on the kitchen table under the kerosene lamp or reread his favorite stories from Poe, "The Murders in the Rue Morgue," "The Gold Bug" and "The Mystery of Marie Rogêt." He would then prepare his canvases with the new mixtures, and during the day put them out in the sun to dry until he had a sparkling background on which to apply his paint; a background which gave the paint an added luminosity.

How bitterly difficult it is to learn what we really are, he thought. How ceaselessly we strive to find our way back to the simple fundamentals of our own nature. Some men never do, they are lost forever in the forest of other people's thoughts. Others struggle long and hard, but never succeed because there is nothing to return to: no core, no base. Some crack the shell of their own nature underfoot, only to find it empty of meat; others peel off subcutaneous layers of orange in a hopeless effort to reach the sweet juice of their own natures and end up with nothing but rind.

12

When after many months of solitary labor he grew tired of himself he enrolled in the famous Acadèmie Julien. His teacher was Jean Paul Laurens, a heavy, bull-jawed fellow. John felt that if anybody could teach someone else how to paint it would be a ruggedly honest man like this. The painters worked all week without criticism or correction, and then early on Saturday morning Laurens started around the room, analyzing each canvas so that everyone in the room could hear and understand. Laurens had a genius for going to the heart of a man's weakness, illuminating it in a fast brutal sentence. It was with a quick smile that John heard him grunt:

"Not so bad, Noble."

Each spring and fall Laurens awarded a prize for the best painting produced by one of his students. John started a night seascape, with a lopsided moon low over the horizon, the waves thick and oily and a small fishing boat making its way through a trough. He called it *Path of the Moon*.

Laurens stood in front of the canvas and barked:

"First prize to Mr. John Noble for *Path of the Moon*."

That night John wrapped the canvas in heavy brown paper, nailed it into a wooden crate and sent it to his father in Wichita, a gesture of love for the older man's patience and generosity over the years.

By act of winning the Laurens prize, he automatically graduated himself out of the academy. Hearing that Henri Matisse might be willing to take on a few more students, he applied early the next morning at Matisse's *école*.

Matisse wore a neatly trimmed beard and well-fitted spectacles, dressed fastidiously and carried himself with the poise of a banker. He said, "Ah yes, John Noble. Jean Laurens has told me about you."

"Then I may work here in the school, Monsieur Matisse?"

Matisse looked around the big, bare salon of what had been a religious school before the French government took it over and leased it to him for a pittance. About thirty young American and English students were working at their easels. John saw Matisse shake his head in amused despair.

"To each new student as he comes in the front door I say, 'Don't become a little Matisse, don't imitate or copy me. Learn what I can teach you about technique, and absorb it into what you already know,' *mais mon dieu . . .*"

He took John on a tour of the studio. Nearly all of the young students were painting Matisse themes, highly decorative in nature and with the conscious eliminations and distortions which Matisse made in his drawing, the better to achieve his effects: but where Matisse had eliminated details to highlight what he was trying to say, and all elements fitted into an indigenous whole, the imitating students were using Matisse's mechanisms without understanding, accomplishing quite absurd results.

"I see what you mean, monsieur," said John grimly.

At the end of his first week at the art school he was invited to Matisse's flat for the evening. It was his first dinner in a private home in a very long time. Madame Matisse was a scrupulous housekeeper, every inch of her apartment scrubbed and shining the way he remembered his mother's house in Wichita. The Matisses had three small children, and John knew the story of how Matisse, who had been making a fair living by selling conventional, academic canvases, had one day suddenly sickened of the technique and destroyed a canvas which he could surely have sold, the money from which he very much needed. The Matisses had paid heavily for this revolt: they had had to send their two sons to their grandparents in the country; sometimes there had been far too little food in their flat; at one period Madame Matisse had had to open a hat store to support them. But Matisse's judgment had been sound and his craftsmanship the finest to appear in Europe since Paul Cézanne. At this point he was beginning to sell some of his new and radical canvases.

When he sat down to the table with the Matisses, the three youngsters full of high spirits, the family talk commonplace and salutary, John suddenly became homesick for the wonderful hours he had spent at the Noble dinner table in Wichita, homesick for the confidence and love of his parents and brother and sisters, homesick for the solid friendship of Dave Leahy and Victor Murdock, and, above all, homesick for Frances Birchfield.

In his youth and ignorance he had imagined that artists must be free as the air and wild as the wind, able to come and go, to work or loaf, to paint or talk, to change localities, loves and ideologies as frequently and swiftly as one changed one's shirt; that marriage and a home and children would nail an artist down to the mundane realities, make a conventional being out of him, one whose life would be devoted to putting food into mouths and clothes onto backs. Yet here was a man whom nearly everyone in Paris conceded to have inherited the cloak of Whistler, Manet and Cézanne, living a conventional bourgeois life, happy, working constantly, and creating brilliantly.

All of his years of chaotic drifting suddenly overcame him. Why had he not married Frances and brought her to Paris with him? They could have had a home, had their children, their companionship, their devotion to each other, and he could have lived just as arduous a life with his paints as he could have wanted. Because of these internal churnings he was unable to eat very much of Madame Matisse's delicious dinner; in a stumbling way he poured out the story of his fear of permanence and responsibility . . . and now of his realization that Bohemia was not the only place where authentic art could originate.

"It is no use marrying because you think you should be married," Matisse reassured him; "you must wait until the love and the urge are so powerful that you cannot conceive of living without that marriage."

"Love is not like painting," added Mrs. Matisse quietly. "You don't need years of study and training, of experimentation and failure in order to achieve success. Someday a woman will appear before you, your eyes will rest upon her and your voice will say, 'I love her! This is she.' And your love will be as perfect and complete a work of art as that Cézanne *Bathers* we have on the wall above the buffet."

"If that ever happens to me," mused John, "I will indeed believe in miracles."

Because of his newly found nostalgia for home he found himself going more often to the American Art Association Club. The billiard room had a change of paintings on its walls every twenty-four hours, but John found that the conversation concerned itself more with baseball and women than it did with the newest exploits of *Les Fauves,* or the Wild Animals, a group name now being given to Picasso, Braque, Rouault and Dufy, who were attempting to overthrow Impressionism as a romantic movement and to replace it with a lyrically interpretive realism.

He became better acquainted with Alexander Harrison, who was taking the nude models out of the north-light studios and painting them in the open air with the warm sunlight on their bodies; and with George Luks, the exact opposite of Le Grand Harrison, who was painting deep-bitten subjects, most of them out of proletarian life, people and scenes which had not been considered worthy of the artist's time, yet setting them down with such an intense love and inner force that what had been called sordid and vulgar now shone with a beautiful inner illumination. With George Luks he organized the first American baseball team that ever played in Paris.

He painted often at the Art Students Club where there was no instructor and everyone chipped in to hire the models. Harrison propped his easel beside John's, leaning over from time to time to study John's canvas. One morning he said:

"You're *sui generis,* John, a loose and wandering star in the heavens, with no prescribed route or place. It's futile for anyone to attempt to classify or categorize you. The more I see of you and your work the more I'm convinced that you are a natural-born anarchist, and that you will never concede the existence of hard and fast lines in time, space or reality."

13

He awakened feeling cold inside, not merely exhausted, but actually abandoned, as though everything and everyone had moved out of his head and he had been left alone.

He extricated himself painfully from the bedcovers and doused his face in cold water. Then he looked about him and saw that it was foolish to imagine that he was alone or abandoned: all around him, giving dimension as well as boundary, was the result of his hard and faithful work since he had moved to this studio: dozens of canvases stacked against the walls and lying face down in unused corners.

The ambition of every painter in Paris was to have a one-man exhibition. Very well, he would stage his own one-man show. There would be no eager, nervous, bustling little gallery owner, no officials from the Department of Beaux Arts, no officers from the Academy or Salon, no crowds of people such as he had seen so often at the Vernissage of the Independents or the Salon d'Automne; the room would not quickly be filled with smoke and the sound of excited, disputing voices, and no pictures would be sold. He would have to serve as the gallery owner, critics from the journals, and the crowd of gallery followers who were forever seeking some new and fashionable departure.

But that was as it should be: standing in the middle of his room and his world, he felt that it was time for him to act as spectator, critic and analyst. If these paintings were good he could use their warmth to melt the coldness inside him, the lush richness of their paint to quicken his faint pulse, the excellence of drawing and structure to brighten his eye and refresh his mind.

He propped the pictures against the long walls, framed and unframed canvas standing shoulder to shoulder, and when this space was solid he got out string and tacks and covered the walls all the way up to the ceiling. By making a quick count he judged that he had almost a hundred paintings in varying stages of completion.

He began at his immediate left and studied the canvases, edging slowly along the room, his eyes piercing every stroke of the brush, every concept of organization, every idea behind the drawing. There was no need to hurry; he had not hurried in painting them, he had never added a layer of fresh paint onto still wet paint, had never added the fresh idea on top of half a dozen crusts of error, but had always scraped and cleaned and gone to a fresh new surface both on the canvas and in his own mind.

His disappointment was sudden, unexpected . . . and crushing. Those canvases which were unmistakable imitations he brushed aside quickly: he was not and never could be a skilled pointillist; his café interiors were unrecognizable Toulouse-Lautrec because he had used Pissarro's heavy brush stroke where Toulouse-Lautrec had had the genius to know that such subjects could be captured only with thin flat surfaces; and his efforts to copy Monet by picturing the vague shimmering outlines of a railroad station or a cathedral sacrificed his own ability to draw.

But what about those others which were the fruit of his own creation? What had he painted that extended beyond the borders of the frames, that suggested an infinity behind the simple finite statements? He could not ask less of himself than he demanded of others. Where was the inner glow, the vibrating essence, the divine illumination which he had demanded even of the masters in the Louvre, and without which he had passed a picture by as being amusing or decorative or clever storytelling or photographically accurate, but without a living and permanent importance because it was uninspired?

And where was God in any of these paintings?

If God was not in his work, then for him nothing of genuine beauty or meaning was in it: a painting without God was like a dark room without a light or a prairie wagon without wheels. His draftsmanship was strong and true; his chemical experiments had taught him a great deal about mixing colors; he had rejected petty or meaningless subjects and stuck to heroic themes; he had worked always with force and warmth and love. Then where had he failed? At his wrist, his finger tips, the brush end? For it seemed to him that despite his mightiest efforts none of his feelings had been transferred to the canvas, that he had succeeded only in painting still lifes, empty ships upon an empty sea, a dead sun in empty heavens.

He took the canvases off the walls with slow, exhausted movements, cutting them to pieces with his knives and heaping them in the center of the floor for some convenient annihilation by fire. As the piles grew larger and the walls barer, he began to feel aseptic . . . and more and more dead.

He had deceived himself about the relationship of work to God. He had gone on the assumption that he would find God through his work: through his integrity and rugged dedication to the task on hand. But he was no closer to God now than when he had arrived in Paris. He knew that he had been a fool. No man had any right to search for God: He was not a fact, not a substance, and never a demonstrable reality. Except in the religious sense He was unfindable, or at least unrecognizable; to the individual who insisted upon facing his own particular God, He was uncreatable. God can create man. Man cannot create God.

His hunger and his search had been based on his need: but why did there have to be a God just because he so desperately needed one? The answer was plain to anyone who dared to face it: there was no God. He would no longer search for God in his painting. He would no longer paint.

He felt himself left bare-handed and bare-hearted, the past too painful to look back at, the future too meaningless to contemplate.

He entered the nearest bar and began to drink; he did not know who brought him home nor how long he lay across his bed. He awakened to find it dark outside, feeling sick to his stomach.

Two ways inside his head revealed themselves quickly: he could go back to his thoughts of yesterday or he could go back to the blessed oblivion of alcohol, finding release from the terror that still clutched him, able to dim the harsh reality that, if he could never paint again, his life was over. How devastating, he thought, to discover about one's self that there is no self, that the beautiful box, so colorfully wrapped, contains no gift, that the box and the wrappings are all!

He searched about the studio in drawers and clothing, found a handful of bills and once again went out into the streets. When his money was used up he found that his credit was good in the dozens of Parisian cafés where he had eaten and drunk over the years. He did not care whether he was drunk or unconscious but there was no state in between that he could endure. The moment he awakened, no matter where it was, in his own studio or slouched over a table somewhere, he had but one thought: more drink to wipe out the ability of the brain to think and of the heart to remember.

"What's the matter with John?" his friends asked themselves. "Why is he staying drunk so long and so continuously?"

Yet they did not despair when he refused to answer or explain: for they knew of his solid months of labor, they knew that painting, like childbearing, carries with it the terrible exhaustion of afterbirth.

"You'll be all right, John," Alexander Harrison said when he became boisterous at cafés, telling everyone how little he thought of Paris and how great was the Southwest.

"You'll work out of it, you will get enough of this and go back to your easel," said George Luks.

"Take it easy, boy. Let's go home now," said Charles Hawthorne, "and sleep it off."

But the voice inside his head cried, "I am so lonely, I am so lonely," and he knew that what he meant was, "I want to be dead. I want to be dead."

Whiskey was expensive, and when his credit ran out at the cafés where the proprietors had lost hope that this was but a spree, he turned to absinthe, which was cheaper, more readily available, and the effects of which lasted longer. He almost never touched solid food; he had no concept of how he looked, going about unshaven, unwashed, his hair matted, his clothes reeking of the alcohol which drenched him inside and out. Strangers turned from him in disgust; only his oldest friends stood by, managing somehow to get him home, a heavy inchoate bundle of unconsciousness.

One evening he was approached by a tall, gaunt man with a Vandyke beard and wonderful soft black eyes. His coat was also black, and under it was a high white clerical collar.

"Mr. John Noble of Wichita, Kansas? I'm the Rev. Mr. Van Winkle of the American Episcopal church here on the Left Bank. I received a letter from the minister of your church in Wichita, Mr. Noble. He says that your mother has not heard from you for a long time. She is worried."

John drank deeply to drown out the minister's voice. The Rev. Mr. Van Winkle wrote to Elizabeth Noble urging her not to send John any more money, but rather to send it to Foinet, the color merchant. When John learned what had happened he stormed into the dealer's store to demand his money; the color grinder remained firm: the funds had been sent from America for paint and canvas only.

"Very well, then give me paint and canvas! All of it that my money will buy."

Shrugging helplessly, Foinet did as he was ordered. John squeezed the tubes of paint wildly onto a canvas, mauling it around with his fingers and exclaiming:

"There, you have my masterpiece! Who said I was not a great painter? Look, could anyone have portrayed better the meaninglessness of life?"

The color merchant refused to handle John's money any longer. The Rev. Mr. Van Winkle then wrote to Wichita urging that the checks be sent to a bank in Paris. When John learned of this shift in maneuvers he put on his cowboy outfit, strapped his two revolvers about him and charged into the bank, firing shots into the ceiling, terrorizing the clerks and the clients, and demanding every last sou credited to his account. The cashier obliged him in crisp franc notes and gold, but he had no sooner reached the sidewalk than he was arrested. The next day, when the judge learned that he had taken only his own money, he found no grounds for prosecution. John paid the costs of repairing the holes in the ceiling and was dismissed.

He had now been drunk for such an interminable time that the Latin Quarter changed his name from Buffalo John to Whiskey Bill. There seemed to be no limit to the degrading means he would use to obtain more liquor. When he was drunk, but not drunk enough to have wiped out all sense of being alive, he went from café to café down the street, wheedling drinks from strangers, emptying whatever glasses might be standing about on the tables. He was turned away from in revulsion, ejected by waiters and proprietors, picked up by gendarmes and carried to the police station to lie in torment.

When a check arrived and he managed to buy a full bottle of whiskey he took it with him to the Café Bullier at the crowded apéritif hour, poured the content into his dirty Stetson, cried out:

"The guy that drank from Lillian Russell's slipper had nothing on me!" and downed the full quart in one long gulp. By the time he reached the middle of the drink he knew that this could kill him, and a voice he had not heard for many months, a quiet, sensitive, inner voice, commented:

"Go ahead, destroy yourself. What do I care? How can I exist further in this shambles that is John Noble?"

14

He awakened to find George Luks sitting before his easel sketching rapidly.

"George. Why . . . are you . . . here?"

"I'm Mohammed, come to the mountain."

John went to the washstand, poured some cold water into

the bowl and dipped his whole head in, sloshing water over his long unkempt hair.

"Please, George, no riddles, not with a head like mine."

"It's a good head, John. Well shaped, plenty of character. That's why I'm painting you."

"I don't want my head painted. There's nothing in me to paint. You'll come out with a completely blank canvas."

"Maybe you would, if you tried a self-portrait. But I know what I want to say. I've got the coffee boiling. Take yourself a cup and then sit down here and behave like a good model."

John protested, but he sat for the portrait at least twenty times in the following month: in the studio, at a dozen different sidewalk cafés, in the homes of complete strangers whom he picked up while drunk, but always with George Luks trailing him and sketching steadily. Then, for the last few days of intensive work, Luks brought a case of liquor up to John's studio where he kept him captive until the portrait was complete.

During all this time John had shown not the slightest interest in Luks's work. Now, suddenly, it seemed important to him to know what George had to say about him. The impact was like being smashed in the face with a heavy fist: for although he had seen the contempt in the eyes of strangers as he badgered them for drinks or spilled liquor or tobacco over his clothes; though he had known that his friends had despaired of him, saying that he was finished, crazy, hopeless; though he had been called every foul name by storekeepers, café proprietors, the Parisian police, and had known them well earned, still all of this censure had meant nothing to him personally, had never managed to get beneath his skin.

But now as he stood before the George Luks portrait he faced with a terrifying clarity and finality the irresolution, the weakness, the self-indulgence, the decay of the pale flesh, the weakening of the blue, watery, almost unfocused eyes; the death's head peering out timidly from what had once been a strong and bold personality. He saw himself for what he was: a self-deceiver, a sick one, too weak of mind to meet harsh realities, to endure uncomplainingly in a meaningless world, to carry on with courage the omnipresent farce by means of which men pretended that life was good, beautifully designed, that it ended with meaning and purpose. Dimly he understood that each man's tragedy is uncommunicable; other people endured the same as he, but silently, carrying on their jobs, burying their grief, shouldering their part of the load. His pretentious cant about having lost God, of being unable to endure life in which there was no manifestation of divine power, all of this had been a façade, an elaborate metaphysical excuse used as the justification for abandoning his work, his responsibility, his place in society, and that last of all imperatives, his self-decency.

To his own image, gazing back at him from the canvas, he whispered:

"We are all alone on earth."

He sat on the rough kitchen chair before the portrait, his eyes closed. His mind went back to the trestle high above Wichita, where his comrades had betrayed him by crying, "Jump! Jump!" when he could have jumped into nothing but the shallow water of death. He saw himself running through the fields and the streets of the town, into the back door of his house and up to his room where he had thrown himself on his bed and wept in humiliation.

Then he felt his mother put her arm about him, comforting him, wiping away his tears, saying:

"You see that North Star, son? It's always there, unfailing. No matter what happens to us or to the world, that star is steadfast. It will never change, never disappear, never fail you. As long as you can find the North Star, you will know that you are secure."

Aching to have his mother by his side and her arm about his shoulder, her soft voice in his ear, he reached inside his shirt to find the North Star she had given him before he left home. But the string was not hanging in its accustomed place. He fumbled about his throat and neck, groping, tearing with his nails. Then he ripped open the shirt and searched frantically.

As suddenly as he began, he stopped. The North Star was gone. He had lost it. It had disappeared somewhere in one of his drunken orgies, had fallen off him while he ran through the street or lay unconscious in some strange alley.

But then, hadn't he known all along? Hadn't he actually lost the North Star on the day that he awakened feeling ill and empty, when he had told himself that he was an utter failure, that he was finished, that his work was of no value and could never be of any value?

Unable to bear the excruciating pain in his heart, he picked up a bottle of the whiskey which Luks had brought, tipped it vertical and drank deeply. When he could swallow no more he sat on the edge of the bed holding the bottle, waiting for the physical revulsion to pass, the sense that his stomach and his insides would rise of their own accord and vanish forever through the exit of his mouth; and when it had passed he drank again long and hard, until he could no longer see George Luks's portrait, no longer realize that the North Star was gone, no longer remember what he had thought and known about himself as the ultimate and bitter truth.

15

He could feel hard pavement under him; the rest was obliterated. There was no single light to be seen anywhere; the stores and shops, which always kept a small light burning toward the rear of the merchandise, were tonight like oblongs of pitch.

He looked up. There were neither stars nor moon. Even the slight light of darkened skies was missing. He looked again toward the houses in search of a light, then realized why he could perceive no smallest trace of illumination under doors or windows: there were no doors or windows or shop interiors.

Had he passed out of the city's environs, gone beyond all buildings to open fields? He tried to pierce the darkness, but he could see no more of fields or trees than he had of houses or shops.

Then he felt his first fright: he could not see his feet or shoes, moving out so rapidly ahead of him. Nor his ankles, nor calves, nor knees nor thighs! He doubled over quickly. Yes, he could feel them, he was at least here.

He raised his hands, stretching his eyelids wide, rubbed his eyeballs with the heel of his palm until they pained. Ah yes, his eyes were still there, and his hands too. They could feel each other, know each other through the intimacy of touch.

He let out a scream, but it burst and shattered inside his bosom. Why had it taken him so long to understand? There were stars up in the sky, as bright as ever; the moon was at its third quarter, illuminating the few drifting clouds; the night lights were on in all the houses: in downstairs hallways, in children's rooms, at the rear of shops. There had been no failure in the lamps, the gas, the supply pipes, the night habits of the city.

The light had gone out inside his head.

For years he had said, "The night is just as bright as the day, only it's a different kind of light." But this kind of night, black in front of one's eyes, and black behind them, this sightlessness, was akin to death.

He turned around and quickened his step. He must get home, get into bed, get into sleep. There lay security. Then, when morning came, he would awaken to the bright sun, and all the world would be bathed in light. What matter if the night sun had set permanently inside his narrow-boundaried skull? A man was not supposed to have his own world of light, operating independently of the sun, moon and stars. A man was supposed to see by day and be blind by night. No great loss, no tragedy in being like other men!

He had been jogging along in a slow steady trot. He had walked the streets so often at night he knew every cobblestone, every crossing, every *place* and *pont* and gate. Surely instinct would carry him home now?

But he could recognize nothing. The hardness under his feet was unfamiliar. He could not tell whether he was going in the right direction or carrying himself farther and farther away. He continued to walk, faster and faster. He stumbled, fell. Only then did he realize how foolish he was. Why should he be terrorized, run as though his life were over if he did not reach home under cover of darkness? What did it matter where the light reached him: home, in bed, or here in this strange field or unfamiliar street? When the sun rose it would be light, light for him as it was for everyone else. Time enough to see when there was something to see.

He felt his senses slipping. Was it sleep? Unconsciousness? He knew only that for a considerable period there was a blank in which he felt and thought nothing. Then, slowly, feeling cramped, tired, he waked.

Now at last it was a different world, the morning for which he had waited. Outside he heard the beer wagon rumbling slowly over the pavements, the children chattering in their high voices on the way to school. Below him he could feel the heavy movements of fat Madame Lacouste as she cleaned her flat, her heavy heels shaking the building. And to his nostrils came the tantalizing odor of morning coffee. His lids still closed, he put his hands under him to push up from the strange floor. But this was not a bit of earth nor collection of irregular paving stones. This was his own bed.

He made his way to the windows, fumbled for the shade string, heard the blind roll upward. Only then did he open his eyes, having awaited the moment when the sun would flood over his face, hot and bright, wiping out the night terrors.

But there was no sun. The day, like the studio, was dark.

He could see nothing, not even the opposite side of the court. But why? Had he wakened too early? Was it still night? Had his ears deceived him? Had he been longing so hard for the day that he had imagined he heard the drays on the cobblestones, children chirruping on the way to school, Madame Lacouste cleaning her rooms below?

But if it were still night, what was that heat on his face, that burning sensation on his fingers as he held them on the open sill? The sun! It could be nothing else!

He sank down on his haunches below the window, lay there like a lumpy sack of flesh, all life drained out of him. To be blind in the night world, yes, that was akin to death. But to be blind in the world of light, for a painter not to be able to see that which exists in the universe, or that which he has recreated in microcosm on his canvas, that was death in the world of the living.

He pulled himself up slowly, found his way to the bed and fell across it, his feet and legs hanging over one side, his arms and head over the other.

When his mind slowly edged back to awareness he sensed that he had been lying here in his studio for a very long time. He tried to open his eyes but could not raise the lids; he tried to move his arms and then his legs but he was powerless to command them. During the past months, no matter how drunk or weak or sick he got, no matter how ardently he had reached out his arms and spirit for cessation there had been moments of clarity, rare moments when his alter ego, the life force, the other side of the shield cried out, struggling, fighting as best it could infinitely resourceful and patient, determined to save him; at the base of his brain had lain the assurance that the quieter, decent man, the inner spirit, was the true master of John Noble, and that the loud, dirty, foul-smelling mass of sick flesh was the slave who could be brought up short at any time and controlled. Now he sensed that it was too late; that this was the end for him, a final brief awakening inside his brain, a brain which no longer had the power to control the rest of his body, an awakening to give him the knowledge that the struggle was over. That he would lie here until somebody broke in and found his dead body.

That is, unless he could summon forth the strength to raise his exhausted body, to swing his legs out of the bed, to sit up, to stand on his feet, to pull himself back from oblivion and destruction, to breathe again, to walk with the feel of solid living earth beneath his feet and the heat of the living sun in his face, to stretch his arms upward and cry:

"I live!"

He felt all of his crumbling strength shoot together toward a focal core, and he knew himself to be out of the bed and standing on the cold wooden floor, trembling, faint, weak, feverish, hollow . . . but alive.

He heard footsteps mounting the stairs, then voices. Maud rushed in, followed by Alexander Harrison and George Luks. She ran across the room and put her arms about his waist.

"John, you're all right? I was in here an hour ago and couldn't feel your pulse. I thought you were dying. I ran and gathered up everyone I could . . ."

John walked slowly to the bed, then smiled up at Maud. His head turned from Harrison to Luks. There were more hurrying footsteps on the stairs and Gerald Addams came in with Dr. Bogard from the American hospital. The doctor crossed quickly to John, ran his hand over his forehead and down the long, near-white hair.

"You look awfully alive for a ghost," he said. "I thought I was being summoned to sign the death certificate, and here you are ready to take nourishment."

"I'll go get some milk," said Maud. "What else can he have, Doctor?"

Dr. Bogard said with a laugh, "I wouldn't give him a beefsteak, he doesn't look as though he has had solid food for a very long time. Start him with a little broth. Here, Mr. Noble, put on your robe and sit in this chair for a while until we get things organized."

John could find no words, nor wind to voice them if they had formulated. All he could do was to smile with a smile they had not seen since his collapse.

Maud stayed behind and nursed him, feeding him the medicine prescribed by Dr. Bogard. His friends came in now, took one quick look to reassure themselves, saw that he had let a barber shave him and cut his hair, that he was bathed and attired in a fresh flannel nightgown, that the studio was swept and scrubbed, and that he was stone sober, able to joke with them a little and tell them that he was feeling better every hour.

"Thank heavens it's over," they said in unison. "You'll never have any idea what you put us through!"

The Rev. Mr. Van Winkle brought a check from Wichita. "It's been a bad time, son. If ever I saw a man possessed by the devil, it was you. But now you are purged and well again and I know that you are going back to work."

"Thank you, sir. You have been wonderfully kind."

The minister smiled whimsically. "You will pay your medicine bill at the pharmacy first, won't you, and then the doctor? And your friends who have used their money to buy you food and take care of you?"

At the end of a week he took a carriage to the Bois to sit on a bench in the sun midst the crisp gray-clad nursemaids, as he had on his very first day in Paris. He settled his outstanding bills, then went to Cartier's where he selected an amethyst necklace. He invited Maud to dinner at the Brasserie Universelle, ordered champagne for her but drank nothing himself. When they had finished eating he presented her with the oblong velvet box, so like the one in which he had received his five twenty-dollar gold pieces for knocking out the California Crusher.

"This is a poor way to repay you, Maud, but take it as a token of how grateful I am."

Maud ran the necklace through her fingers, touching each of the purple stones in turn, but to John's surprise her lips were unsmiling.

"What's the matter, Maud, don't you like it? Maybe you would rather have had earrings or a brooch?"

"I don't like presents," she said; "the more beautiful and valuable they are, the less I like them."

"But why?"

"Because they're always farewell gifts. It's happened to me before."

"No, no, Maud, I'm not going away. There's nothing farewell about this."

Maud laid the strand of amethysts carefully into its box, snapped it closed and put the gift into her purse.

"George Luks and Harrison are going down to the Côte d'Azur tomorrow. I heard them talking about persuading you to come."

16

His room in the Hôtel Savournin had a balcony facing south, overlooking the Mediterranean. He spent his days there with the warm spring sun on his face, its heat and energy pouring into his body. By the fourth evening he felt willing to go down to the dining room with his companions. He rummaged around in his suitcase for a clean shirt and caught a sudden gleam of metal. He quickly picked up a pair of old work pants, fumbling with the belt and found a broken, blackened piece of string wrapped around the buckle. Aware only of the pulsation about his heart, he broke the string and drew forth his North Star.

He went out on the balcony, the silver star cradled securely in his hand, and sat on the railing. The sun was just sinking beyond Cap d'Antibes and covered the still water with a heavy layer of color from the lightest of rose through the deepest vermilion. He turned to look behind him at the Alpes Maritimes, their snow-clad peaks reflecting all the colors of the sea beneath, but stopped short. Standing in the patio overlooking the sea was a girl. The rich brown colors of her hair was fired with shafts of golden light; her eyes were so voluminously deep he felt he could fall headfirst into them, his whole bulky, awkward body be submerged in their warmth. Her beautifully shaped lips seemed to be excitingly alive. He reached out his hand, as if to touch her cheek, and heard Madame Matisse's voice as clearly as though she were standing beside him.

"Someday a woman will appear before you, your eyes will rest upon her, and your voice will say . . .

" 'This is she!' "

He returned to his room, shaved carefully, wet his hair and combed it, fitting it meticulously to the shape of his head. He retied the North Star about his neck, then took his best suit from the wardrobe, the dark blue flannel which the garçon had already pressed, donned a clean white shirt and spent considerable time selecting one of his long black flowing neckties.

The stairway turned a sharp angle to the left, bringing into view the heavy-beamed lobby and the girl seated in a chair by the window. His friends heard his footsteps descending the stairs; they came forward to greet him.

To Harrison, John said, "Who is that girl? Do you know her?"

"Yes, I've spoken to her a few times."

"Would you introduce me?"

Harrison searched his friend's face. "Of course, John."

The older man led John across the lobby to the girl, bowed gallantly, then said, "Mademoiselle Peiche, may I have the pleasure of presenting my confrere and countryman, Mr. John Noble."

Amelia acknowledged the introduction with a slight nod. John slipped into the chair beside her, unabashedly devouring her face with his eyes. Her glance seemed to seize him by the throat; he felt a compulsion to speak.

"Have you ever heard the fable of the White Buffalo and the warring Indian tribes?" he asked.

She did not reply.

"I first heard the story from an old Comanche chief, sitting before a night fire in the Osage mountains . . ."

Amelia listened to his tale without moving, then in precise English said, "I enjoyed your story, Mr. Noble, but I have no idea why you told it to me."

"Neither have I. It just came to my mind when I saw you. Will I see you again?"

"It's likely. I'm to be at the hotel for another week."

"No, no, I mean . . . just the two of us. Couldn't we take a walk tomorrow?"

She smiled slightly at the importuning quality in the voice of this tall, broad-shouldered man with the handsome large-featured face and long light-colored hair; feeling herself moved, bewildered.

". . . we'll walk up into the hills . . ."

"Very well," she heard herself reply. "Say two o'clock, after luncheon."

"Make it ten o'clock, after breakfast: that comes sooner."

He rose and left her without making any adieus, going quickly to the round table in the dining room where his friends were awaiting him.

"Did she agree to pose for you? Are you going to paint her?"

"No, I'm not going to paint her."

"Then what was all the fuss about?"

"I'm going to marry her."

His statement was received by the men with an outburst of incredulous laughter. He felt a pair of eyes burning deep into his back, turned, and saw Amelia standing in the doorway of the dining room. She gave no indication of having heard.

The morning was already warm when they left the hotel. Below, the Mediterranean lay quiet as a powder-blue lake, the shore line running in an arc to Nice and Monaco. They walked up the winding hill streets of Cagnes, past the narrow whitewashed houses, Moorish in architecture and designed to keep out the all-year sun. On the hilltop there was a church and a fourteenth-century castle, surrounded by cactus, pale mimosa and the heavy scent of orange blossoms.

Down from Grasse came the fragrance of acres of violets, roses and carnations, almost ready to be crushed for perfume: heady, insupportably sweet. Amelia walked with her head thrown a little to one side. She closed her eyes, took a deep breath. He watched the line of her abdomen and thighs, the firmness of her small breasts as she stretched to fill herself with the scent of the full-blown flowers; and with a painter's eye he knew that her body too was vital and magnificently proportioned.

She is pure essence, he told himself.

Amelia opened her eyes suddenly, catching him in full confession. Tiny spots of color mounted high in her cheeks, but she sought no escape.

"This secluded valley with its fragrance of the flowers," she murmured. "I could build a house right on this spot and live here forever."

"You're a romantic, aren't you, Amelia?"

"Incurably so."

"Incurably? You can't be very old . . . twenty? And I doubt if you've seen much hardship or ugliness. Would you continue to be romantic if life grew sordid around you, if you were forced to throw your illusions overboard, one by one, and nothing that you planned came right?"

"Being romantic has nothing to do with the external world; it has to do with one's nature."

"Are you in love, Amelia?"

"Yes . . ."

His heart plunged into his bowels.

". . . with life."

He began to breathe again.

"But not with any one man?"

"I'm engaged to an old friend in Strasbourg. He's a nice, well-to-do Alsatian who is going to inherit his father's business. He has always looked up to me as an artist, and tells me that I don't belong in a kitchen, but with a pen and brush. He's rather proud of that."

"Then why are you hesitating?"

"How did you . . . ? My mother tells me I don't know how lucky I am, especially as my family has lost so much money and they can give me only a small dowry. Now don't laugh at me, Mr. Noble, dowries are terribly important in Europe. But I just let things drift. I'm happy as long as I don't have to make a decision."

"Love isn't something you decide about, Amelia."

"I was referring to marriage."

". . . it either reaches out and catches you in a death grip, or it just isn't there at all."

"I thought you called me a romantic?"

He felt a warmth rising to his cheeks; he hadn't blushed for so long that it made him feel like a young boy again.

"How do you happen to be on the Côte d'Azur"? he asked.

"I was on a vacation at Cannes with my aunt and uncle, and when we were taking a trip to Nice I saw this little village perched on top of the hill. I decided to come here for a few days to paint. My aunt and uncle did not like the quiet, and so they went back to Cannes."

Her voice had a vibrant, surcharged quality, as though it were a safety valve for a great compressed spirit.

"And you've been happy, all by yourself?"

"Completely. I get up early, paint from the top of the hill until noon, come back for lunch, and then return to my painting until sunset. The only one I've spoken to all week is your friend, Mr. Harrison. He said he was intrigued by my enthusiasm and hard work."

"Did you study in Strasbourg?"

"Only painting china dishes."

They had reached the top of the hill. He opened the box he was carrying, took out a small canvas and began sketching quickly, not even realizing that this was the first time he had worked in months, or that he had been convinced he would never set brush to canvas again. Amelia sat slightly behind him, watching him hurl himself at his canvas with a torrential force which overwhelmed her.

An hour went by in silence, two hours. Then she saw the picture begin to take shape. She who worships beauty was deeply moved by this strange male hurricane who had the power to create beauty almost at will. She understood that he was the first real artist she had ever met; and in some dim fashion knew that she would never paint again.

He stopped work abruptly, turned and saw what was in her eyes.

"I have never seen anyone work the way you do," she said. "You paint as though you were in confession, seeking absolution from your sins."

"Put into more Protestant terms, I would say it is a reaffirmation of faith."

"In God?"

He quivered, as though he had been struck across the face by a fine reed.

"You believe in God, don't you, Amelia?"

"Oh yes, with all my heart."

He thought, God is in her. I must never let her go.

17

They set out early the next morning with a basket lunch and climbed steeply upward to the Grande Corniche, the road which Napoleon had built to conquer Italy. They found a cove with a running stream, and here Amelia quickly spread the crisp white tablecloth on the grass, setting out the silverware, buttered French bread, the roasted chicken, fruit and pâtisseries. She worked with sure, graceful movements. John never took his eyes off her.

"You're indefatigable, aren't you?"

"I suppose so."

"That's good. You'll need to be."

"Stop talking in riddles, and have a piece of this chicken. What do you like, white meat, dark . . . ?"

"You know, Amelia, some people stop existing at the outside circumference of their skin. Others, like you, and my mother, you reach out . . . project . . . embrace people, make them feel warm and friendly, happy to be alive."

"What is your mother like, John?"

"They say about my mother in Wichita that she will run a full block so she can get on the streetcar first and pay everybody else's fare."

Encouraged by Amelia's quick, appreciative smile, he went back to his earliest memories and told her the story of the Noble family from the time his mother and father left Todds Point after their marriage and went west to the tiny gathering of huts on the vast Kansas prairie. It was the first time he had ever talked of his family's life on the plains, and he found the rich, homely truth infinitely more colorful than the tall tales he had fabricated in Paris.

Then, in turn, he wanted to hear about Amelia. ". . . every little detail, all the things I missed by not knowing you during the years you were growing up."

There could be no doubting the sincerity of his tone. Amelia spoke slowly at first, stumbling a little; for her too it was the first time she had shared these intimacies, and gropingly she perceived that this exchange was a subtle form of mating.

"Have you ever been to Strasbourg, John? It's a delightful town on the main road between France, Germany and Switzerland. The river Ill flows through it, and there are beautiful quais. We used to have an apartment near the Orangerie, the beautiful park where everyone comes to hear the music in the open air. There is a lovely terrace where we sat and ordered hot chocolate with whipped cream and Kugelhopf. Then there's the Kaiser's Palast; in order to get to the Palast you have to take off your shoes and put on huge brown felt slippers. My sister May and I used to slide through the corridors when the guards weren't looking."

"Tell me about your parents, Amelia."

"Father owned a small bank. He was a happy, trusting and generous man, very optimistic, in contrast to my mother, who was quite pessimistic. We children had only to wish for something and, as if by magic, there it would be. He was a very romantic-looking man with fair skin and light curly hair. He loved life. It was a real adventure to go out with him, and he took me everywhere. He understood music better than he did painting but he used to buy me prints of famous paintings for my birthdays. His greatest joy came from reading. He taught me Italian so I could read the works of Leopardi and D'Annunzio, and English so I could read Shakespeare."

"And your mother?"

"She is beautiful, with large brown eyes and a lovely figure. Never in her life has she touched cosmetics. She was very happy in her home life, but serious-minded and very conservative. I was allowed to go into the drawing room only to practice my piano and on those rare occasions when the family went in, we had to put covers over the silk and velvet chairs before using them, and walk around the rugs.

"We were very comfortable while Father was alive, with two maids. We even had special linen just for breakfast: the napkins and tablecloth were white and blue, the butter and honey were served in separate silver dishes, the cocoa had whipped cream floating on top, the croissants were hot and crisp. On Sundays we always got up at five: Mother would put on one of her silk or velvet dresses. My sister and I dressed alike, usually in red. After church we would go to the Orangerie for Kugelhopf with large raisins and almonds. Then in the evening friends would come in for supper, oh, many friends, twice as many as Mother expected . . ."

There was a note of nostalgia, almost of sadness, in her voice.

"We still have the house. But Mother seems like a person reluctantly alive, with Father gone. The house is quiet."

"Do you think your family is going to like me?"

"Like you?" For the first time she was startled. "Why? Were you planning to visit Strasbourg?"

"Most assuredly. For years I've been wanting to eat Kugelhopf on the terrace of the Orangerie."

On the way back to the hotel they stopped at the home of Auguste Renoir, who had answered John's letter with a cordial invitation to drop in to tea. John had often stood before Renoir's paintings unable to believe that any one human being could create so much imperishable beauty. But now he and Amelia found this seventy-year-old artist in a wheelchair in the garden, crippled by the rheumatism which had plagued him for twenty years, his fingers so stiff they could not hold a brush. Yet he was painting as they walked toward him on the garden path, painting with a brush strapped to his wrist, his face deeply lined, tortured by the pain . . . painting warm glowing female nudes on a grassy bank, surrounded by gaily colored flowers that seemed so real and living that one wanted to reach out and smell them. A protesting cry was wrung from John's innards:

"Why paint any more, Monsieur Renoir? Why torture yourself?"

Renoir turned his old man's face to them, the eyes sweet, even innocent.

"The pain passes, the beauty remains."

John and Amelia gazed into each other's eyes, a look deep and probing.

"A man could build a life on that," John said quietly, and in Amelia's steady look he thought he saw assent.

They were riding along the coast on their way to Cap d'Antibes on saddle horses John had rented. He reined in his horse, putting out a hand to restrain Amelia's rather nervous animal.

"Your friends warned me against you last night," said Amelia. "They told me you were a serious drinker. What did they mean by that?"

Her tone told him that she had no concept of what drinking meant, had probably never seen a really drunken man. He was determined to be honest with her.

"They meant . . . that sometimes . . . when I have been unhappy . . . I have drunk too continuously."

"But it's all over now?" Her voice had the solicitude of a mother asking after a small boy's stomach-ache, and he knew that she was hopeful for his sake rather than her own.

"Yes, Amelia, it's all over now."

They had reached the outer tip of the Cap. John tied the horses to the slim pine trees, set out his easel and began to work. The motif of his picture was a sun, a lopsided sworling mass of Midi heat and light, as seen imperfectly by the human eye; a blue sky, the sky of antiquity which one sees at night; the sea, Mare Nostrum, the mother of all seas; the sail, with a barely discernible ship beneath it, representing all ships, and the external hills, the solid mass that evolved from what once had been all whorling liquid sun, all blue sky, all fathomless liquid sea; the solid sand onto which life had crawled, and where man now lived; sun, sea, sky, sail, land; not all independent, separate, living apart and alone, but all one, indistinguishable parts of a whole.

At noon he stopped work to have lunch and lie on the pine needles with her hand in his, looking across the water toward Africa and the Near East. Indicating the half-completed canvas, Amelia observed:

"You're deeply religious by nature, aren't you, John?"

"Religious! Certainly not. I haven't been inside a church in years."

"But the things you try to paint are essentially spiritual."

"All painting is spiritual in nature, even the ugliest and most sordid subjects. All I want is to feel deeply about simple things. You don't see any seraphim floating on that canvas, do you?"

"Your sun, the sea and the sail, that could be your way of painting the Father, the Son, and the Holy Ghost."

He flushed.

"Don't read fairy stories into my pictures, Amelia. I'm interested in the graphic arts; I leave fiction writing to my friend Dave Leahy of the Wichita *Eagle*."

He saw that his rough tone had hurt her, for she was looking away, and her eyes were clouded. He put his hand on her arm, gently. She turned back to him.

"I'm sorry, Amelia."

"My parents were both deeply religious. I too went through a very devout period: during the first year of my communion, when I was interned in the covent, my fervor was so great that I would kneel by my bed saying my rosary for hours at night, and kissed the floor in penitence. When I was at home during vacation I got up at five in the morning to attend an early mass. Just going to the Cathedral was a thrilling experience for me. It was so majestic, so dark, so mysterious. I would've given everything in life to become a nun in a long white veil kneeling in the beautiful chapel with the flowers, incense and music."

She sighed deeply. "I look back on it as a beautiful period."

"And then?"

"Then, like all ecstasies, it passed. I always had to keep things happening. In Strasbourg, John, when a girl finished school she was ready for marriage. Only when I finished school I wasn't ready. Life was wonderful and noble, and I wanted to play a heroic part in it. But just exactly what that would be, I didn't know. And my mother . . ."

"She wanted you to be practical and marry your young man. Did you have many romances?"

". . . no . . . none. I never went out unless chaperoned. At the dancing classes we would sit with our mothers on one side of the room, with the university boys on the other. After class a young man would escort me home, and my mother as well."

"Were you so carefully chaperoned that you couldn't even get yourself kissed?"

"Oh, the boys stole a kiss once or twice in a fleeting sort of fashion." Her face was serious and a little puzzled. "Tell me, John, is a kiss really as exciting as the romantic novelists describe it?"

He hesitated for a moment before answering.

"Truthfully, Amelia, I've never found it to be a soul-shattering experience . . ."

The words failed, the viscera spoke. He took Amelia in his arms, lifted her up against him and kissed her passionately on the lips. They clung to each other for a long time. Then they stood glaze-eyed, a little frightened and considerably in awe of each other. John was the first to break the silence.

"Anyway, now we know."

The week passed quickly. In the evenings they sat close to each other on a big leather sofa before the log fire while she mended his ties and cleaned the finger marks off his Stetson. He had resisted all previous attempts at domesticity, but now he even enjoyed the joshing he took from his friends about it. The days they spent searching out new and exciting places to paint. He could not seem to get enough of her company, for each moment revealed an additional delight in her nature: she was gentle, yet with a fierce pride; she was completely self-reliant, yet never egocentric, always interested in other people. There was little that she missed; he was constantly astonished by her hypersensitivity and her devotion to beauty in any form or fragment. When she exclaimed, "How lovely that is!" her eyes sparkled and her whole figure trembled with joy.

On the last morning of Amelia's stay they walked over the hills to the sun-drenched town of Grasse, where they passed a perfume factory with its shop attached. He took Amelia inside, buying her bottles of Rue de la Paix and Après l'Ondée.

"John, you mustn't get me so many."

"I'd like to buy you the world."

"Is it for sale?"

He stopped short, put the bottles back on the counter and burst into delighted laughter.

"I sounded just like your well-to-do Alsatian friend, didn't I? No, Amelia, I don't want their old world, it isn't good enough. I'd like to create a whole new world for you."

On the ride home he was uncommunicative. Back at their hotel he placed her belongings in the rear of the carriage, then lifted her up to the driver's seat. She was touched by his thoughtfulness and attention, but what was she to say against his heavy dejection as he clicked the reins and started down the hill?

When her train came into the station he took her to her compartment, kissed her moodily on the cheek and walked away. Sitting at the window of the compartment, Amelia felt let down. Whenever she had gone to see a friend off, she had stood on the platform waving her handkerchief and smiling broadly until the train had disappeared from sight. But these Americans, what strange creatures they were! As the train left, she recalled her first impression of him, of how tender and humble he had been, with a simplicity that touched her, and her own feeling that she wanted to do things for this tall, strong-looking man because he had seemed so forlorn, so lost. This was probably the last she would ever see of Mr. John Noble of Wichita, Kansas.

Back in his room, John sat forlornly before the little hotel desk. He had said to his friends on the night he met Amelia, "I'm going to marry her." But now as he gazed at the photograph he had persuaded her to leave behind, he asked himself how such a thing would be possible. What kind of life could he give Amelia?

Years before, while working in George Israel's studio, he had looked into a mirror and penetrated to the basic truth about himself. The hour had come for another such recounting, only this time it was infinitely more important: for there was something crucial at stake, the happiness of the girl he loved.

What had he to offer a woman by way of permanence? In marriage one slept at night, and worked during the day, ate breakfast in the morning, and supper when it grew dark. One established a routine, settled down in one place, begat children, walked with them in the park on Sunday. The picture of the Matisse family flashed into his mind; Matisse working constantly, brilliantly at his painting, but still having enough energy and tenderness to be a good husband and father. But could he live that way, alternating as he did between misery and exultation, living in a world of his own creation, moody, erratic, fluid of emotion, never knowing what to expect of himself next, racked by doubt and indecision, putting everything vital into his work, leaving little for love, for marriage.?

Amelia's eyes seemed to gaze back at him from her picture, clear and sparkling and intensely confident. After all, she was no shallow doll. Amelia was strong; she was flexible; she was wise as the best of women are wise. She loved painting and knew how it tore the heart out of a man to create even the tiniest fragment of beauty. If Amelia loved him she would take the good and endure the bad; whatever adversity she could not conquer she would outlive.

18

He arrived in Strasbourg on the night train, his clothes dusty and wrinkled. The carriage driver took him to a hotel where he left instructions that he be wakened at six. He asked that his boots be shined, but forgot all about the condition of his suit. He slept fitfully and was out of bed at the first step of the bellboy in the long corridor.

The sun was just edging above the horizon when he emerged from the hotel. The city was sound asleep. He walked along a parklike avenue under chestnut trees in full bloom and found his way to Amelia's house. He rang the bell, waited, rang it again, then pushed it hard and continuously. At last a sleepy-eyed maid opened the door the barest crack.

"Say, where is everybody? I've been ringing this bell for over a half hour. Where is everybody?"

"Sleeping."

"Amelia still sleeping? Go up and tell her I'm here."

"Who is you that's here?"

"Oh, I forgot. It's John Noble. How about letting me in?"

The maid stepped aside, though reluctantly, and John managed to squeeze himself into the hallway.

"I don't like to wake her now, Mr. Noble. It's not seven o'clock yet."

"How long is she going to sleep?"

"Well, I'll tell you, Mr. Noble, maybe three, maybe four hours yet."

"Three or four hours!" He took off his Stetson, handed it to the maid. "Which is her room?"

"The one just on the right side of the stairs, Mr. Noble. But I don't think . . ."

"You just go back to your breakfast. I'll be all right here."

He called from the bottom of the stairway:

"Amelia! It's John. Come on down."

His words echoed up the stair well and along the top hall. He moved up a few steps at a time, calling, "Amelia, wake up!"

He reached the top of the stairs and knocked on Amelia's door. A very sleepy voice answered.

"Go away, please."

"Do your sleeping at night, Amelia. This is morning now. The whole town is awake. The streets are crowded with people. It's me, Amelia. Wake up."

There was a brief silence, then he heard Amelia getting out of bed.

"John, is that really you? What are you . . . doing in Strasbourg? And at this hour?"

"Hurry up, Amelia, it's almost noon. I've been waiting for hours."

"John, please go downstairs. Tell the maid to give you coffee. I'll be down right away."

He went down to the dining room. It was furnished in carved oak with a large grandfather's clock in one corner. The maid brought him a cup of coffee with some rolls and honey. He ate hungrily, turning his head every few moments toward the door. It was a full hour before Amelia emerged. She was dressed in a beautiful blue negligee with a blue ribbon tying up her curls at the back of her head. John rose eagerly and took her hand in his.

"Amelia, after you left Cagnes, I just couldn't stay any longer. I couldn't even think, let alone paint. . . . Amelia, you're not listening. Aren't you glad to see me?"

"Yes, John, I'm very glad to see you. But why must it be seven o'clock in the morning? Heaven only knows what my mother will say."

John pulled out a chair for her at the table. "Seven o'clock isn't early. Why, out West, women get up at the crack of dawn. My mother used to grab her double-barreled Winchester and shoot game for her breakfast before the sun even started to rise over the horizon."

"But, John, this is not out West."

Mrs. Peiche entered the dining room, followed by Amelia's sister. Both wore negligees, and the mother was in a state of shock. She was a woman of about fifty with a fine satiny skin which she had bequeathed to Amelia, and bold streaks of gray running through her hair. She was of medium size, but at this particular moment she looked bristling and formidable.

"Amelia, I take it this is your American painter friend from Cagnes?"

"Yes, Mother. May I present Mr. John Noble. John, this is my mother, and my sister May."

Mrs. Peiche's grim expression had struck John dumb; all he could do was blink and nod.

"And to what do we owe the pleasure of this nocturnal visit, Mr. Noble?"

"Nocturnal? That means night, doesn't it? This is the daytime. Look, the sun is out." He walked to the window, pushed aside the crisp white curtains, wrinkling them in his pawlike grasp. When he looked back to Mrs. Peiche he saw that she was still waiting for an answer. "Well, I . . . I came to marry your daughter."

Mrs. Peiche stiffened, looked quickly at Amelia, but got no help from that source.

"How interesting, Mr. Noble. Then am I to take it by indirection that you are in love with Amelia?"

"Certainly! Didn't she tell you?"

"Now, John, how could I have told anyone," protested Amelia, "when you never even told me?"

Mrs. Peiche went to the window and straightened out her wrinkled curtain. Only young May seemed to be enjoying herself.

"Suppose we sit down and have breakfast like sane people," said Mrs. Peiche. "Then, afterwards, we can talk this over quietly."

"That's a great idea," boomed John gratefully. "We'll have breakfast, then you can dress and we'll go down to the City Hall."

Amelia's eyes opened wider than he had ever seen them before.

"City Hall . . . Why, John, what are you talking about?"

"Marriage, of course. You yourself said it isn't noon, it's only eight o'clock. We have plenty of time to catch the afternoon train back to Paris."

Amelia and her mother exchanged hopeless glances. Then Amelia said in a very firm tone:

"John, I haven't yet said I would marry you. But even if I had, it would take a long time. First the banns have to be published. Then the engagement cards have to be printed. We have to reserve the Cathedral. Besides, there's my trousseau to be got together. That will take many weeks. And the plans for the wedding party."

"Who ever heard of making all this fuss? What do you want printed engagement cards for? And that Cathedral, now. That's just a lot of unnecessary bother."

"John, all my life I've wanted to be married in the Cathedral. No one's going to talk me out of it. What's more, it's going to take weeks of sewing and fitting to get my wedding gown just right. Besides, I must say, this is the strangest proposal any girl ever had."

"I can't push you around like a dumb longhorn, can I?" There was admiration in John's voice. "That's good. I wouldn't marry any woman who wasn't my equal."

"Just a moment now," said Mrs. Peiche. "As of this instant, you're not marrying anybody. First I want some information about you. Are you a Catholic?"

"Catholic? No."

"Have you ever been baptized?"

"If you haven't been baptized, John," broke in Amelia, "you can't be married in the Cathedral."

"I don't intend to be married in the Cathedral anyway."

"I'm glad to hear you say that, Mr. Noble," replied Mrs. Peiche acidly. "That means we will just have to get along without an American painter in our family. Besides, Amelia is engaged to a very sound and prosperous businessman here in Strasbourg."

"She loves me."

"That is a matter which my daughter and I will debate in private," declared Mrs. Peiche; "that is, assuming we are going to get any more privacy. Don't you think you might at least tell us something about yourself, Mr. Noble: who you are and where you come from?"

Mrs. Peiche's manner threw John completely. He put on his most disarming smile.

"Why, of course, Mrs. Peiche. I was born out in the wilderness, on the Santa Fe trail. Everyone had to carry a six-shooter then, even when we went to a dance. Each man made his own law. The strong lived, the weak died. That was the West for you. They built cities overnight. They punched cattle without sleeping for weeks at a time. They're giants. Why, I remember living with a bear once out in the mountains . . ."

Amelia's sister, her eyes wide, asked, "You mean a little bear?"

"Little bear?" He leaped to his feet. "Why, that fella stood up this high." He lifted his hand several feet above his head.

There was a gasp and then an icy silence from Mrs. Peiche. Amelia suggested, "Mother, don't you think we might all go into the drawing room?"

She rose quickly, went across the hall and moved back the big sliding doors. The drawing room was olive green, with black furniture, velvet- and satin-covered chairs, and a beautiful parquet floor. The pièce de résistance was the long, handsomely carved sofa which had been preserved over the years with meticulous care. No one was trusted to touch The Sofa, as it was known in the family, except Mrs. Peiche; in her mind its proud bourgeois respectability stood as the foundation stone of the family fortune.

She expected that once John lowered his bulk carefully, tenderly, onto The Sofa he would realize how solid and irreproachable was this family he was intending to marry into. Unfortunately John knew nothing of the place this heirloom occupied in their minds. He dropped heavily onto The Sofa, sprawling his large frame across it with his knees crossed, and with his elbow pushing its white lace doily askew. Mrs. Peiche was now certain that this man was not merely an American, but a native American Indian.

John resumed the account of his background.

"When I was in the Panhandle, the only hotel there had one sleeping room upstairs; they'd string wires overhead and then drape blankets between the beds for privacy. When you paid for your bed the manager told you he'd have to rent the other half in case he needed the space. Well, I woke up in the middle of the night, seeing an enormous fellow standing next to my bed, with spurs on his boots, two revolvers and a flock of knives in his belt. You know, he didn't even bother to take off his hat! He just pulled down the covers and jumped into bed with me. Every time I moved the other fellow moved too, and I could feel a pistol or a knife sticking into my ribs. Oh, he was a killer all right. I knew that once I fell asleep I'd be murdered in cold blood. At dawn the killer climbed out of bed. He saw me staring at him and said, 'Sorry if I disturbed you last night, friend; I guess I was a little under the weather. I don't generally go to bed with all my clothes on.' Do you know who it was, Amelia?"

"No," replied Amelia bluntly, wondering why he felt it necessary to tell these preposterous stories, "who was it?"

"Temple Houston, son of Sam Houston. You've heard of Texas? Well, Sam was the first president of Texas. Now, was there anything else you wanted to know about me, Mrs. Peiche? I'll be glad to tell you everything I can remember."

Mrs. Peiche asked the maid to summon Amelia's uncle. He

was an expensively dressed, chunky, bristling man with stiff waxed mustaches. He gave John's hand one abrupt shake and then tossed it aside.

"An artist, eh? No, no, Amelia, you must never marry an artist. Nothing personal meant, you understand, Mr. Noble."

John nodded that he understood.

"Artists are always poor. I invited one to come for supper. When I met him later, and reproached him, he said he couldn't come because he didn't have any decent clothes. When I insisted that he should have written, he said he couldn't because he didn't have any money for postage stamps. Is that the kind of life you want to lead, Amelia, being unable to write me that you can't come to supper because you have no money for stamps?"

Amelia rushed to the rescue.

"But Mr. Noble is an American, Uncle, and in America everyone is rich."

"That's right, Uncle," agreed John, "even the starving artists."

Uncle's mustaches began to sag.

"But I don't understand . . . how can a starving artist . . . be rich . . . ?"

John pulled a huge wad of bank notes from his trouser pocket. "You've heard about the streets in America, how they're paved with gold?"

". . . yes . . . I heard rumors . . ."

"Well, when an artist is hungry, he just gets his pickax, goes into the street and digs up a few gold bricks."

May, who was greatly taken by John, shattered the confused silence that followed by asking:

"Mr. Noble, how did you begin to paint?"

For a moment he was amused at the question, and inclined to toss it off with a light quip. Then all the deep, indigenous conflicts of the artist flooded over him, the hours and the years of work and struggle before a naked canvas. The furrows deepened in his wide brow, and he turned so that he could stare sightlessly out the open window.

"How does anyone begin anything? You are born for certain things, you grow up and enter those things, and that's all you know. You find yourself in the middle of some distant, inexpressible longing that gradually begins to press on you. You are sad at first, because inside your heart you feel something stirring, though you don't know what it is. You know that it's got to come out of you if you want to live at all. And at first you don't know how to let it come out. There are so many things that you begin to sense, so many things that happen and have strange meanings, but which you can't explain. It's as if a dam had been thrown across the seething river within you, and unless you find the way to tear down that dam and let the river gush out, you'd go mad."

Mrs. Peiche was stirred by the ringing sincerity in his voice.

"What do you want to paint? What sort of subjects?"

The emotion had by now drained out of him. He felt a little sickish at having exposed himself.

"I want to paint the nothingness of things."

"Nothingness?" The uncle studied his face. "But who will buy nothingness?"

"I don't know, Mr. Peiche. I paint what I must paint, and not what I think other people will buy."

John gazed intently at Amelia, saying to her, inside his head:

Don't believe it, darling. What I want to paint is not nothingness, but everythingness, the whole answer and solution to the riddle of life and death. I can't ever explain it to you, but stay by my side, and one day you'll understand because there it will be, up on the canvas, unmistakably, and caught forever.

Then, feeling that he had behaved badly, he made retribution by agreeing to return to Paris and have the Rev. Mr. Van Winkle baptize him.

19

Back in Paris he bought himself two suits, one a blue serge, the other a gray Irish homespun with small green dots. He also shopped for new shoes, white shirts and black Windsor ties. On the way home he stopped in at a barbershop.

"Give me the works: shave, haircut, singe, shampoo . . ."

An hour later the barber straightened him up in the chair.

He stopped next at the concierge's apartment on the ground floor of 7 Rue Belloni, gave the concierge a five-franc note and asked him to please bring up the iron tub in which his children were bathed, and several buckets of hot water.

He was large and the tub was small; he had to fold himself at various angles and scrub one area before he went on to the next. He had dried himself with the rough turkish towel and stood naked on the little rug, his skin glowing, when suddenly he glanced down and noticed the grimy string around his neck. It did not seem fitting to be baptized in this now wire-hard, black string. He cut the end just below the knot, so that he could use it again, removed the North Star and dropped the piece of string into the hot water of the tub. The string disintegrated completely; nothing could be seen of it except black blobs in the water.

"I knew it!" he exclaimed aloud. "For years I've been telling people that soap and water are harmful. I'm just lucky it wasn't me that fell apart like that in the tub."

An hour later, dressed in his new finery, he opened the box which had come from Wichita during his absence. He took out of it a gleaming white Stetson which his mother had sent. He placed the hat with an almost conservative rigidity straight on top of his head.

A few moments later he was walking up the street to the Episcopal church, a modest building set far back from the pavement. He mounted the short stone steps. In front of the small arched doorway he hesitated for one moment, the thought passing across his mind: Should I really do this thing? After all, baptism is irrevocable.

But he knew it was idle speculation. He took a last pull at his cigarette, flipped it into the street and entered. It was cool inside, and the light coming through the stained-glass windows was soft and mellow, illuminating the narrow aisles and pews. After a moment the Rev. Mr. Van Winkle came in from a side door and walked up to the altar. John called out:

"Rev. Van Winkle, I want to see you for a moment."

His trail-herder voice hit the wooden beams behind the altar, bounced back and forth between the walls and finally shattered noisily in the four corners. The Rev. Mr. Van Winkle whirled about, saw who it was, and came quickly down the center aisle.

"Why, John, it's good to see you again."

"Rev. Van Winkle," said John huskily, "I want to be baptized."

The minister blinked the lids over his big, soft, black eyes.

"John, I'm happy. I can't tell you how happy. This repays me for the nights I've pursued you to the far ends of Paris. When do you want to begin your studies?"

"Studies? I want to be baptized today. Right now."

"But, John, you can't be serious." Shock and gentle protestation were in the minister's voice.

"Of course I'm serious."

"What is your desperate hurry, John?"

"I've got to catch the next train back to Strasbourg. I'm getting married."

The Rev. Mr. Van Winkle studied John's face. "Then

there's no need to rush things, my son. Marriage lasts for a lifetime . . ."

"Mine will," interrupted John.

". . . if the girl is the right sort, and really loves you, she'll wait for you. Does your family know about her?"

"Yes, I wrote my mother several weeks ago. Aw, come now, let's not make this any more complicated than it has to be."

"Look, John, you go home and get yourself a night's sleep, and we'll talk about it again tomorrow. I couldn't baptize you today; for one thing, we have no witnesses."

"Witnesses? That's easy. I'll go out and lasso the first Frenchmen that pass."

The Rev. Mr. Van Winkle had the strongest disinclination to perform any holy ritual over John in his excited state of mind, yet he knew that John would never leave the church until he was baptized.

"All right, John, I'll christen you, but first you must give me one assurance . . ."

"Anything, Reverend, anything."

". . . that this is a good girl. From a respectable family."

Suddenly all the noise and bounce and presumption drained out of John. He stood humbly before the minister, and his voice was quiet.

"That much I assure you, Reverend. She comes from a fine Strasbourg family. I've been in their home. No family could be more decent or respectable. Amelia is the most wonderful person I've ever known, like my mother, really. She should never marry me, I'm not good enough to polish her boots, but with her by my side I know I can do good work. You'll see that I will, sir."

The Rev. Mr. Van Winkle knew that John was speaking the truth; his humility, his ardent love, which glowed in the darkness of the church, all these reassured him.

At the railroad station he learned that there would be a two-hour wait before the next train left for Strasbourg. He sat with his face in the sun at the café, drinking innumerable cups of coffee while the saucers piled up before him. After what seemed an interminable delay he boarded the train and found his way to a second-class compartment. The train was a local, and it would be many hours before he reached Strasbourg. After the conductor took his ticket John leaned his broad shoulders against the windowpane, let his back sag a little, and gazed out the window. Soon they had left Paris behind and were riding through the factory district, then the suburbs with the houses surrounded neatly by hedges and trees, then the farmlands with the grazing cows. He tilted the immaculately white sombrero over his face; the train's clicking became rhythmical, and he fell into a deep sleep.

He was wakened by somebody shaking his arm. He realized that he must have slept for a considerable time because the lights had been turned on and the compartment was now filled with its component of eight passengers. Over everything was the pleasant, warm odor of worn plush and the food that his fellow passengers were eating from the packages on their laps. Once again he felt someone shaking his arm.

"Pardonnez-moi, monsieur, but is this yours?"

John stared dumbly at the paper for a moment and then recognized it.

"Yes, yes, it fell from my pocket. Monsieur, do you know what this paper is? It's my christening. What do you think of that, monsieur? I was just baptized this afternoon."

The well-dressed Frenchman with a thin dark face and thin dark hair was quietly amused.

"I would say it was a bit late in life, monsieur."

"Well, frankly, I would never have thought of it myself. But my girl's family, they thought we couldn't be married without it. I'm on my way to Strasbourg right now to get married. Were you ever married, monsieur?"

"Mais oui, monsieur, I have been married for seven years." He rubbed his wedding ring on his coat to brighten it. "Is this not a beautiful ring, monsieur? My wife and I exchanged them at our marriage."

Suddenly John awoke completely.

"Monsieur, tell me quickly. Does the man . . . am I supposed . . . a ring for your wife when you get married?"

"Mais certainment, monsieur," replied the Frenchman with an astonished tone. "You buy the ring. You carry it in your vest pocket. At the end of the wedding the priest takes the ring from you and puts it on her finger. Every man must buy his wife a wedding ring, monsieur."

John shook his head, dazed and a little angry.

"First I had to be christened! Now I have to buy a ring!" He jumped out of his seat.

At that moment the engineer applied the train brakes, and John was lurched back into the seat again. The conductor called out the name of the small town.

"Monsieur, tell me quickly, how far out of Paris are we?"

The Frenchman took a heavy gold watch from his pocket, studied it intently, then replied:

"We are exactly three hours and forty-three minutes out of Paris."

John climbed to his feet, exclaimed, "All right. I'll go back and get a ring. But, so help me, this is the last thing I'm going to do!"

He climbed several flights of narrow wooden stairs and then knocked on a dirty white door in the Impasse du Maine.

"Maud! Maud! Let me in."

A hoarse and sleepy voice asked from inside, "Who's there?"

"It's me, John, for heaven's sake, let me in. I'm in trouble."

He waited for a moment while he heard her get into her robe and high-heeled mules. Then she opened the door. He went in and closed it behind him.

"You're drunk," she said.

"Maud, I'm not drunk. I've never been more sober in my life."

The strange quality in his voice made her look at him for the first time.

"Why, John, you are sober. And where did you get those new clothes?" She came close to him, sniffing at the now faint scent of the barber's eau de cologne. "I can hardly believe it: you smell as though you've had a bath."

"Maud, I want you to do something for me. Right away. Will you get dressed and go shopping? I need a wedding ring."

Maud suddenly stood still, peering up intently into his face.

"John, you're not serious?"

"I'm getting sick of that question," he bellowed. "Every time I want to do anything, whether it's get baptized or get a ring or get married, people tell me I'm not serious! Maud, will you please take these five hundred francs and go out and buy a wedding ring?"

She stood quiet for a moment, a quizzical uncertain expression lighting her features.

"Please, hurry," pleaded John, "I have to get back to Strasbourg as soon as possible."

Maud was disappointed, but not for long.

"I thought it couldn't be me. All right, at what store did you buy the engagement ring?"

"What are you talking about?" He flipped his cigarette out the window to the street below. "What do you mean by engagement ring?"

"John Noble, do you mean to stand there and tell me you

174

don't know the difference between an engagement ring and a wedding ring? How do you know she's going to marry you if you haven't become engaged? Don't you know you have to give a girl two rings before you can get married?"

"Two rings?" he whispered hoarsely.

"Of course; the first ring is to make the engagement official. Then when you are getting married, you put the wedding ring on her finger next to the engagement ring. That makes two rings."

"I'm not going to stand for it," he shouted. "First it's one ring, now it's two rings! That's your confounded European way of doing things. In America a woman considers herself lucky if she gets a marriage certificate!"

"No, John, it's the same all over the world. If you love this girl, whoever she is, you'll want her to have an engagement ring. It will cost you about five hundred francs. And a good wedding ring will cost you about another hundred."

He took out his billfold and thrust the money into her hands.

"All right, take it. But I wouldn't let you do this to me if I wasn't in such a hurry."

When Maud left he began pacing up and down in front of the open windows, smoking. He figured it would take her fifteen minutes to find the two rings and bring them back. By the time he had finished a full pack of cigarettes he realized that several hours must have passed. He had a strong impulse to go out and look for Maud, but he knew that this would be hopeless. At length, exhausted from his pacing, he threw himself down on her bed. In a moment he was asleep.

When he awakened the windows were already dark. Maud was standing over him, shaking two little boxes in front of his face.

"John, here's your two rings. The engagement ring cost me four hundred francs, the wedding ring cost sixty. Don't you think that was a bargain? And I didn't let them fool me, either, I bought the two best rings in all Paris."

He sprang up, went to the window, and saw that it was indeed night.

"Where the devil have you been for the past eight hours?"

"I've been shopping," she replied, a little breathlessly. "I must have been in every jewelry store in Paris. Some of them turned their noses up when I walked in. But when I put your five hundred francs down on the counter, you should have seen those sales people bring their noses down!"

"Thanks, Maud. I've got to get to the station now."

He put the two boxes in his pocket.

"Aren't you even going to open them? Don't you want to see what I got you for your money?"

"All rings look alike."

20

When he returned to Strasbourg he learned that Mrs. Peiche had mailed out white announcement cards with a golden border. He was relieved; this could only mean that Amelia's mother was going to oppose him no further. He engaged the most imposing suite at the leading hotel, and this, added to the two beautiful rings Maud had selected, finally reassured Amelia's uncle and Mrs. Peiche that in America even starving artists were rich. He went with Amelia to the Cathedral where he signed a statement relating to children. Then the Monseigneur opened his enormous marriage ledger and wrote down:

Amelia Peiche and John Noble: June 10, 1911

Because she would not be able to give her daughter a substantial dowry, Mrs. Peiche assembled a lavish trousseau with fine tablecloths, napkins, sheets, down comforters and pillows, and dozens of embroidered nightgowns, camisoles, chemises, petticoats and handkerchiefs for Amelia. When the trousseau was completed it was laid out in Amelia's bedroom and all of her girl friends were invited in for a party. John too was invited.

He stood in the open doorway in front of Amelia's bedroom, gazing at the white muslin curtain which circled her bed and was tied back at either end with a large satin bow. From the top of the bed hung a blue glass ball.

"I always look into that glass ball before I go to sleep at night," Amelia told him. "I love it because things get reflected in a funny kind of way."

On her bureau was a music box; the beautifully dressed doll perched on its lid revolved while the music played. In the corner of the room was an altar with all of Amelia's favorite saints, many candles, and angels with silver and golden hair. John slipped an arm around Amelia's waist and whispered:

"When you go to your reward you will probably take a pot of gold paint so that you can glamorize heaven."

Amelia had ordered several silk robes with long trains and

176

wide sleeves and trimmed with gold braid, which she thought would be wonderful for an artist's studio. She also had a robe of light blue, a copy of the one Marguerite wore in *Faust;* and her dressmaker had made two corduroy suits in a matching dark green, one for Amelia and one for John. He gazed warily at the extensive collection.

"How are you going to cart all this around with you? You know we'll be moving from place to place . . ."

"That beautiful carved oak trunk, it all fits in there. It will be no trouble to use at all, John. No matter how far we may travel or what fantastic lands or climates we end up in, I will always carry Strasbourg with me."

"But that heavy oak trunk! It must be more than a yard long and a yard tall, and weigh at least ten times as much as the things you are going to put in it! Couldn't we just buy you a couple of suitcases?"

"No, John, this trunk has been my hope chest since I was a little girl. I've always intended to carry it with me . . . and I shall."

John shook his head at her with an expression of prideful despair.

The wedding day turned out sunny and fine. When John called at the house at ten in the morning he found Amelia starry-eyed and breath-takingly beautiful in her wedding gown of antique satin with its shirred bodice and long train. She wore a crown of silver to support the voluminous duchesse lace veil. He stole a quick look in the mirror and decided that he looked rather dashing himself in the Prince Albert coat with the light gray trousers and patent leather shoes.

The chapel was filled with Amelia's friends, relatives and the hundreds of townspeople who had come to see the first American ever to be married in the Strasbourg Cathedral. John thought the walk down the side aisle to the Chapelle de St. Marc was longer than any trip he had made across a Southwest prairie, but from the happiness on Amelia's face he knew that she could continue walking endlessly to the horizon. When the ceremony was over, and John had kissed her, he caught her for a moment before the onrushing guests took possession.

"Your lips are moving, darling; what are you saying to yourself?"

"I'm praying, John, praying to God to let me make you happy, to help you to become a great artist, to help you bring beauty into the world."

That night they stood on the dark station platform waiting

for the wagon-lit that would take them to Brittany for their honeymoon. Over everything lay the powdered mist of full moonlight.

"You see that moon, Amelia? It's lighter than the sun. Most people don't know that, but it is. It has a white far whiter than the day. The night isn't dark, there is never any darkness, not really, it's just a softer, more subdued type of day. That moon, there, for instance, and those stars, they aren't dim and weak. They are burning with fire. You can't see the stars in the day, can you? There is too much light. The night light isn't as loud as the day, that's all."

His voice was quiet, blending with the silence about them, and with the church bells tolling behind them. Amelia moved a little closer, nestling her shoulder against him.

"Do you see the road the Milky Way makes across the sky? And there is the Big Dipper." He pointed it out with his finger. "If you'll follow the handle of the Big Dipper, it will lead you to the North Star. It's the brightest one out there. Can you get it?"

"Yes."

"It has been the great star of all the ages. The moment the sun went down behind the hot prairie, and dusk came, the first thing I did was to look for that North Star. It was a guiding star for me. Out on the plains, if you don't know where it is, you simply lose your way. Every cowpuncher knows that. Sometimes clouds come and cover the sky; then you can't find it, and you lose your course. There's nothing to do then but stay where you are, and wait. Never forget that star, darling."

She turned to him, her eyes alight with love. He took her in his arms and kissed her, tenderly. Then he whispered:

"We'll never be apart, darling. No matter what happens to us, it will happen to the two of us, together. Will you remember?"

She kissed him in turn.

"I'll remember, John. That assurance will be my North Star."

Book Three

BRITTANY

The Treasure

THE HÔTEL des Voyageurs in Pont Croix had been built in the fourteenth century, and the Nobles found that little modernization had been attempted since. Their bedroom had rough wooden boards for a floor, and the solid oak headboard of the bed leaned inward at a precarious angle.

Two husky laborers carried Amelia's trunk into the room, grumbling, "What does Madame carry in here, iron?"

John tipped them generously. He closed the door behind the men and lifted up one end of the trunk. "I told you we ought to leave this in Paris, Amelia. You'll have little use for your lovely things here in Brittany."

"Now, John, we've been over all that before. How can a girl go away on her honeymoon without her trousseau?"

The rain that had greeted them at the railroad station continued to come down in a permeating drizzle, and so they spent the next days in their hotel room. On the fourth evening John said, "I think I'll start work in the morning. This is beautiful country, even in the rain."

He slept fitfully, rising an hour before dawn. When he was fully clothed he wakened Amelia and helped her dress under the covers, for the room was bitterly cold. They were the only ones up; no breakfast was available.

They passed the Pont Croix chapel which dated back to

the Druid age, and made their way to the farthest point of land projecting out to the sea. There were wind-swept skies, somber and silent. On the beach a few fishermen were working on boats whose once bright-colored sails were now faded and hung with a melancholy droop in the rain. Down from the church came a religious procession headed by the priests dressed in their white surplices, followed by the fishermen and their families, the wives wearing the ancient headdresses indicating the part of the country where they were born. The fisherfolk were carrying brightly colored banners, one of a solid dark green set with a red cross, the other a tall gold banner with a madonna and child. The procession came down to the water's edge, giving its traditional blessing and thanksgiving to this sea which was their life and hope, their dismay and tragedy. The Bretons were deeply religious people with a strain of mysticism; most of the women wore black mourning dresses all of their lives, for there was almost no family that had not recently lost one of its men at sea. The sun had now come out a little, elliptical in shape and burnt orange in color as it tried to pierce through the misty veils which hung over the water.

He set up a sketchboard where the Bretons had uttered their prayers, engrossed in his theme. Amelia grew cold, but she did not interrupt his work. It was midafternoon by the time he was satisfied that he could do no more. When they returned to the hotel to get something hot to eat, the proprietress said:

"Dinner was served two hours ago. As you see, the fire has gone out."

They went back into the water-soaked streets and walked to the town's only café, one large room with a huge fireplace over which hung polished brass pans. This fire too had been allowed to go out. An old Breton woman came to the table and stood above them soundlessly.

"Could we trouble you to give us something to eat?" asked Amelia in French. "No? Then would you have the kindness to bring us some coffee and rolls?"

They sat at the table for a very long time, but they did not see the old Breton woman again. An hour passed. Amelia was shivering; John lost his temper and pounded on the table. A man rose from one of the dark corners, introduced himself as the town's schoolteacher and explained that the owner did not like to serve food at the inn during the afternoon, for that was the time to sell beer and wine. They returned to the hotel to wait for supper.

180

With the passing of the days John grew more and more absorbed in his studies of the fishermen, the boats and the ever-changing light on the sea. Amelia insisted that he wake her every morning. Unlike John, who was generating his own heat, she suffered from the continued rain and cold but did not want to be left behind in the dreary hotel room. She was grateful when, wanting to light a cigarette, he handed her his heavy paintbox and palette and then forgot to take them back, so that she trailed him like a squaw but at least gained warmth by carrying the heavy objects under her arms.

One night he was awakened by muffled sounds. He sat up in the darkness and listened. It was Amelia, her body racked with cold, keeping her head under the covers in an effort to quiet her coughs and not waken him. He took her in his arms and held her very tight, warming her, until the coughing subsided.

"Are you all right, darling?"

"Yes," she whispered, "I'm all right. It's just this wetness. They told me downstairs that today is the fortieth straight day of rain. I don't think my feet have been dry since the moment we got off the train."

"I'll get us some wooden sabots in the morning."

But the following morning Amelia felt feverish. She did not want John to think her weak, a woman who would be a burden to him.

"You go ahead and work, darling. I'll just stay in bed and rest."

When he was invited to sail with a sardine boat for several days and excitedly assured her that this was a great opportunity to paint the men while they were engaged in their struggle with the sea, she said:

"Go with them. I can see how much it means to you."

He returned at dusk of the third night, his clothes reeking of the sardine catch, but with a full notebook of hard-bitten sketches of the Breton fishermen. Back at the hotel he found the schoolteacher waiting for him.

"Monsieur, I must apologize for interfering in your private affairs. I realize it is an impertinence. But Madame Noble has been so pleasant to us . . ."

John's notebook dropped to the floor; a chill seized him. Why was the schoolteacher speaking . . . almost in the past tense . . . about Amelia?"

"Monsieur, here in Brittany we do not believe in pampering women, they must work and suffer, that is their load. But your wife is ill. You must summon a doctor."

John stammered his thanks, then rushed blindly up the flight of stairs to their room, threw open the door, and fell on his knees by the bedside.

"Darling, I've neglected you, I've let you freeze day after day, gone out to sea while you were ill . . . yet I love you more than anything else in the world."

He put out his powerful hands to clasp her to him, and for the first time perceived how thin her body was. He felt her warm tears coming down his cheeks. He kissed her a hundred times, on the eyes, the forehead, the mouth.

"Oh, Amelia, I've got so much to learn; I've never had responsibility for another human being before."

2

The Pont Croix doctor gave Amelia medicine, and John stayed by her side constantly, only going out to buy little gifts or to find books to read to her. He ordered flowers to be delivered every day, and at mealtime set up a table by her bedside, plying her with broth and broiled meats. Never once did he look at his sketchbook or paints.

At the end of two weeks they left Pont Croix and went along the Channel coast to Etaples. Here everything was bathed in hot clear sunshine: the cobbled market place, the narrow streets faced on either side by low white houses with green shutters, the flower gardens in front and the vegetable gardens at the back. The most famous house in the little town was the one which had been occupied by Marshal Ney, Napoleon's second in command; a small but rambling building with large windows, without plumbing or lighting or running water and yet the most expensive house for rent in the village.

". . .which is probably the reason it's still available. Do you like it, Amelia?"

Amelia went through the entrance and found herself in a large living room with a broad fireplace. Off to the right was a bedroom with a canopied bed and a window opening onto a garden with fruit trees in bloom. At the rear of the living room was a kitchen with a door leading out to a vegetable garden, and above the whole first floor was an attic which had been turned into a studio.

She ran from room to room, her cheeks flushed with pleasure.

"John, it's beautiful. Look at these fine wood floors . . . and the low ceiling that gives the house a feeling of intimacy. And this canopied bed, just like my own bed in Strasbourg."

It took them only a couple of hours to unpack their valises, settle Amelia's oak chest by the side of her bed, and shop in the market place for the supplies with which to fill the empty kitchen shelves. Then they walked past the quaint twelfth-century church whose tower rose high above the town, and made their way over a bridge between tall, slender poplars to the beach. Here John rented a cabana and a boat for the rest of the summer. They lay side by side on the sand, letting the sun burn their fair skin, then rowed the boat out into the surf, and after a quarter of a mile dove off its sides into the calmly rolling sea to swim and laugh and kiss in the warm water.

He started out at dawn the following morning and spent the day painting two fishermen on an ultramarine-blue sea, both of them wearing yellow smocks and working under a green sail. The next day he painted a canvas called *Launching the Boat,* a fisherman leading his white horse out into the surf, pulling his one-sailed boat off the sands, his son helping to push the boat into the water, the whole scene bathed in the gentle yellow luminosity of an early summer morning. The following day he painted *Toilers of the Sea,* a group of men straining and hauling to pull their boat into the water, working in a murky overcast, everything obliterated but the grim struggle and the mystical outline of the boat and men. The next day he painted *Low Tide,* the fishing boats high and dry on the sand, the men repairing their nets, and in the background a design of bigger boats against the overwhelmingness of the sea and sky. Then he took to working nights, painting *Etaples Moonlight,* the village seen from out at sea: water against boats, boats against land, land against houses, houses against hills, hills against a sky almost powdery white in the moonlight; then by contrast, *Blue Moonlight,* the village with its ships and sea, houses and streets, hills and sky all related and held in unity by a phosphorescent blue moonlight.

All theories and preoccupations fell away from him, for now his life and his work had come into glorious fulfillment. He no longer had to think about style or technique or subject: he had been swept into a period of power and creation. Here with the sea, which was akin to the prairie, his nature came into harmony. He knew that this happened only rarely in a painter's life; it might be a short period or a long one, but during it everything went easy. It was a period caught between two wars, cut out of a world of conflict and confusion, a mating in which happy lovers came together. And his canvases glowed with an almost unearthly light.

On one of their first mornings, when Amelia had risen before dawn to prepare his breakfast, John asked:

"Wouldn't you like to go into the market and hire one of the young village girls to help you?"

"Not right away, dear. I would like to keep our first home myself. I want to cook our own food and make our own bed and wash our own dishes and floors. Is that sentimental of me?"

"Yes, and wonderful. Everything about you is wonderful. Now that I've had time to come to my senses, I'm glad I married you."

As they lay side by side in the intimacy of their bed, she would ask:

"What are you thinking about, John?"

"It's odd, but my thoughts keep going back to my childhood."

"Was that a happy time for you?"

"Happy? No, not in my relations with people. But when I remember the sublimeness of the level prairie extending from horizon to horizon like an ocean . . . how beautiful it was, especially at night. And what stars! I have never seen the atmosphere so clear; the plains made one feel that all the world beyond must be beautiful."

"I've never seen or felt anything like that, John. All my life has been spent in cities . . ."

"Cities! In cities I am only half alive. Ah, but the plains that stretch to infinity, with nothing to catch hold of your thoughts, to break the sameness; with everything so flat that your mind soars to great space beyond the unmarked road. And the early hours of the morning, when the plains are still dewy, and you can see the faint outline of the tumbleweed against the horizon; there is beauty greater than all the poems or pictures ever painted. The barren plains are like a world without end, Amelia."

"I can see it clearly, John, the way you describe it. Those prairie deserts of the West, they're like the deserts in which Jesus and Mohammed found their solitude and worked out their own deliverance."

He stirred, uneasy, then turned and took her in his arms. She was so fine, so good, so precious, and her lips were so sweet against his.

"I don't know about Jesus and Mohammed," he replied, his voice low, "but to the artist the passion of embodying emotions and thought and perception in a visible form is at once the romance and the reality of his life."

"I know that, darling," she replied, "and I'm not jealous. It's strange, but the more you give yourself to your work, the more I seem to have of you."

During the first weeks he deposited his still wet canvases on a rear porch. By the end of a month Amelia brought them into the house and placed them about on the walls and furniture. When she looked at *Launching the Boat, Blue Moonlight, Toilers of the Sea, Low Tide*, she found them held together with a force and a vitality which shed a benign, all-embracing warmth that gently seized her and made her part of the picture itself. *Land's End*, painted in its hour of silence with a luminous sun about to descend into the brilliantly lighted waters, and the little village flowing down from the hills above it into the sea below it, shone with an inner radiance.

"It's happiness coming through," she exclaimed when he came in from work that evening.

She reached up and kissed him on the cheek: before their marriage his work had been incomplete, unrealized; now that he had come into a creative surge she felt she had a right to believe that their love had a great deal to do with it. John read all this in her soft brown eyes, and remembered the line which had resolved his doubts in Cagnes:

"Whatever adversity she cannot overcome, she will outlive."

3

He got caught in a heavy squall and made his way home thoroughly drenched. In one corner of the living room he found Amelia, her hair done up in a kerchief, at her feet a bucket of soapy water and the brush with which she had been scrubbing the floor; in the other corner stood Marty Buckler, surrounded by suitcases. Marty and Amelia were gazing at each other in hostile silence.

"Why don't you live where a man can find you?" growled Marty.

John laughed, put an arm about Marty's shoulder.

"Say, you've put on weight. Frances has been feeding you too good."

Marty looked down at his tightly vested middle.

"I just don't get any exercise. The boys started a new game, golf it's called, but every time I go to hit the ball I see my father's starved face staring up at me. Guess I'm too old to learn to play."

"You did pretty well in Paris your last trip over."

Marty's eyes lighted, the tension lifted; he was about to speak when he looked at Amelia, who was still sitting dejected in her chair. John went to her, kissed her.

"Could we have a celebration dinner, Amelia? Marty's my oldest friend, I've told you about him."

Amelia shot him a quick look, rose and walked out of the room.

"What happened between you and Amelia, Marty? The atmosphere in here is as thick as a stale chocolate pudding."

"When I came to the front door I saw her scrubbing the floor," replied Marty sotto voce. "I thought she was the maid and asked if Mr. or Mrs. Noble was at home. She looked at me without getting up from her hands and knees, then said something in French about not speaking English."

"I see."

"Frances is tremendously curious to know what kind of a woman you married." Marty began pacing the room in short concentric circles. "She has images of her as a regal creature, cultivated and cultured." He stopped short and faced John, his eyes shining as though in triumph. "Wait till I get back and tell her! John, how did you happen to choose a . . . a farm girl?"

John smiled. "Well, you know me, Marty, I always wanted a simple horny-handed lass of the soil, one who could milk cows and plow in the fields, a woman who would never be 'sicklied o'er by the pale cast of thought.' "

"That's Shakespeare, isn't it? But how do you get along, if she speaks no English? Last time I saw you, you didn't know ten words of French."

"You're right, Marty, it's tough to have a wife who can only sign her name with an X; but I'm slowly teaching her to read and write. In a few years no one will suspect that she never wore shoes until the day of our wedding."

"Will Frances be amazed!"

"How is Frances, Marty?"

Marty's elation collapsed.

"She hasn't been too well, John. Nothing serious, lassitude, the doctor calls it. She has grown thin as a split rail. The worst part of it is, the thinner she gets the taller she seems . . . while I, since putting on all this loose weight, look shorter every day. She travels a little: went out to southern California last winter, took a boat ride to South America."

"By herself?"

"She takes one of the Wichita women for company. I can't seem to interest her in my plans any more. I don't know why, it's not like I failed, or talk about things I don't follow through with."

"Maybe Frances thinks you've got enough money."

"How can anyone have enough money?"

"When you set your sights low, boy, you arrive at your destination too soon. The trouble with spending your life driving for money is that you can get it. Man is only happy pursuing the distant, the difficult, the barely perceivable. Any kind of completion is another tavern passed on the road to death."

Marty pulled a black cigar from an upper vest pocket, burnt the edge with a match and blew smoke into John's face, obscuring not only his friend's words but his expression as well. John backhanded the smoke away as though it were an acorn-beaded portiere hung between two doorless rooms.

"That's the fascination of the arts, Marty: trying to grasp the truth, trying to portray life's meaning, suffering, beauty, things which can never be completely captured. Even the greatest of the geniuses, an El Greco or a Cézanne, a Shakespeare or a Dostoevsky, can make only the barest beginning."

"Aw, cut out that arty stuff, John, you know it's over my head."

"Then I'll let you in on a secret about women and love: they like a man who is eternally struggling; the one thing they can't get excited about is a *fait accompli*."

Marty had stopped listening. He knocked the ash from his cigar into the cuff of his trousers.

"Why didn't you bring Frances with you, Marty?" asked John.

Marty looked around the room exultantly.

"Yes, I should have done that. Maybe if she saw how you lived . . . Frances has all sorts of romantic notions about the glamorous life you lead. If I could show her now . . . primitive . . . I think she'd come to her senses."

John could not think of any answer to this, and suddenly, in the silence, Marty sensed how gauche he had been. He quickly began shoveling words into the open manhole between them, telling how he owned parts of banks in Kansas City, St. Louis and Chicago.

". . . they came to me and wanted to make an exchange

187

of stock. Our banking combine is now investing its funds in industry: railroads in New York, steel in Pittsburgh, oil in California . . . I must be on about a dozen boards of directors."

"Well, what do you know, you're a millionaire at last!"

As Amelia came in from the kitchen to announce dinner, he cried, "Darling, do you know what that makes me? Half a millionaire! Say, Marty, I've pyramided that hundred dollars high enough; I better pull out before you make me just too damn rich."

Marty's eyes glazed. He turned away. To Amelia there seemed to be a number of words half formed in his throat before he managed to put breath behind them.

". . . actually no cash . . . everything being reinvested . . . You know, John, you can't take money out of an expanding empire. . . ."

After she had done the dinner dishes Amelia opened her Strasbourg trunk and donned a blue silk robe with wide-flowing, gold-trimmed sleeves. It was the first time she had worn any part of her trousseau. She removed the kerchief from her hair and swept the soft blond curls high upon her head. Marty gaped in astonishment when she came into the room.

"I might have known it," he exclaimed to John; "you've been pulling a Dave Leahy joke on me."

"Don't you think you earned it?"

Marty rose, went to his suitcase and took out a long, narrow box. He stood behind Amelia and clasped a string of exquisite pearls about her neck.

"I brought this as a wedding present," he whispered.

The next morning John and Marty walked barefooted along the shell-studded beach.

"There are a lot of your old friends from the Ruche living close by, Marty, and some other fine painters I'm sure you'd like to meet. Your name is known to them because of those canvases you bought at the Beehive. I'm going to tell them you are here."

Marty was flattered; he made only one demurrer. "Those pictures have never been anything but a liability to me; they're still in their original packing cases."

A few nights later the painters came to call: Karl Leipsche and Giuseppe Donello walked from a neighboring village; Oscar Magozanovic made the trip from Neufchâtel with Pablo Anza, the wistful-faced, silent Spaniard; Anton Van der Meetch came up from Le Touquet with Ichiro Kunogi.

They embraced Marty like a long-lost brother, asking numerous questions about the state of painting in America. Donello asked whether he had come over for the express purpose of adding to the Buckler Collection.

"No, I just . . ."

"Of course Marty is here on a buying trip," interrupted John. "Why else would I have asked you to bring your newest canvases? Get your pictures on the walls, boys, the Martin Buckler Purchase Show is about to open."

Marty received thunderous applause. His lips trembled a little as he seized John by the arm and in a husky undertone said, "Look, John, I kinda expected something like this . . . but you got to do something for me in return."

"Anything, Marty."

"Then take me to Paris for a week. I been dreaming about the times we had ever since I was here last."

"But you can go to Paris by yourself."

"No, no, I don't know where the places are. I couldn't find the girls . . ."

"Nothing doing, Marty."

"Then no pictures bought."

John glanced about at the men busily placing their canvases.

"All right, but there are other pictures in Paris too, many fine canvases painted in the past few years that the Martin Buckler Collection would be incomplete without: Braque, André Lhote, Rouault, Dufy, Picasso, Van Dongen . . ."

"Now, John, have a heart!"

". . . Duchamp's *Nude Descending the Staircase,* so far the greatest of all the Cubist paintings."

"A nude, eh? I know a wonderful spot for it behind the bar in the Elks Club. Say, Johnny, did you hear that your Cleopatra was all patched up and sold to a carnival? I saw it in a side show down in Missouri, ten cents to get in, and the electric light still goes on and off, making her look real."

John winched.

When the last of the painters had left, Marty stood in the midst of the canvases John had selected.

"They're none of these pictures worth anything," Marty grumbled, "but even so yours would sure win the booby prize."

The wind went out of John; it was the first time Marty had commented on his work.

"Don't you like the new canvases, boy?"

"I hate them." Marty's whole body bristled.

John stood staring at *Toilers of the Sea,* which was resting on the mantelpiece. He was unable to understand the violence of Marty's reaction.

"But what is it that antagonizes you, Marty? You never broke out in a rash about my paintings in Paris."

"Of course not. Why should I? They were just like everybody else's. But now you're trying to make fools of us by painting something we can't understand. Why do you think that makes you smarter than the rest of us, just because you're making yourself mysterious? What are you trying to hide in those pictures?"

John studied his friend's face: it was quivering with rage, the protruding cheekbones a dead white.

"It's strange, your reacting with such intense emotion to the pictures, Marty. What is it about them that frightens you?"

The rage flooded out of Marty's face, and he stood trembling before his old friend, tears in his eyes.

"Because you're painting something I could never know anything about. Why, John? Why do you have to make a world that I could never enter?"

John suddenly felt good inside himself, where he lived as a painter.

"There must be something awfully strong and real and penetrating about the canvases, Marty, to earn such passionate rejection."

"No, Johnny, they're bad." Suddenly Marty began talking very fast, like a carpenter throwing up the façade of his own structure. "Look, boy, I'm gonna build a block-square department store in Wichita. It'll be six or eight stories high, the biggest thing west of New York. We'll sell everything made in this world: household goods, clothing, jewelry, stationery, music, books. And art works, Johnny. You could be in charge of that department, you could come to Europe each year to buy paintings and tapestries and anything else you wanted for the section. What do you say, boy, have I got it all figured out for you? Come back to Wichita with me and help organize . . ."

"You're still trying to make me over in your image," interrupted John quietly. "Why, Marty? I've never tried to make a painter out of you. Why do you consider my way of life some kind of frightening menace to your self-respect and to your security?"

4

When the pelting autumnal rains began driving in from the ocean, John and Amelia moved to Paris and found a studio in the Rue Falguière. Amelia spent her days sewing draperies for the windows; John had a hundred quick Brittany sketches which he hoped to convert into major themes. He drew deeper and deeper inside himself, bolting the windows and doors to the outside world. He found that the man who had no need to get God on his canvas could do very well without Him. One painted the sea, which had about it a touch of the prairie; one painted the fishermen who were akin to the trail herders and mountaineers; one painted the ships which were like horses or buffalo traversing a wide plain.

Since the day he had lost faith that God could be found through one's work he had neither thought of God nor searched for Him. God was a myth, a fiction, something pursued by fractional, unhappy, lonely creatures. When the impulse to remain alive had caused him to spring out of his deathbed he had not done so because he had faith that he could come back to a God-inhabited world; it had been a primordial instinct of self-preservation which had rescued him. Then in Amelia he had found the perfect substitute: the man who had found love had no further need for God.

Amelia was learning that in Paris the word "studio" was used as a romantic handle with which to rent the most bleak, cold, cheerless, barnlike enclosure. John could not understand what it was about the studio on the Rue Falguière which marked it off from any other, but Amelia felt that it had the makings of a cheerful home. She hung golden draperies full length to the floor, found a set of red velours divan and chairs, a brilliant oriental rug, many brightly colored lamps, an altar for her saints and a tall rubber plant like the one in the parlor in Strasbourg. She filled the studio almost to overflowing with books, candelabra, vases of flowers; then as a concluding touch she bought some gold paint and gilded the window frames, doors and low-lying coffee table. When she had finished the studio was warm, gay, cluttered, homy. John awakened from a concentrated stretch of work, looked about him for the first time; his face broke into a delighted smile.

"It's just like I told you in Strasbourg," he said; "when you go to your reward you're going to take a pot of gold paint with you to glamorize heaven."

"You're not poking fun at me, John?" she asked. "You really like it?"

He held her against his chest, hard and ardently; she was so anxious to please . . . and so utterly defenseless.

"I love it, darling, it's the first real home I've had since I left Wichita; if I stumbled into this room a thousand miles from Paris I would know with one glance that it was yours."

"I'm glad you like it, because now I want to give a big party and invite all your friends."

"Not a pink tea!"

"Take the horror out of your voice, John. You are a respectable married man, and you should entertain your friends on Sunday afternoons, just the way your mother did in Wichita. Besides it will be a good chance for them to see your new pictures."

His first and automatic reaction had been one of shrinking within himself at the thought of showing his work; but his ear caught a quality of pleading and pride in her voice.

"You're right, Amelia, let's invite everybody we know."

Amelia hung John's Brittany canvases on the walls, filled the vases with bright flowers from Les Halles, prepared enough food and drink to keep the party provisioned until midnight, and invited almost a hundred guests, practically every painter John had known in Paris, and a number of people from the American Club.

They arrived early: Marcel Charbert, Angelo Verdinni of the Ruche; George Luks, Fred Waugh, Charles Hawthorne, from the American Club; Harrison and Tanner, back from Etaples; Gertrude Stein with a retinue that had come to her studio for Sunday morning breakfast; the Fauve, or Wild Animal group, from the opposite side of town: Picasso, Braque, Juan Gris, Rouault, Lhote, all the men whose paintings John had made Marty acquire on their trip to Paris, in particular Marcel Duchamp, who was enormously grateful to John for selling the *Nude Descending the Staircase*. John did not tell Duchamp that his picture was destined for the Elks Club bar. The Rev. Mr. Van Winkle of the Episcopal church came, as did the Third Secretary, now the First Secretary of the Embassy. John regretted that Henri Matisse and his family had moved to the south of France; he wanted to say to Madame Matisse, "How right you were about love."

As the big studio filled with his friends John realized that this was more than a grand reunion; it was a recapitulation of his ten years in Paris; the first excitement over the great paintings in the Louvre; his loneliness; the rattlesnake vest and six-shooters at the Pompeian Quatz' Arts ball; the wonderful comradeship at the Ruche; Maud; the solitary studio on the Rue Belloni; the struggle to master his craft, to find something lasting and universal to say; his defeat, despair, near-death. There was no one here but knew what he had been through; there was almost no one here but had believed him incapable of marriage, domesticity; and to the last man they had feared for Amelia, or for any woman unfortunate enough to marry him.

"Mrs. Noble, you've brought about a miracle," said Charbert, his eyes resting on John with his corn-white hair freshly cut, his suit freshly pressed, his body lean and hard, his skin clear from the months in Brittany. "We didn't think you could do it."

But the greatest excitement was caused by John's work. The men walked about studying the many canvases and their luminescent quality. They looked at *Blue Moonlight, Toilers of the Sea, Low Tide,* and were happy for John's sake; he had worked so terribly hard to reach this point of fruition; but hadn't they all come through anguish and terror, hadn't they all worked faithfully and hard? Much as they liked him, they could not understand how the paintings of the loudest, drunkenest, most exhibitionistic of them could suddenly become the most spiritual.

"What's your secret, John?" asked Gerald Addams as he gazed at *Land's End* with its fiery sun about to descend into the brilliantly lighted waters.

"Is it that Feigenmilch you were working on?" insisted Angelo Verdinni.

John chuckled. "I've even forgotten what went into that formula."

"It must be something he does to the canvas before he puts the paint on," observed Tanner.

"We're all stupid," said Alexander Harrison, shaking his handsome leonine head; "it's not specially prepared canvas or chemically balanced paint that is creating the sense of exultation we see shining over the paintings. It's his own glorious sense of fulfillment coming through."

In a corner of the room Amelia was standing with George Luks. "You think his work is good?" she asked.

"Good!" exclaimed Luks, who less than two years before had painted John as a death head; "dear lady, you can fool the critics, the dealers, the Salon judges, the public. But no painter ever fooled another painter. John's stuff is completely original, unlike anything else being painted in Paris . . . or in America, for that matter: the subjects are strong, the motifs daring, the mood is deep, the technique is genuine: and they exude joy: joy in the world, its people, its force, its beauty. Yes, even in its tragedy. There's a strong hand and mind and faith behind every stroke."

Amelia looked with pride to where John was talking to a slender bald-headed man in immaculate cutaway coat and striped trousers who had come in with Gertrude Stein. She watched him talk excitedly to John about one of the large canvases, then reach out his hands in a gesture both of bestowal and appeal. She saw John stiffen, the color leave his face. She went quickly to his side.

"John, what is it?"

"Amelia, this is Mr. Frazer from the Chicago Art Institute. He is over here to get pictures for the 1912 Annual Chicago Show. And he's just asked if he may take back *Toilers of the Sea.*"

Addams and Harrison had been standing close by. They wrung John's hand, calling out the news to everyone in the studio. There was a moment of silence, then a deluge of exclamation.

". . . how wonderful, the only American in Paris to be invited . . . it's the beginning of great things for you, John . . . it should happen to us . . . as good for the Art Institute as it is for John . . ."

Amelia stood on tiptoes and kissed her husband full on the mouth.

John looked at the men about him and smiled wistfully.

5

Because their thoughts went back so often to the happy months in Etaples they decided to find a permanent home on the seacoast. On New Year's Day they took the train to Brittany and walked to Trepied in the sharp winter sun. Just before they reached the tiny village they saw a sign, HOUSE FOR RENT, made their way down a small lane and found themselves before a farmhouse, low and long in structure, its white walls covered with vines.

The owner was a tall, lean, weather-beaten Englishman.

"I've been called back suddenly, it's likely I'll never be able to return. Would you be interested in a long lease?"

He opened the front door for Amelia, and they stepped into a large dining room. The sitting room was behind this, with picture windows overlooking the back garden. On the opposite side and running the full length of the house was a room which the Englishman had used as a drawing room.

"This would make a wonderful studio for you, John. Here's a door to the back garden when you wanted to work outside."

John walked up and down the long room, getting a sense of spacious austerity from the painted floor, light blue plaster walls and simple moldings. He was excited and happy.

They remained in Trepied for several days, John signing the papers for a five-year lease, while Amelia worked out the plans for a family-sized kitchen and designed the furniture for their bedroom to be made at the local wood-turning shop.

They returned to the studio in Paris and the rest of the winter passed quickly. They rose at the first touch of light in the east, John painted all day, and then at four o'clock they set out, arm in arm, to ransack the antique shops for furnishings for the house in Trepied. First they discovered a fifteenth-century Italian sideboard, next a fine set of wicker furniture for the sitting room, its French toile de Jouy patterned with large birds and flowers in brilliant colors on a blue and white background. When they came upon a bright red rug for the sitting room they took everything down to Trepied, where they decorated the sideboard with a set of Brittany plates. Two weeks later they made another trip because their bedroom furniture had been finished. Amelia painted it blue, placed the bed and dresser on a blue rug, painted the walls yellow and put white net curtains on the windows. She stopped suddenly, a paintbrush in her hands, demanding of her husband:

"Why do people always make their bedrooms so dark and grim? I think it should be the gayest room in the house."

"I guess that depends on one's attitude toward . . . lovemaking. If you think it's beautiful and joyous . . ."

". . . John, stop . . . it's the middle of the afternoon . . . the paint is still wet on the bedposts . . .

They moved into the Trepied house on the first day of spring. John set up his easel in the big studio, tacked his dozens of rough Brittany sketches on the walls. Amelia planted marigolds in the center of the front garden, climbing roses

195

around the front door. In the back garden she planted sweet peas, poppies and daisies,

"I'm the vegetable man," John insisted. "I'm going to put in carrots, lettuce and corn, then strawberries, and red and black currants."

From their back garden a winding path took them to the tiny studio of Myron Barlow, a tall, good-looking, shy man from Detroit whose canvases invariably consisted of a picturesque farm girl trying on blue slippers: always the same girl and the same slippers. Next to Barlow lived Tanner and his wife in a large well-kept house that looked like a house in Paris. Mrs. Tanner was a tall statuesque blond Swede. Tanner had an extra seat attached to the back of his bicycle and they made a charming sight riding through the country, Tanner leaning over the handlebars, pumping furiously, while Mrs. Tanner sat tall and upright behind, surveying the landscape with poise and aplomb. Further on was the house of Austin Brown, with magnificent flowers that were the envy of Amelia's life.

By the first of July the colony at Trepied was complete: Alexander Harrison had arrived with two lovely young models; Gerald Addams, who had been painting in the museums of Italy most of the winter, was both proud and perplexed by his first commission: to deliver an exact replica of the *Mona Lisa* to an art gallery in Boston.

"What do they think I am, a professional copier?" he groused to John. "It's a good thing they offered me two thousand dollars, or I would have been insulted."

"I wish someone would insult me like that," replied John. "I haven't earned a dollar from my work since I sold that drawing of the Dalton gang to the Wichita *Eagle*."

He spent his days roaming the coast line, always perceiving bolder themes. He ruled all browns off his palette, concentrating on the colors that were fine for glazing: lemon yellow, cerulean blue, cobalt and French ultramarine, viridian, emerald green, alizarin crimson, vermilion. Alongside the low key picturings of Pont Croix he did some that were yellow and pure white, where everything was bathed in a high shimmering vibrant light with the components blending mystically into each other, the sun being part of the sea, the sea being part of the beach.

Again it was a period of tremendous production, and some of his older friends became frightened for him; it was a pace impossible to maintain. No man could feel or think or project this deeply without utterly exhausting his emotions, using up the reserve of past years and digging deeply into the ore of the future. Yet they knew too that no artist could turn himself off: the fruit must be plucked when ripe.

His themes were indigenous to the life in Brittany, a blending of the prairie, the sea and John Noble: an inland canal with ships silhouetted against distant houses life on the fishing boats, both at sea and when hauled up on the shore; wrecked trawlers, seaweed gatherers in the moonlight, children on the beach; the fishermen mending their nets, baiting their lines, sailing their four-masted schooners into the hot-sunned horizon. He painted sailing boats almost flying the crest of the wave, painted them like phantom ships caught in misty moonlight or before whirling suns; painted the ship's wake in the path of the moon. He painted ships and men caught in full life and full sail, and he painted them locked in wreck, in death, in decay; painted mystical ships with mystical white wings sailing on mystical seas, uniting heaven and earth.

And his loneliness was gone. Since finding Amelia the terrible pain of being alone had vanished. Now there was always somebody by his side to accompany and to complete him, to keep away the fear that he would walk through cities and crowds and people and not be able to communicate with them, to let them know that he was there.

It was so simple. The White Buffalo was love.

6

There was a good deal of visiting back and forth among the artists for evenings together. The communal spirit allowed for little jealousy or envy; no one family seemed to have more than the other, the few dollars needed for rent, for food, which was cheap, and for painting supplies. Amelia remained the radiant bride and invited the painters in for supper several times a week, happy at long last to be able to use the lovely tablecloths and napkins her mother had provided in the trousseau. She was a good cook and a warmhearted hostess who took pleasure in seeing her husband surrounded by friends.

There was only one cloud on her horizon: the fact that John rarely let her leave his side; she must be up at dawn to accompany him on the daylong painting trips, and never go out of the house when he was working at home.

"But, John, why can't I go for a walk in the hills overlooking the sea? You don't need me for anything, and I have supper already prepared."

"No, darling, please, take your walk in the back garden where I can see you."

"But I must market. I thought I would stop on the way back . . ."

"Wait until I have finished work and I'll go to market with you."

And so, not wanting to argue further, she walked the little path in the back garden, but it was a small garden and grew monotonous with the passage of the weeks; she had a great deal of energy and she loved to walk in the hills as she had during all of her youth. Finally one day she said, "I wish you would let me go out, John. This back garden is getting to be a little like a prison."

"We are all in one kind of prison or another," he replied quietly, not looking up from his easel. "If you're happy in your own particular prison, then there's no sense in looking out longingly through the bars."

"But, John, I can't understand why you're so unwilling to be left alone for an hour or two. After all, you've spent most of your life alone . . . just you and Wichita Bill out on the trail . . ."

He saw that she was distressed and so he put down his brush and sat her on his lap, placing her arms about his neck. He reached into his shirt and brought forth the North Star which he now wore on the end of the heavy silver chain Amelia had given him for his birthday.

"What this North Star really represents is love, Amelia: love the fixed, the constant, the never-varying. That was what my mother meant, that I must find love and steer my life by it. During my boyhood the North Star was my love for my mother. Now it is my love for you."

He kissed her tenderly on the lips, and then continued to speak, as though to himself.

"When I can see you, hear you, reach out my hand and touch you, then the specter of loneliness is vanquished; loneliness cannot exist in the same world with you: with your eager voice, your bright infectious laughter, your inexhaustible interest in every phase of life. Even when I'm so absorbed in my work that I appear not to see you, or to know you are in the room, when I eat mechanically because you tell me to, work all night and fall asleep at midday in my clothes, even then I can remain in the world of my painting

198

only so long as I know you are close. If you disappear, I come back as though through a dense fog to the present, actual world, and I am made ill by the too rapid transition."

Amelia felt that perhaps this was because her husband was so utterly without God. She prayed for him when she awoke and when she went to sleep, and attended services every Sunday. John walked with her to the church but he would not go inside, waiting somewhere, sketching until she reappeared.

"You're an enigma, darling," she exclaimed one Sunday morning; "your paintings are so spiritual in tone and yet you are so devoid of religion."

"A man's religion is a solitary thing, Amelia," he replied. "There is no way to organize the relation of a man to his universe. Way back in Wichita I decided that religion for me could never be a prescribed group exercise, that any set doctrine would be too rigid for my needs. It's just that I'm a maverick. . . ."

"Are you sure you're not romanticizing yourself?" she asked gingerly; "this need to be different, to walk alone? Is it a disparagement of the truth to say that it is so magnificently clear and understandable that all people can see it and worship it? Surely God is strong enough to make His own truth discernible to all people? If He can create the people, He can at the same time create their understanding of Him and give them the courage to worship together in a commonly held and beloved religion. If one believes in God, then one must believe that to Him all things are possible."

"Even the making of John Noble? Are you denying the power of God to have created one man in a slightly different pattern? That's sacrilegious of you, Amelia. Perhaps God is using me as an antibody; someone whose function it is to exist outside the Church, in order to provide the mass of people with a threat which would unite them the more tightly. If I serve this purpose, then surely God must love me as well for the good I do."

"You're too clever for me!" cried Amelia, on the verge of tears.

"No, no, Amelia, it's only a vocal cleverness. Pay no attention to it. You are right; go on praying for my immortal soul. I'm sure God loves you, and it gives me a feeling of security to know that someone as good as you is appealing my case and cause."

Instead of turning toward the hills and their own house they continued onward to the *plage*, went into their cabana, slipped into their swimming suits and struck out through the surf to a raft which was anchored about a hundred yards offshore. Here they lay on their stomachs on the rough wooden planks, feeling wonderfully wet and cool and yet at the same time warmed by the hot August sun directly overhead. John threw an arm clumsily about Amelia's back and laid his cheek against hers.

But these reassuring moments grew farther and farther apart: for Amelia was faced by the irony that the happier John grew in his work and marriage, the more completely he neglected her, plunging for days into the world of images which he wished to transcribe to canvas. They sat down alone to the luncheon or dinner table, for now when he was immersed in a large canvas he refused to go out and visit, or have their friends in. Sometimes the tears would roll down her face because he failed to ask after her needs, to pass her the bread or sugar or butter. She thought, I'm not really of any importance to him. If his work goes well, he's content. If it goes badly, he's miserable. Our love doesn't even serve as a leaven. . . .

When she pointed out to John that he never spoke of their love or marriage in considering his state of happiness, he replied brusquely, "That's not true. Our love is the basis on which all the work, yes, and all the business, is built. That is *entendu,* and what is understood between two people does not have to be the subject of daily conversation."

While obsessed by a task at hand he rarely talked to her at all; sometimes if a color tube or a particular brush was missing he would cry out to her, blaming her for the loss, since she was the only one who cleaned the studio. Then, an hour or a day later, he would come with a few flowers in his hand and a penitent half-smile on his face to ask her forgiveness.

"I suppose it is all right, John," she would reply quietly. "You have just lived too much among men. I wish you had been with women more before I met you. . . ."

Then, a little sad, and a little lonely for Strasbourg and her family and the house in which she had been born and raised, she would go into John's studio and there she would see the new canvas on the easel, completed, glowingly beautiful, so beautiful that one could not imagine a mere human could transfix it on canvas. And she pitied John as she tried to envisage the agonies he must have endured in creating his picture. It was terrible and wonderful to be an artist; for she knew that an artist was a man possessed; that it was not until his work was completed that he realized the demons had been angels in disguise. She resolved to remember that: it would help her in the difficult hours, in the days when John did not know she was in the same room, the same bed, even the same world: if she were a partner, then she would endure the losses with the gains.

In September the director of the Pennsylvania Academy of Fine Arts visited Trepied. He asked John for his *Breton Fishing Village* to hang in the 1913 Annual Show in Philadelphia, probably the oldest and most important exhibition in America. The following week Mr. Frazer arrived from the Chicago Art Institute, informed John that his *Toilers of the Sea* in the last show had attracted a great deal of attention, and this time selected two canvases for his 1913 show. The director of the Salon d'Automne came to Britanny for a study of the work being done in the colony and chose one of John's *Processionals* for the most important of all the Parisian exhibitions. This represented recognition by the French government, an official recognition which was quickly followed by an invitation to exhibit at the Société Nationale des Beaux Arts.

Because John was the only American who had been tapped for all the important American and French shows, Amelia prevailed upon him to let her give a big party for the artists' colony in Brittany. George Luks had found a beginning success in America by exhibiting with John Sloan, William Glackens, Everett Shinn, George Bellows, and their teacher, Robert Henri, as a group which the academic critics had labeled the Ashcan School because they chose to paint realistically the life about them; but the majority of the Americans painting in Paris were still unrecognized. John had no wish to be granted the outer forms of success while his friends were still struggling and unacknowledged. His expression when he greeted the guests was a little sheepish and off focus. Alexander Harrison, the oldest and wisest of them, said:

"No, John, we don't feel that way. We're happy for you. Not only because you deserve it . . . your work is the best being done now . . . but we know what torture you've been through."

"You're the only one who really has descended to Dante's City of Dis, at the very pit of Hell," added Addams; "and we're happy to know that there is a road back."

"Amen!" said Tanner, his white teeth flashing. "May it happen to all of us, please God!"

After the party, when everyone had congratulated John

once again and Amelia had bid her guests good night, John put his arms about his wife.

"Are you happy now?" he asked.

Amelia thought for a while, then replied, "I guess marriage is like painting: composed of nearly equal parts of agony and ecstasy. There are troubled and confused times, failures along the way, frequent inability to grasp, to understand, to reduce what seems like chaos to some kind of sensible order. But along the route if it is creative . . . of fine hours of companionship . . . of help and partnership in times of trouble and crisis . . . of good work . . . of children . . . then it has justified itself. I've decided that to make a marriage a success takes as much devotion as painting does; the Sunday wife will create little more than the Sunday painter. . . ."

John turned her by the shoulders so that she had to look directly at him. There was a quality in her voice, an expression in her eyes he had not seen before.

". . . what was that about . . . children?"

She flushed. "Well, what about it?"

"I'm asking the questions. Was that an aside or was it thrown in for a purpose?"

"For a purpose."

"I thought so. Are you?"

"I are."

"Why didn't you tell me?"

"I just told you."

"But are you all right?"

"Of course I'm all right."

"Then you won't mind the . . ."

"No, darling, I won't mind, any more than you mind when you're painting a picture: the pain passes, the beauty remains."

She walked about the sitting room gathering up ash trays, straightening cushions on the chairs.

"It was a lovely party," she murmured. She went to John and kissed him on the cheek. "I'm proud of you, darling. You wear your success with such humility."

"I'm built to withstand success, Amelia," he answered; "it's failure that I'm not equipped for."

7

Winter set in and they moved back to their studio in Paris. The big art shows opened. The Parisian critics wrote long articles about the emergence of a "new American out-of-doors-school," naming John Noble its leader and strongest voice, and praising him for creating another Barbizon School of landscape painters.

The most individual work being done today is that of John Noble. He paints in a low key with wonderful strength and solidity of color. What is most noticeable is the atmospheric quality of his work. He is a new colorist of unusual depth and individuality. There is no one painting today that catches so vividly and with such a sense of eternal life the out of doors; the sea with the hills overlooking it, the white sandy beaches against the powdery blue sky and the powdery yellow sun, the infinity of land beneath an infinity of sky arching to meet each other in a great circle of light dominated by a powerful pulsating sun.

To the newspaper reporters he talked with sober good sense about painting and the journals ran his statements under reproductions of his pictures:

To really paint a man must put his soul into his work. He must paint from the heart rather than according to mathematical rules. But he must never be content with that which meets the outer skin of his eye: he must also create his own world and transcribe that world to canvas.

Though he had given his pictures to no dealer for the purpose of sale, two buyers found their way to his studio: one a dentist who had taken care of Whistler's teeth and had accepted paintings in lieu of non-existent cash, and now paid John five hundred dollars for his *Launching the Boat,* and the other an American who had a home in Passy, who selected two small canvases. Then to his astonishment a foursome arrived from Wichita, one of Marty Buckler's banker friends by the name of Davidson, who bought *Moonlight at Pont Croix,* and his friend Mr. Amidon, a lawyer who bought *A Breton Fisher Village* and ordered a portrait of his wife.

"I'm terribly grateful," said John, "but I don't know anything about portraits; I have never painted one in my life."

"How about the portrait of Cleopatra in the Mahan bar?" asked Davidson.

The five Wichitans enjoyed a hearty laugh, after which

John told the story to Amelia. However Amelia wasn't listening; the moment John stopped speaking, she said, "John, of course you can do a fine portrait of Mrs. Amidon. They came to you as the outstanding American painter in Paris, and you have no right to turn them down."

"She's right," said Amidon. "We are offering fifteen hundred dollars for the portrait."

The banker added, "Better take it, John; it would be all my life is worth to go back to Wichita and tell Marty that you turned down a fifteen-hundred-dollar commission."

John's face suddenly lighted, the smoky protest disappeared from his eyes and they became a clear, transparent blue.

"I accept. Amelia, how much money have we received in the past few weeks, including this fifteen-hundred-dollar commission?"

"Something under three thousand dollars, John."

"Good. I want you to go to the bank in the morning and transfer the funds to Wichita. Then we are going to cable my mother and father that I am sending them money to make the trip to Chicago and Philadelphia to see my paintings in the winter shows. There will be enough for my sister Belle, her husband and child, also my sister Elizabeth and my brother Arthur. And if there is money enough they are to take Marty Buckler and Frances with them too."

Their child was delivered at the American Hospital in Neuilly by Dr. Bogard. When Amelia's senses cleared sufficiently for her to get a good look at the baby she decided he was quite beautiful, with a large head, strong features and smoky eyes. John came into the room at that moment.

"Meet your son, John."

He bowed from the waist, saying formally, "How do you do?"

There was a knock at the door and George Luks came in carrying a huge armful of flowers which he had picked up in stall after stall at Les Halles shortly before dawn. He dropped the flowers at the door of the bed, spreading them over Amelia's feet like a colorful afghan.

"It's a boy, George," she said while John stood by, mute and pale, studying his son's face. "Do you think we ought to make him a painter?"

"No, no," cried Luks, "make him a banker, then we can all borrow money from him."

At the end of ten days the family made the return trip to

Trepied. Though he could now use his son's growth as a measuring rod, John was still completely atemporal. He noticed that his painter friends, at the end of the summer at Trepied and more particularly on New Year's Day, liked to tot up their books: so many months had passed, so many drawings, sketches, studies, paintings had been completed, hence the summer of the year had been well or ill spent and justified quantitatively; and so the books could be balanced and closed. But for him time was an ever-flowing river, rising in some high and inexhaustible mountain spring and flowing smoothly, uninterruptedly to some distant sea. He rarely knew the time of day or day of the week; he almost never knew what month it was or what precise calendar year. When Amelia chided him for his total unawareness, he replied as he had years before in Wichita:

"I know the seasons by the color and substance of the foliage; by the shape and movement of the clouds, and by the heat or chill of the sun. What more do I need to know?"

"I have to know when it is eight o'clock, twelve o'clock and six o'clock in order to feed the baby."

"You only think you need to know; when the boy is hungry he will yell, and when he yells you feed him."

He worked practically all the time, even when he was walking with his son cradled strongly against his shoulder in the back garden or eating his dinner in communal quiet with Amelia. He never stopped working inside his mind, thinking through canvases he had imagined were finished but now saw could be repainted to heighten the tonal effects, or remembering scenes and analyzing what was unnecessary and could be eliminated, how the various elements could be brought closer together in space arrangement to make a more harmonious whole.

One morning as he set out a new large canvas, *Fisherman's Homecoming,* to dry, Amelia said, "That's your finest canvas, darling. It's so beautiful . . . it's like . . . like God . . . shining through it."

The blood mounted a dull brick-red up his neck and through his cheeks and forehead clean to the hair line.

"Don't ever say that to me again!"

His voice was angry and rough. The tears came to Amelia's eyes.

"It's a . . . yes, it's a stupid thing to say. I paint a simple scene, a white horse pulling a white boat up on the white sands . . ."

"Please let me explain, John. I see God in that yellow sun

205

caught for an instant of eternity in those purple and gray clouds; I see Him in that white-masted fishing boat, which seems almost like a mystery ship which God would sail between two worlds; I see Him in that wonderful old white horse who somehow seems like a figure of eternal work and eternally silent suffering, the lot of man and beast alike."

The blood had drained from his face now, and he was pale; she could see his jaw muscles quivering and she shook her head in despair.

"I won't have you talking that kind of nonsense," he shouted, "do you hear me? I forbid you to say any such thing again! It's several years now since I put away all thoughts of God, just as I did my toys in Wichita when I grew up. Since then I have been able to live, and be happy and creative. I forbid you ever to talk about my painting in that mystical fashion."

"All right, darling, I won't do it again."

He reached out his arms for her. While rubbing the rough stubble of his beard against her smooth cheek, he said:

"Amelia, forgive me, but you can't know how dangerous this talk is. . . . I want to paint and live like this without an interruption all our lives, sober, quiet and well-behaved."

He left the house, walked down to the beach and crouched on the dark, wet, hard-packed sand, scratching random designs with his fingernails. Then he rose and stared over the murky waters in numb fright, for the first time since he had come to Trepied a victim of his own doubts and misgivings and torments. Could a man come out of the misery and torment of his own unhappy years, a man who had been all his life possessed by a demon, and live a calm, unperturbed life . . . or were the seeds of his own destruction contained within his own nature? Had the demon really been vanquished, or was it just lying still and quiet somewhere at the base of his brain, knowing that this was the wrong instant to strike, that it could accomplish nothing at the moment but must patiently bide its time, watch every word and every move, ready to spring at the first opportunity and once again become master?

No, no, that was all over, it would never happen to him again. His work was good now, he had mastered his medium, matured in his craft. This could not be a temporary, a passing phase.

He spent an hour a day tending his corn in the garden, in his long painting smock and white Stetson, the first thing he put on in the morning and the last thing he took off at night, holding a large ruler against the stalks to see how much they had grown. Then kneeling down, he would dig up the earth to see how the roots were behaving. Though his father sent him prize seed from Wichita each spring, when the painters of the neighborhood held their annual Corn Show he was invariably awarded the booby prize for the runtiest corn . . . doubtless the result of poking at the young roots with his ruler to hasten their growth.

The French farmers laughed at the painters, demanding, "Whoever heard of eating corn? Why, we feed that stuff to the cattle!" There were other tussles with the farmers of the neighborhood: once John had to rescue Alexander Harrison from the local gendarmerie, for Harrison still liked to paint his nude models in the warm sunlight of his garden, and the neighbors finally had him arrested. After John bailed him out the two men pitched in and built a high stone wall around the garden . . . only to find, after it was completed, that the selfsame farmers had come during the night and broken peepholes through the wet plaster.

On New Year's Day of 1913 the colony learned that an attempt was being made to stage a show of modern art, in the 69th Armory in New York City, which would display for the first time in America the new and radical approaches to painting which had been exciting European art for many years, the work of Cézanne, Van Gogh, Pissarro, Toulouse-Lautrec, Gauguin, Matisse, Picasso, Braque, Dufy, Rouault, Duchamp, Kandinsky.

John sent a cable to the New York sponsors which read:

MARTIN BUCKLER OF WICHITA KANSAS HAS FINEST COLLECTION OF MODERN PAINTINGS IN AMERICA. AM SURE HE WOULD BE GLAD TO LEND FOR EXHIBITION.

A few days later he received a cable from Marty:

FOR HEAVENS SAKE STOP. DONT WANT TO LEND ANY PAINTINGS STOP ARMORY SHOW WILL REFUSE TO ACCEPT AND I WILL BE EXPOSED AND REJECTED IN THE BARGAIN. PLEASE STOP.

John then cabled to Frances to intervene, and apparently this device worked, for the following week he received a second cable from Marty:

COLLECTION CAUSED SENSATION AMONG JUDGES. AM STUPE-
FIED OR SHOULD I SAY JUST PLAIN STUPID STOP FRANCES TER-
RIBLY EXCITED. ·

The Armory Show caused the greatest excitement and
hair-pulling in the history of American art; and as John
learned over the following weeks the Martin Buckler Collection was at the heart of the storm. The most controversial
canvas proved to be Duchamp's *Nude Descending the Staircase*, for try as they might no one could find either the nude
or the staircase. The picture was reproduced in several of the
New York papers along with a picture of its owner, the cap-
tion reading

NUDE DESCENDING THE STAIRCASE

In smaller type it was explained that Mr. Martin Buckler,
pictured above, was the owner of this famous-infamous picture: and Martin Buckler with his burned stubble hair, confused purple eyes and bony face became known throughout
the country as the *Nude Descending the Staircase*.

John chuckled heartily as he read how Marty had been invited to talk to the members of the National Arts Club. He
tacked the newspaper clipping onto a wall in his studio, and
under it a cable from Marty:

DAVE LEAHY WOULD BE PROUD OF US.

8

Gerald Addams was the first to take the war talk in Europe seriously and book passage home.

"John, why not come back to Boston with me?" he asked,
his silver spectacles sliding up and down the hump of his
nose excitedly. "You don't want to get caught here when the
shooting starts."

"This is my home, Gerald. We plan to buy the house."

Calm, easygoing Alexander Harrison was the next to close
his studio.

"John, you'll find that war simply paralyzes an artist. Of
one thing we can be sure, the United States is never going to
get embroiled in any European quarrel."

"But how can I leave Brittany now?" John's voice was hurt

and confused. "I'm happy here; I'm doing good work; there are so many scenes I want to paint, so many canvases to complete."

Charles Hawthorne was returning to Provincetown to prepare for the annual summer session of his popular art school. "Come with me to the Cape, John. Imagine a thin, solitary finger of land crooked out in a vast ocean, with a harbor where a thousand ships would be safe, and the little barn and fishhouse village with the Portuguese fisherfolk who look like they come right off the island of Capri. From sea to sea the four miles of land are covered by oaks, pines, juniper, sassafras and blueberry moors covering the dunes. The colors of the sea alter every few moments: pale blue, deep gray, and at sunset the masts of the fishing boats make long lavender shadows . . ."

John shook his head. "No, if I'm forced to leave I'll go to my aunts' place in England. Then I will be within a few hours of my studio here."

Nevertheless he accelerated his pace, working ever more concentratedly. He gave up his hour in the vegetable garden, no longer walked with his son on his shoulder, and took to painting nights on his unfinished canvases.

"Do you think there will be a war, John?" asked Amelia anxiously.

"No, of course not. It's just a lot of politicians coming into town for a Saturday night brawl and shooting off their firing irons in front of the saloons."

He kept insisting there would be no war, even after the remainder of the American painters had given up and gone home, the Englishmen had crossed the Channel, and Amelia's family had written from Strasbourg warning that the conflict was imminent.

"John, don't you think we had better do something?" urged Amelia, "for the boy's sake, if not for our own?"

"Oh, there's no rush," he replied. "I've got a number of subjects I want to paint yet. . . ."

They were in the casino a few days later; the orchestra was in the middle of a lively tune when a wave of excitement swept over the room. The waiter who had taken their order for tea and cakes cried, "I cannot serve you any more. I am a soldier now!" and the band stood up and played the "Marseillaise."

And so they were caught short, the last Americans left in Brittany. The American consul advised them to leave the following day or they would miss the final boat to England.

John packed his paintings carefully in great piles and roped them inside protective blankets, while Amelia stored the household goods they could not possibly carry with them, then stuffed some of her most precious silverware and dishes into her trousseau trunk.

"What are you putting that stuff in there for?" asked John suspiciously.

"Because I am taking it with me."

He grinned. "Here it's so late we're liable to be blown up by the bombs and you're busy packing your trousseau . . . when you haven't even had a piece of that fancy lingerie on your back in the three years since we came from Strasbourg."

She straightened up from the trunk, the big iron key in her hand, and faced him with blazing eyes.

"It's not my fault that we're late; you refused to listen to all advice. I'm going to take this trunk with us."

"I have carted that chest for thousands of miles, half of them on my own back, and I'm not going to move it one more inch. It's not going with us. It's a sample of the Old World and all the futility it represents. If it wasn't for things like that crazy trunk and all those crazy German politicians we wouldn't have to move out of here. Now come and help me pack these paintings."

Amelia seated herself on the chest.

"If we go, the trunk goes; if the trunk stays, we stay."

"Confound you stubborn, illogical sentimental women," he cried. "All right, the trunk goes. Now get up off it and start moving. That last boat leaves Boulogne at ten in the morning."

They worked all night to get their things in order, then made a wild dash to the port. They arrived in Boulogne a little after nine in the morning. Here they learned that John had made a slight error: the boat sailed at ten that night.

Amelia sat down on her trousseau trunk utterly exhausted, wondering how she was going to keep her son comfortable for the next twelve hours in the dismal boat shed. She looked up at John for help, but his face was turned away, studying a group of stevedores who were loading cargo, and soon he was at his easel and paints, blocking out a canvas.

9

The long black car sped past glass greenhouses, continued along the circular driveway which edged a well-kept lawn, and drew up in front of Beckfoot. The chauffeur opened the door and a butler came down the steps of the baronial mansion to take their luggage. From the reception hall they stood gazing into a huge fireplace which centered an overstuffed drawing room. The butler then led them up the stairs to a second-floor bedroom with windows overlooking the garden. Amelia stood in the doorway of a bathroom surveying the white porcelain fixtures with tears in her eyes.

"What are you crying about," asked John, "haven't you ever seen a bathroom before?"

"Yes . . . no . . . John, I thought the story of your wealthy aunts and their estate was just one of your fabulous tales."

After they had rested from the rough crossing of the Channel and the long automobile ride to the north of England they went down to the drawing room where they found John's aunts awaiting them: tall aristocratic Mary, her iron-gray hair parted in the middle and drawn in a tight knot on her neck, wearing a low-cut evening gown of beaded velvet, diamond earrings and a diamond necklace. Standing considerably behind her was Elizabeth, the second of the two spinster sisters: small, drab, with heavy features, small gray eyes and an overly large mouth which she kept bunched together as though to reduce its size, wearing a threadbare evening dress belonging to some long-vanished era, with a skimpy string of crystal beads about her neck. It was as though their parents had exhausted themselves in producing regal Mary of the flashing dark eyes and imperious manner, and had only vestiges left for little Elizabeth.

Mary knew that John had been living in France, but she ignored the fact.

"It's about time you came home to England, John. I don't see how you stood it in America all these years. Why, when I visited your family as a young girl they would go out just before dinner and catch the chickens and twist their necks; I heard them squawking, so how could I have been expected to eat a single bite?"

"Hasn't changed a bit," drawled John in his broadest trail

dialect. "My mother still has to go out on the prairie at dawn and shoot herself a buffalo in order to have fresh meat for breakfast."

A short, muted chuckle came from behind Aunt Mary. Everyone turned to look at Aunt Elizabeth, but she was silent and innocent-faced.

Mary crooked her arm for John. They walked together into the mahogany dining room. He and Mary reigned at either end of the table, their faces lighted by five-pronged silver candelabra while Amelia and Elizabeth sat on either side, lost in the center darkness.

After dinner they sat in the oak-paneled library where Mary brought out her most prized possession, a minutely documented genealogy of the Noble family on which she had been working for some thirty years.

"I have succeeded in tracing the family back to the fifteenth century," she told John with great pride. "The Nobles have reached the top of every profession in England. Only one Noble ever deserted: your grandfather, who went out to Illinois."

"In our country, Aunt Mary, if a man traces himself back far enough he'll eventually find that he comes from horse thieves."

There was an enormous Chinese gong in the downstairs hall which a maid boomed once to inform the Nobles that they had better get up, the second time to inform them to dress, and the third time to tell them to rush downstairs as the food was about to be served. At breakfast there were bowls of oatmeal, eggs, bacon, fish and coffee. They had hardly left the table when the Chinese gong boomed again and they were back in the mahogany dining room for cold cuts from the lamb roast of the night before, boiled vegetables and a tapioca pudding. After lunch they went for a ride in the motor, with Aunt Mary and John ensconced in the back seat and Elizabeth and Amelia sitting on the narrow jump seats. At five o'clock they were back at Beckfoot before the sound of the gong had faded, having tea in the center of the flower gardens by a large stone sundial: slices of bread and butter, fresh scones, fruitcake with white icing; and then at seven o'clock the gong again for dinner.

On Sunday morning Amelia went with Mary and Elizabeth to the village of Brampton to attend the Episcopal services. After the services the congregation came to shake hands with the Noble women even before speaking to the bald-headed minister: for most of the church, including the stained-glass windows, had been donated by a Noble.

"If you painted that church at Brampton maybe your aunts would buy the picture," suggested Amelia as they went up to their bedroom for the night. "We haven't a franc or a shilling left to our name."

"Every time I pick up a paintbrush that confounded gong rings; how in the devil can a man work on such a full stomach?"

Occasionally he and Amelia would escape through a side door, climb the hill on the east end of the Beckfoot estate and descend to the creek where they would take off their shoes and stockings and wade in the cool waters. Little John played here for hours, the sun beating down on his plump naked body.

"The boy is flourishing," said Amelia happily. "Those four meals a day that are killing you are doing wonders for him."

"I think I'll take your advice and paint the church over at Brampton," said John, restlessly juggling two small rocks in his hands. "Maybe do a study of the house seen through the peach trees."

He did the two paintings and considered that they turned out badly. Aunt Mary was enchanted with them.

"We must take you to London, John, and introduce you to all the great English artists."

"Would you like to have these two paintings?" asked Amelia timorously.

"Certainly, certainly. I have every intention of acquiring them."

"What does Aunt Mary mean by acquiring our paintings?" asked Amelia when she and John were alone. "Take them in return for room and board?"

"Stop worrying, Amelia," said John. "British troops have landed in France and the French have defeated the Germans in Alsace. In another month or two we will be back in Brittany."

But immediately thereafter the news became bad. Every paper John read brought accounts of German victories: the Allies had to retreat to the Somme, the Russians were defeated by Von Hindenburg at Tannenberg, the first airplane bombs were dropped on Paris. Like everyone who loved France, he was stricken at the thought of the burning villages and harrowed land. He left Beckfoot for days at a time, tramping the surrounding countryside in hopes of finding paintable scenes. At first he rejected everything he laid his eyes on: rolling hills, tiny villages at the end of narrow winding lanes, plowed farmlands, sparse sandy dunes, dark green forests, the fog-shrouded Solway Firth, for nothing moved or excited him. Then in fear that he was rejecting these characterful scenes out of indolence he cast aside all principles of selection and for weeks painted everything he stumbled upon: the pretty, the obvious, the banal, the empty, the unpaintable. When the cold lashing winds swept across Cumberland and the December snows made the narrow roads almost impassable he continued to paint blindly . . . most of the time not even bothering to take the canvases back to Beckfoot with him.

On the night before Christmas he returned from a trip to the Cheviot Hills, on the border of Scotland, his face red and chapped from the cold, and tossed a still wet canvas onto the bed, cursing volubly.

"I did better work at the Ruche ten years ago. What do you suppose has happened to me?"

Amelia glanced at the paintings; they were dark, confused.

"The subjects are new to you, John, and perhaps not sympathetic; you're not accustomed to the English atmosphere and countryside. But surely you're entitled to a fallow season? You worked so hard for three years; why not spend the days with the boy and me . . . until we find out what's going to happen to us."

They were sitting in the library that evening playing bridge. Everyone was depressed by the stalemate in France, the German submarine raids on British seacoast towns and the crushing Austro-German victories in Russian Poland. John's optimism about a quick Allied victory had given way to the certainty that this would be a long and bitter struggle. When he looked up from his reverie he heard his Aunt Mary speaking.

"You take this English fruit, how delicious it is; your American fruit is just terrible."

"It's true that here in England and in France the fruit is very fine," replied John softly, "but it's almost prohibitive in price. Our fruit is not handled with such delicacy, but it is available to everybody. I guess that's the major difference between an aristocracy and a democracy."

"Wait until you are master of Beckfoot, then you will understand . . ."

"Master of . . . ? Aunt Mary, what are you talking about?"

"But surely, John, you know that you are the next in the

male line of the Nobles? Beckfoot would have gone to your father, but now that he's dead . . ."

John stared at his Aunt Mary, bewildered. He had had a letter from his father only the week before, a long newsy, rambunctious and affectionate letter, the kind which usually accompanied his monthly check.

"John, don't tell me you didn't know your father had died?"

". . . no, nobody told me . . . when did he . . . ?"

"We received a cable from your mother while you were out on your last painting trip. We thought you didn't want to talk about it."

Numbly John said, "No, my message must have been missent. . . ."

He went to his room and huddled his big frame into a chair, thinking back to his father as he had grown up with him; practical-minded John Noble who had supported his son all these years even though he had little use for painting. He remembered their pack trips during the long summers, voyages on horseback into the Rocky Mountains and the plains of the Southwest. He remembered their terrifying quarrel about his not returning to school, how his father had struck him across the face . . . and how they had both drunk themselves blind to forget.

Then he remembered the proud letter he had received from his father after the family had made the journey to Chicago and Philadelphia to see his paintings in the two museum shows:

I understand now what you meant when you said that the West was not a place but a state of mind. Painting is to you what the prairie wilderness is to me: wide-open country with no fences or borders or staked-out claims: a place where a man can live his own life and build his own empire.

His father had given him the greatest and rarest of all gifts: the right of absence; for like Alexander Harrison he had learned that his son was a loose and wandering star. Much as his family loved him and missed him they knew he was better off in distant and strange parts; that Wichita could do nothing for him but create unhappiness. What better proof could his father have given him of his love than to have left him free in space and time?

10

"We must invite Blanche Marchesi down for a week end," said Aunt Mary. "She will see that you are a great painter and introduce you to London."

"But how can you be sure I'm a great painter, Aunt Mary?"

"You're a Noble, aren't you?"

With that she picked up her long train and swept out of the room. Aunt Elizabeth started a low chuckle, then suppressed it. "I have a better way of knowing, Johnny: I have seen your Britany pictures."

Several days later he returned from another trip into the country to find Aunt Elizabeth gone . . . and a dozen of his paintings as well. Aunt Mary was pacing the drawing room, a baffled expression on her face.

"She has gone to London. Simply commandeered the motor and left."

"But why?"

"To take your paintings to Blanche Marchesi."

"I thought she had been invited here?"

"She couldn't come, not for six or eight weeks. Your Aunt Elizabeth must love you very much indeed to be moved to this revolt, John: she hasn't done anything without my consent since our parents died, some twenty years ago."

Aunt Elizabeth returned three days later to inform John that Miss Marchesi would be pleased to give a reception for him, Sunday a week.

Blanche Marchesi, the famous singer, whose mother had taught the young Melba, had a large and beautiful house in St. John's Wood to which came all of musical Europe. Blanche was a tall, heavy woman with white hair and a voice which even in casual conversation was pure music. She was as interested in painting as she was in music, and her drawing-room walls were covered with canvases. John stood in the doorway, his heart pounding in his ears, for Blanche had hung six of his Brittany paintings between her Corots, Turners, Rousseaus, Millets and Daubignys. She came toward him with a hand outstretched.

"How do you like the company you're in, John Noble?"

"It's a cruel test to put a man's canvases immediately next to the finest things that have been painted in a hundred years."

She searched his face. "How do you think you come out?"

"I don't know," he replied gingerly.

"Well, I can tell you that your paintings stand up extremely well."

Guests began to arrive, not singly but in bunches. First he was introduced to three sculptors: Jacob Epstein, an American, Clare Sheridan, an Englishwoman, and Meštrović, a Balkan. Next came a group of musicians: Ysaye, the Belgian violinist, Gans, the pianist, Vladimir de Pachmann, a Russian pianist, John Runciman, the English music critic. Then it was the writers' turn to pour in: H. G. Wells, George Moore, Bernard Shaw, Frank Harris. The guests came in such profusion that John was barely able to distinguish their names, but among the painters he was enormously happy to greet Augustus John, whom he considered to be the finest of all the English painters; Walter Sickert, who lived and painted in Whistler's old studio; Fred Mayer, a water-colorist who had lived close by in Trepied during one summer; George Turnhouse from the Ruche, still dressed in his incredibly wrinkled suit of tweeds. Society was well represented too, for Clare Sheridan brought her aunt, Lady Randolph Churchill, H. M. Cleminson, Manager of His Majesty's Shipping, and a Countess Lewenhaupt-Falkenstein, a large, breezy California woman who had married into the Swedish nobility. The countess embraced John as a fellow Westerner and carried him off to a corner of the salon to tell him the fruitier stores of European society. There was music and food and drink and, despite the scattered uniforms and war stories, good conversation about painting, sculpture and literature.

"I owe this all to you," said John as he hugged his Aunt Elizabeth.

He received a dozen invitations to parties, teas, dinners, receptions, all of which he accepted and none of which he remembered; but it was Augustus John who finally stood on a chair in front of Blanche Marchesi's fireplace, took off the wall John's *Breton Fisher Village* and said:

"Come along to my studio. I want to talk to you and get acquainted."

Sitting quietly in the hansom, John had a chance to study his new friend. He thought Augustus the handsomest man he had ever seen, with great flashing eyes and long lashes, soft yellowish hair falling loosely over his ears, and a soft yellow beard and mustache.

Augustus John's studio at 33 Tite Street in Chelsea was big, disheveled and filled with a tremendous quantity of char-

217

coal, pencil and wash portraits in various stages of completion. In one corner stood a big black box filled with hundreds of coins. Augustus explained:

"Whenever I sell a canvas I drop the money into this box. My family and friends all live off it until the money is gone, and then we wait until I sell something again. I have so many wives and so many children, I have to hire a bus when I want to take them all out together. Fortunately I have been selling pretty steadily of late, so I haven't seen the bottom of that black box in several years."

"Why did you take my picture off the wall at Blanche Marchesi's?"

"Simple reason. I am going to show it at the Grosvenor Gallery Exhibition which opens next week."

"The Grosvenor Gallery? But the selections are closed. I read about it at Beckfoot."

"I'm going to give up my space to you."

"Give up . . . But why should you make that sacrifice? Besides, they probably won't like my canvas . . ."

"The gallery can't afford to turn me down, my friend. And when the art world learns that I think your picture so important that I have given up my hanging space in the annual Grosvenor show . . . together we shall enjoy a *succèss fou!*"

Augustus John was right. For three days in advance of the opening the newspapers carried stories of the historic substitution of canvases, with photographs of the John Noble and Augustus John paintings so that the public could make its own comparison. When the show opened all London came to see the John Noble canvas and, having come largely out of curiosity, remained to admire and to clasp John Noble to its bosom, the first American painter to have been accepted so warmly since the latter stages of James McNeill Whistler's stormy career in London.

11

It should have been easy: for three solid years he had painted so gloriously, everything he touched had throbbed with life and beauty. He had with him dozens of rough sketches; he needed only to set up his easel and canvas, squeeze the paints onto the palette and do the same work he had done in his winter studio in Paris while working from the Brittany sketches. He was the same man, the same eyes, brain, hand, feelings, and yet when he put the paints on the canvas the pictures came out dull, meaningless.

Why?

He took his easel, canvas, palette and brushes out into the streets of London to paint Waterloo Station, Westminster Abbey, Gray's Inn; he painted inside the glass-covered dome of Paddington Station, he tried to capture the shops and jammed busses at the corner of Regent and Oxford streets, painted St. Paul's Cathedral seen from Ludgate Circus, the greenery of Regent's Park and Tower Bridge from a barge on which he had rented space for several days. He tried painting along the Thames River, thinking the water scenes might excite him; he did the Battersea Bridge which Whistler had made famous; and with the first warmth of spring went down to the docks where the weather-beaten ships from Africa and the Orient unloaded their exotic cargoes.

He destroyed all these canvases. He had not been able to paint at Beckfoot, or anywhere in Cumberland, and now he had painted London like a stranger, catching only the barest external aspects of the houses and streets.

John and Amelia were now living as much in London hotels as in Beckfoot. At a party for writers and painters which Walter Sickert gave for him in Whistler's studio, John met Sidney Whitman, who was a political writer, tall, thin, bent, with a black skullcap covering his bald head. One day Whitman took the Nobles to the home of Sir Thomas Barclay at 61 Nevern Square, a five-story house of large red stone. Sir Thomas Barclay was stationed in Paris for the British government, but his German wife was afraid to occupy the house alone while England was at war with her country.

Amelia and John entered the front door, walked through a narrow hall into an oak-paneled library lined with priceless books and with glass cases of art treasures. They followed Whitman up a narrow, carpeted staircase to the second-floor greenhouse with inlaid mosaic stone floor and green palms around a pool. On the third floor they found themselves in a tremendous drawing room with massive velours sofas and mahogany armchairs covered with valuable petit point. On the fourth floor were half a dozen bedrooms, the largest of which had high ceilings and white walls, a huge bed, dressing table and chest of drawers with carved outlines etched in real gold. Pale green curtains edged the windows that admitted bright sunlight and overlooked the garden of Nevern Square.

"How would you and Mrs. Noble like to live here, John?"

asked Whitman after the tour of inspection. John stood speechless.

"Live here? But . . . can we afford it?"

"Tell me what you can afford, and that will be the rent. Sir Thomas wants the house occupied. He is particularly keen to have someone who will appreciate his art collection."

For several days after they moved in John watched the activity about the house: tradespeople coming and going with supplies of food and liquors, domestics being instructed by Amelia in the midst of household cleaning. When on Saturday morning a group of cooks and butlers took possession of the house it was no longer possible to think that these were routine activities. He found Amelia in the vast subterranean kitchen with a short, redfaced mustachioed Frenchman.

"What's the meaning of this, Amelia?"

"We're going to have an 'at home.' Tomorrow. Sunday."

"You'll do nothing of the sort," he shouted. "I won't be a host at a pink tea!"

"Now, John, you can't go to luncheons, dinners and receptions all over London and not reciprocate." She added tenaciously, "Besides, I've always wanted to have a first-rate salon. . . ."

John stomped out of the kitchen swearing that he wouldn't be there when the guests arrived.

She had arranged for his friends to come early. Sidney Whitman arrived in midafternoon to grunt his approval of the preparations and of John in striped trousers and cutaway coat. Augustus John came in a hansom with Jacob Epstein and Blanche Marchesi.

Amelia took from the oak trunk her loveliest trousseau outfit, a green shantung gown appliquéd with jade satin flowers. She stood at the head of the large staircase while the butler called out the names of the hundred and fifty guests whom Blanche Marchesi had helped her assemble from the cream of the British painting, writing, musical, theatrical and social worlds, an increasing number of whom were now in the services.

"You look like a Christmas tree," murmured John, between guests. "And you've got stars in your eyes."

Amelia flushed, then turned to greet the Maharajah of Benares, and Mr. and Mrs. Sidney Webb.

During the evening Pachmann played the piano, Ysaye his violin, and Blanche sang. It was in the midst of the reception, when Lady Randolph Churchill was entertaining a group of writers and members of Parliament with tales of her American childhood, that John's inner ear heard the butler, with an almost imperceptible edge of disapproval, announce:

"Mr. and Mrs. Martin Buckler."

He hurried to the head of the staircase, saw Marty and Frances standing in the small foyer, dressed in traveling suits. Frances looked toward him eagerly, a high spot of color on either cheek. John saw that she did indeed seem taller, almost fleshless. He ran down the stairs, took her in his arms and kissed her. She quivered all over, like a ship that has been struck. There was a long moment before he was able to speak.

"Marty, how did you get to England with a war going on?"

"I'm over here on a banking mission. President Wilson insists we're neutral, even after the sinking of the *Lusitania,* but, boy, if you could know how many millions of dollars we have invested in the Allies!"

John led the Bucklers to Amelia, introduced them to his friends.

At midnight when the last guest had called for his hansom and gone home, Amelia took Frances up to the white and gold bedroom. John lay sprawled on a leather divan in the library, his cutaway coat, starched collar, stiff-bosomed shirt and striped trousers strewn over the floor. In a chair across the room slumped Marty, his deep purple eyes baffled and hurt, just as John remembered them from the early days of insecurity in Wichita.

"John, you made a fool out of me!"

"What in hell are you talking about, Marty?"

"For years I've been telling Frances how wrong she was to think there was anything romantic about a painter's life. I told her about the dirt at the Ruche, how everything was old and broken and smelly; I told her about your house in Etaples, how you had no running water, even had to use an outhouse . . ."

"That was all true."

"You urged me to bring her over, so at last I did . . . and what do you do to me? I find you living in a mansion. . . ."

Marty was crushed. He sat in the chair, his legs out stiff before him, his head down.

"Frances will never forgive me . . . she'll think I was lying . . . talking you down in order to build myself up . . ." He sat with his eyes closed for a moment, then added quietly, "But even so, I want you to know that I'm mighty proud of you. I was wrong, John: now I see you're a great painter."

"Thanks, Marty, but what's made you change your mind?

You couldn't have seen any of my work since you got to London."

"I don't need to, your success is perfectly obvious: living here like this, all the great people of England coming to your parties . . ."

Jonn rolled over so that he could look directly at Marty.

"This is lovely irony. You brought Frances to gloat over how badly we lived and stumbled into Amelia's soirée. In Brittany I was painting gloriously and you hated my work. Now, when I've been in England for a whole year without painting one worth-while canvas, when my brain is as thick as cold porridge and my hands are made up of a dozen thumbs, you congratulate me on becoming a great artist. You're even with me, boy."

"Aw, cut out the arty talk."

12

The following day John took Frances to lunch at a small French restaurant in Soho. They sat in silence for several moments while a waiter served them from the hors d'oeuvre cart. Frances was the first to speak.

"I'm divorcing Marty. Did he tell you?"

"Oh no, Frances, you wouldn't do that to him . . ."

"We're strangers, John, accidentally locked in the same house. I started proceedings in Wichita but Marty begged me to make this trip before I did anything final. I think he meant to show me how much better off I was than your wife. . . ." She was quiet for a moment, then shook her head abruptly as though to throw off the thought. "There's just one thing I can't understand," she went on, "it's this reputation as an art critic that Marty has built up."

". . . it came about gradually . . . he naturally mixed with painters when he was with me at the Ruche . . ."

"You bought those paintings for him, didn't you? And you made him memorize those things he told the reporters and the audience at the National Arts Club?"

"You'd be surprised how fast he learned. . . ."

"When I saw those collectors and museum directors talking to him so respectfully at the Armory Show I was dumbfounded. . . ."

"You're misjudging him, Frances."

"Am I? Prove it."

"All right. We'll set up a Martin Buckler Purchase Show here in London. Marty told me last night that he wanted to add the best English paintings to his collection."

"And he will know, all by himself, which are the best of the English paintings?"

"Just wait and see."

"I guess everything you say is true," sighed Frances.

John ventured, "Marty told me you'd been getting along better since the Armory Show, that you've become excited about modern painting."

She leaned across the table, her face close to his.

"John, I'll drop the divorce if you'll help me get something I want very much."

"What's that, Frances?"

"You remember how you hungered for the sight of good painting during the years you lived in Wichita?"

"Of course."

"Well, we have nothing more today. As far as Wichita is concerned there is no such thing as art. I want to build an art gallery in Wichita."

"Have you told Marty?"

"I've offered to provide the land, a beautiful site I bought years back, down the river. John, can you know what that would mean to me? I would have an interest in life . . . become alive again. I could give to the young people of the Midwest a chance to see the work that's being done; they wouldn't have to grope blindly, unhappily . . . flee to other countries . . . as you did . . . and be lost to those who love them."

John felt the years drain away between them.

"He'll build it," he answered quietly.

That night he spread word among the painters, with Augustus John, Sickert, Turnhouse as couriers, and among the sculptors through Jacob Epstein and Clare Sheridan that his friend Martin Buckler wanted a show assembled for the purpose of acquiring new art works to take back to America. He then went to the American Club and secured permission to use their social rooms for the purposes of displaying the paintings and sculpture. The English artists did not know much about Martin Buckler's taste or judgment, but there was one thing they did know: he bought. For days the parcels and crates arrived from all over England.

"Look, John, I'm scared," said Marty. "If I make mistakes,

pick the wrong ones, or say something stupid, Frances will know I'm a fraud."

"There's nothing to worry about," replied John. "We'll go through the show on the night before the exhibition and make a list in your little notebook of the paintings and sculpture you are to buy. Then as you walk through the rooms you will pick out the titles you've got jotted down."

Two days before the hanging was completed John received word that his Aunt Elizabeth was seriously ill. He caught the next train for Beckfoot, sat by her bedside for some thirty-six hours, until it became certain that she would recover. Then he returned to London, but too late for the opening.

He walked quickly to the American Club and to the exhibition rooms. As he made his way along the walls he found that Marty had selected the strongest, the most radical pictures in the show! He had even chosen two of Jacob Epstein's crude, powerfully sculptured heads.

He sank slowly onto the divan in the center of the big room. How had Marty done it? Had he really learned about modern art? He sprang up from the couch, made his way to the Claridge and pounded on Marty's door.

"Marty, you're wonderful. You picked all the finest pieces in the show. How did you do it?"

"It was easy," grinned Marty. "I remembered how in Paris, when I saw canvases that looked like they had been drawn by children or lunatics, those were always the ones you made me buy. So this time I just passed by everything I liked and picked out the craziest things in the show."

John threw his arms around his old friend and hugged him delightedly.

"You're a genius. Now I know why you're such a phenomenal success in Wichita."

"Glad you appreciate me at last."

"Yes, I do, Marty. And you're ready for your next big step. . . ."

"Now, John, this purchase show set me back fourteen thousand dollars . . ."

John pretended not to have heard him.

"The next thing you're going to do is build a gallery for all these fine pictures in Wichita. . . ."

"A museum of art! Do you think I'm plumb loco?"

"Marty, you must build the museum."

He had spoken in a low, flat tone. Marty stared at him, searching for further explanation, yet at the same time fearing it. After a moment he lowered his eyes and muttered:

"All right, John, if you say so. But it's going to be called the Martin Buckler Museum of Modern Art, do you hear me?"

"I hear you."

13

He did a canvas of Amelia and little John on the balcony overlooking Nevern Square; it had a sweetness of sentiment, nothing more. He did a camouflage painting of warships in their docks so patterned with paint that they would be invisible from the air; the Admiralty thanked him for the new idea in color striping, but the picture itself was poor. In the fall H. M. Cleminson asked him to do a three-paneled decoration for his music room; John spent the long dark months of their second winter in London making sketches for the mural, immersing himself in the pleasant anesthetic of a commission. The center panel, which he called *My Family*, a mother, father and child picnicking on the beach, had a little warmth to it, but the end panels of *Morning* and *Evening* were thin and banal.

He went about the city to the homes of his friends hoping for a newborn vitality. Everywhere there was talk of the German use of poison gas, the opening of the long-expected Allied drive in the west and the compulsory Military Service Act; and everywhere he went people immediately demanded, "When in heaven's name is America coming into this war?" How could one paint in a world in flames? How could one start a big canvas today when tomorrow German Zeppelin bombs might blow one's home and canvases into a thousand fragments? How to paint in the midst of hundreds of people, parties, receptions, discussions, "at homes"? Painting was a lonely art.

"I told you I'm only half alive in cities," he answered Amelia when she commented on his restlessness. "I need lonely places, where I can paint elemental things."

"Then let's find a lonely place."

"Where?"

"On the North Sea; some small fishing village . . ."

He considered the idea soberly for several moments.

"Maybe I can find the counterpart of the Breton villages. But it will be pretty cold and bleak along the York and Dur-

225

ham coast. And you are having such a grand time here in London."

"I would rather be cold with you on the North Sea than warm and alone here."

They packed lightly and made the pilgrimage from town to town: Hornsea, Skipsea, Bridlington, Scarborough; north to Blyth and Amble in Northumberland. In spite of the sporadic cruiser raids, John worked feverishly on the raw rugged coast, trying to catch the fishermen, their boats and nets and villages. He found picturesque scenes and sympathetic characters . . . but his heart weighed heavily, and he painted mechanically, like a laborer who hates his job and works only for the wage.

"It's no use, Amelia," he said one night in March after they had been out for six weeks, "we might just as well get out of these cold inns and go back to the house in London. I don't understand these people, their boats or their villages or their sea."

Back in London he dug into his Breton notebook again, transferred several Trepied studies to canvas with all the right colors and with a composition he knew as intimately as the knuckles on his painting hand. Yet nothing exciting emerged, just paint and canvas.

At last he came to the realization that he could not paint at all. Not because of any of the reasons he had given himself: for these reasons had been excuses, rationalizations, delaying actions, keeping him from admitting what he had known deep in his mind, that he stood empty, abandoned, to let. Art in any form was a sometime thing: now a man was good, now he was great, now he was mediocre, and now he was bad; and he could never know in advance which would be coming next. All of a painter's work put together made one integrated picture: the complete story of everything he was, everything he felt, thought, lived, created, failed in: his autobiography.

He had been at the crest where he had created at the fullest; now he was in the trough, obscured, sunk deep, powerless, able to do nothing . . . like the boat he had painted, rolling dead in the trough of a Brittany wave. Would he ever ride the crest again, reach a peak of creation? He had no way to tell. But if he should be through now, what had he done to justify himself? He looked at his Brittany canvases one by one: how good they were, how strong, how deeply felt, how they spoke to one of things infinite like the sea and the plains. Yet he could hardly remember having painted them.

. . . It seemed impossible that he could ever have painted that well in the past, he who could not paint at all in the present.

It was the end of July by the time he locked his studio door behind him, after still another four months of wasted effort. He had never counted time, but now he pulled out an old calendar and computed that he had been in England for two years.

He rose at no particular hour in the morning for there was nothing to get up for; he had coffee, much coffee, but he had lost his appetite for food. He roamed the various floors of Sir Thomas' elaborate house, then settled himself in a big chair to read the newspapers, all he could lay his hands on, letting them fall to the floor as he finished with them.

He went out. He did not tell Amelia where he was going because he did not know where he was going, and was ashamed to say that he would simply be wandering. He did not tell her when he would come back for he did not know when he would come back. He thought it the better part of kindness to get his irresolute bulk out of the house and keep it out.

He went to the galleries and looked at good paintings; he went to the homes and studios of his friends for talk and argument, he went to the families who were buying his pictures and helped them select the best room and the best wall for his work. Everywhere he was welcomed. But when people praised him as a painter he would think:

You should be talking to the pictures, feeding them, praising them, befriending them; for they, and not I, are the living reality.

When the most respected art journal in England said of him, "John Noble is a poet; he creates a world not real but more true than the physical world about us," he mocked silently, See, now I'm a poet.

He managed to alternate the people he visited so that, since each group saw him only one day a week, they had no way of knowing that he was not working the rest of the time. Not that they would have cared: for they had judged him first-rate; and a first-rate man produces when and as he can; the torture of not producing was infinitely worse than the burden of creation. They admired him for what he had been and what he would be; what he happened to be at this moment was an accident of time and circumstances.

When there was nothing left to do and no place to go he meandered home. But there was little reason to be at home either; an unhappy man can bring no joy to his family.

"Why not try again, John, now that the summer heat is on?" urged Amelia. "We could go to Devon or Cornwall. Everyone says it's so beautiful there. Isn't it better to turn out unsatisfactory canvases than none at all?"

"No, there are enough millions of mediocre paintings already in the world. I want to produce only what I know is my best. I've been trying for over two years now and haven't painted even one good canvas. Think of it, Amelia, not one . . . not even by accident!"

She saw him wandering, forlorn, suffering inside his head, without focus or purpose, filling the days with noise and discussion and theories and increasingly loud laughter. For the first time she could charge that he was failing to fulfill his promise: what was happening to him was happening to him alone; there seemed no way for her to share his burden. Now she too became unhappy, for her marriage had become a fractional one. He had said that she was his partner, that in his joy and security at having her by his side he could turn out good work. But she was not helping him now. Had they become too much involved with the world? These were John's friends, he liked these people, and the acclaim and prestige were his due, as it was the due of any artist who had achieved recognition through good work. Hadn't he told her in Trepied that he could withstand success? Here in London he had had a solid success; this elaborate house which she loved, the striped trousers she made John wear to receptions, the Lord Fauntleroy velvet suits for little John, and her "salon" . . . John might grouse about them, but weren't they helpful in getting him the attention of critics? And was not this success a part of the cycle of their lives, even as failure would be? She knew now how right had been her instinct before marriage: in John's work they would find their love and happiness. What did they have without it: half a shell each, but together still making an empty shell.

John saw in Amelia's face her growing doubt and puzzlement, saw it when he came upon her wandering in Hyde Park with their little boy or weeping in her bedroom over the French defeats at Verdun; when he came home late and found her sitting alone at the dinner table, her food untouched; when she rose early to go to church and make a special novena for him. He knew that he was closing her out. But out of what? He was so empty there was not even love to share.

He was dressing for a party at Blanche Marchesi's, looking

in his closet for a suit that had apparently been lost at the cleaner's, when in a far corner he saw his rattlesnake vest.

"My old pal from the cow country," he murmured, taking it from the hook. He tried it on, decided it still fitted him well and searched through an unpacked valise for his two-gun holster. He donned his white Stetson and gazed at himself in a long mirror.

"I look beautiful," he grinned, "this is a fine uniform, except they don't want men over forty."

He went quickly down the stairs onto the street, acknowledging the amazed expressions of the passers-by with a broad tipping of his hat, laughing as he saw them hurry away when he placed his hands on his guns.

At Blanche's he enjoyed the commotion he caused, regaling the party with stories of the Southwest and the Chisholm Trail. He had no need to make himself the hero of the tales, but in the days that followed he acted them out with tremendous gusto wherever he happened to be: in the squares, in the stores buying the rationed supplies, in the Grosvenor Gallery or the exhibition in the Royal Academy.

He knew that he was staging a performance; and Amelia knew it too; for by now she had learned from his tone, by the way he cocked his shoulder and took the stance of a man carrying heavy guns, that he was fabricating for his own amusement. She did not try to stop him; rather she was glad: for this was the only time she saw his body alive, heard his voice booming. Sometimes he would return at midnight to find her sitting with her hands clasped in her lap behind the tightly drawn curtains of the blackout. He sat beside her in silence; then the Boy Scouts came bicycling through the streets shouting, "Take cover! Take cover!" and they rushed down to the basement, Amelia carrying the boy and John carrying paintings. They huddled in the darkness listening to the explosions of the Zeppelin raids, waiting until the "All clear!" before climbing the four flights of stairs to their bedroom. Sometimes this happened three or four times a night; John slipped into his old habit of sleeping only when he needed to, regardless of the hour of day or night.

Amelia watched him as he smoked endlessly, shut up inside himself, his eyes staring out through the room and the walls, through the war and the years; she did what she could to comfort him.

"I know you're unhappy about not being able to paint, darling, but in the meantime there are so many things to be grateful for: our boy is growing strong, we have this lovely house, we have friends in London, and a secure place in the art world; we are selling well?"

"Yes, I should be happy . . . but I'm miserable."

Nonetheless he was repentant, and the next day they would take the bus near Richmond and go out to Hampton Court, which had been built for Cardinal Wolsey. Another time they went down the Thames to Windsor Castle, had luncheon on a beautiful terrace overlooking the Thames.

One day Amelia handed him a letter from his Aunt Elizabeth asking them to come back to Beckfoot and take over the estate.

"What do you think, John, shall we stay in England and become citizens? Beckfoot is so beautiful."

"No, Amelia," said John, shaking his head. "I can't live where I can't paint."

He reached across the table and impetuously took her hand in his, as though to say, I'm sorry.

"So be it," sighed Amelia; "for a while I thought I was going to become a great English lady."

"You'll be a great lady wherever you go," replied John, and leaned over to kiss her. They were both consoled, a little.

14

He was locked in a room. It was pitch-black, airless, smelling of dankness and decay. Though he could not see his hand pressed so tightly against his face, he knew that there were thick stone walls on all four sides, walls that could not be breached. What was it: a dungeon? the basement of his house during an air raid? Beyond these walls he saw other people's homes, art galleries, clubs and restaurants; saw himself being greeted heartily, his hand wrung by an ever-increasing stream of bright people with eager faces expressing their delight in meeting him. He heard their praises . . . one of the world's great artists . . . style of his own . . . Then why was he not there? For he knew he was here, in this black cave which was nowhere. Why were all these people participating in this farce? Was it a conspiracy?

If it had seemed strange in Wichita so many years before that he should go among people, shake them, shout at them and they should not know he was there, it was infinitely stranger to him that now in London he should be entombed in this black abyss, sitting in the deepest silence yet watching himself parade all over the city where people welcomed him with open arms.

He scrambled to his feet from the cold rough floor, ran to the walls, beat against them with his fists and made an exit: so that now he was in the Leicester Galleries where Epstein was showing his new *Venus,* with an admission charge, and people stormed out of the galleries demanding their money back; or accompanying Lady Randolph Churchill to an opening at the Grosvenor Gallery because she liked the way he evaluated pictures. Even as he was engulfed by his friends, he cried out:

Why do you talk to me when I am not there? Why do you pretend to see me when I cannot see myself?

And he found himself running for home, until he was standing by the lily pond on the inlaid mosaic floor, with Amelia beside him asking:

"John, why are you so silent, so utterly deep-plunged silent? You haven't spoken to me or little John for days. Are you worried about something? Have you had bad news? Are you unwell?"

He shook his head, unable to push words out of his throat.

"I'm frightened and unhappy, John: something is happening to you that you are not sharing with me. You've gone away. I can't find my North Star, John. . . ."

The North Star had vanished for him too. Not the silver replica given him by his mother; that was securely bound around his neck on the silver chain given him by his wife. It was the star in the heavens that was gone. Why? How had he fallen into this impenetrable cave from which no light, no star could be seen? How strange to walk around, a prisoner in solitary confinement, and yet conceal the fact by putting up a convincing front composed of all the words, expressions, gestures, movements so well remembered from the days of vital life. How many of these vivacious, active, energetic people were fooling him just as he was fooling them? How many of them, like himself, were momentarily dead but making a great fuss and racket the better to conceal it? How did one find out about the others? Was there a secret password? But no, this was one fraternity in which the members did not want badges. Each man was a secret order unto himself so that if the fateful day should come when he returned into full life, no one, not even himself, would remember that he had once been dead.

Dead?

No, that was not now. That was Wichita, many years before. He had wandered through a long valley carpeted with bleached white bones, and he had thought that he had found his White Buffalo. Later, before his easel, he had heard a voice tell him that the White Buffalo was work; he had persevered; long, hard, futilely. Then he had found love; in his happiness and surge of creation he had imagined the White Buffalo to be love.

But now what could the White Buffalo be except one's self? That was what men pursued all their lives and rarely found, or in the finding were seldom content. Was that what he had been pursuing so ardently, right from childhood: his self? Searched through long summer months in the saddle, over wild country and unexplored mountains, searched through long winter months in books, in paintings? Was that what the North Star was too: one's self . . . the only possible constant in a changing world, the only dependable, trustworthy, omnipresent lodestar? Was that what his mother had meant on the unhappy night in Wichita when his companions had betrayed him: that he must not build his life on others, but only on himself; for if he could always find himself, always get his bearings, always know that in a changing, chaotic world he at least would be constant, then he was safe, he could survive.

Death. Work. Love. Self. None of these strong enough to pull him up out of this abysmal darkness or break through these concrete walls. Perhaps his White Buffalo was pure illusion, Fata Morgana, the great lie that Man had invented and in which they all played roles, each knowing that he was a fraud; knowing that Man was nothing, a physical organism like any other animal life, yet striving mightily to keep this fact from himself and from the world? Wasn't Dave Leahy the greatest artist of them all, coming closer to the truth about men and about life? Wasn't the White Buffalo a Dave Leahy hoax built to such proportions that even its inventor came to believe in it, just as he had come to believe that there was a baby at the bottom of the well?

He saw himself back in his house in Trepied, standing in the center of the long studio room, the bright sun lighting his row of Brittany canvases: *Low Tide, Launching the Boat, Toilers of the Sea, Breton Fishermen, Baiting the Line.* Around him were Addams, Hawthorne, Tanner, Harrison, looking up at his canvases with puzzled faces.

"What's your secret, John?"

"There's no secret, Charles."

"It's that Feigenmilch you were working on in Paris."

"I've even forgotten the formula."

"It's the way you treat the canvas before you put the paint on," cried Tanner.

"There is no special treatment."

"John's right. The glow in the pictures is his own happiness."

Was that all it had been, just plain happiness? If happiness could make a man paint the way he had painted in Brittany, wouldn't there be many many great painters instead of a mere handful? Gerald Addams had exclaimed, "If marriage can make a man paint like that, I'm going out and find me a wife . . . any wife."

Yes, love had helped; happiness had helped; his years of hard work and experience had helped; and all of the men he had learned from, painter and teacher alike; perhaps even his chemical experiments had helped, who could tell? But he still had love, experience, skill, energy, devotion to his craft. Why then had he been so magnificently alive, sensitive and creative during those other years . . . and now was stumbling through the months so cold and dull and unmoved? What had he had then that was gone, or lost, or used up now?

God.

The darkness was dispelled, the walls crumbled. Light poured upon him, there was space about his elbows, the infinite space of the prairies, the heavens and the seas.

What had been shining in him so gloriously in Brittany had been nothing less than God Himself! He, John Noble, had been possessed by God . . . at the very period when he had repudiated all concept of Him and was living happily for the first time in his forty-odd years.

All during the years in Brittany he had been painting nothing but God, and it was God who gave his canvases their inner glow and intense beauty. Having devoted himself to his work, his love of Brittany, its people, its eternalities: then, and only then, had he been possessed of God; and he knew now that every whorling sun or star-studded night, every calm or stormy sea, every tiny sailing boat or great ship, every human being and horse and ox, everything he had painted shone and quivered and lived in God's great light. This was what everyone had seen in his canvases; and this was why his work had been so fine and so feeling and so mature.

Amelia had known all along! She had said to him when they first met, "The mystic is a religious man; religious in the sense that he believes there is a universe beyond that which his senses can perceive."

He had grown angry with her when she had said these things; in his fear he had shouted and warned her never to speak of God again. But she had been right; all the time she had been right. And he felt that he could never again unlearn the fact that God was and always would be the hero of his life, the central pole around which his brain and his flesh, his acts and his hours would be built. He no longer needed to ask, "Is there a God?" Now he had demonstrable proof. Neither did he need to ask, "Where is God? How does He manifest Himself?" For in Brittany God had been within him. Perhaps that was what inspiration meant: that an individual, sometimes an unworthy one like himself, was taken up by God and possessed by Him for the purposes of creation.

He recalled how Amelia had complimented him on taking his success with modesty and how he had replied, "I am built to withstand success." Now he understood why in the midst of his best work he had felt exultation rather than egoistic pride: a man who has been possessed by God, even though he does not know by whom or by what he has been possessed, has a realization that he is not working singlehanded, that he has a collaborator; for he can remember back to the struggling pedestrian days when he had to create solely with the awkward implements of his trade.

In Brittany he had said that the White Buffalo was love; now he knew that God wore many faces: Death and Work and Love and Self. His White Buffalo was God.

He knew too that when God entered into a man He could withdraw at any moment, any hour. But when He had entered into a work of art there was no possible withdrawing. His countenance shone there eternally. That was why the work of art was greater and more enduring than the man.

Weeks, months went by, and he had no desire to paint. He tried occasionally, experimentally, to see if the appetite had been reborn, but he knew even as he picked up the brush that it had not; he painted a little, destroyed what he had done. He wondered sometimes whether, if he could recross the Channel, get back into his studio in Trepied, he would become creative again. Then he would shake his head: for a return to Brittany would be a flight into the past; it had been a phase, a cycle, an epoch; now it was over, done with, irretrievably closed.

Where to go then, when he was free to go?

To Wichita, to Kansas, to the prairies, the vast mountains and plains of the Southwest for which he was sometimes so homesick? His mother was still alive; his sisters were married and had children and would welcome him. Marty and Frances were there, and the gallery was building; Victor Murdock and Dave Leahy were there, both of whom he loved and trusted because they had had faith in him. And yet . . . and yet . . . he could not go home. Why? For the same reason that every man flees his past: the fumblings, the uncertainties of childhood, the painful memories, the failures and inadequacies. He was not strong enough, sure enough: Wichita would throw him off balance, expunge everything that had happened in the intervening years. In Wichita he would once again be a groping, unhappy boy with the cry of "Jump! Jump!" ringing in his ears. No, he could not jump . . . back into the shallow childhood waters of Wichita.

More and more he thought of Provincetown, of the solitary cape jutting out into the sea. For years Charles Hawthorne had urged and written him to come and settle there. It was lonesome country, like the plains of Kansas and the sea off Brittany, where people stood face to face with the primordial, with their universe.

Perhaps there he could come alive again, paint and create as gloriously as he had in Brittany. This was what he must live for, no matter how many years it took. And if all the waiting brought only one short hour, one small canvas, it would still be justified, still be sufficient cause and reason to survive no matter how bitter the emptiness or how deep and shattering the misery between. He must have that great hour again: he must endure.

Book Four

NEW YORK

The Reward

THEY rented a house from Charles Hawthorne upon their arrival in Provincetown several months after the end of the war. It had a narrow staircase that was as steep as a ship's companionway. This was the first time Amelia had left her bedroom since the birth of her second son ten days before, so John carried her down the stairs and into the large sitting room with its floor-to-ceiling windows which faced the street and the harbor. The town clerk of Provincetown had been sitting on the edge of the narrow black horsehair sofa, waiting impatiently. He grabbed his official record book and ran across the room.

"Mrs. Noble, we simply cannot give you any longer to name that boy. My records . . ."

"Hold on now, you can wait long enough for me to put my wife in the rocking chair," replied John.

"I think the boy should have an Indian name," insisted Amelia, "since he was born in America."

"This is no longer a country of Indians." John was half angry, half amused. "We now have a few Anglo-Saxons mixed in."

"But, John, it isn't my fault if I think America primitive country. . . ."

"Well, we did have a ranch outside Wichita," he muttered sotto voce; "called it Towanda, I think."

Amelia gazed out the window to the harbor filled with fishing boats and white sailboats. "Towanda? Lovely. Would you please enter that in your official book, Mr. Town Clerk?"

"With the greatest of pleasures," exclaimed the clerk, scratching his rough pen across a white line which had been left vacant. He took a blotter from the side pocket of his black business suit, jabbed it hurriedly at his own writing and departed.

"Bring the baby and the crib down, will you, John? I want to sit here and watch the harbor."

John did as he was asked, then went out into the bright spring sunlight, made his way up Commercial Street through the little shopping center and down to the wharf where the trap boats were unloading their heavy catch of whiting and mackerel. He had spent considerable time with the Portuguese fishermen since his arrival in Provincetown a month before, going out in their boats in the darkness before dawn as he had with the fishermen of Pont Croix. He exchanged a few sentences with each of the boat crews, commenting on the size of the catch, his mind's quick pencil making sketches of the fish, the men at work, the sails on the sparkling sea, the two streets of shops and houses and then the hills and dunes which rose above the bay.

He left the town behind him, crossed the railroad tracks, went up a sand hill, then found a trail which crossed blueberry moors, went downhill again into a pine woods, across a little valley covered by a profusion of wild lilies and through chokecherry trees and gnarled beach plum bushes until he came to the crest of the dunes, and his new magnificent world spread out before him.

His whole being filled with joy as he gazed out at the sea: for Cape Cod was another Finistère: a world in itself, jutting strong and bold into the vastness of the Atlantic Ocean to the east and north, its beautifully sheltered harbor lying below him on the west with hundreds of trawlers, dories, lobster and fishing boats, and beyond them the deep blue Cape Cod Bay. This was the harbor where the *Mayflower* had landed in 1620, where great whaling fleets had centered and prospered for a full century, and where for many years the swarthy, emotional, dour Portuguese and the light-skinned, cool, dour New Englanders had shared the end of the earth. He could see nothing but the Cape and the sea; together they constituted a universe: for Massachusetts was but a blue haze on the horizon on clear days.

In the few weeks he had lived here the simple little village had become the place he loved more intensely than any he had known. He felt that it was in the truest sense home: more than Wichita with its painful memories; more than Paris, where he had been a transit guest; more than Trepied, for although he had known three years of glorious fulfillment in the Brittany villages he had never really got inside the heart or mind of the Breton. But in Provincetown everyone was his neighbor and friend. He rode the bumpy bus up Commercial Street and back, round trip, just to become acquainted with the passengers; he went into the drugstore to visit with Adams the owner, have a chocolate soda and talk to whoever sat next to him; he stopped on his walks to chat for an hour with a man who was cutting his front lawn, a housewife planting flowers, the fishermen cleaning their fish.

At sundown he went to the Beachcombers, a club for artists and writers which had formerly been an old fishhouse. Each Saturday night two new painters were introduced, and as initiation fee had to cook supper for the fifty-odd members.

He was given a boisterous reception, for here were many of his oldest friends from Paris: Charles Hawthorne, who had opened the first painting school in Provincetown at the turn of the century; Frederick Waugh, who was known as one of America's finest marine painters; Max Bohm and George Elmer Browne, with whom he had worked at the American Club in Paris; Gerald Addams, who came over every Saturday from Boston for the parties. He stood in the doorway of the big clubroom watching the men smoking, drinking wine, talking animatedly, saw not only painters and sculptors but a group of young writers: tall, gangling, redheaded Sinclair Lewis, completing a novel which he called *Main Street;* Wilbur Daniel Steele of the spare figure and craggy face, whose short stories John felt were closer to his own painting than any writing being done at the moment; Max Eastman, handsome radical young journalist; Harry Kemp, bohemian poet; Floyd Dell, intellectual out of Chicago's newspaper world, working on two novels of his youth. Then there were George Cram Cook and the group around the new Provincetown Playhouse who had converted an abandoned fishhouse into a theater and were producing the one-act plays of a melancholy Irishman by the name of Eugene O'Neill.

238

For John this was an authentic art colony, composed of what the French called *hommes sérieux,* without idler, poseur, crank, fraud or dullard. Beyond a nostalgia for the simple living to be earned from their work, there was little talk of money among them. The painters were older than the writers, better established, but not enough to turn their heads or to give them more than the barest living; most of them had to teach in order to support their families. He found a sense of camaraderie here and of sharing which verged on brotherhood. Painter and writer alike had a need to be close to the essence of life in the same way that a tree needs to grow out of the soil.

Amelia was right in saying that he was having a love affair with Provincetown; he was completely enchanted with the sea, the village, the dunes against the infinite skies. He felt alive and vital as he had in his earliest days in Brittany. The four barren painful years in London already seemed long ago and far away. Standing on the dunes overlooking the sea, he saw a hundred pictures he wanted to paint. But he was not desperate to start. This was too good, too sure, too exhilarating to inspire haste. He said to himself:

Take your time; this is the best, it is not going to vanish, it is not a case of "get it down, for tomorrow it will lose its beauty or character for you."

He must learn everything that was indigenous and meaningful in Provincetown before he grappled with its underlying reality; absorb its atmosphere, design, arrangements in space. A painting was like an iceberg: only the top tenth of what the artist has known or felt can appear above the surface; the rest lies submerged, yet always there to buoy the top tenth, to give it solid substance.

2

Long tables were set up in the main room of the Beachcomber; the two novitiates brought in the tureens of hot food from the kitchen. A discussion arose over the traditional versus the modern in art, with Zorach, the sculptor, maintaining that modern art which put aside the photographic and the sentimental was the best being produced because it best represented its age, while Richard Miller, the leader of the traditionalists, demanded:

"Best in comparison to what? Your work is so new and so

raw that there is nothing to test it against. But when we paint conventional pictures we can set up standards of excellence because we can compare them against five hundred years of art."

"What do you say, John?" called out Hawthorne. "You have seen everything being painted in Europe, both traditional and modern. Which should we turn to?"

"Why must we categorize ourselves?" replied John. "I learned in Paris that there is little use going in for a school or a fad or a movement because it sounds new or exciting; all we can do is express what is native to our own temperament."

One of the younger abstractionists cried out at Miller, "You're more afraid of comparison than we are: you won't even let us hang our modern paintings alongside yours in the exhibitions."

"I'm afraid that's an academic question," interrupted Hawthorne. "We can't hold shows here any more because the place isn't big enough to handle a fraction of our canvases."

"There should be a permanent art gallery," volunteered John. "We all intend to stay here for a very long time . . ."

He was greeted with laughter.

"A great idea . . . we've been trying for fifteen years . . ."

"It's easy," replied John. "All you need is a good organizer, someone who can collect money up and down the Cape."

"Know anybody who will take the job, John?" asked Hawthorne.

"Sure."

"Who?"

"Me."

This time the laughter was derisive.

"You as an organizer . . . no artist could possibly . . ."

"You're wrong, friend," answered John quietly. "The artist is not unqualified to be an executive: the organization involved in even the simplest picture is so intricate and demands such infinite understanding, such a grasp of the essentials and of self-discipline, that the organizing of business detail is uncomplicated by comparison. Any first-rate artist could make a first-rate business executive; the only reason he doesn't is because he doesn't consider business important enough. What's more, every artist wants to prove, just once, that he could have been a great executive . . . if he had thought it worth bothering about."

"Okay, John. Set up the plans for a permanent gallery, and then go out and get the money and put up the building."

John took the big white hat from his head and held it out to the men. "As an opening shot every one of you will empty your wallets and purses into my Stetson. All right, skeptics, shell out."

He left the house every morning at seven and made the rounds of the fishing wharves, the shops, the homes, the hotels and tourist cabins, up and down the streets all day in his ten-gallon hat and flowing black silk tie and broad amiable smile, selling the permanent Provincetown people on how much good the Provincetown Art Association could do them businesswise. Most of the merchants put their hands in their pockets slowly, fumblingly came out with a dollar bill which he accepted gratefully. He then spun a yarn of the wild West, told it with all of the humor and excitement he had developed over the years: of how he had been the first white child born in Wichita, a pal of Wild Bill Hickok, how he had run the first herd of cattle up the Chisholm Trail and across the Staked Plains. By the time the story was over he had collected another five- or ten-dollar bill and was on his way to the post office or to Adams' drugstore where he gathered a crowd around him at the fountain, treated everyone to sodas, told how he had fought at Custer's Last Stand . . . and then passed his hat. He also solicited the one-day tourists coming off the boat from Boston.

Summer came on with its intense heat, yet he attired himself impeccably each morning, wore a freshly pressed coat even when the collection was to be taken among the Portuguese fishermen. He did not begrudge the time that was passing, for he was collecting with one hand and making sketches with the other, filling dozens of notebooks while he walked the length of the Cape gathering contributions from the Coast Guardsmen and the farmers further up the peninsula. He was absorbing, growing surer; he felt certain that one day he would break forth with the full power of creation. He was content to go forward to this tryst slowly, lovingly.

By the end of the second month, when he had assembled almost enough money to begin his building, he knew every mile of dune and marsh and bog, of hillside and scrub pine; knew the bay and the ocean from every angle, the beaches under the blazing sun and the full summer moonlight; the constantly changing colors of the sky and water, the subtle shades of dawn and sunset, the movements of the fishing boats as they made their way through the summer days and deep ocean waters.

When he was only one thousand dollars short of the needed sum he went to the richest woman on the Cape, a widow who was passing the time by learning to paint. It took him almost twelve hours around the clock, but when he left he had a thousand-dollar check in his pocket and the rich widow had been promised a place of honor in the opening art exhibit.

Several weeks earlier he had purchased two large rambling houses and had had them moved together. Now he hired carpenters and masons, spent hours discussing how the bricks should be laid for the front entrance. He decided on a herringbone pattern, gave the workmen the go-ahead signal. In a miraculously short time the Provincetown Art Association was completed, the members brought pictures for the opening exhibition, and invitations were sent to everyone important in the art world of New England and New York.

On the morning before the opening he used his passkey to get into the gallery. He was alone there now for the first time, in a series of spacious rooms, well lighted, with ample hanging space.

"Oh, my gosh," he exclaimed aloud, "I forgot all about that rich widow's painting!"

He dashed down to the basement, found the canvas, came upstairs to the main salon. Gerald Addams entered through the open door, stood with a shocked expression on his face as he watched John adjust the pictures in the center of the panel. John turned, saw Gerald and commented:

"Any time before this summer I would have loathed this chromo; any time after summer I shall cordially detest it. Right at this moment I think it the most beautiful picture in Provincetown."

"But, John, you can't give that poster the place of honor," protested Gerald. "By so doing you proclaim it a fine painting, and that would be an artistic lie."

"Tut-tut, as an artist I am concerned with truth," replied John, "as an executive I am concerned with success."

That afternoon some three hundred painters, critics, curators and well-wishers gathered in the new gallery to dedicate it and make speeches about the wonderful job he had done.

"And now as a climax to our ceremonies," said Charles Hawthorne, fingering a square velvet box, "we wish to present you, John Noble, with this token of our appreciation."

Amidst bravos of approval John took the object out of the box, fondled it for a moment, then said:

"How beautiful! What is it?"

242

"A watch."

"What's it for?"

"To tell time."

"Time? What's that?"

Everybody laughed.

"You know: the device by means of which we learn whether it is five after ten or ten after five."

"And you can tell all these wonderful things just by looking at this little gold ornament?"

"Yes . . . providing you wind it."

"Wind what?"

"This little stem here."

John turned the watch over a number of times, marveling.

"You've got to hand it to our scientists, the new machines they invent. I can't thank you good people enough: now I'll always know whether it's night or day."

3

He was not aware of the exact moment at which he started; he did not will it consciously nor determine that on such and such a day at such and such an hour he would begin. He was standing in his studio above the garage when suddenly he picked up a palette, squeezed color onto it, took his brush in hand. It was so effortless that he could perceive almost no transition between not working and working.

Almost at once the pattern of his intent evolved: to recreate the whole of Provincetown: not merely its routine of living but its symbolism as well. To this end he painted all that seemed significant to him: boats in the harbor; the village on the hill; the moon in the sea; the port against the sky; houses caught between sea and land; white sails against a white sun; a sea gull against a wave; a street against houses; a sickle cutting hay; morning, as seen by land, sea and sky; the old boat horses; the rocks and the wrecks; the sentient world bathed in mist and fog. Rarely did humans appear, and then never as the important element in the picture but only as an accessory or adjunct, small foreground figures as in *Sardine Fishermen*. In *Mending the Nets* one saw the village, the sails, the sea, and only the impression of men mending nets. What he painted was not an inhuman world but one in which man was but a transitory species, not master of the universe but one of its tiny components and, when posed against the eternalities, not very important in the over-all pattern.

Having seen no English canvases anywhere in John's home or studio, his friends from Paris and Brittany had avoided the embarrassing question of what he had done with the four war years. Now they watched him caught up in another magnificently creative period. They knew that he was at work before dawn every morning, that he could not sleep because of his excitement over the prospect of seeing the sun rise and spread its first colors in the eastern sky. They saw him striding energetically about town with his easel and paintbox, a ruggedly built man in a white sombrero with the ascetic face of a cleric, like some itinerant clergyman of the Southwest. He painted Provincetown as he had painted Brittany, with a religious fervor and a religious purity, expressing all that was best in himself and in the universe. For him art was basically a religious impulse which brought one closer to the inscrutability of life, its mystery, its flow, its constant re-creation within itself: the highest form of activity in which a man could participate.

Like all creative artists he rearranged nature and evaluated the accidental: for the existing fact was not necessarily the truth, it could be tangential or distortive; the rearrangement, the artistic fiction, might be the permanent and universal truth. His pencils and brushes became extensions of his right arm, the palette an extension of his left; not external objects divorced from his breathing or the circulation of his blood but organic parts of his body and brain. He worked intuitively now, at one with his medium and his subject, plunging directly to its essence, creating it on canvas without going through the endless process of the conscious craftsman.

The painters were enthralled by his work; the only adverse comment came from a group of Worcester art teachers who saw on the walls of the gallery three of his Breton and three of his earliest Cape Cod paintings.

"They're beautiful; the paint is like crushed jewels," said the first of the teachers, a gray-haired, sensitive-faced woman who could not know that the man next to her in the white sombrero was the artist they were discussing; "but his range is so narrow: nothing but fishing villages and boats."

"Maybe that's his limitation," added one of her younger companions; "that he can work in only one field."

"The world is so large," continued the tall, gray-haired woman. "How can any artist be content to confine himself to such a restricted area?"

Gerald Addams came to visit the next morning. He was now the most successful copier in America, with a commission from a Pittsburgh museum to go to Florence, Italy, and copy Titian's *Venus of Urbino* in the Uffizi Gallery, and another from Kansas City to copy El Greco's *The Assumption* in the Church of San Vicente, Toledo, Spain. He was handsomely dressed and drove an expensive car, but was unhappy. Only his battered silver spectacles had not improved with his rise in the world; they still slid up and down the hump of his nose when he was perturbed.

"John, this is not what I spent all those years at copying for: just to get chained to it for the rest of my life. You know I copied only to learn how the great masters had done it, so that I would have a solid basis on which to create an original style of my own."

John shook his head in wistful negation.

"Gerald, you could not have spent all those years copying over the face of Europe if you had not had a natural affinity for it, not only enjoyed the copying but done it extremely well. Remember how lost you felt when you were with us in Brittany and tried to paint from nature?"

". . . all right . . . I'll admit that . . . but I always believed it was temporary. I was waiting for the day when I would be ready for my original work."

"Look, Gerald, little as we may like it, each artist has one thing he can do well; one and no more. We may thrash about, try different mediums, genres, materials; we may squirm and protest and revolt at being fractional, flee into all kinds of styles, but in the end we have to be content with our own little segment. Some art teachers I overheard at the gallery yesterday were criticizing me for being narrow, restricted, but that's true of all painters; between us we make up the component parts of one great painter: a painter who captures the whole universe."

Gerald's expression lightened. He hit John a rough affectionate blow with the back of his hand.

"Yeah, you're right; I guess I ought to be happy that I can do something better than anyone else. There are millions of Americans who can't go to Paris or Florence or Toledo and who will see absolutely faithful copies of the world's greatest paintings because of my peculiar genius. Thanks for the consolation, John."

"Don't be silly: I was consoling myself. Those confounded art teachers cost me a night's sleep."

4

September came, yet the weather remained warm, the skies a brilliant blue and the sea an apple green in the morning and flaming purple when the sun plunged into its western depths at night. The art students dispersed to the four corners of the nation; many of the painters returned to their winter homes. But for John Cape Cod was the world in microcosm. Though everything was small, almost in miniature, it seemed quite large because it was in perfect scale: the scrub pines were low and hence made the hills seem high; the houses were narrow and made the streets seem wide; the boats were small, and so the harbor seemed enormous. Everything depended upon the perspective: Provincetown existed in its own dimension.

That winter the wind from the northwest was cold and bitter, and when it shifted to the southwest the gales whipped Provincetown, not only the ships in the harbors but the houses on the little hills and the people inside their walls. The fishermen made sporadic attempts to fix their gear, but for the most part the village was locked up. John put up storm windows, cut and laid in a huge supply of wood for the fireplace, then went out to paint *Provincetown in Winter,* with the boats locked in the ice floes, the masts gaunt against the snow-covered hills beyond; *Provincetown, Winter,* looking down from the village to the breakwater, a cold fragmentary sun sinking into a cold black horizon. He painted *Streets, Provincetown,* with the sea beyond and the church spire extending up to heaven and the houses locked tight. He painted *The Ice Cutters,* a group of men hacking out blocks of ice. When the northeast storms made it impossible for any living creature to remain out of doors, he lit a big stove in his studio and painted from his notebooks.

Amelia converted the large upstairs bedroom facing the bay into a sitting room and bought some new unfinished furniture, painting it all a bright golden color. John exclaimed:

"I see you are glamorizing us again."

She looked up from the floor, holding the damp paintbrush in an upright position.

"It's because I'm happy."

"Then you don't miss Sir Thomas Barclay's house and your brilliant social whirl in London?"

Amelia shook this off as unworthy of answer.

"John, your pictures are not only as beautiful as the ones you painted in Brittany, but you are far happier creating them. There are no long silences, no endless reveries. For me, it's like another honeymoon. Perhaps we should have come home to America sooner, right after we were married."

"No . . . things have to work themselves out in their own tortuous fashion. I wouldn't change any of it, not even the bad period in Paris before I met you, or the sterile years in London. Never quarrel with any part of a success, Amelia: we worked wonderfully for three years in Brittany, and now I'm working better than ever, and I know that what we have now is going to last, and be good, right up until the final minute: until I have painted everything I wanted to paint and said everything I wanted to say. No price is too high for that kind of fulfillment."

"Amen."

Frances Buckler arrived in Provincetown the day before Christmas, laden with gifts for the children. Marty had promised to come up from Washington where he was serving his first term as a United States senator. John was amazed at the change that had come over Frances; in London she had been gaunt, with deep shadows under her eyes, seeming as tall and awkward as a man on stilts. Now her figure had filled out again, she was holding herself proud and erect and no longer seemed tall at all, but rather gave the appearance of an interesting woman, alert, vital, colorful. Even her clothing which he remembered as being drab in London had been completely revolutionized, for now she wore a deep red, loose-flowing tunic, and between her breasts hung a beautiful Indian cornflower necklace. She led her own life quite apart from Marty, traveled extensively and was making friends among the world's painters, for she understood them and bought their best canvases. In the Midwest she had become known to the young aspiring painters as a blazing black-eyed woman of infinite kindness and helpfulness, and so had in middle age conquered her barrenness.

After an early Christmas breakfast, when the boys were playing with their new toys, he and Frances made their way up to his studio above the garage. John lit a fire. Frances went directly to the canvas that was locked securely on the easel: a picture of the town, the hills, the harbor painted in rich colors with blues, greens and purples predominating, and here and there broad touches of red. In spite of the vigorousness and power of his conception and the brilliance of the paint, the values were so carefully balanced that it had the feeling of a low-tone color scheme. Frances studied the scene for a considerable time, then turned and exclaimed:

"John, it's good. It's stronger yet more subtle than the Brittany canvases. I've always liked your method of portraying only the essential characteristics. Everything in this picture has a sense of reality, and yet again it's the exact opposite of realism."

"One of the painters around here, Jerome Myers, says that I envelop my pictures in a religious fog."

"That's not true." Her cheeks flamed at this deprecation of his work. "It's simply that there's an over-all poetic feeling . . ." She broke off, then without looking at him, said, "John, could I have this painting? I mean, buy it, of course. I wanted to have some of your things in London but I didn't dare ask you."

"This will be your Christmas present, Frances. But I would like to show it first at the opening Provincetown Art Association exhibit in the spring. The important New York dealers come up to see that show."

"Of course, John." She went close to him and hesitantly slipped her hand in his, letting it rest so lightly that he was not even sure it was there.

"John, it's good to know that I wasn't wrong. Right from the beginning, when we were kids, I felt that there was something strong and individual and different about you, and that regardless of what happened to everybody else in the world you would somehow fulfill yourself." She looked about the studio, letting her eyes rest long and exultantly on the dozen Cape Cod canvases he had completed. "These canvases must surely be among the best painted and the most satisfying being done in America today."

He left her side and walked about the studio studying the results of his work, his attention on each canvas as he passed it.

"I don't know how good they are objectively; I can only tell you that I am working at the height of my power."

It was easier for her to speak to him of intimate things now that his back was turned. She started hesitantly, in a low voice, but gathered courage as she went.

"John, for a long time . . . I thought that loving you . . . had ruined my life. But now, having managed to live through the years of adversity, I understand that having loved you is bringing me a good and beautiful life. People might think I'm old because I'm fifty, but actually I'm only beginning. . . ."

Can you understand that, John? The first half of my life was thrown away; now I'm going to live to be ninety in order to make the second half count for something."

He went to her side.

"Frances, you look as young and beautiful as the girl I used to go with in Wichita."

She flushed, but her eyes were clear and smiling.

"Wait until you see the Martin Buckler Museum of Modern Art, John. It's one of the most beautiful in America. Marty gave me a handsome sum for the spring and fall purchase shows of young Americans."

She told him of further plans; she was assembling a collection of art books which were largely unavailable in the Midwest; also etchings, lithographs, drawings and color reproductions of the world's paintings.

"I want to establish a complete art reference library in connection with my colony."

"Colony?" John looked up at her sharply, an amused glint in his eye. "Are you out to create some sort of Utopia?"

"No, just a colony in Wichita for young painters and sculptors to come to to live and work without cost, so that they can have at least one year in which to learn what they are driving toward."

"Still giving young people a chance at home that I never got, eh, Frances?"

Her gaze was steady. "Marty has made millions, I don't think even he knows how many. I'm determined to spend every last dollar of it before we die, and spend practically all of it on painting and painters."

Marty arrived three days later in a Pierce-Arrow limousine that looked like a locomotive. At long last his face had filled out to match his plump body, and he had even found a barber in Washington, D.C., who had encouraged his red stubble to grow and be combed back long on his head. The two men bundled up in heavy sweaters and went for a walk on the beach.

"I'm sorry I couldn't get out to Kansas to help with your campaign, Marty."

"To the contrary, Johnny, you were very much present, perhaps the strongest single influence: there are plenty of bankers in Kansas, and industrialists too, but where else in the state could they find the combination of financier and internationally famous patron of the arts? So help me, John: not a soul talked about my political platform or my experience as an executive; but you should have seen the miles of space about the Martin Buckler Museum of Modern Art, and my great collection. I used to think you were making me pour my money into adobe pits, but man! I've had offers for some of those pictures you forced on me in Paris: ten thousand for the Renoir that cost me four hundred . . ."

"You always said you had a genius for making a profit."

"This is a funny country, John; we're supposed to be materialists, worshiping machines, engines, factories, dollars; yet no matter how many banks or railroads I owned, nobody outside those board rooms cared a damn for me. But after the Armory Show I became a celebrity. Why?"

"You got me, Marty. Nobody is excited about putting my picture in the papers. Or my paintings, for that matter."

"Even now the newspapers say Senator Buckler (R), Kansas, as quickly as they can, and then go on to talk about me as an art critic. I'm on the Senate Banking and Finance Committee, and doing a mighty good job. But when I go to New York or Chicago or Boston, do the reporters ask me about how I'm stabilizing the currency or planning to fund the war indebtedness? Hell, no. They want to know when I'm going to Europe again for a purchase prize exhibition! The only thing I know about, money, they don't want to discuss; the one thing I know nothing about, painting, I can never escape. It's like living in a tent on top of a live volcano: not a night of my life goes by but I wake up in a cold sweat, seeing my picture on the front pages: MARTIN BUCKLER A FRAUD. *Multimillionaire Senator Proves Ignoramus About Painting.*"

"Stop worrying, Marty, I'm the only one who knows your secret, and I'll never tell."

The wind blew John's words out to sea. Marty continued:

"Look, boy, I want to return the favor."

"How?"

"Easy. There's a whole new industry set up in New York called public relations. They get your picture in all the papers, invent exciting news items about you, make you a favorite subject for the columnists. One day you'll wake up to find John Noble a household name, like Gold Dust Twins or Ex-Lax: and then you'll be the most famous painter in America."

"You mean the most notorious."

"What's the difference?"

"My paintings have got to speak for themselves; no amount of publicity can make them one jot better. Lay off me, you hear?"

"Not a chance, Johnny m'boy. You made me famous, and now I'm going to return the compliment."

5

During the next months he completed his panorama of Provincetown in winter, momentarily atrophied, gripped by nature. These scenes were like so many he had done in Paris from his Brittany sketches, cold to the eye but not to the mind or heart: for under the ice and the stillness he felt the dormant vitality, the sense of life waiting to burst forth.

Having lived a full cycle of the seasons on the Cape, he found that he had finished painting his version of Provincetown, its people, sea, ships. He now began to construct the ingredients of an imaginary Provincetown, symbolic of all ports and seas and men, to paint a highly personal creative fictional world which he knew could not be located anywhere precisely, and yet was the prototype of all men and boats and seas since the beginning of time. He did not paint surfaces, but spaces and depths, all of which spoke to him, moved him deeply, as though he were in communion with the supergerminal forces of creation.

Prior to the war he had been known among art circles in New York, Philadelphia, Boston and Chicago as part of the American Group in Paris; but it was five years since he had exhibited except with the Provincetown Art Association, and he found that both his name and work had been largely forgotten. Now, in the early spring, the Daniel Gallery in New York City opened a show of fifteen of his canvases.

One New York paper said that his art leaned heavily on the work of the Post-Impressionists, another maintained that he leaned upon the Florentines and El Greco. One claimed that he followed tradition, another said that he broke with tradition; one pointed out that he had a feeling for color, still another maintained that he had no appreciation for the fact that there is a harmony of texture. It was the New York *Tribune* which made the most definite statement and launched him on his American career:

John Noble is a dashing, audacious painter with rich color, sharp in contrast, and flung onto the canvas with a gesture that, if seemingly rough at times, is very skillful and into the bargain very personal. His accent is frankly assertive and he works with an uncompromising direct touch which is his essential distinction.

It was the critical conflict as much as the praise which made his exhibition a success.

When Frances Buckler received the New York papers in Kansas she immediately picked up the telephone.

"John, I'm so happy for you. Would you let me bring your pictures out to Wichita? I think it's about time the prophet got a little honor in his own country."

"I'd like that very much, Frances; I'm sure Marty'd get a boot out of it: THE MARTIN BUCKLER MUSEUM Presents JOHN NOBLE."

The long-distance call from Wichita gave him the idea. He had often written to his mother, urging her to come to Provincetown, but now he telephoned and would not hang up until she had agreed to come the very next week. He was waiting at the depot when she got off the train, went forward slowly, tentatively, for it had been many years since they had seen each other. But in their love they had never been apart, and the space and time between them as dispersed as they went quickly into each other's arms. Then he held her out before him, his powerful hands gripping her by the shoulders.

"You're not one to be dimmed by the years, are you, Ma? I swear your complexion is as pink and white as it was when I was a boy. And what about your piecrust, is that as delicious as ever?"

"So they tell me in Wichita."

Her tone was light but her eyes were serious as she probed her son's face, for she knew that he had been through bad times as well as good. But now she saw that despite the passage of the years he looked sturdier than she had ever known him in Wichita: his eyes penetrating, forceful, happy, his body overflowing with vitality.

He linked his arm possessively through Elizabeth's, took her home to Amelia and her two grandsons. The two women embraced, then they all went to the upstairs sitting room where John, Jr., and Towanda were bathed and dressed and anxiously awaiting their first sight of their grandmother.

After dinner that night Elizabeth had John bring in the large, heavily roped cardboard box she had carried with her.

"I wondered what kind of present I could bring you, son, and at last I decided that this was the one thing you would want."

John cut the ropes, opened the box and took out his father's enormous buffalo coat. It had been the older John Noble's pride and joy and was known throughout thousands of miles of the Southwest. Elizabeth had had some of the worn hides replaced and the lining renewed. John slipped into the coat, wrapped it securely about his body, felt the heat and the weight of it. There were tears behind his eyes, but he did not let them show.

"I feel as though I have Father's arms around me."

With summer, Provincetown was once again crowded. A kind of contagious jubilance permeated the colony, for it had been a year of amazing arrivals: Sinclair Lewis had emerged from obscurity with his *Main Street,* which the critics said introduced a new era in American literature; the Provincetown Players' production in New York of Eugene O'Neill's play, *Emperor Jones,* had earned him the position of America's most important young playwright; Floyd Dell's novel *Briary Bush,* a sensitive portrayal of the growth of a young artist and intellectual, had been received with critical hosannas, while Wilbur Daniel Steele had been given a special award by the O. Henry Committee for maintaining the highest level of merit among the short-story writers. A number of the painters had had successful shows in New York, while four of them had had canvases purchased by museums.

In the still, sleepy heat of midafternoon John took his family out for a sail in the knockabout he had rented for the season. Amelia and their older son swam off the side of the boat in the cool blue water, while John stayed with his mother, sketching the sea and the land from different anchorages. On Sunday afternoons Amelia held open house, when some thirty of their friends would come in directly from the beach in dungarees and jerseys, their faces glowing from the sun, ravenous for good drink and food and animated conversation. Elizabeth watched her son with his painter and writer friends, saw him move freely and companionably among them, and was deeply gratified. She acceded to John's plea to stay on, remaining in Provincetown until mid-August.

By now the Nobles had become well-known characters on the Cape, Amelia tripping along the sidewalks with her quick short steps under a gaily colored parasol which she had painted herself; John, under his white Stetson, recreating the legends of the old West, telling them ever funnier and more ferociously, yet with so much charm and grace that after a while most of Provincetown understood that John Noble, the artist, was creating a fictional time, place and character for himself; understood that the wild West Noble was just a cloak he wore to conceal his gentleness, his hypersensitivity; a protective covering to hide, even from those with whom he did not need this gentle dissembling, his soft, almost woman-like nature.

He was up before daybreak, painted straight through until midafternoon. After supper he visited with the family for an hour, then went back to his studio until midnight. When Amelia protested that he was not getting enough rest, he exclaimed, "There are so many ideas rattling around in my head that I can't turn myself off."

When at the end of the summer he assembled all of his canvases he realized that he had come through a second complete cycle. During the first year he had painted Provincetown as he had seen it, with the detail strained through his own craftsmanship. This second spring and summer he had used the Cape as a point of departure, mixing its character with the product of his own imaginary world, so that the canvases became half Cape Cod, half John Noble.

Now he knew that he must make the transition into a third stage: he must paint Provincetown as it might appear to God; not as it would be seen through the end of a long telescope but rather as grasped by an over-all force which stood above the existing earth. He had never doubted since coming to Provincetown that whatever he had had in Brittany had come back to him and was pervading his every moment and every brush stroke. He knew that the ultimate use of his talent and his craft must be to paint the interior of God's mind, to capture and represent on canvas God's intent.

The full pattern of what he was after had nothing to do with man; it had to do only with God's universe: the recreative, indestructible, immortal.

6

He went out during the coldest of winter, warm and comfortable inside his father's buffalo coat. In the spring he was re-elected director of the Provincetown Art Association and planned stimulating exhibitions for the summer months. He finally acceded to the demands of a group of young students to start a teaching class, but found that he had no talent for this kind of communication; his art was largely an instinctive expression. Try as he might, he could not articulate the things

254

he felt so deeply. He ended by painting the students' pictures for them.

Late in August he assembled the final exhibition of the summer. The critics came for the opening not only from Boston, but from New York, Philadelphia and Chicago. That night Provincetown held its own Quatz' Arts ball in the Town Hall; everybody danced till dawn, then waited for the newspapers to see what had been printed about their show. The Boston *Post* said:

Any painting, which by its sheer strength and force alone can raise the whole tone of a large exhibition, must necessarily possess sterling qualities. Such a one is John Noble's view of Provincetown. It is because of the power of his brushwork, the correctness of values in his low-toned color schemes, his method of recording only the essentials that the artist has given to this harbor scene a rugged strength and a sense of reality which sets it apart as a distinct artistic triumph.

Last summer he would have considered this high praise. Now the Boston *Post's* review proved to be more of an obituary than a commencement; the lines had a hollow ring, praising him for qualities he had abandoned as fragmentary.

He began by-passing projects he formerly would have seized upon eagerly. By sheer self-discipline he forced himself to start two new paintings . . . and then for the first time since he had come to Provincetown abandoned them half completed. Next he developed a distaste for setting up a new canvas on the easel, squeezing paints onto the palette or picking up a brush. Then his revulsion grew so strong he could not bring himself to enter his studio.

He told himself he was tired, momentarily painted out; perhaps even a little ill, needing a complete rest. He told himself there was nothing to be concerned about: in the past three years he had produced what most men would have been content to do in ten. One day his energies would flood back along with his enthusiasm and his perception, just as three years before he had instinctively picked up his brush and been halfway through a big canvas before he said to himself, "Look John, you're painting." In a few days or a few weeks he would run excitedly up the steps to his garage studio, nail a canvas onto a board, take the caps off the tubes of paint, squeeze them into a widening circle on his palette, dip his brushes and begin.

Yet even while he was reassuring himself he heard a contrapuntal voice telling him that this was wishful thinking, rationalization. He had done his job fully, skillfully, passionately, but in his last self-imposed task he had failed. There was more in God's design and God's mind than John Noble had been able to paint . . . because there was more than John Noble would ever be able to perceive. No man could enter God's mind, understand the pattern of His intent; achieve this identity while still on earth. Always there would be the ultimate gap, the unbridgeable chasm . . . as there was between the visual reality of his canvases and what he had hoped to create on them. In spite of their heavenward flight both the artist and the paintings were earthbound. He could paint only what he saw as a man, what he could understand from his position within the confines of his particular corral, from the train window of his particular roadbed.

For him this was no longer enough. How could he be content to paint that which was visible to man's eyes when he had striven so mightily to paint that which was seen by God's eyes? How could it be anything but a painful journey backward . . . to that which he had already said and done? Could he be satisfied now to paint the fragment when he had so ardently pursued the whole?

What could he do with the remainder of his years? What awaited him in the boundaryless time which had to be filled with eating, breathing, thinking, feeling, a bottomless pit into which he must shovel the ingredients of living: a pit which he could never again fill?

It was not possible for him to hide from Amelia the fact that once again he had stopped working. He could leave the house in the morning, wander the countryside and not return until nightfall; he could lock himself up in the studio to dream, to sleep, gnawing away at the hours as a dog gnaws at a meatless bone. But how to explain this transition from a man vibrantly alive, happy, creative to one who was dull, apathetic, unemployed?

Amelia was not upset; they had survived four barren years in London.

"It's just that you've worked yourself into exhaustion again, John. We have no money worries, and you have enough completed canvases to exhibit for several years. Why can't you just sit back and relax, enjoy yourself, spend your time with your boys?"

How could he tell her that this was not merely a transition

in the cycle, a period of recuperation? That he despaired of ever working again? He could not say that. He could not even intimate it. Yet what did he do about that little gnawing point of death which already sat heavy in his innards like some indigesible, poisonous food?

For the first time in many years he felt terror: the same terror he had felt in Paris when he had abandoned all hope of finding God, of finding Him through that one last avenue of approach, work.

The following week he received two telegrams from New York City. The first was signed Awards Committee, Salmagundi Club, and read:

YOUR PAINTING BRITTANY MOONLIGHT HAS BEEN AWARDED THOUSAND DOLLAR FIRST PRIZE. CAN YOU COME DOWN TO ACCEPT AWARD PERSONALLY?

The second was signed by Childe Hassam, whom John considered one of the two or three greatest living American painters.

HAD ALREADY AWARDED FIRST PRIZE WHEN I FOUND YOUR PAINTING HANGING BEHIND DOOR. IMMEDIATELY TOOK BACK PRIZE AND GAVE IT TO YOU.

Amelia was tremendously excited. "I know there are more important art awards from the viewpoint of the public, John, but to have the painters themselves give you first prize . . ."

"I'm not going to New York," he interrupted pugnaciously.

"But, John, why not? A trip away from Provincetown will be refreshing."

"No, I . . ."

"Take the morning train. Spend a few days in New York and then come back on Thursday. The train gets here at seven. I'll have supper waiting for you."

He had managed by holding a hard, tense grip on himself to keep away from the drink he so desperately wanted when he reached Grand Central Station; the two or three more drinks he wanted when he entered the Salmagundi Club at 47 Fifth Avenue; the dozen or more drinks he wanted while he shook hands with old friends from Paris and Brittany and London, stood on the platform and was awarded First Prize to applause from the several hundred artists and writers seated before him. But once the ceremonies were over he

257

rushed out to the nearest speakeasy, a dark little basement on East Twelfth Street, and began drinking, slowly at first; then as the alcohol numbed his anxiety he talked to the people about him, buying them drinks and letting them buy him drinks in turn. He knew only two things: that he was getting drunk and that he was carefree for the first time since he had stopped painting.

He awoke late the following afternoon in a dingy hotel room. His first thought was of Amelia; he must get up, find a barbershop, have his suit pressed and rush back to Provincetown. But no, Provincetown was where his life lay: his barren studio, his failure . . . Besides, he did not have to go home yet, Amelia had said Thursday, and this was only— what? Tuesday? Wednesday? He was sure that he still had another day or two of freedom. He dressed, searched in his wallet to make sure he had money and went out to find a few drinks, a few companions, a few more hours of release.

The days that followed were blurred: he found himself drinking in a speakeasy or sleeping in a friend's house or beating on the door of the Salmagundi Club. Then early one morning he awoke lying face down on a bed in an attractive room. He rose, went to the window, saw that he was in a hotel overlooking Times Square. He sent for the hotel barber to shave him and cut his hair, gave the bellboy sufficient money to buy him fresh linen and a tie at the haberdashery store in the lobby. He then sent a telegram to Amelia telling her he would be home on the next train, and went out to buy gifts for his two sons.

7

During the next weeks he spent a great many hours roaming the harbor, the hills and the dunes looking for a scene he had not painted before, one which might suddenly arrest and excite him. When this stratagem failed he locked himself in his studio for long stretches, going over his drawings and experimental compositions, forcing himself to put something down on canvas, knowing that he cared little what would emerge.

The days were not so bad. He could walk, find somebody in the village to talk to for on hour, even read a few pages; but the nights, after he went to bed and the lights were out, were full of interminable anguish. He tossed, he turned, he writhed, he got up and smoked, went down to the kitchen for coffee, got back into bed and lay there stiff as death, resolved not to turn or twist again but to fall asleep if it were the last thing he ever did. At dawn he was still awake, feeling that inside himself he had grown thinner, more tired and withdrawn.

But he kept from drinking; the memory of the week in New York was fresh in his mind and the terror of what would happen if he lost control was even greater than that of the sleepless nights.

When he could stand it no longer he went to a newly arrived doctor in the town, told him of his insomnia and asked for a prescription for sleeping pills.

"Glad to oblige. These pills are pretty strong, so take only one or two at the most."

Shortly after lunch he swallowed one of the pills and stretched out on the bed. An hour went by while he waited for the potion to work. Nothing happened. He got up and took a second pill, drinking a cup of black coffee with it. Again he reached out his aching, exhausted mind and body toward sleep . . . but sleep drifted farther and farther away. In desperation he went back to the kitchen, emptied the contents of the bottle into his hand and gulped them all down at once.

His first sensation was not of sleepiness but of being stifled, of needing air. He ran out of the house and made his way into the hills behind the village. He wandered for hours, sometimes walking, sometimes falling in a heap in the sand or in the woods until the sun had set, the night grown dark and cold. He kept plunging on ahead blindly, and finally at one in the morning made his way up the street to his home, pushed in the front door and fell unconscious on the floor.

He came to on the couch with Amelia and Dr. Hiebert, who had delivered their son, leaning over him.

"Darling, what have you done to yourself? We found this empty bottle in your coat pocket. Where did you get these sleeping pills? Why did you take them?"

". . . that new doctor . . . he told me one or two . . . but they didn't work . . ."

"I'd better use this stomach pump," said Dr. Hiebert; "then I'll check with the other doctor and find out how strong these pills were."

That was the last John heard. He lost consciousness again. When he awakened it was morning and he saw Dr. Hiebert and the doctor who had given him the pills standing over him. He could not make out their words too clearly, but he did hear them say that ". . . pneumonia is inevitable . . ."

To the amazement of the doctors and the entire town he was up and around in a few days. He knew that people were saying he had tried to commit suicide; but it wasn't true. He had merely tried to escape into sleep. Now he knew that this was impossible: sleeplessness was caused by fear. Very well then, there was a way to drown out fear.

The taxi owners in Provincetown got him as much bootleg liquor as he wanted: grain alcohol mixed with water and spiked with juniper, scotch, rye or rum flavoring. When he had a bottle of liquor in each pocket of his buffalo coat he made his way to the Ship, a little restaurant on the beach. The waiters were art students and the clients came almost exclusively from the writers, musicians and painters of Provincetown. No liquor was allowed inside the Ship, so he stood in the bushes behind the shack taking long pulls at the raw alcohol. After the third swallow he began to feel better, the hard edges blunted within him, he decided that he had been a fool, a romantic idiot, to have taken his fatigue and satiation as anything more than momentary. By the time he had finished the first quart bottle and hidden the second one in the bushes, he was feeling fine.

Inside the Ship he found a little booth, listened to the piano player improvise on such popular songs as "Say It with Music" and "Chicago," then hummed for him the tunes of "The Dying Cowboy" and "Dinah Had a Wooden Leg," and began to sing the songs. Pretty soon the whole Ship was joining in for choruses.

Feeling happy now, warm and friendly, John went through the kitchen and out the back door of the little café, drinking deeply from the second bottle. When he returned he began telling his earliest tales of the West, and once again he was Charles Goodnight and Grat Dalton and Crazy Horse and General Nelson A. Miles.

Suddenly, after two more trips out to his hidden bottle, while in the middle of a yarn, he sprang up and cried:

"What am I doing here? I should be back at my studio working!"

He ran all the way home, set up a canvas on the easel and blindly threw paint with his palette knife.

At first he was peaceable, hurting only himself; but it took ever larger quantities of alcohol to bring him up out of his despair. Then one night he went to the Ship roaring drunk, gathered a few of his remaining admirers around him and suddenly shouted:

"Would you like a slow death or a quick one?"

He picked up the steak knife that was lying on the table and brandished it in mock ferocity. The owner, Inez Hogan, who kept bromo seltzer in the kitchen for the purpose of containing John's drunkenness, hid the other knives and called for the police.

The officers put him in the jail in the basement of the Town Hall to sleep it off.

After his arrest he lost all vestiges of responsibility. Amelia, Dr. Hiebert or one of the friendly taxi drivers followed him around at night trying to keep him out of trouble. When he was too drunk to be handled, the doctor would slip knock-out drops into his glass and the taxi driver would carry him out to the car.

One evening he was sitting in a booth at the Ship alone, muttering to himself, when he heard a group of youngsters in the next booth discussing him:

"Used to be a good painter."

"Just a bum now."

"Broken-down drunk."

He slumped on the hard wooden bench, stone sober, more sick at heart than at any time during the past months. Was that what he was now, after all the high hopes and the great soaring flights? Just a broken-down drunk? If that was all that was left of John Noble, why hadn't that bottle of sleeping pills done its work? Why hadn't he been able to gulp down enough of prohibition's crude alcohol so that he would never need to wake up again crumpled somewhere on a sandy beach or dune?

He rose from the booth, sober and steady, walked out without a backward glance at the young students. He found Amelia sitting in the big rocker by the window, her eyes and ears riveted to the outside street, fearing that he would be drowned, be run over, that he would in some way do harm to himself or someone else. He threw himself down on his knees before her, cradling his head in her lap.

"Darling, this is awful, awful what I am doing to you. I've got to stop it. I've got to stop hurting you."

"John, but how? We've tried everything. Why are you so unhappy? What has happened to us?"

"Amelia, we must get out of Provincetown. Let's go to New York, find a new home there, start all over again. I don't want to hurt you any more, Amelia, you know that."

She lifted his face in her hands, kissed his haggard eyes, the hollows in his cheeks.

"I know you don't want to hurt me, my dear. That's why I can endure all this. But if you would only let me help, if you would only tell me what it is that makes you drink."

". . . I don't know . . ."

8

They found a second-floor apartment on Stuyvesant Square in a beautiful old house which was shared by a doctor who lived below and a painter by the name of Auerbach Levy above. From the front window they could see the clock of St. George's Church, the trees and fountains in the square. There was an enormous front room with high ceilings, double sliding doors leading into a small dressing room whose ceiling was painted with cupids and roses, and beyond that an equally large back room with a balcony overlooking the garden.

Amelia ransacked the antique shops and secondhand furniture stores of New York for a vivid oriental rug, red divan and chairs. When the furniture had been placed she sewed yellow draperies for the windows and borrowed a tall ladder so that she could give a coat of gilt to the cupids and roses on the ceiling, to the window frames and door. She had an altar built for her saints, bought a rubber plant which looked like a lineal descendant of the one in her Strasbourg parlor. Then she went out to find brightly colored lamps, candelabra, antique glass balls, vases for her flowers, and a hundred-year-old Madonna with real golden hair and a light blue satin brocade cloak embroidered in silver. John surveyed the room with amused resignation.

"Amelia, wherever you go you take your own world. Once we close that front door we're back in Paris on the Rue Falguière."

"Do you like it?" she asked anxiously. "You were so happy in the Rue Falguière studio. This north light will be good when you pull the draperies . . ."

His momentary sense of pleasure vanished like rain water in an underground sump. "If you're an artist, Amelia, and you have something to paint, you can paint in a barn. Look out for the artist who has to have everything just right. . . . Say, what are all those packages?"

"New clothes for John and Towanda. They start school at the Friends' Seminary tomorrow."

"What do they need new clothes for? They should be brought up like children on the Western frontier. Why, my mother made my clothes out of buffalo hides."

She knew from his grumblings that he was pleased; and when he set up his easel by the front windows and pulled the curtains back so that the light flooded in from the square she found herself hopeful again for the first time in months. She made a simple supper for herself and the boys, put them to bed in the back room and joined John in the studio.

"John, it's dark in here, don't you want me to turn on the lamps?"

"No, I like the darkness; come sit by me."

All night he sat in the comfortable chair before the blank canvas and talked to her intermittently as the hours passed, planning the design, telling her of the colors he would use and of the effects he would achieve and of the technique he would employ. Amelia was exhausted from the day's work of getting them settled in the apartment; several times she asked tentatively if he wasn't ready for sleep.

"No, no, I've got to stay with this."

He heard the milkman rattle his bottles against the metal basket at the door, then heard the boys awake and Amelia getting them dressed, giving them breakfast, taking them to the Friends' Seminary for enrollment.

For four consecutive nights he sat motionless before the canvas, keeping Amelia by his side, no longer speaking. She dozed occasionally in her chair; that was all the rest she managed.

Late in the afternoon of the fifth day he began working. It did not take him long to paint the picture, for nothing was involved beyond the mechanics of setting down what he had resolved so completely in his mind. When dawn lightened the tower of St. George's Church and the milkman rattled his bottles at the door, the picture was done. The sun edged across the big windows and focused its sharp clear rays on his canvas. It was a picture of the square outside his window and St. George's steeple. He studied his space arrangement, examined the juxtaposition of colors, followed the linear relationships. Technically the work was excellent; he had lost nothing of his surety.

He continued working this way for several months, sitting motionless for long nights in front of his easel, then getting the painting down on canvas in a rush. Whenever he felt a gnawing uneasiness he pushed it out of his mind and began a new project: *The Run*, picturing the scene at Hunnewell just after the starting gun had been fired; *The Big Herd*, thousands of buffalo extending across infinite plains to some remote horizon, in the foreground a White Buffalo, belonging to the others and yet a creature apart, remote. He agreed with Amelia that their move to New York had been most wise.

During all this time he never looked at the canvases locked in the closet. Then early one morning he realized that he could no longer keep himself from facing them. He waited until the children had gone to school and Amelia was shopping; then he took out the paintings and placed them about the big studio, hanging some along the walls, propping others on the tables and mantelpiece as he had in Paris.

The sun was streaming in the front windows, lighting the entire room with its brilliance. He walked from canvas to canvas, pulsating with a numb, unthinking kind of joy: and then suddenly his heart seemed to stop beating. Was this shining light coming from within the pictures themselves, or was it the external light of the sun pouring through the windows?

He turned abruptly, walked to the front of the studio and pulled the long golden curtains shut. Slowly he went back to his paintings . . . and in the darkness saw only darkness: no warmth, no radiation, no inner glow, no spirit and essence beyond its immediate detail, that which made a picture extend beyond its frame to the point of infinity without which all was a dry river. Oh, he might pass these canvases off, exhibit them in galleries, perhaps sell them. He might even fool some of the critics for a time because the craftsmanship was so solidly based. But the one person he could not fool about them was himself.

Calmly, feeling terribly cold inside himself, he started cutting the canvases with his palette knife and stuffing the pieces into Amelia's golden wastebasket.

9

He had told Marty Buckler in Brittany that an artist's work was never done because, no matter how long he lived or how valiantly he strove, he could hardly do more than scratch the surface of truth. Yet where did one find the fortitude, the endurance to hobble from hour to hour, from year to year? Time had been his friend: a smooth, amiable creature which simply went away when one was not interested. Ah, but now! Here was every relentless second, ticking loud and hard and inescapably so that he might not lose count.

He went to the miniature trunk in which Amelia kept the family jewels, and there he found the vast accumulation of time which he had neglected over the years: the slim, silver Elgin his father had given him when he left for Paris, the small, beautifully carved black marble clock given them by Amelia's uncle for their wedding, and which he had allowed to adorn no mantlepiece, the gold watch presented to him by the Art Association in Provincetown. My, what a lot of time was represented here, millions of hours, really, which he had neglected. But he would neglect them no more! He wound the marble clock and set it over the fireplace, wrapped the Art Association watch about his wrist, put his father's Elgin in his trouser pocket. Now every part of him would know that time was present and beating. He would make up for all the wasted hours by living half a dozen seconds for every one that passed!

There was one escape . . . one only. . . . A few drinks, and he would no longer be concerned about the future.

Wanting the company of old friends, he hurriedly dressed and made his way to the Lafayette Hotel where the restaurant and bar were replicas of the places he had enjoyed in Paris, even to the marble-topped tables. Here he met a young editor from the Longmans, Green publishing house, who to John's surprise exclaimed:

"Mr. Noble, I've been planning to get in touch with you for quite a while. The writers in New York say you're the best storyteller they've ever heard, and that you know more about the old West than any man alive."

The heavy depression which had settled on John's chest rose somewhat as he replied, "So much has been written about the West . . ."

The young editor's eyes were bright with excitement.

"I've already talked to the publisher about the possibility of your doing a book for us. We even have a title for you: *The Chisholm Trail.* What do you say, Mr. Noble?"

John's need for a drink disappeared. He began to talk excitedly: "Do you really want the truth about the West? For example, I could tell the story about the Bender family who took tourists from their covered wagons into their homes for meals and lodgings, and then murdered them for their possessions. Their farm used to be right close to our home; I can remember digging around the pits near the murder house for the skeletons."

"Of course, that's good, great flavor and character, just the stuff we need!"

He remained at the Lafayette all afternoon telling his best yarns; but when he returned home he had to confront himself with the fact that the Bender family had lived in Coffeyville, not in Wichita, and had vanished some twenty or thirty years before he was born. Could he erase himself from the stories he had been telling? The book would be a long job, probably take him several years. Could he keep himself so completely occupied that neither he nor his fellow artists would know that this was an act of replacement?

Amelia came in, saw him pacing, asked for the news. When he told her she urged him to sign the contract right away.

"You could work up your outlines here in New York for the rest of the winter, John, and then in the spring we could go back to Provincetown . . ."

"No, not Provincetown, Amelia: it has too many memories for me, they would get in the way of my writing. Let's look for a place up in the mountains where we've never been."

The spot they found was Lyme, Connecticut. they rented a two-story house in the peaceful countryside and here John transported all of the papers and notes he had accumulated about the West. At night after Amelia and the two boys had gone to sleep he sat at a large table in the living room surrounded by books and structural plans. Over the winter months he had read everything that had been published about the Chisholm Trail, the settling of the West, and had decided he would write the story chronologically. But he was unable to work in this fashion: all he could do was set down the best of the human dramas he had read or remembered from his early days in Kansas. By morning the table, the chairs and the floor were covered with endless sheets, some scribbled, some torn, and cigarettes, ashes and matches.

He slept till noon and after lunch took long walks through the countryside with Amelia and the boys, or sat in the hammock on the front porch swinging back and forth. Then he noticed that the edges of the leaves were beginning to crinkle; and soon Amelia announced that they would have to be going back into town for the opening of the boys' school.

He took the one hundred and fifty-odd pages of manuscript which he had managed to get into coherent form, started reading at ten o'clock of a Friday night and by the next morning had finished. When Amelia came downstairs she found a fire blazing in the grate, with all of the pages of the stillborn *Chisholm Trail* reduced to a thin wavering gray ash.

"Oh, John, no! Why did you destroy the manuscript?"

"Because no man can blithely exchange his paintbrush for a fountain pen. It isn't as though I didn't know better: I've watched the writers up in Provincetown work, and writing is just as difficult and complex an art as painting. . . ."

"But you were doing so well."

She was not only disappointed but frightened. He reached out his hand and drew her to him.

"No, Amelia, it wasn't good. But anyway it did use up a lot of time."

When they reached their apartment in Stuyvesant Square that evening they found a telegram stuck into the crack of the front door. It was from John's brother in Wichita, informing him that his mother was dead.

10

Elizabeth Noble's last ride seemed more like a civic parade than a funeral procession: for most of Wichita closed down to pay her homage. Nor was there any sadness at the final services in the cemetery: rather a sense of exultation that such a woman should have lived at all. Standing beside his mother's grave, John realized that Elizabeth had been a real pioneer, for Wichita was now a metropolis, a great and durable city which his mother and father had helped build from a few shacks pasted insecurely against a flat prairie. Elizabeth Noble had lived precisely her threescore and ten years, and to her son it seemed as though she had been a completely happy human being.

He lay awake all night in his old bedroom gazing out the window at the North Star. Though most of his adult years had been spent away from his mother he knew that the cord had never been cut. In the morning he went down into the parlor which Elizabeth Noble had opened for her son when he first needed a room in which to work. He remembered having protested that he might spill paint, and he heard his mother's voice say as clearly as though she were in the room:

"Things are to be used."

When he had left Wichita, some twenty-five years before, his easel had been standing in the center of this parlor. Now he saw that it was still there, pushed to one side.

He had several cups of black coffee, then walked quickly to Hyde and Humble's stationery store where he had bought his first painting supplies, returned home to the parlor and put a canvas on the easel. His mind went back with an almost terrifying vividness to that first day in this cherrywood parlor when he had stood like an awkward breathless boy without the faintest notion of what to do with these luscious buttery paints he had squeezed onto his palette and transferred thickly to the canvas just to see how it felt to work with a brush. That had been such a raw, amateurish beginning; something before a beginning, actually.

He had no conscious knowledge that he was painting a picture: he painted it instinctively, as though he were talking to his mother and saying good-by to her. When he finished he saw that he had pictured a phantom ship which would carry her from earth to heaven, had created for her his conception of immortality, said in the only medium in which he knew how to express himself that her place in the universe was fixed and beautiful. He named the canvas *Phantom Ship,* and felt that it was stronger and more beautiful than anything he had ever painted: for God was here in His finest sense. But he was not deceived by this knowledge; just as that first bungling canvas he had essayed in this room a quarter of a century before had been something before a beginning, so too this canvas was something after an end. The *Phantom Ship* would be hail and farewell not only to his mother but to his painting as well.

At nightfall he went down to the Wichita *Eagle,* climbed the flight of stairs and made his way into Dave Leahy's cluttered office. Dave's hair had grown gray, his figure heavier, his personality even more deeply encrusted with pipe smoke; but he was still the irrepressible Irish storyteller, recording not only the actual happenings and anecdotes of the pioneer country but setting down its legends and apocrypha as well. Dave was not altogether happy.

"Johnny m'boy, I wanted to write great history books about the Southwest and the Territory," he groused; "but what have I actually turned out? Just thousands of newspaper columns, most of them yellow and forgotten by now; and worse yet, half of them not even true."

"Dave, a critic in London said, 'John Noble creates a world not real but more true than the physical world about us.' You taught me that: the difference between information and wisdom."

"Thanks, Johnny, that's a great compliment."

Victor Murdock came in, shook hands warmly and said, "If you really want to see a cockeyed world in operation come with me to Congress. Poor Dave, he was unhappy there because what was going on in all seriousness put even his best hoaxes in the shade."

"Do you see much of Marty in Washington, Vic?"

"Sure, we have lunch together once a week. You know, that boy's not doing a bad job as a senator. He understands money in a sense that none of the rest of us do. It speaks to him, tells him its innermost secrets . . . as though he were a lover . . ."

The next day John sent to the art colony which Frances had completed. She took him through the gallery, then the main house where there was a communal dining room, a social room, library and studio porch overlooking the river. They walked through the wooded acres where she had built some twenty cabins in which the painters and sculptors worked in privacy for as many hours of the day as they wished.

They returned to the main house just as the sun was setting beyond the Arkansas River. While John sat on a rattan lounge watching the sunset colors deepen, Frances came back from the kitchen with some coffee and fried chicken which had been left from luncheon. She set the plate before him, spreading a napkin on his lap.

"I'm sure you haven't eaten any solid food since you arrived in Wichita."

She leaned back in the hard straight chair and gazed at him with wide, accepting black eyes. John thought, How beautiful she is now. . . .

She said, "I can see you sitting across our dining-room table with the sun on that white-gold hair of yours, with your skin roughened from the weather and your lips parched, your shirt open and your lean ribs showing through. I can remember as vividly as though it were this morning how faint I felt while I watched you devour that food."

The life flooded out of his face. When he spoke his voice was hoarse.

"Yes . . . well, the years have been good . . . some of them anyway. . . ."

She leaned forward, anxious. There was a weary fatalism in his voice.

"A man is as old as his courage, Frances. There are no more pictures left in me."

He reached across the coffee table and took her long slender hand in his, holding it tightly.

"But that must not mean that you are to stop your work."

She threw back her head with a prideful toss. Her voice was clear and resolved.

"No, John, I can't stop now, not even if you do. These last ten years of getting close to the heart of a great art, assembling exhibitions and writing and printing books, having all these young people come here to try their wings in their first known security, all this has given me another dimension. I want to go on for years, always learning, helping more and more young people to have an opportunity to develop themselves. When your happiness is born out of misery your courage can never be exhausted."

11

He was aware of a long valley of bleached white bones. It seemed like that very first valley in Wichita, only now when he looked around him it was not just one valley, but somehow a world full of bleached white bones which he was seeing from above as a great circular mound of parched skeletons: for what was life on the earth beneath him but a relentless journey from the pain of birth to the pain of death?

His sight cleared. He grasped that this vast white forest was made up of living, breathing creatures, moving about, working, playing, hoping, planning. Yet to him they were already half dead because they knew that one day they must die: the unbroachable secret held by all, uttered by none. Gazing down from his heights upon earth and mankind, he felt that what he saw was trivial, meaningless, mundane, perishable: the valley of death. Where then was the valley of life? He must find some other world or sphere where there was no death, where there was only the timeless and spaceless universe. He remembered how he had described the plains of Kansas to Amelia when they had first been married:

"The plains stretch to infinity, Amelia, there's nothing to catch hold of your thoughts, there's nothing to break the sameness, yet there's beauty in it all, because everything is so flat that your thoughts must soar to great space beyond the unmarked road. The barren plains are like a world without end."

That was where he wanted to find his way: to the great spaces beyond the unmarked road, the world without end. He looked below him to earth from his uncertain, precarious midway position and reviewed the whole of his own life, saw it in a suspended continuity, clearly visible. He understood how it had been dominated by his love of God. He had thought that he could remain on earth and have God within him; miracle of miracles, this had happened not once but twice. How blessed he had been, for through his work God had enabled him to burst into flame. That was more, much more, than any one man had a right to expect.

It was no longer possible for him to equivocate or evade. If he wished to walk again in God's serene glowing light he would have to go into God's realm, make his way to the side of the Lord of Creation. Death was not a renunciation, it was an avowal; it was not ugly, it was beautiful; it was prompted not by fear, but by the certainty of one's place in God's universe. Wasn't that the primary wish of all life, to make its way swiftly and painlessly through its travail, through time, through space, through pain, through death, into God: a temporary journey through the dark and cold and rain, emerging into the warm mellow sunlight? If God was love, then death too was love: the wedding ceremonial which joined man and his Maker. For him death would be not a chute leading out of life, but a gateway leading into life; to join God, that was not to die, that was to be born.

He had always imagined death and God to be antithetical: if the White Buffalo was God, then one lived joyously, worked energetically, and from that living and working emerged a good and intelligible pattern; the meaning of life was at all times clear, its flavor sharp, zestful, inspiriting. If the White Buffalo was death, as he had thought in Wichita and Paris, then there was no purpose in work beyond the pleasure in the exercise itself, no meaning in life beyond carnal experience. But when at the end the two merged; when death became only one small phase of God's will, just another servitor of God's design, having its own good and functional purpose, then the conflict ended, the terror and the tension passed, death became a mountain pass; the ascent might be steep and rocky: but ah, the vista from the crest!

He struggled long and hard to get his eyes open. When he suceeded he could see nothing. The room was black, airless.

He was lying on a narrow bed with a heavy covering over him. His head burned with fever. He shivered a little, then his teeth began rattling and his arms shaking in their sockets. When he was exhausted the chills lessened and he lay still and cold, covered with perspiration.

After a few moments he threw the buffalo coat aside and struggled up from the sofa. His bones felt splintered through his skin. Around his brow and across the back of his skull were steel bands joined to each other by thongs and pulling ever tighter. He beat around the room blindly, knocking over a lamp, then pitching headlong over a low coffee table into the floor.

It was here Amelia found him. She soaked a towel in water, dropped to her knees beside him and raised him up so that his head was cradled in her arms.

"What has happened, darling? What hurts you, John?"

His gaze wandered over her face, beyond her to the walls and ceilings of the studio.

"Then . . . I am not . . . in Wichita?"

"Of course not, John. You're here with me in New York. You've been home for several days."

He reached out, took her hand and held it against his cheek.

"I'm so lonely."

"Lonely? But, John, how can you be lonely? You have me, and the two boys, and all your friends."

"It hurts to be so alone."

"Let me get you some coffee, darling. It will make you feel better."

In a few moments she came back into the room, helped him up into a chair and pressed the hot black coffee to his lips.

"Drink some of this, darling. Then I'll get you some soup."

He nodded in agreement. Relief came to her eyes. He waited until he heard her moving about in the kitchen, then he rose, slipped into the heavy buffalo coat, put on his ten-gallon hat, went out the front door and stumbled down the flights of stairs, trying to be quiet but bumping against the walls.

She stopped in the midst of ladling out a dish of barley soup with square-cut pieces of beef. She stood at the stove, her head down, her heart beating painfully, knowing that she must let him go.

12

He started from such an abysmal low that the whiskey had little effect on him; he drank all night, mostly in the speakeasy on Twelfth Street, and then moved downtown as the more respectable places closed, ending at dawn on the Bowery. Even after the consuming of three bottles of bourbon he did not feel drunk or even exhilarated, but only a little less cold and frightened and lonely.

He slept for a time with his arms, head and shoulders sprawled over a beer-soaked table; when he awakened the bar was already lined with the early birds even as the Mahan bar had been in Wichita that bright morning when Carry Nation had come in with her cane and rocks. He ordered drinks for the house. He began telling stories, stories of the Chisholm Trail. The audience was attentive and swelled in size as word spread that free liquor was being dispensed.

At noon he hailed a cab and rode to the Salmagundi Club. He wanted to be with friends and talk about painting. But when he entered the front door, walked to the dining room and saw twenty of his comrades gathered about the luncheon table in a discussion meeting, the friendly liquor suddenly turned mean, he cursed them for their respectability and security, denouncing them as sugar-bowl artists. The chairman merely called:

"Go home, John, and sleep it off."

He was about to turn away when a voice within him urged, Do something dreadful, something irrevocable so that they will throw you out and you can never come back. These are your friends, this is your organization; after you've lost them it will be easier, you'll be closer to home.

He strode to the table with a bellow of rage, gripped the long white tablecloth with his powerful hands and gave it a sudden tremendous yank. It was pulled so fast that it came off the table leaving all of the dishes and glassware behind, their contents spilled in an inglorious mess.

Strong hands seized him and he was pitched out of the club.

He found another speakeasy and drank steadily for several hours, trying to bring himself back up to the point where he had been when he left the Bowery saloon, for his accomplishment at the Salmagundi Club had depressed him further. By three in the afternoon he had once again eaten away the rigid borders of reality and was putting on a show for the men in a Tenth Avenue saloon, killing Indians, capturing desperadoes, holding up railway express cars, bringing the Dalton gang into Coffeyville.

At five o'clock he found himself uptown, entering the Milch Galleries, where one of the Milch brothers was in the process of displaying a John Noble canvas to a client. He stood in the shadows just inside the door listening to the sales talk; it was good talk, highlighting his own lifetime philosophy about painting. At any other time it would have been deeply satisfying to know that a gallery dealer understood one's work so thoroughly and could present it in such a sympathetic and captivating manner; but now the words, the jargon of painting, reverberated in a hollow tympanum inside his skull. He stormed up the the client, crying out:

"Don't believe a word he tells you!"

"Now, John, please . . ."

"Look, mister, I painted it and I ought to know whether it's good or bad. Don't waste your money, this is junk, I'm just a third-rate artist."

Milch stood stupefied. John took a threatening step toward the buyer, shouted, "Get out of here before I cut your throat!"

The air became fuzzy after that: he remembered running, finding new saloons, speakeasies; drinking, shouting, cursing, telling stories, fighting, then everything blacked out. When he came back to consciousness he was lying in a lot near the East River huddled over a pile of mortar-covered bricks which had been torn out of an abandoned building. It was deep in the night, he had no idea of what night; he picked himself up, ran a finger over his face and pulled away several blotches of dries blood. He felt in his pocket; he still had money, and so he started walking toward the center of town. After what seemed like agonizing hours he found a cab and thickly muttered his address on Stuyvesant Square.

Once home he fumbled in his pocket, found the house key and went heavily up the flight of stairs to the second-floor flat. He had never thought of food but now suddenly he was hungry, terribly hungry, and he wondered how long it was since he had eaten: two days, three, four . . . ?

He did not want to wake Amelia. He made his way from the hall into the little pantry where she had the supplies neatly arranged on shelves, the eggs, the cheese, the vegetables and cans of fruit. He decided he would make himself an omelet, it was just the thing he needed, but he could not see very clearly and he thought the eggs were on the top. He climbed up several shelves, tried to balance himself, then fell with a tremendous crash, pulling the structure down with him: eggs, milk, bowls of cooked food spread about him, and he lay silently for a moment in the midst of the havoc until Amelia came rushing in, picked him up off the floor, helped him into the living room, got him out of his reeking clothes, then donned her rubber gloves and went back into the pantry to scrub up the mess.

Remorse seized him and made him as drunk again as though he had lifted a bottle of Sunnybrook and downed its contents. He went to his closet, put on a fresh suit, ran out the door and down the flight of steps before Amelia could stop him.

His money lasted for another twenty-four hours during which he drank steadily, sinking ever deeper into a despairing triumph . . . descending a jagged, broken ladder, tearing his flesh with each rung but pulling the structure down behind him so he could never get up again. Then, when his money ran out, when he had to find his way back to those speak-easies where he was known and could get credit; when his credit was used up and he started wheedling and cadging drinks at strange bars, all consciousness of the years between vanished and he imagined he was once again in Paris.

When next he came back to consciousness he saw that he was in Times Square. The lights were still on but there were no people in the streets. His head felt cold; he put up his hand and found that his white Stetson was gone. So was his necktie. His clothes were a rumpled sack of alcohol and filth. What day was it, what night? How long had he been away from home? And why were these policemen standing around him in a circle, holding their clubs, a determined expression on their faces. He tried to listen.

". . . one we want all right . . . wife's had us hunting him for a week . . . I caught up with him the other night over on Tenth Avenue but he knocked me down and ran . . . he's not going to knock anybody down this time, boys, let's close in and take him. . . . But look out, he can kill a man with those hands."

He started to run. Something hit him, whirled him about. He struck out blindly with his fists, started to run again, then felt a heavy blow and sank wearily, almost gratefully to the sidewalk.

13

One eyelid twitched open, slowly, painfully. It seemed like a matter of hours before the other eye opened. All he could see above him was a dim, white expanse. He tried to move but there was something tight which chained him across the middle. He raised a hand to rub the thick stubble of his face and help awaken himself, but the arm too was held.

Where was he? By lifting his head a trifle he could see dim white walls. Was he dead?

He strained his ears. He could hear nothing; it was like lying in a coffin or in a tomb. Then slowly sounds came through: faint breathings, tortured moans, stifled, deep aching groans.

He strained against the binding across his middle, pulled hard on the vise that gripped his wrists, managed to get an elevation so that he could look down at himself and try to learn where he was. Across his stomach he saw a heavy brown leather belt and on his wrists the same kind of belt securing him. But to what? He tried to focus his attention and at last saw that he was on a bed: high, white, hard.

He sank back. He felt strange, as though he were disembodied; not the weary, sick, disenchanted, almost spiritual convalescence after a long drunken siege, but as though he were floating above this white bed and above these hard brown straps which bound him down; as though his body had permanently been put out of pain and all that remained of consciousness was some little sight, some little sound, some little sense of being.

A touch of strength returned. He raised himself again on his elbows. He saw that he was in the middle of a large room with the lights very dim, and in it a number of men like himself were stretched out on hard white slabs. He tried to focus on their faces: chalky, toothless, sunken-cheeked. Over everything hovered the murmur of deep unconscious moaning, yet he could see no sign of sound escaping from the lips of these corpses.

By concentrating on as many of the sheet-covered forms as he could embrace in his narrow vision he saw that his comrades sometimes moved: a head pulled up, a shoulder dropped, a leg twitched in a writhing circular motion. Now he heard the surrounding sounds more sharply; sounds of men in mortal agony: subdued, throttled, impassioned, breaking forth not only at the throat but at every pore of the skin and the senses. And he knew that he could not be in the morgue, that these men were not dead; they had passed through the morgue, passed through death and had come out on the other side into Purgatory.

A groan escaped him, and only then did he realize that these same muted sounds had been escaping his own lips, joining with those of the others. Well, that was as it should be: this was the place for penitential suffering, for the expiation of sins. But why did he have to be chained? He had no will to leave, to escape.

He lapsed. Sounds and sights vanished. He did not awaken again until he heard a familiar voice which floated in slowly, making its way with difficulty across the jagged floes of ice that ground inside his skull. Then, when he was sure it was Amelia, when the phantasm of dead men and Purgatory receded, he pushed his inner ear outward to pick up the words.

". . . sure my husband will be all right . . . once the spell is over . . . if you will let me take him home now . . ."

"I'm only trying to protect you, Mrs. Noble. Your husband was brought to Bellevue in an advanced state of alcoholism; I never thought he would awaken."

"But he's done this before, Doctor. His friends told me he did it even when he was young. It doesn't seem to do him any harm, once he gets over it. He'll be quiet now if only I can take him home and nurse him."

He heard a moment of pause, of thinking silence, then he felt two firm fingers touch his eyelids and push them back. He held them open, studying the doctor's face and managing a tiny woebegone smile at Amelia. He tried to talk but strangely enough he had no voice and like that inside ear which he had to push out through his aural canal and suspend somewhere midway in the room in order to catch any sounds at all, so now he had to drag his voice all the way up through his viscera and throat and make an almost superhuman effort to croak:

". . . Mrs. Noble . . . right . . . go with her . . . these straps . . . let me free . . ."

14

Time bulked; time dissolved; bulked again, melted away, vanished . . . bulked again. Inside himself a voice kept saying:

"Dear God, let me out! End my misery!"

Yet he could not put an end to his life by a simple decisive act. No frontiersman had ever killed himself: the Westerners were too strong, too bold, too resorceful, too devil-may-care to indulge in such a sickly, introspective pursuit as suicide. They might court death in gun fights, trail-blazing, rounding up thunder-crazed cattle, for they were men of carelessly worn courage. They might drink themselves to death; hard drinking was one of the honored traditions of the Southwest. But who ever heard of a cowboy taking his own life?

And so he proceeded slowly, painfully, the only one to know that what was being played before the public's eyes was not a rollicking comedy but a tragedy: that he was not seeking laughter and noise and excitement and conviviality, but rather to drown out intolerable pain.

Nor could he reveal to his wife what he was thinking and feeling so that she would have the boon of understanding to help her over the tortured nights when she brought out a folding cot, set it by his easel and lay there, sleepless, watching the stars and straining for the sound of his returning footstep. How could he make her understand when her concept of God was so different from his? If he said, "I hunger for God, I can no longer endure without Him!" she would cry with joy, pull him down beside her on their knees to pray; say over and over again, "I always told you you were religious!" He pitied her, and in his pity loved her the more deeply.

As for the rest of the world, he lived in perpetual terror lest someone find him out, mock him as a mystic, expose him to ridicule. The more he yearned for Him, the more often he asked silently, "Can you understand how a man can love God so passionately that he can no longer endure this humdrum life?" the more he tried to hide it by conduct which made him look like a stupid, guzzling, insensitive clod. This was his mask, his armor, his shield of defense; he willingly allowed his image in other people's eyes to be destroyed in order that no one should penetrate behind his disguise and learn the real truth about him. God would not care what John Noble was doing to himself, so long as he remained faithful. The body passes, the flesh decays: only love is indestructible: and the ultimate love is for one's Maker.

How often had he been in Bellevue? He could not remember. How many days and months had passed since that first long drunken spell when he had awakened and thought himself in Purgatory? How innocent he had been then, how naïve. This was Purgatory, here on earth.

He sat in the big chair before his easel, turned at an angle to look out over the trees and fountains in Stuyvesant Square. This last bout had been the longest and the worst. Loosely, without organization or discipline, his mind wandered over the fragments of memory that remained from the past weeks of almost total obliteration. He remembered the ugly scene when he had gone into the washroom at the Milch Galleries and taken the small bottle of paraldehyde from his pocket, the sedative which the friendly doctor downstairs had prescribed for when he should feel faint from hunger or seized by the need for a drink. Milch had come into the washroom as John stood with the bottle tipped in the air, had assumed that it was alcohol and struck his arm so violently that the bottle of paraldehyde smashed to the floor, setting up an immediate pungent odor. He heard Milch's voice yelling, "Get out of my gallery and never come back!"

He had gone home roaring drunk and created such havoc in the apartment that Amelia had been forced to call the police; but the moment he heard the officer's footsteps on the stairs he had sobered up, straightened his tie against his shirt, combed his fingers through his long white hair and, when the officer came into the apartment, exclaimed in a loud authoritative voice, pointing to young John:

"Officer, arrest that boy. He's drunk and disorderly."

The policeman had had young John down the stairs and onto the sidewalk before Amelia was able to convince him of the truth; by the time they got back upstairs John had escaped through the back garden. The next day John, Jr., had determined to go to sea; being refused permission, he had brought the captain of the ship home, and the father had denied the son the right to freedom which the first John Noble had accorded all these years to his own son. John, Jr., had defied him and gone away . . . and he was glad.

He recalled the quarrel with his younger boy Towanda; Towanda, who was in revolt as young John had never been. He had been walking up Broadway with Amelia and Towanda and, suddenly stopping in the crowded thoroughfare, had gathered an audience about him, spinning yarns of the Southwest, putting on a show with his Stetson and two-gun holster so that Amelia and Towanda had melted back into the crowd, not wanting anyone to know they were with him. He heard Towanda's voice while he lay in his studio, only partly conscious, Towanda crying out, "Why does he behave like this? Why does he do this to us? Why can't we live like other folks? Can't we do anything to stop him?" and Amelia's forbearing voice replying:

"You mustn't judge your father harshly, Towanda, he is unhappy, tormented, he is suffering far more than we are, believe me, my dear. We must be patient, we must try to help him."

He remembered having been found by Amelia in Union Square, and how she had tried by main force to get him into a taxicab and take him home; how when everything else had failed she asked a passing policeman for help . . . and he had jingled a lot of silver dollars in his pocket, whispering, "This lady . . . er . . . she has been annoying me . . . you know the kind, officer, no better than she ought to be." Whereupon the policeman had started to take Amelia away . . . and she was saved only by the fact that she had a passport picture of Mr. and Mrs. John Noble in her purse.

Then he recalled being committed to Lloyd's Sanitarium, carried to the hilltop hospital which looked as black and abandoned as a haunted house. He had been taken down a long corridor devoid of all furniture, with the calcimine peeling off the walls and ceiling; hustled up two flights of stairs by burly attendants, led through iron doors which clanged behind him and then thrust into a room with nothing but a bare cot and a heavy door which was locked behind him. When he had sobered up and been allowed to come down to the common ward with the other inmates: the alcoholics, the dope addicts, the manic depressives, the schizophrenics, the dementia praecoxes and all the deranged senile cases, he had gathered them about him as though they were children in a schoolroom and told them his most gruesome stories of the Southwest until he had turned the place into bedlam.

And lastly he remembered being locked in the attic of some strange house for four or five days, kept under heavy sedatives, the attic of some doctor's house, and the powerful male nurse who had been there to watch over him. When both the alcohol and the sedatives had worn off he had picked up a knife from his dinner tray and threatened the nurse with it. The attendant, with the knife only a few inches from his throat, had at last managed to whirl and run, leaving the door open behind him so that John could make his escape. But even as he heard the nurse half stumbling down three flights of stairs he had called after him:

"Don't be frightened, it's not you I want to do harm to, it's myself."

Through how many eternities must he live and suffer until he could find escape?

He turned back to the easel in front of which he sat when sober, staring at blank canvas, trying to imagine a picture or even remember one, to hollow out the scene, conceive interesting space arrangements, think in terms of bold or subtle colors, exciting design. But the power to project was gone. He began looking about the half-lighted room at the dozens of his canvases on the walls, the cream of his production from both Brittany and Provincetown. He murmured aloud:

"If I can't create new pictures, at least I can perfect the old ones."

He took the canvases down from the wall one by one and locked them onto the easel, turning a strong lamplight upon them so that he could face them in all of their naked reality. How incomplete his thinking had been, how superficial: for there was too much sky on this picture, too vaguely sketched in, out of proportion to the sea and the shore and the ships: and so he took his palette knife and cut off several inches from the top of the canvas, several inches of sky which he cut off and threw away; and felt better because he had improved his picture. Then he took another one down from the walls, a study of the dunes and the village of Provincetown flowing down to the sea; no, he had not been very astute when he painted this picture, for he had pulled the dunes too far to the south, made the scene top-heavy on one side, which caused that side to sink and pull the rest of the picture into a spin. He must balance this picture now, he must perfect it, he must cut out its crudities of proportion and arrangement: and once again he took his palette knife and slashed off a portion of the dunes.

At that moment Amelia came into the studio. She stood paralyzed at the door, trying to understand what was happening, then rushed at him and seized the arm which held the knife.

"John, what are you doing? Have you gone crazy?"

He did not look at her but gripped the knife firmly in his

hand as he studied still a third canvas which he had put on the easel.

"If I can't paint any new pictures, Amelia, at least I can improve the old ones. I can look at these paintings objectively, in cold blood, see what is wrong with them and cut it off."

She gripped his wrist which held the knife, gripped it with an almost maniacal force as she cried out:

"Cold blood! The only thing cold blood is good for is to die. You painted these pictures in hot blood, and that's where their quality lies. Anything you do to them now will ruin them."

He stood glaring at her, forcing the knife down slowly toward her bosom, overpowering her strength. Then just before he touched the skin he released his pressure.

"Aren't you afraid of being killed, Amelia?"

She stood facing him head on, her eyes blazing.

"I'd rather you destroyed me than your pictures. They are all I have left now to justify our marriage and our years together."

The knife dropped from his hand, fell noiselessly onto the rug. Only then did he realize that this action too had been a way of destroying himself, hacking away at his pictures until they no longer existed: for then he would be truly dead and nothing would remain except this useless battered carcass which somehow held grimly onto life.

Amelia hung the pictures back on the wall, then sat down on the couch and held her head in her hands. He sat beside her, took her hands from her face and placed them on his own.

"It was bad luck for you, Amelia, bad luck the day you rode along the Riviera and saw the Hôtel Savournin up on the rocks at Cagnes."

She kissed the corner of his mouth gently as though he were one of her children.

"No, darling, I don't think that, I never think that; all life is interesting . . . even when it happens to you."

They heard a heavy car door slam in front of the house. In a moment Marty bounded into the room with a broad grin on his face. He had with him boxes of newspaper and magazine clippings, many of them featuring the most bohemian of John's photographs with the flowing white hair and flowing black tie.

"I wanted to bring you the first batch of clippings myself,

John, and show you what a great job my public relations counsel is doing for you. Here, look at this full-page newspaper spread from Chicago; it tells how you and Toulouse-Lautrec were pals, used to spend your nights making the rounds in Montmartre and end up in jail supposedly drunk but actually carrying on the most brilliant discussions about art . . ."

"Toulouse-Lautrec was dying by the time I reached Paris."

"So what? Look at this double-page magazine spread of you and Paul Gauguin at the Dôme café in Paris, with Gauguin's Tahitian girl sitting alongside him in her native garb of brilliant colors: orange, blue, red, green . . . and with a parrot perched on her forefinger matching the colors of her outfit."

"Gauguin was in the South Seas when I first emerged from the Gare St. Lazare."

"Who's going to know over here? By making you the intimate of all these famous painters we make you great too. In public relations it's called Establishing Through Association. But here's the best article of all, I'm really proud of this one: five pages in a syndicated Sunday newspaper section, seen by twenty million Americans . . ."

"What did I do in that one?"

"Gave James McNeill Whistler his comeuppance at a party in his studio. We've got reproductions of three of his paintings and three of yours. In our story Whistler, who was always insulting everyone else, turned to you when you were studying one of his paintings, and asked, 'Well, young man, what do you think of my work?' You reply, 'Why don't you let some of God's sun shine on your canvas?' "

"What does that make me, insulting one of the great creators of our modern art?"

"Why, it makes you his superior as a painter, obviously!"

John was silent for a moment, then replied, "It won't work, Marty."

"Of course it will work, John. You don't know the power of the press. I don't care if I have to spend a fortune to make you the most famous . . . painter . . ."

He stumbled, stopped, frozen by the expression on John's face.

"I'll admit the power of the press, Marty, and even more the power of your money. But when it comes to inventing Dave Leahy hoaxes, I can beat you at your own game."

"What do you mean?" demanded Marty, offended. "This is no hoax. You're a great painter, aren't you? We're just selling

283

you to the public, the way we would market any other commercial product."

"I can unsell faster than you can sell, Marty. I've alienated every gallery dealer in town, so that not one of them will show a picture of mine. Every time I meet a critic or a museum director I behave like a drunken, vulgar lout . . . so that they've dismissed me as worthless . . . won't even discuss my painting any more."

"But why, John? Why should you destroy your lifetime work?"

"Have you ever loved anything so much, Marty, that you couldn't share it?"

There were tears in Marty's eyes. He rose, gathered his clippings and turned away.

"John, it isn't fair . . . why must you always defeat me . . . ?"

15

He disappeared for nine days, then stumbled home blindly, managed to pull himself up the flight of stairs, get in the front door, make a diving motion toward the divan on which he usually slept . . . and fell in a heap on the floor beside it. Amelia came running from the back bedroom. She tried to lift him up, to get him on the divan, but he lay there like a dead weight. Finally she went to the closet, took out his buffalo coat, covered him with it, put a pillow under his head and ran downstairs to the flat below.

The doctor stripped off John's clothes and gave him a thorough examination. After a considerable time he looked up, shook his head in bewilderment. "He has the kind of body the Greeks used to carve onto their friezes. If not for that he would have been dead long ago."

"Then he'll be all right?"

"I don't know, Mrs. Noble. It might be better if he were dead, better for himself and certainly better for you."

"No, no, Doctor, you must not say such things, any life is better than death, no matter how bad it may seem."

"Perhaps. But I'm frightened for you. I've seen the police reports. He is growing progressively more violent . . ."

"No, no, John isn't like that," she interrupted; "he's soft and gentle inside. He wouldn't hurt anyone. It's just that when he's drunk he thinks he has to play the wild West desperado."

"Whatever your explanation may be, I'm convinced that it is no longer safe for you to live with him. You must leave him or have him committed to a state institution."

They heard a faint moan from under the buffalo coat. John gazed at them through bloodshot eyes, the encrusted lids half closed. He reached out blindly for Amelia's hand.

"Amelia," he said hoarsely, "you won't do that to me . . . you won't put me in an asylum with all those crazy men?"

"No, darling, never. I won't send you away."

"And you won't leave me, Amelia? You know how terrible that would be for me. I love you, Amelia, you believe that, don't you, in spite of all the terrible things I am doing to you?"

She felt the hot tears coming down her cheeks.

"Yes, John, I believe it. You promised me on the station in Strasbourg the night we were married that whatever happened would happen to us together. I made you the same promise that night, John, and I'll never go back on it."

He fell asleep then, in her arms. She looked up to give the doctor a reassuring smile; but the room was empty.

16

He awakened feeling icy cold, his body drenched. He did not know why he was so cold and wet. After a long painful struggle upward he finally realized that once again he was in the psychopathic ward at Bellevue; that the icebag they had left on his head had broken and the cold water had run down over his chest and abdomen.

And he knew that he was going to die; not from this last wild drinking spell in which he had been determined to drown out the life force itself; but through a stupid accident, through a weakened or badly used icebag which had broken during the night and drenched him with its cold fluid. He had only a few hours left, but he had no intention of dying here in Bellevue. He wanted to die at home in his big chair in front of the easel.

The day shift came on at six o'clock. The male attendant entered the room, saw John lying there with his eyes open.

"What, you again?"

"Yes, my friend, but for the last time."

"That's what we've thought for several years now, but you always come back."

"Would you call the doctor, please? I don't want to die here, I want to die at home."

"I'll call the doctor, but you're not going to die anywhere; as far as we're concerned it looks like you're going to live forever."

"It only seems that way," he whispered.

He lapsed into unconsciousness, but awakened later when he heard Amelia's voice.

"Please . . . please . . . let me take him home . . . I'll get a nurse . . . we can care for him there."

"Your husband has a high fever, Mrs. Noble."

"But, Doctor, you said he was going to die anyway. He has always begged me to bring him home . . . not to let him die in some strange place."

John opened his lips several times, wetted their cracked dry skin with his tongue. "Let me go, Doctor . . . let my wife call an ambulance. I promise never to come back, never to trouble you again."

The ambulance attendants carried him upstairs on a stretcher and laid him down on the big couch in the studio. Amelia heated some water, shaved him carefully, then cut his hair until it fell in a clean shapely line over his head. Then she put him in a fresh white nightgown and propped him up on a pillow. His eye followed her every move, lovingly, hungrily. When she had finished her work she sat by him on the sofa and held his hand in hers.

"Amelia, I have just one thing to ask: you'll bury me in my Stetson, won't you?"

"Yes, John."

"The pictures belong to you. Watch over them. You'll have a hard time for a while because I've done so many stupid and ugly things. People will hold my conduct against the pictures. But that will pass, they'll forget about everything I did: and only the pictures will remain. That's all I want, Amelia, just that they be judged for themselves, and that they find their rightful place."

"I'll protect them, John; and I'll see that they find their place."

He gripped her hand. Slowly his hold loosened.

He plunged backward in time and space: through New York and Provincetown; through London and Brittany; through Paris and the later years in Wichita; back to the moment when he was a child, hovering on the top of the bridge above the Arkansas River. He heard the boys' voices crying, "Jump! Jump!" and he looked below into the shallow waters. He did not see the grim, bony visage of death mocking him, but rather the gentle faces of his mother, of Amelia . . . and unformed, indistinguishable from the waters and the reflections of the clouds, another gentle visage.

He felt his body falling through space, entering the waters headfirst, his knees doubled protectively under his chin, felt the water warm and benignly restful, dark and friendly as the waters of the womb from which he had emerged at the beginning of his long travail. The passionate journey was ended.

Other SIGNET Books You Will Enjoy

☐ **THE CONVENTION by Charles Beardsley.** This fascinating, no-holds-barred novel tells of the chaotic whirl of a three-day convention to open a new hotel and the way-out people who link up there. (#Q5152—95¢)

☐ **SEASONS AND MOMENTS by John Haase.** When a handsome, talented architect, bored with his button-down collar existence, meets a beautiful global gypsy, it is love at first sight, and the twosome are soon whisking off around the world, leaving wife and business world behind. ". . . genuinely moving . . ."—The Los Angeles Times (#Q5124—95¢)

☐ **EDSEL by Karl Shapiro.** Meet Edsel Lazerow. Poet on the loose in an up-tight university. Long-time rebel of forgotten causes. Male on the make among the restless campus wives, rebellious coeds, and lovely lewd ladies of the town. Put it all together and you have the unforgettable hero of the wildest, wittiest, most outrageous and devastating novel of the year. (#Y5123—$1.25)

☐ **BIRDS OF AMERICA by Mary McCarthy.** When Peter Levi goes to the Sorbonne, he takes us on a tour of Paris that travel folders never show. Befriended by a group of French bird-watchers, trapped in a student-police confrontation while out walking a house plant, guest at a ferociously "American" Thanksgiving dinner at a NATO general's home Peter just flaps his wings and glides through it all. "Mary McCarthy at her very best."—National Observer (#W5001—$1.50)

THE NEW AMERICAN LIBRARY, INC.,
P.O. Box 999, Bergenfield, New Jersey 07621

Please send me the SIGNET BOOKS I have checked above. I am enclosing $_____(check or money order—no currency or C.O.D.'s). Please include the list price plus 15¢ a copy to cover handling and mailing costs. (Prices and numbers are subject to change without notice.)

Name_____

Address_____

City_____State_____Zip Code_____
Allow at least 3 weeks for delivery